COUNCIL

BY GREG TOBIN FROM TOM DOHERTY ASSOCIATES

Conclave
Council

COUNCIL

Greg Tobin

 A Tom Doherty Associates Book
New York

COUNCIL

Quotation from *Gift and Mystery* by Pope John Paul II reprinted by permission of Doubleday
Broadway Books, a division of Random House, Inc.

A Forge Book
Published by Tom Doherty Associates, LLC.
175 Fifth Avenue
New York, NY 10010

www.tor.com

Forge® is a registered trademark of Tom Doherty Associates, LLC.

Library of Congress Cataloging-in-Publication Data

Tobin, Greg.
    Council : a novel / Greg Tobin.—1st ed.
      p. cm.
    "A Tom Doherty Associates book."
    ISBN 0-312-87353-0 (alk. paper)
    1. Popes—Fiction. 2. Catholics—Fiction. 3. Catholic Church—Fiction. I. Title.

PS3570.O29 C68 2002
813'.54—dc21

2002023512

First Edition: August 2002

Printed in the United States of America

0 9 8 7 6 5 4 3 2 1

This novel is dedicated to the "Three Monsignors,"
who have inspired and instructed me:
John E. Doran
Robert J. Wister
William Noé Field (1915–2000)

Who, then, is a faithful and wise servant? It is the one that his master has placed in charge of the other servants to give them their food at the proper time. How happy that servant is if his master finds him doing this when he comes home!

—Matthew, 24:45–46

The [Second Vatican] Council has pointed to the possibility and need for an authentic renewal, in complete fidelity to the word of God and Tradition. But I am convinced that a priest, committed as he is to this necessary pastoral renewal, should at the same time have no fear of being "behind the times," because the human "today" of every priest is included in the "today" of Christ the Redeemer.

—Pope John Paul II, *Gift and Mystery,* 1997

Mysterium fidei. Let us proclaim the mystery of faith.

The Vatican, October 22, 2002

Mulrennan regarded his friend and mentor, Leandro Biagi, who had been his luncheon guest in the papal dining room and stayed for an afternoon coffee. It was lonely being pope.

Cardinal Biagi was sharing confidentially with the new pope what Innocent XIV, the Filipino who had been elected in January and assassinated in July, had said to him shortly after his election. It only confirmed what Timothy Mulrennan, Pope Celestine VI, had known in his own heart for a long time.

"Holiness, I believe you should hear from me about a conversation I had with your predecessor—a number of conversations, more accurately," Biagi said. "The first time he mentioned his intention to convene a council was during Holy Week. He approached it rather mischievously, if I may characterize it that way. He said to me: 'Dear Cardinal, it is time to shake the foundations of our Holy Church. Not in a destructive way, but again to test and reinforce the basis of the True Faith.' Of course, he said it with a smile and must have watched my face turn three shades of red.

"Over the course of a few meetings, he explained his thinking this way: 'Time has accelerated and the world has changed radically in a very brief period, just a generation since Vatican II. If we wait until we fully "absorb" all the new teachings and initiatives of that council, we will fall far short of addressing the needs of so many people around the world. And the forces of reaction will continue to build strength, as they have over the past few decades.' He knew he was playing a dangerous game, Your Holiness, but he seemed determined to move ahead."

"Was this why he was murdered?" Mulrennan asked. He had his own dark feelings about the assassination that had caused the vacancy in the Holy See and led to his own surprise election; early information had tied it into Muslim-extremist terror cells—but the financing had apparently come from other sources in the West. Unspoken for now were his suspicions about the role played by the secretive lay society, Evangelium Christi. . . .

Biagi, the diplomat and politician, shrugged. "That will be for the police investigators to determine, not me. He kept it very close, spoke to only a very few others. Perhaps they leaked it, perhaps there was a spy in the papal household. In fact, it's possible that there still is. I would recommend that you commission a thorough security study of the Apostolic Palace—quietly and professionally. There are so many opportunities for leaks and sabotage. After all, you are sovereign of the Vatican City State as well as Supreme Pontiff of the Church."

"Sure, I need to be reminded now and then just who I am." He smiled ironically at the man from Florence who would have been at home as a Chicago ward heeler or a county chairman. "And what to do. I must remember that God speaks through other human beings, even you, Allo."

"Holy Father, I choose to believe that you mock me because you love me."

"I don't mock you, my friend. I can speak my mind openly with you as with no one else. And you can do the same with me, to lead me and correct me. I am most grateful to you—that is, when I am not silently cursing you."

"The late pope's scheme was only that when he died. It was unformed, and he must have shared it with the wrong people, I think. The only positive thing was, it had not gotten into the press."

"Which is not to say it won't or can't. I wonder if that would be so terrible?"

"I believe you should make that determination yourself— either put it out openly as an idea that you choose not to pursue, or quietly decide and plan another approach."

"You mean do it—convene a council? That is the most au-

dacious move I could make, not that it hasn't crossed my mind a
few times already in the quiet dark night when I can't sleep. I
cannot imagine the response, the consequences. Is it necessary? Is
it the right time? Am I the right one to do it? It blows my mind,
as we used to say in the sixties." Again the smile; he could not
help himself. He loved this man with olive skin and the most
exquisitely formed bald head he had ever seen. Biagi was a
churchman of the classic mold of Consalvi or d'Ailly and in another time would surely have been elected to the papacy himself;
and Timothy Mulrennan thought he would have made a damn
fine pope. But the American, not the Florentine politico, had been
placed upon the Throne of St. Peter. "It would be wrong, I think,
to do it just because De Guzman had begun to entertain the notion. There must be a deep institutional justification and need."

"Look into your heart, Holy Father. Ask yourself and ask
God for the answer. You will be shown the way, I am confident."

"And you? What do you think I should do, Leandro?"

The tall seventy-five-year-old shrugged his red-robed shoulders with profound ambiguity. "I am not God, my friend—and
neither are you."

"No, but neither am I any closer or farther away from God
than any little old lady of the Rosary Society or any seminarian
studying his ass off to become a priest."

A seminarian, Mulrennan thought . . . what a far distance
from there to here—yet in those years of his formation as a priest
his soul had been marked and changed, and his feet had been set
upon the path that led him to the cathedra of the Universal Pastor.
Mulrennan prayed daily for the young men and women throughout the world who had committed themselves to lives of service
to God's people. It was a most difficult path to follow—the understatement of the ages!—and he respected them so much,
prayed for them and for others to follow them. Miraculously, at
the dawn of this twenty-first century since the death and resurrection of Jesus, the number of vocations was on the increase:
incrementally, to be sure, and too early to call a real trend, but
encouragingly, desperately needed larger numbers. This despite—
because of—the devastating scandals and problems that had

rocked clergy and laity in his native United States. Were these seminarians and novices like the Tim Mulrennan of forty years ago? He had no doubt that they were, and the thought filled him with hope. He had promised himself shortly after his election that he would visit as many universities and seminaries and convents and monasteries as he could . . . for he had been a seminarian once.

Feelings of grandeur and mystery mingled with the hard-won humility of his heart, just as water mingles with and is transformed with the wine in the chalice.

A council. Could it come anywhere near to fulfilling his vision of such a gathering? How would the bishops respond to the summons of their brother and shepherd-in-chief? How would the Christian and non-Christian worlds respond? And, most importantly, would the Holy Spirit be "on the move" among the children of God in this hour and place? Did a time of inspiration or a time of darkness lie ahead? Only the Father Almighty knew these secret and sacred answers.

PART I

Fisher of Men

CHAPTER ONE

Jersey City, New Jersey, September 11, 2001

The archbishop, a lean, almost ascetic figure, tall with broad shoulders that filled out the flowing emerald-colored chasuble, bowed deeply toward the altar in a gesture of obeisance and reverence as he deliberately pronounced the words that sacred Tradition and Scripture attribute to Jesus Himself: "This is my body." He paused for a heartbeat, then continued: "Which will be given up for you." Timothy John Cardinal Mulrennan lifted the host, a thin wafer of unleavened bread that had, with his words, become the body of his Lord Jesus Christ. He held the host aloft before the gathered attendees of this special, early-morning mass, then replaced it in the plate and genuflected before it.

Next, he took the chalice of wine intermingled with a drop of water and pronounced the similar words of consecration in a clear, measured cadence: "This is my blood, the blood of the new and everlasting covenant, which will be shed for you and for all, so that sins may be forgiven." Again, he breathed silently before he added in a near-whisper the admonition that had brought Christians together for two thousand years: "Do this in memory of me." The gleaming upraised vessel reflected the blameless sunlight that shot through the windows of the chapel, in St. Peter Hall on the college campus, which were open to a bright, cloudless new day.

Cardinal Mulrennan had returned from Rome less than twenty-four hours earlier, ending a brief vacation trip combined with a visit to the Holy Father. He had been emotionally shaken by the sight of the old man whom he so loved—a bent and shrunken shell ravaged by age, disease, and the woes of the world, and still suffering the aftereffects of an assassination attempt twenty years before. Yet, never had he known the pope to be so mentally acute, attuned to the spiritual currents across the globe, even prophetic in his words and his attitude. The pontiff—the holiest man Tim Mulrennan had ever known—had sadly predicted a renewal of evil and darkness in the earthly kingdom, which very soon he would depart. . . . Difficult to believe on such a warm and glorious September day that war, pestilence, and famine might descend upon the people of God. Mulrennan smiled to himself as he continued the sacramental rite of the Eucharist, through the Lord's Prayer and the Agnus Dei and as he served Holy Communion to the community which had gathered for the planned events of the day—another busy, overcrowded schedule for the cardinal who was responsible for the care of one and a half million souls in the Archdiocese of Newark, within hollering distance of Manhattan island.

God is in charge, his spiritual director, an old priest colleague and mentor, Father Joel, always reminded him. Let God do His job and try your very best to do *yours*. Simple as that. Though Timothy Mulrennan's job was quite demanding and complex and highly public; still, he strove for simplicity and focus amid the heavy challenges and responsibilities that he faced nearly every day.

Like the pope himself, Cardinal Mulrennan was a successor of the apostles, a member of the worldwide college of bishops which is charged to teach the ancient faith and tend to the far-flung flock of Christ. Yet he also believed that the Bishop of Rome was indeed first among equals, a direct inheritor of the ministry of St. Peter and the living representative of Christ on earth, His vicar and chief servant. Not that he spent a lot of time thinking about the meaning of the apostolic succession . . . he was more often too busy with the day-to-day affairs of his diocese to soar into such elevated theological realms. In front of him each day was laid a crushingly packed agenda of activities—masses, talks, meetings, charity dinners, parish visits—that would cow any corporate CEO. But he liked it; in fact, he thrived on it.

The trip from which he had just returned, which had included a several-day holiday in Ireland, his ancestral homeland, was the very first lengthy break he had taken since his appointment to this archiepiscopal see. Occasionally he had taken a two-day "weekend" (in the middle of the week, of course) or squeezed in a round of golf on the Essex County public course, or a few days on retreat, which was always more work than relaxation. So, he actually felt refreshed and ready to tackle this first full working day, feeling blessed that he was in a job assignment that he loved. He was grateful that his five years in a curial position in Rome had ended with his appointment to the archdiocese where he had been born, raised, and educated.

In fact, in his homily this morning, after the Gospel reading from Luke, in which Jesus calls the apostles to join Him in His ministry, Mulrennan spoke to the forty or so professors, deans, and administrators from St. Peter's College about their connection to the apostles and their role in proclaiming the Good News, and he urged them, too, to be grateful for such a vocation. This mass with the archbishop was a part of their day-long convocation to mark the beginning of a new academic year.

"Push your boats out farther into the waters and let down your nets," he preached, echoing the words of the evangelist. "The fish you will catch, even after you think there are none left to harvest, will astound you—even as Simon Peter and his men were astounded. Let yourselves be surprised by God and His power to work such miracles in your lives and the lives of those you touch through your profession." If every Christian, and every Catholic, were to heed the simple instructions of Jesus, how the world would be transformed and the light shine through any darkness or disaster that might befall God's people. "They left everything behind to follow Him—all the way to His death and resurrection and beyond, to the end of their days. And today He calls us, his latter-day followers, to do the same. His message is changeless, asking us to change and become fully who the Father created us to be."

When the liturgy ended, at about 8:20 A.M., the archbishop stayed for a quick cup of coffee with the college president, a Jesuit priest friend of many years, along with the other academicians and religious who pressed him for details of his *ad limina* Vatican visit and asked after the health of the Holy Father.

"As you know, he is planning a trip to Armenia, the oldest Christian nation in the world," Cardinal Mulrennan said, "and is still determined to travel to Iraq some day. And I certainly would not bet against him—based on strength of will alone. His physical body is failing him, certainly as it does everyone, but his mind and spirit are stronger than I have ever seen, and I have known him for almost forty years." He had first met the future pope at the Second Vatican Council when the Pole was a young bishop—had observed the philosopher-pastor's fertile, restless mind at work even then. "I pray for him every day. And he prays for us."

By eight forty-five he had extracted himself—gracefully, he hoped—from the gathering and made his way to the car in the crowded college parking lot. A young priest named David Gallagher awaited him and would drive him back to Newark. Mulrennan got into the front seat instead of the back, pulled on his seat belt, and turned on the radio as the driver pulled onto the narrow street. He sat back and closed his eyes. A news bulletin caused him to jerk upright and turn up the volume: An airplane had just crashed into one of the World Trade Center towers. "David, let's drive toward Liberty State Park, quickly." He caught intermittent glimpses of the towers across the river and saw for himself that smoke was rising from one of them.

Less than ten minutes later, as they headed directly for the park on the Turnpike extension, he witnessed the swift, eerie approach of another airplane and a second heart-sickening explosion, and heard the echoing boom: Both towers were now on fire. "Good God," he muttered. "God, no, no, no." He wanted to bury his face in his hands, but he could not look away from the horror. Father Gallagher, a thirty-year-old who had been ordained less than four months before, drove on until he got to the park, pulled into the visitors' lot. Timothy Mulrennan bolted from the car and ran across the grass and pavement to the water's edge, unable to comprehend the scene he was witnessing.

Irresistibly, his heart was drawn to the sight, though his

thoughts were racing in every direction, tumbling through his brain. What was happening? Instinctively he knew it had to be a terrorist action. But how could something like that succeed? Weren't there security measures to protect our domestic airspace from such attacks?

The sky remained oddly, defiantly brilliant, the air perfect— but for the inky columns of smoke from the giant towers that rose and merged into one evil black cloud.

He and Father Gallagher then sped up to the pier where commuter ferries routinely shuttled back and forth across the water throughout the day. There were a few stunned commuters present and—significantly—a group of Jersey City firefighters loaded down with their equipment, waiting for the next outbound boat, which approached rapidly. One of them called out to Mulrennan: "It's the archbishop! Over here, Father!" With his distinctive urban Jersey accent he pronounced it "fawdder."

Tim jogged over to them, joined them on the deck of the ferry, along with some cops, nurses, and emergency medical workers— about three dozen in all. The ferry captain allowed the few civilians who wanted to make the trip to board, then pulled away from the pier. The waters were calm, clean, reflecting the bright blue day, but as they approached Lower Manhattan the ugliness of the destruction, the debris from the initial twin impact still floated on and above the harbor. The burning towers loomed. Tim Mulrennan looked away for a moment, to the south, to the Statue of Liberty which stood unviolated but a sadly silent witness to the event. She provided no answers. The radio blared news reports but provided no information beyond what they could see with their own eyes: a terror attack, a horror that only grew larger as they moved ever closer. As the boat approached the New York side, the archbishop called the men and women together for a prayer. He had no idea what lay ahead for them when they arrived at their destination. He knew that they would plunge immediately into the burgeoning chaos and put their professional skills to saving lives, as many and as swiftly as possible. God be with them. . . .

"God help us in this hour of difficulty and danger. Please be with those who have been injured and killed in this violation of our homeland. Please give strength to your servants who seek to help others in this terrible hour. We ask in the name of Your Son, the Prince of Peace, and the Holy Spirit, with the Blessed Mother, for your love and support in these efforts. Amen." He blessed the bowed heads with the sign of the cross. The men and women then lifted their faces grimly and turned toward the looming, threatening cityscape. One of the firefighters came to Tim and said, "My brother is a Port Authority cop. He works in there. I spoke to him last night. He and his wife have three boys."

Tim's mind reeled: How many thousands of people were in those buildings, and below ground and on the street, on the trains that fed into the World Trade Center underground? Tens if not hundreds of thousands of souls flowed into the area for work and tourist visits every single day. Now, many were trapped, many had probably been killed. What lay ahead in the next hour? What could he do? He looked around for Gallagher; he had lost track of the young priest. There he was, standing as still as a rock at the forward rail of the ferry, watching.

Then, movement from above, a rumbling that Mulrennan felt in his bones. He looked up as the ferry closed the last hundred yards to the slip. One of the towers splintered near the top and collapsed upon itself. At first slowly, then with increasing velocity, the structure disappeared in a sideways explosion of smoke and debris, falling almost gracefully to the earth. A bloody gray smudge against the sky was all that remained beside the still-erect sister tower, which continued to burn. He looked at his watch: ten A.M.

The ferry finally docked, after an agonizing ten or fifteen more minutes, and the cardinal from New Jersey stood behind the rescue workers, allowed them to debark first and dash directly toward the disaster, followed by the handful of commuters who seemed stunned, scared, uncertain where to go or what to do. A few minutes later, Mulrennan and Gallagher reached the street off the pier and stood there trying to orient themselves when it happened again: The second building, the one with the distinctive three hundred sixty-foot television mast atop, the first to be hit, fell. Gasps and screams from the people in the street.

The earth, this seemingly impregnable island of granite, shifted and vibrated beneath his feet as the giant structure shuddered in its death throes.

"Oh, dear Christ!" he cried, uncomprehending, like a child.

"The world has been changed, forever—by the power of evil. Let us, then, change the world, with God's help—by the power of good." For the second time in twelve hours he preached a homily, this one unanticipated, and this time in the familiar cathedral basilica that was his home church. Sacred Heart Cathedral in the heart of the city of Newark stood majestically on a hill amid the lush greenery of a park and the poignantly stark reality of urban decay, in a "bad part of town," to those who did not live there. From the chancery one could see the Manhattan skyline clearly, now palled by a sinister curtain of smoke and ash illumined by searchlights and bereft of its mighty towers of commerce. The cardinal had opened the doors of the church, which had been designated a basilica by Pope John Paul II upon his visit there in 1995, and hundreds of Catholics and other locals had streamed in for a special prayer service on this day of horror. The people had prayed the rosary with their shepherd and now leaned forward in the pews to hear his words.

"So many in our local community have died, including firemen, policemen, rescue workers, Port Authority officials, and civilians who worked in the buildings that have collapsed. How many? Perhaps thousands of souls have perished. Others are lost, and we don't know whether they're dead or alive. Will they ever be found? Will their families ever know what has happened to them? How can we cope with the terrible grief and anger that we feel tonight? What will tomorrow bring? So many questions, and precious few comprehensible, acceptable answers. What then, are we to do?

"First, my dear friends, we must pray. We must lift up our dead and lost brothers and sisters into God's waiting arms. We must ask our Blessed Mother and all the angels and saints to intercede, as the holy messengers they are, to carry the souls of our loved ones to the eternal rest that is the Father. We say very directly through our prayers: Receive them, Lord, here they are, Lord, those who themselves passed through the horror as we here did not. And help us to find survivors who may be buried, clinging to life—if it be Your will."

His own lungs still burned, and his eyes stung horribly; there were no more tears to cry, but the nerves and blood vessels ached, blurring his vision. He could still smell the stench of dust and death, and he only wanted to go back to the scene, the unspeakable vision of violence and devastation that was now being called Ground Zero—the very epicenter of the handiwork of the Evil One. When this prayer service was over he would return and stand by the men whose task now—indeed an impossible task— was to remove the shattered remains of steel, glass, and concrete that had buried their fallen comrades.

An archbishop never for a waking moment forgot who and what he was: a man set apart from others as their shepherd and overseer. But in these terrible moments, Cardinal Mulrennan had felt as helpless and abjectly human as anyone—a man among his fellow men in their worst time of grief and terror. Still, the bishop's special ministry was such a part of his being that he could not stop himself; his mind and body had switched on a sort of spiritual autopilot—which had not yet switched off.

For several hours he had walked among the people of the city, helped some of the injured find medical assistance, prayed with firemen and emergency personnel, carried water and supplies to the front line of the rescue effort, looked for any familiar face— for any little sign of hope or comfort—but saw none. The rescue work had been delayed for crucial hours by the scary instability of the site, devastated buildings on the verge of collapse, threatening the men on the ground. Police had pushed people toward the north, out of the war zone. A flood of dust-grimed men and women, refugees, flooded uptown on the streets and highways with remarkably little panic. Mulrennan soon realized, after talking with firemen and medical teams who tended to the wounded on street corners, that hundreds of New York City and Port Authority officers—fire and police—had been lost when they rushed to respond to the emergency. Radios were on everywhere and the news reports wafted through the air with the asbestos, soot, paper, and debris across the grid of chaos that was Lower Manhattan. . . .

Father Gallagher had stood with him and walked with him each difficult step of the way, until both men's black clerical suits had turned white with the inescapable dust, their faces unrecognizable behind masks of grime. Every new secretary endured a lengthy training period with his bishop. For some it took a year or longer to get the hang of the job in all its complexity—and to learn the personality of the boss. This young priest was getting an education that neither he nor his archbishop could ever have imagined.

"Second, we must tend to those who are left behind, whose lives have been torn asunder by this evil act. They need us now—and they will for a long time to come: the spouses and the children and the parents, the loved ones in the wider community. As never before, we must stand together in love and solidarity with each other. We must recommit to each other in the name of our Savior."

Mulrennan wore the bright red choir vestments of his office, including the little red skullcap and the golden cross upon his chest. He had stripped off the day's clothing and showered but had not eaten. His staff had attempted to sit him down to feed him something—soup, bread, anything—but he had refused. He desperately craved a smoke, but did not give in to that temptation. He had gone into his personal chapel in the chancery for some solitude and silence. Then he had come directly to the basilica where he greeted the faithful, welcomed them into the candlelit house of worship where he had been ordained a priest thirty-eight years before. Now he was their bishop and they came to him for words of comfort and instruction. What could he say to them that made sense? He had not prepared a homily, but spoke from the gut.

"Thirdly, we all must face judgment, we the living and the dead. The late Cardinal Hume wrote about judgment in this way: 'Judgment is whispering into the ear of a merciful and compassionate God the story of my life which I had never been able to tell.' In this life, even with those we most love and trust, our story is never fully shared. Fear of being misunderstood, inability to understand ourselves, ignorance of the darker side of our hidden lives, or just shame, make it very difficult to share. Therefore, so often, our story is not told in this life. Our brothers and sisters who have gone before us are right now telling God their stories and hearing His compassionate response.

"And finally, we must reclaim our lives after the time of mourning. It may be difficult, perhaps impossible, to imagine our families and our jobs ever being the same. It will require hard work and constant prayer to rebuild our lives. But God calls you to do so, for His sake, and for the sake of our children. Yes, we are afraid. Yes, we are sad. Yes, we are angry at the perpetrators of such a crime. And in such times God calls us more than ever to love our neighbor, to give of ourselves without stint or favor. May we see the countenance of God before us in our efforts to change hearts and to change the world. Now, as we do each day in the Holy Mass, let us exchange with each other a sign of Christ's peace and love."

He stepped down from the pulpit and mingled with the archdiocesan staff and his auxiliary bishops who sat behind the altar. He embraced each man and woman as the tearful congregation did the same, by the hundreds.

Just a few hours before, at about five P.M., young Father Gallagher had "rescued" the cardinal, who would probably still be wandering the gray-shrouded, shattered streets if he had not. Remarkably, he'd had the presence of mind to borrow Mulrennan's pocket date book, and on his cellular telephone he had contacted the chancery up at St. Patrick's Cathedral. He had then pulled Tim Mulrennan away from the field of death and destruction, and the two of them walked the forty blocks uptown, where the New York cardinal's people shoved them into a police car that took them across the closed-off George Washington Bridge at which one of Mulrennan's own men picked him up and transported him safely back to his home.

Home . . . never to be the same again, but always his home.

Rome, December 24, 2002

Kurt Schulhafer sat expectantly in the back pew of the nearly empty church a few hours before the midnight service was to begin that would herald the celebration of the birth of Christ. Years of discipline as an officer of the Vatican's Swiss Guard allowed him to maintain a rigidly calm outward appearance, even as he felt his internal organs churning with fear. The scents of burning candle wax and flowers mingled in the dense, dark air of the baroque structure. He kept his breathing even and shallow, his hands flat atop his knees.

Colonel Kurt Schulhafer, the top uniformed commander of the men who guarded the person of the Holy Father, awaited his secret appointment with a man he had never met before, only spoken to in a brief telephone conversation. He was not accustomed to such cloak-and-dagger maneuvers but understood the necessity of extreme precautions in this situation. An immoral situation of his own creation. How had he come to this place, this turn of events, this evil? Had he not tried to live an upright, even spotless life in service to his Church and his God? When—how—why had it all turned sour and evil and wrong?

He attempted to pray but could not. The words, the feelings would not come . . . the unalterable truth stood in the way. He closed his eyes and tried again: *God*—the single-syllable Name stuck like a fish hook somewhere between his intestines and his heart. The pain only grew worse.

He remembered the first time he had seen Carl Boehmer, a recruit for the Guard, a stocky, rough-hewn mountain boy who knew not what he was getting into, five hundred miles from home and a million miles from the life he had known for his first nineteen years. A raw country recruit like hundreds of others before him. Why had he been different, special?

Seven years ago . . . Schulhafer himself had been that much younger and further removed from his own mortality. He had been a captain of the Guard then, one of three company leaders

of the uniformed group, proud, newly married and expecting a
first child, hoping for a boy. His wife, Marta-Marie, had quickly
lost her seemingly uncritical adoration of the men who wore the
funny bumblebee uniform, as she came to call it. "Marching
around like toy soldiers without guns," she said. "Who do you
think you're protecting—or impressing?" She had spoken with a
smile on her pretty pink lips, but the words stung worse than any
bee could.

"The great Michelangelo created these uniforms," he had pro-
tested.

"I don't give a damn," was her reply. The resentment caused
by those words did not fade away, in fact deepened and hardened
as the years passed.

He sat there on the hard bench in the dark church and heard
her say it—and many other things—again and again. Was she
aware how much her words, tossed at him so casually, had hurt
him, had driven him away? Her voice echoed through his brain
even now in this strange, unwelcoming place. . . .

"Herr Schultz."

The voice from behind and above startled the seated man,
punctured the bubble of silence he had imagined would surround
and protect him from evil. He turned to address the man but saw
only a shadowy black form in the darkness, dimly backlit by a
bank of devotional candles. "Yes," Schulhafer answered, ac-
knowledging the agreed-upon code name. Then he remembered
the proper password response. He said, "Mass will begin soon
for the faithful."

"Well, my friend, we meet at last," the stranger said, coming
around to join Schulhafer in the pew. He spoke in perfect
German, but without an easily identifiable foreign or regional accent, though something about the voice—about him—was faintly
familiar. The scents of cologne and tobacco mingled cloyingly
about him. "There is not much time, so let us get to the point."

"This is difficult for me. I have never done such a thing, you
must understand."

He himself still did not understand how this man had known
to approach *him* at just this time, when he was most desperate

and confused—and afraid. It disturbed and frightened him: an anonymous phone call . . . a proposition . . . a meeting time and passwords . . . If this man, seemingly from nowhere, knew about his problem, then who else did? At least this was a potential solution—a way out—however terrible the method.

"I do. I am a man of business, but also a man of faith. It is certainly not an easy or unconsidered matter we are dealing with. I am prepared to move forward if you direct me to do so. And if you have the money."

"Yes, I have the money." Colonel Schulhafer scanned the nave of the church, looking for any familiar face or indication of threat. He wondered whether he would feel at ease, truly comfortable in his own skin, ever again. In the interior breast pocket of his woolen jacket was the key to a locker in the Termini, the railroad station, that contained a fat envelope of large-denomination, unmarked American notes, mostly one hundred-dollar bills. He had borrowed, begged, and lied to obtain such a large amount of cash—though it had not been as difficult as the decision to end another man's life. He fingered the key in his own pocket. Once he gave it over to the stranger, the decision was sealed. He wanted to ask many questions, but his tongue was frozen with fear.

"Let me review the terms briefly—then I must ask you a question," the man said in perfectly modulated, clipped speech. He sounded to Schulhafer like a fellow military man. "Fifty thousand dollars cash, U.S.—untraceable. Half in advance. The task is to eliminate one Carl Boehmer, sergeant of the Swiss Guard, by whatever means deemed appropriate—" The ghostly figure had kept his face in near-complete shadow, so it was impossible for Schulhafer to get a clear view. He was not a large man but was bulked up by a dark topcoat. He paused, listened to the faint echo of his own voice, then continued. "At the earliest possible time. In fact, I will tell you, frankly, Herr Schultz, that he shall be dead by tomorrow midnight, so you need not worry on that score."

"Do you have to tell me all this?" the Guard colonel interjected, now shifting nervously in the narrow wooden pew.

"Yes, Mein Herr. And I require you to tell me something, before I carry out this mission." Schulhafer felt the killer's eyes bore into his skull. "Why exactly do you require this man to die?"

"You did not tell me this was a requirement."

"I am telling you now, sir. It is what they call a deal-breaker. Although I have a notion, as I mentioned to you before, I must *know*, as a matter of professional interest."

Schulhafer could not see the ghost's face but thought he detected a cruel smile there. He had no choice. He lifted the locker key from his inner pocket and discreetly slid it down and into the other's open hand. Then he spoke in halting bursts. "He has threatened to blackmail me—ruin my family—he claims we had an affair—he is a homosexual and he says he will expose me unless I leave my wife and children. I believe he is insane. This is so wrong—dangerous—my career will be over if this ever becomes known. And my family—" He tightly folded his hands and hung his head in shame. He wanted to be invisible, to die.

"Is it true, what this man says?" the other pressed.

Kurt Schulhafer hesitated. What did it matter now whether it were true or not? Boehmer was as good as dead. And why should he tell this criminal? He decided to bluff and hope for the best. "He actually believes it. I think he wanted to be—that is, he wanted me to be his lover. Usually we are quite able to screen out homosexuals in the application and training process. I don't know how he managed to keep it secret for so long."

"We all have secrets, Colonel Schulhafer." He did not tell the colonel his secret: that he already knew what the colonel had so reluctantly revealed, and more; that Boehmer would, later the same night, "commit suicide" by gunshot into the roof of his mouth.

"We agreed not to use real names," the Guard commander shot back, looking over his shoulder at the low arches behind the two seated men. It's time to go, he thought. The image of Carl Boehmer, the young Guard who had loved him recklessly and unspeakably, would not fade from his mind. He could see the face, the hundred planes and lines and valleys there, the simple handsome eyes that spoke silently and eloquently of hurt and jealousy. The face that would soon be dead and forgotten by the living. He must go now. "No names," he emphasized.

"Yes, you will excuse me, please, for the lapse. We all have our lapses, too. Tell me the truth, my friend. I must know every aspect of the case, for my own protection. Who knows, you might wish to have me eliminated in the future. It is not unheard of in this business."

"I don't see why—"

"The most important thing—more important than you or I—is the truth. That is what this Church stands for, the purest truth man has ever known." He looked up to the ceiling and Schulhafer could now see his profile: a high brow, fine sculpted nose, and strong chin. "Untruth must be eliminated, like heresy. Do you see what I mean, sir?"

"You are preaching to me of truth in this house of God, when we are arranging the elimination of a young man."

"A homosexual blackmailer, a criminal. I can sleep at night, can you? I provide for my family, and I confess my sins. I do what I believe is God's will—even though sometimes I don't like it. Well, I don't have to like it, but I am required to accomplish His will to the best of my imperfect ability. Tell me then, in frankness, between men: Are you afraid of Boehmer because he is telling the truth?"

Schulhafer was afraid as he had never been, for his own life and for his family. What would happen to them if this terrible thing became public knowledge? Yes, he was afraid of Boehmer, a mercurial, uneducated young man. . . .

Often these men were stolid Alpine stock, bred to conform, intellectually uncurious. Only male Swiss citizens under thirty years old, at least five-foot-eight, single, and "of good character" may apply to join the *Guardia Svizzera Pontificia*. The duty is not onerous: eight- to ten-hour shifts, divided among the three squads, known as *Geschwader*, of thirty to forty men. Single men were expected to be celibate, maintain strict moral conduct always. Most importantly, they had to be able to look good in the somewhat ridiculous regalia they were required to don: uniforms of red, yellow, orange, and blue felt strips, plumed metal helmets or black berets, knee socks, armed with halberds and concealed nine-millimeter pistols. The hundred-man military force, separate from the regular civilian-run police force, called the *Ufficio Centrale di Vigilanza* (or just the Vigilanza), has been the pope's personal bodyguard since 1509 and is headquartered off the Porta Sant'Anna entrance to Vatican City. They take a special oath—called the *Giuraménto*—to protect the Supreme Pontiff and, during the vacancy of the Holy See, the *Sede Vacante*, the entire Sacred College of Cardinals, who must bury the dead pope, temporarily administer Church affairs, and then elect the successor within a two- to three-week span. So these modern-day mercenaries, heirs to a noble tradition of loyalty to the person of the Holy Father.

On May 6, 1527, nearly one hundred fifty Guards (of the 189 then in existence) were massacred by German Protestant invaders in St. Peter's Basilica. The surviving contingent helped the Medici pope, Clement VII, escape to the Castel Sant'Angelo, and subsequent pontiffs never forgot that act of self-sacrifice. When Paul VI reorganized the papal security system, only the Swiss Guard remained intact when other units were disbanded or reconfigured. Every year, May 6 is commemorated with special ceremonies and a papal mass.

The usual tour of duty was two years, but Schulhafer was a "lifer," with eighteen years under his belt. He had made it a career, and a somewhat comfortable one, with retirement not far off in the future. He would still be young enough to enjoy the rest of his life in his home canton of Wallis, where his parents and brothers still lived.

Within the past year he had served at two historic papal funerals, occasions of splendor and sadness, complex logistical and security challenges, events that required him and his men to put into practice the intense training they had all undergone. Yes, they were ceremonial adjuncts, but an integral part of the pontifical traditions at such times, a link to the medieval past and guardsmen at the gate of the unknown future. His heart had swelled with pride at the performance of the Guard—crisp, professional, unobtrusive yet ever-present throughout the funeral ceremonies. He had been especially proud of Vice-corporal Boehmer, his protégé and friend, who executed his tasks and led his men almost flawlessly throughout the days of mourning under the glare of international press scrutiny.

How had such love and admiration turned into this—this terrible necessity, this sinful ending of a human life?

The last time he had spoken with Carl Boehmer, several days ago, had been emblematic of the place they had come to in their troubled relationship. Carl had come unexpectedly to Schulhafer's residence in Vatican City, the apartment he shared with his wife and son. Marta-Marie had answered the doorbell, welcomed Carl inside and called for her husband. The boy, Josef, was napping, a blessed and unusual relief for the parents on a Saturday afternoon. It was a scene of apparent domestic stability and serenity, and the younger Swiss Guard officer stood there awkwardly, his broad shoulders hunched, observing the quiet scene. Schulhafer pecked his wife on her cheek and came to the door.

"Carl, what do you want?" he asked, keeping his voice low and even. His own heart thumped wildly within his chest, attuned to the danger and electricity of this potentially unwelcome, unfriendly confrontation.

"Colonel, I am sorry to disturb you at home, but I must talk to you." He looked up at the taller man, his superior and lover, with the penetrating, brown-eyed gaze of a spurned pet.

"Let us go outside," Schulhafer said.

"It's not—I don't mean to intrude in your home, but—"

"I understand. We will go out." The Swiss Guard colonel matter-of-factly told his wife he must leave for a while, would be back soon, and he took his hat and winter jacket as he left with Boehmer. The two men went downstairs and outside, exited Vatican City through the familiar gate with a wave to colleagues at the guard station.

Did any of them know? Schulhafer wondered, more than idly. Or suspect? He jammed his hands in the pockets of the jacket and walked, head down, at a brisk clip until they were several blocks from the Vatican. He had not said a word, nor had Carl Boehmer.

Finally the younger man broke the silence between them. "Kurt, I have missed you. I need to see you, to be with you. Why are you pushing me away like this? What have I done?"

"I told you, we must stop seeing each other. It is wrong."

"Why wrong? When we are together . . . I know it is difficult for you with your family. I will make it as easy as possible. I am not going to upset your life, but I have to see you, I can't end our friendship like this. It's not wrong, not at all."

"It's more than you and me. I mean, my wife doesn't suspect anything, but if we continue she might—she's not stupid. I need her. I love her. It cannot continue, you and me. And we have to work together. It's not right for many reasons, Carl."

"You're afraid. I understand that. I can help you. But don't cut me off, don't end it like this, I beg you."

"Don't say that. Don't make me the bad guy. Believe me, it's not easy for me, either, but I must do the right thing, for many reasons." He pulled his hands from the pockets and held them at his side as they walked, the frosty December air biting at their faces.

Schulhafer hated confrontation, preferring gentlemanly agreement between friends. He had confessed his mortal sin to a new confessor, an American priest, who had immediately required, as penance, that the Swiss Guard commandant end the relationship with the younger man—without delay or hesitation, no matter the emotional upset it would cause either party. He had hoped the American would be more open, more liberal, but had been disappointed—again. So, Kurt Schulhafer had indeed broken off with Boehmer several days earlier. But Carl had not accepted the end of their relationship.

Tears clouded the colonel's vision as he sat in the dark church. Why was this man whom he did not know forcing him to reveal his innermost secrets? As much as he had dreaded taking this step, he now faced an abyss to which he thought he had turned his back. Dear God, I am sorry, I am so sorry, forgive me!

"I thought I loved him, and that he loved me," he finally admitted.

"How could you do such a thing?" the stranger asked. "This is contrary to the law of God and the law of the Church. You are treading very dangerous ground, Herr Schultz." The other man, Boehmer, would pay the ultimate price for his unspeakable crime.

"I do not submit myself to your judgment, only to God's."

"Sometimes God uses men to achieve His works, even imperfect men like you and me. After all, He put us on earth and created us in His image and likeness for some reason—to reflect His love back to Him in the best way we can." The stranger fingered the proferred key, then deposited it inside his coat. His hand lingered there. He turned to look directly at Kurt Schulhafer. "We do what we can for Him," the man repeated. "Especially in these evil times."

"I have tried. God knows—" The Swiss Guard commandant drew in his breath sharply as he saw the dull glint of the knife blade sliding from beneath the other's dark coat. "What are you going to do?" he asked, cursing his own stupidity.

Swiftly, but gently, the killer placed his right hand on Schulhafer's arm and leaned toward him. His left hand pushed the ten-inch serrated blade deep into the colonel's abdomen, puncturing the intestines. He then pulled up, along the rib cage, with a powerful, practiced stroke, like a butcher. The tip of the blade angled up and just nicked the heart. Blood rapidly filled the body cavity and spilled onto Schulhafer's legs.

The murderer removed a dark towel from his coat, wiped his hand, and dropped the towel on the dying man's lap. After removing the colonel's wallet and ID badge and papers, to confuse and delay identification, he made certain that Kurt Schulhafer remained upright. Then he rose from the pew and strode quickly to the church door, moving like a ghost through mist and shadow into the silent night of sacred anticipation, the killing blade secured beneath his own coat.

CHAPTER TWO

Rome, December 25, 2002

In a city renowned for so many elegant and monumental churches, the Basilica of San Giovanni in Laterano, or St. John Lateran, is sometimes called "the mother of all churches," for its fourth-century provenance, its rich architectural history, and its soaring, spectacular beauty. The façade of solemn, majestic white columns was created by the Florentine Alessandro Galilei in the 1730s; the sanctuary, with its gilded arches and holy frescoes, was erected in 1367 and redesigned in the baroque style by Borromini in the seventeenth century. Within its tabernacle are said to be the remains of the heads of the greatest apostles, Peter and Paul, as well as relics such as the sackcloth of John the Baptist, the red robe given to Christ by the Roman executioners, and the cloth Jesus used to wipe the feet of his disciples. The site of the basilica was originally the barracks of the equestrian guard of Constantine—although it is said that in fact he had stolen it from the noble Laterani, the family who held legal title to the property— and that first protector of Christianity eventually donated the property to the pope. For several centuries the Lateran was the administrative headquarters of the Roman Church and the palace of the popes. It is a place of miracles and relics and precious ornaments, including the bronze doors of the central entrance, which came from the ancient senate house of Rome, and one of which is a Holy Door opened only in Jubilee years by the pontiff himself. For some, St. John Lateran is the true heart of Christendom, more sacred even than that relative newcomer, St. Peter's Basilica. And, significantly, it is the pope's own church.

Pope Celestine VI, just five months into his historic pontificate, chose to celebrate mass at noon on Christmas Day in the cathedral of his personal see as Bishop of Rome. Unlike the elaborate midnight liturgy that was broadcast on live television throughout the world, this event attracted a mere two thousand or so of the local Roman faithful, with some several score pilgrims and a handful of reporters and editors who covered the pontiff's every sneeze and eyeblink.

The first American pope, who had been Archbishop of Newark before his surprise election in the second conclave of a tumultuous year now ending, began his homily by welcoming visitors to the monumental cathedral. He greeted the local faithful, whose pastor he was, the third foreigner in a row—that is, non-Italian and (more importantly) non-Roman—delivered to them for their skeptical appraisal. He had found them open and curious, if a bit world-weary and unmoved by the prospect. Perhaps they were little different from any parish in his own home diocese; they always, naturally, sized up the new man. In his white and gold chasuble, designed to accommodate his six-four height, and white silk zucchetto, or skullcap, he stood before the altar, a lavalier microphone discreetly attached to the neck of his pallium, loosely worn on his shoulders as the symbol of his universal jurisdiction. Even in these sacred vestments whose significance dated back hundreds, even thousands of years, the slender man from North Auburn, New Jersey seemed as contemporary and immediate as any media-created celebrity. The difference was that he quite consciously placed himself in the apostolic line of succession as the 263rd Vicar of Christ and Servant of the Servants of God since St. Peter himself. Sometimes in quiet, private moments that were all too infrequent it nearly overwhelmed him, but he could not and would not put it aside; he lived with the thought of it and the grave responsibility it represented for twenty-four hours each day of his life.

From the moment of his election, Timothy John Mulrennan, a fit sixty-four years old and nearly forty years a priest, experienced what so very few men ever have: the full weight of the cross of responsibility for Christ's universal Church.

Now, as he looked out over his flock gathered in this magnificent structure, memories of the distant past and hopes for the dimly imagined future collided in his mind, and he forced himself to stand squarely in the present moment. A human life was built of memory and hope; the philosophers may attempt to analyze the existential or phenomenological significance of these manifestations and their origin, but a man simply lived them, built on them, worked and dreamed and suffered—despite rather than because of any school of theology. For this man, there was no turning back, only moving forward, one foot in front of the other . . . with the constant prayer that God's will be revealed and fulfilled. He knew no other way.

He spoke the first part of the homily in painstakingly rehearsed Italian.

"My dear brothers and sisters in Christ, as we celebrate the birth of our Savior and His promise of salvation for all mankind, let us open our hearts as never before to the call of the Father, the sacrifice of the Son, and the silent but certain prompting of the Holy Spirit. Let us listen to the cry of the baby who lies in the manger. Such a cry naturally concerns and inspires us. It is the unfamiliar voice of the God of Israel in a very familiar, inescapably human form."

The pope noted that the cardinals and bishops and priests who were concelebrating this mass with him sat to each side of the altar and stared stonily into space or at the floor as he delivered the meticulously prepared text of the homily. His friend and Secretary of State and twice *grande elletore*, or great elector, in the recent conclaves, Leandro Cardinal Biagi, was not there, nor his personal secretary, Monsignor Philip Calabrese, one of several "refugees" from Newark now serving on the papal staff. These two close advisers were back at the Apostolic Palace in the pontiff's office awaiting his return; they both knew what he was about to announce, in fact they had each had a hand in the draft of the statement.

As recently as two weeks ago, both men had been skeptical and concerned—and had expressed their feelings bluntly to Pope Celestine. He expected nothing less of them, and he had listened to their cautions and reservations.

Calabrese, a former seminary instructor whom Mulrennan had enlisted a few years previously as assistant vicar and director of communications and public affairs for the archdiocese, was a Jersey City native with a laid-back professorial demeanor and a sharp mind for the intricacies of human behavior in the realms of business, politics, the academy and, most importantly, the Church. He had served a few years as a parish priest a dozen years ago, when he had been completing his second master's degree, in Scriptural theology, before embarking upon his doctorate. Amazingly, for such a young man, Calabrese had been able to balance intense studies and pastoral work, earning high marks in both. The pope valued the clarity of his observations and his writing skills; at forty-two, he also provided a younger and more contemporary point of view that was lacking—to say the least—in the Curia. In contrast to the aristocratic Cardinal Biagi, who had descended from medieval popes, princes, and patrons of high art, he sometimes peppered his speech with street language that betrayed his urban roots.

Phil Calabrese stood five-eleven, with a longish mane of silver hair and laughing brown eyes. His face was scarred from childhood acne and lined beyond his years. He spoke with his hands as much as his mouth—which was the subject of some good-natured ethnic ribbing from colleagues. As the pope had read his rough first draft of the Christmas homily-announcement, the American monsignor had paced the length of the study in the papal quarters, a perfectionist deep in the throes of creation.

"We need to simplify it, Phil," the pontiff had told him, "more for me than anyone else. I don't want to invite criticism for any hidden or double meaning or potential ambiguity. And I have to be convincing in Italian."

"Yes, Holy Father. I'll take another crack at the sonofabitch." Then he caught himself. "Sorry, I didn't mean to say it like—"

"I know what you meant, Father. And you should say what you mean, especially here. You can be certain these walls have heard profanity before."

"Forgive me, Holy Father. I'm still learning. I get over-excited sometimes . . ."

"This is exciting stuff, for me at least," a tensely smiling Pope Celestine said. "I won't get to hear the sotto voce cursing of my holy brothers of the Curia, so I must settle for yours. I suppose there is no way to soften the blow for them." He looked to the Secretary of State.

"Short of a fully loaded encyclical, this will be the most important statement of your pontificate," Biagi said. "It should reflect your thinking exactly, clearly." The cardinal had sat near the pope, reading each page as Mulrennan passed it to him. "However, do not underestimate the value of ambiguity, when wisely and judiciously applied. I believe the American politicians call that 'wiggle room.' "

"You're right, of course—as always. But don't expect me to do everything you tell me, my friend."

"I know how stubborn you can be, Holy Father. I have a good memory of the conclaves."

"Too good, if you ask me. I hope you don't influence Father Calabrese against me." He turned to the younger priest. "And I cannot caution you enough to be wary of this man—you can see how he ruined my life!"

Calabrese laughed, and Biagi gravely shook his head to deny the accusation. The pope treasured these light moments; they were rare in the highly charged atmosphere of the papal apartments in the Vatican. The pontiff stood by the large-paned window of his private study and peered out at the cold expanse of St. Peter's Square below. It was inaccurate and unfair to consider himself a "prisoner" in this place, but he felt the weight of history and expectations close around him in these thick old walls. He was incredibly grateful to Biagi and Calabrese.

The pope had thanked them and asked them to keep the information to themselves until he had told the rest of the world. He expected that the rest of the world would be as surprised as they had been at first. There had been no rumors, no backroom whispering or second-guessing—because he had kept his intentions *in pectore*, secretly within his own breast. Perhaps the word surprise was an underestimation of the expected response: Shock might fit the situation more aptly.

Then, early this morning before he left the Apostolic Palace for the mass, the pontiff had learned of the deaths—the murder and suicide—of the commander of his Swiss Guard and one of the vice-corporals. He received the word in silence and sorrow, went to his chapel for a special prayer for the dead men, then pulled himself together for the day ahead.

"As Christians," Celestine VI continued, "we believe the authentic revelation of the Hebrew Scriptures and the New Testament; we receive the holy Tradition handed down to us through the apostles and evangelists and the early Church fathers. The Scriptures are the recorded manifestations of the Word of God, and the doctrines of the Church are drawn directly therefrom.

"Think of the wondrous events we celebrate in this holy season: the Savior's birth as a man, the shepherds' vision of the angels' choir, the visitation of the wise men from the East, the miraculous escape from Herod's sword. In later ages, martyrs, saints and holy men and women have been moved to great deeds by the voice of God in their own hearts. And in our day we have the divinely inspired event of the Second Vatican Council as a vivid and immediate example of the stirrings of the Holy Spirit, the giver of life and divine messenger from the Father, calling us to reexamine and reform the dogmatic and liturgical representations of the Body of Christ, His Church in the modern world."

The speaker paused and brought his hands together. He touched the Ring of the Fisherman that he now wore as a sign of his apostolic office, the ring that would be taken from his finger upon his death and broken into tiny pieces with a silver hammer, just as his body would disintegrate into dust within a cold dark tomb. He believed, however, that his own physical mortality and the passing of material things were outweighed on the great scale of existence by the revealed knowledge of immortality. He asked himself: What role shall I play—a weak human being who, whether by accident or design, has been assigned a mark upon the stage of the world—in the unfolding drama that is the Church?

The words of a favorite hymn played upon his heart: *Reclothe us in our rightful mind; in purer lives thy service find, in deeper*

reverence praise . . . O still small voice of calm. In myself, I matter
not very much at all, but what I do and how it affects others will
be remembered and judged by God and by history.

"Brethren, I wish to make a statement to you, and to our
Christian and non-Christian brothers and sisters throughout the
world." Mulrennan had made a very deliberate choice from the
first day of his pontificate to use the singular personal pronoun
rather than the royal and papal "we" when addressing the faithful. Some of the Curia's hard-liners still had a difficult time with
that. "And to the college of bishops, and to our dedicated clergy
who serve you humbly and lovingly as earthly vicars of Christ,
and to our self-sacrificing religious around the world, I also send
this message."

A few of the gathered eminences with whom he shared the
altar pricked up their ears at Celestine's words and the change in
the tone of his voice. They had learned to expect surprises from
this American who seemed from the moment of his election to
chafe at the suffocating traditions of the Vatican. Even though he
had served for several years in the Church bureaucracy himself,
and as much as he respected, even revered the institution of the
papacy, this pope had grown increasingly impatient with the diplomatic subtleties and indirect style of communication inherent in
every aspect of life and work within the Apostolic Palace. It had
taken every ounce of patience and tact—bolstered by many hours
of prayer—for him to contain his temper even as he confronted
the frequently passive-aggressive behavior of the Roman Curia and
the long-entrenched Vatican apparatus. He now self-consciously
shifted to his native English for the balance of the homily.

"At this moment the Vatican press office is distributing a release in sixteen languages that will reflect exactly what I am about
to say to you." Pope Celestine VI breathed deeply, felt the increased warmth in his own cheeks and the moisture upon his
brow. It was a cold Roman day outside, but sunshot and cloudless. Inside, the basilica was close with incense, candle smoke, and
human warmth.

"To you, my spiritual family, I announce a new general or

ecumenical council for the Holy Catholic Church, to convene in approximately a year, to be held here, in the Holy See. This proposal will no doubt surprise many of you. You might understandably ask, Why now? It has been 'only' forty years since the last one, but it is self-evidently the time. Why so quickly? I know that there were more than three years of preparation for Vatican II. In the electronic age, however, we require substantially less preparation time—every document can be shared instantly and there need be less travel time for all the bishops before, during, and after the council sessions.

"We are commissioned to be fishers of men, to preach the Gospel to all nations, even unto the ends of the earth. I say we shall go there, to where the people and their priests need us. In the act of convening a council and discussing the crucial issues and problems of our time we shall be fulfilling Christ's commission. Yes, I know there will be some elements of disagreement among the bishops and the laity about this idea. But remember, this is an ancient custom of the Church, to achieve reconciliation with the contemporary world. From the first such council in Nicea in 325 to the Vatican Council of living memory to so many of us, there have already been twenty-one councils—and we faithful Christians must benefit greatly from such a gathering of today's senior Church leaders.

"I have reflected upon the words of His Holiness, Blessed John XXIII, when he first announced to a select group of cardinals his plan. He said, 'We earnestly pray for a good beginning, continuation, and successful outcome of these proposals, which involve hard work directed toward light, improvement, and joy for all Christian peoples, toward a renewed invitation to the faithful of the individual religious groups, for them also to follow us with friendly courtesy in this seeking after unity and grace which so many souls from every part of the earth eagerly desire.'

"Today, in the early years of the twenty-first century, we can say virtually the same thing, though the particularity and urgency of the crisis is much different. We now live in a world of unspeakable terrorism and abuse of human beings. We seek unity among Christian denominations; we seek understanding between Chris-

tians and Jews; we pray for dialogue between Christians and Muslims, between Christians and other faith traditions of the world.
These ecumenical concerns are not merely theological, but, at
their core, *human* concerns. To solve the problems of our people,
we must address the concerns of all people. As protectors and
transmitters of the deposit of faith, we are obligated, by the very
content of that faith, to share it and to learn from others its truer
and dearer meaning. We are charged to bring peace to a world
at war with itself."

He had been a seminarian when the Vatican Council was convened by Pope John XXIII in 1962, a very new priest during the
subsequent sessions. In fact, he had served as a secretary to one
of the operating committees under an American archbishop,
which kept him close to the action and informed about the debates as they progressed through the autumn of 1965 when Paul
VI closed the council. Ever since, as priest and bishop, Mulrennan
had become a student of Vatican II; he had absorbed the council
documents and the volumes of commentary and reflected on them
for four decades. He also read about the past ecumenical councils
of the Church, from the first meetings in Nicea, Constantinople,
Ephesus, and Chalcedon to the first Vatican Council in 1869–70,
which had never been officially closed, rather aborted, when
French troops loyal to Pope Pius IX abandoned the city to the
Italians during the Franco-Prussian war and the bishops and cardinals fled to their homes—after the acrimonious debate and vote
on the definition of papal infallibility.

Twenty-one such councils over eighteen centuries: Some were
little more than squabbles of eastern Mediterranean bishops over
now-obscure heresies (with fistfights and excommunications
aplenty), while others grappled with universal issues and dogmas
and schisms that rocked the very foundation of the apostolic institution that lays claim to the *depositum fidei* handed down to
Christ's own earthly disciples.

Vatican II, then, was the last such gathering of the college of
bishops—the last that most Catholics now living had expected to
see for at least another century. Yes, there had been intimations
and encouragements in the 1990s, just short of a full-out discus-

sion of the possibility of a council. No one had expected the long-reigning John Paul II—nor his immediate successor—to call for a council. Karol Wojtyla had been a young bishop in the early 1960s, a full participant in Vatican II, indeed a product of that crucible. His pontificate, his teachings, his very being were all tied directly to the council which had finally and definitively opened the Church to the modern world.

Priests, bishops, theologians, religious, and laity throughout the world were still, at the turn of the new millennium, processing the effects of Pope John's council. Very few seriously expected that the first American-born pope and successor to St. Peter would be the one to turn the Church on its head with the call for an ecumenical council. Now? Why? Where? Timothy Mulrennan knew this and savored the element of surprise, as Blessed John XXIII had in 1959. This new pope, however, had long held such an idea in the silence of his heart, like an unspoken petition to God. And Pope Innocent XIV's thinking only confirmed his own. But never had he dared to expect that he would be in the position in which he now found himself, the place from which to issue a call to the successors of the apostles to meet in a body once again for the sake of the whole Church.

As he faced the congregation in St. John Lateran on this Christmas morning, Mulrennan felt himself perspiring, his heart pounding within his chest.

"Already in effect, with the release of this call to the council, three colleagues will be, with me, co-presidents of the council. These are Leandro Valerio Cardinal Biagi, the former Archbishop of Florence, now the Secretary of State for the Vatican; Bernard John Cardinal Tyrone, the former Archbishop of Armagh and Primate of All Ireland now serving as prefect of the Congregation for the Doctrine of the Faith, and Archbishop Ignatius Min of Taipei, Taiwan. These three men are only slightly less surprised than those of you hearing my announcement today, and in the spirit of brotherhood and unity they have accepted my commission."

Cardinal Tyrone had been as stunned as any of his fellow Curia members, upon hearing the news in a confidential meeting with the Holy Father a mere seventy-two hours earlier. "We are your advisers, your senate, your brothers," he had said to the pope through clenched teeth, his large Irish face redder than his choir cassock.

"Bernard, I did not mean to shock or embarrass you," Pope Celestine had said. "I will announce to the entire world in a single statement, and I do not want to risk a leak to the news media. You very few are the only ones who know for now."

"You do not trust us . . ."

The pontiff paused before he spoke, choosing his words with some care. "I have not yet learned to trust all of my curial administrators, dear Cardinal. However, you are not one of them whom I doubt. I trust you with my life and with the life of the Church."

"I do not seek a pat on the head, like a spoiled child."

"Nor is that my intent when I talk to you in this way. I mean what I say, whether you like it or not."

Tyrone saw the pope's jawline square up as it did when he was on the verge of anger himself. But he did not back away; that was not his style. "Holy Father, we are the men who elected you to hold the keys of the kingdom, to govern and guide us here on earth. This is a responsibility any of us would avoid if we could, but you were courageous enough to accept it. You have my personal loyalty, which means that I shall speak my full and honest mind to you at all times. To do otherwise would be shirking my responsibility."

"I understand, Your Eminence. Truly. And I am grateful to you. At the same time, I expect no argument with the premise upon which I have based my decision. That is, the bishops of the world must answer the summons of their servant and shepherd and come together for the good of the whole Catholic Church."

"Is it for the good? Have you thought through all the implications of such an action, prayed about the unforeseen consequences?"

Mulrennan moderated his voice, aware of the prying eyes and ears of the handful of other cardinals who were hearing the words exchanged between these two men. His words, and his breath, came in low staccato bursts: "You may fight me every step of the way, but I'll be damned if I have not prayed and reflected with all my being on this decision—and you are way out of line, dear Cardinal." He felt like the army officer he had once been, dressing down a subordinate.

Bernard Tyrone, who loomed several inches above the Vicar of Christ, took the scolding in silence, head bowed. He said nothing further during the rest of the meeting.

That had been some days ago. True to their word, none of the curial cardinals had leaked word of the impending announcement.

At the Lateran, the pope turned dramatically, his golden chasuble sparkling in the intense single spotlight that was trained on him, to the several Curial cardinals and archbishops to whom he had not spoken and who, try as they might to conceal their astonishment, were obviously dumbfounded. "As my brothers in the hierarchy of the Church, you know of the dangers and the opportunities that lie in front of us this very day. I speak of this council not with fear or apprehension, but with honest joy and anticipation: I believe with all my being that we are being called by our Almighty God and Father, in this time and in this place."

The pontiff was also well aware that of Pope John, *Time,* in the November 1958 issue had said: "He did not tiptoe into his reign; he stomped in boldly like the owner of the place, throwing windows open and moving furniture around." What would the media and the public—and the mavens of the Curia—say of the new Pope Celestine now?

The pontiff watched one of the Curial cardinals more keenly than the rest: Bernard Tyrone, the prefect of the Congregation for the Doctrine of the Faith. The Irishman remained expressionless but stiffened noticeably as the pope spoke the words that would electrify the Church at large. This one will oppose me with as much strength and skill as he can muster, Mulrennan thought. Yet, he is a sincere and worthy opponent—a man I respect, a man of God. Pope Celestine had left nearly all of his predecessor's choices for the Curia in place, including the fiercely orthodox theologian who was both beloved and reviled, in roughly equal measure, throughout the Church.

The Irish prelate's face remained unmoving, noncommital, uncertain. The pope turned again to the congregation.

"To the lay brothers and sisters, to the press representatives, and to members of other faiths who have come to this Liturgy of the Eucharist on such a special day, I invite you to participate fully in the council with your prayers and observations, be they supportive or critical—God does not ignore any well-intentioned human utterance. Even so, I cannot necessarily say the same of myself or the bishops of the Church." Much of the audience laughed, in part politely, in part with recognition of the truth of Celestine's remark. "I can only assure you of my commitment to the discovery and pursuit of the very best course of action. Again quoting Blessed Pope John, one of his favorite maxims was: 'See everything. Disregard much. Correct a little.' I believe we are called upon to correct a little of what we see is wrong, both within and outside the body of the Church, and to do this work in a spirit of lightness and joy, as an example to the world."

Mulrennan smiled and bowed his head for a moment, the white silken zucchetto a bright contrast to his steel-silver hair, which he kept cut severely short, a habit from his long-ago days of military service. He prayed silently with and for the congregation for the space of a few heartbeats, then returned to stand at his throne beside the altar to recite the creed, the statement of belief that always punctuated this phase of the mass. Later, as he sat during the presentation of the gifts, he watched the senior men discreetly whispering and gesticulating among themselves, communicating in gestures and with few words the way priests do.

The pontiff managed to focus on the sacred liturgy of the mass for the next forty minutes or so that it took to conclude the celebration. As he served the host to a number of the people he looked into their faces, listened to their responses of "Amen" to his presentation of the thin white wafer: "The Body of Christ." What did he see there, what did he hear, what did he sense in their inflections and body language? It was impossible, beyond his mortal abilities to know. . . .

The remnants of incense invaded his nostrils and made his nose itch. Mulrennan, Pope Celestine, ended this Christmas mass with his blessing in Italian, English, Polish, French, Korean, Vietnamese, and Spanish. He processed deliberately with his entourage down the central aisle of the basilica; he carried the tall crosier in his left hand, paused to touch the outstretched hands of the people and to offer his blessing in abbreviated motions with his right.

He enjoyed these moments of contact with people, however brief and glancing, and made a mental note to request that more of the traditional larger, public audiences be scheduled, despite the very legitimate security concerns of those charged with protecting the person of the pope. No doubt the first successful assassination of a pope in seven hundred years had shaken them severely. He felt them closing in around him as he was escorted to the limousine that would take him home. He hadn't even the time to change his vestments—he would do that when he reached his private quarters for a "post mortem" with his advisers. No doubt they awaited him impatiently.

Perhaps, he thought, I should engage a private security consultant, as Biagi had advised—more to ease others' minds than my own. He, in fact, cared little about his personal safety. That consideration had died a quick death five months ago.

Mulrennan vividly, viscerally recalled the moment of his election: the feeling, the tears, the doubt, the decision, the simple words that had sealed his fate forever, "I accept." *Accepto.* The Holy Spirit had filled the dry and empty vessel of his being in that instant and had never since left him empty of grace. Try as he might to share what he had been given, it came back to him in abundance. *Your will be done,* he prayed silently, as the black papal limousine whispered savagely across Rome behind a screaming police escort. *Not mine . . .*

CHAPTER THREE

New York City, January 29, 2003

From across the gilded dining room of the St. Regis Hotel, the silk-wrapped and bejewelled fiftyish woman accompanied by a wide-backed, balding man could not keep her eyes off the rather exotically handsome man engaged in animated business conversation with two other men at a round corner table. Arturo Sebastian Wilderotter-Mendez was well used to such attention in public settings. He found it both unsettling and challenging: After all, one came to New York not only to accomplish business goals, but to live life to its fullest extent—which extent could only be discovered by expanding the limits as far as one could possibly push them. However, this time he did his best to avoid the woman's inviting signals in order to concentrate on the conversation at hand.

"It may provide a lift to the Cuban economy and the Church there, as you say, but at what price? If the bishops support marriage in the priesthood, for example, that will only divide the Church throughout the world. If they open the question of the ordination of women as priests—no matter how it is resolved— that will drive such a wedge through the middle of the Church, it will take many decades to recover. Look at what has happened since Vatican II. We can expect the same—or worse."

Wilderotter gestured with his perfectly manicured finger, jabbing the air dramatically. His fine black hair, touched with gray at the very tip of the razored sideburns, was swept back and held in place by a scented gel. He wore a spread-collared snow-white shirt beneath the gray Brioni suit, accented by a gold patterned silk tie and jade cufflinks. Although not an athlete, he kept his stomach flat with regular workouts and a strict diet. He smelled good and looked good and he knew it. But he also took it for granted as the result of good genes: an Austrian father and beautiful Latin mother, both now deceased. He was forty-six, well married to the daughter of a wealthy Argentine industrialist, and father to two good-looking teenagers, a boy and a girl. Currently he held a post in his country's delegation to the United Nations, a representative for economic development with ambassadorial rank, which entailed seemingly endless committee meetings, cocktail parties, and dinners such as this one with two American tech investors—who were understandably skittish in the wake of the terrorist crisis, Argentina's woes, and the volatile world markets. Arturo Wilderotter could not, however, divorce his deeply held, passionate Roman Catholic faith from his passion for business and diplomacy.

"The world is changing, yes, at a very rapid rate, beyond our ability to keep pace—or I should say *my* ability." He smiled ingratiatingly at the two Americans. He had taken their measure immediately upon meeting them earlier in the evening: young men with too much money on their hands, seeking to invest in foreign markets to spread their risk and gamble on an upsurge in high-technology sales in South America. Upon discovering, after gentle probing, that both had been raised Catholic in northern California, Arturo had steered the conversation to the subject of the upcoming Church council. He was also feeling them out on the possibility of involvement in the lay movement Evangelium Christi. Wilderotter had been an active member of the controversial organization since he was a teenager.

"You're not doing too bad," one of the Americans said.

"I have been blessed with the best education possible—at my father's knee. He understood how to get the best out of numbers and out of people. His drive to achieve efficiency was almost religious. Yet, he truly cared about people." The elegant Argentine's English was impeccable.

"Our country was fortunate too that my father influenced the business community, helped stabilize the national economy through many years of political uncertainty. He was never as comfortable with the military as with the civilian leaders. He was a man of peace. He believed in productivity as the solution to almost any political problem. And—perhaps most importantly, to me—he was patient. Never in a hurry to accomplish anything. Yet he always achieved his goals, no matter how long it took.

"For example, before the recent disaster we had painstakingly reformed the tax structure in my country to make our labor costs more competitive and largely cleaned up the corruption in government agencies, as well as in the private sector. We are now in the process of strengthening both democracy and the national economy. I know there have been many very difficult days in my country, but if you look back to just a few years ago you will see a very different situation from today—and, more importantly, tomorrow."

His dinner guests were an incurious pair, at least about the past. They wanted to hear about how they could make more money—as if they needed any more than the few billion each claimed as his net worth. Through the main course and dessert and coffee, Arturo Wilderotter painted as positive a picture as possible of the deeply troubled economy in Argentina, encouraged them to consider substantial investments in several companies. He offered personal introductions to businessmen in Buenos Aires. Then they adjourned to the King Cole Bar for after-dinner drinks. As the Americans spun their brief—and, to Arturo, boring— biographies in the buzzing, elbow-to-elbow cocktail lounge, his thoughts traveled homeward.

Nine months ago he had visited the dying Hans Hermann Wilderotter for the very last time. He had replayed the scene in his memory many times.

Arturo Wilderotter's father lay in an oversize hospital bed in the cavernous master bedroom of the family's Buenos Aires mansion, which had been fitted out as a hospice facility with twenty-four-hour care by nurses and attendants. The room itself looked like the chamber of a medieval grandee, with forty-foot ceilings and twenty-foot windows shaded by maroon draperies, a vast woven rug across which the medical personnel padded to and from their trays and machinery, and a huge oil portrait of the fading patriarch and chairman of one of Argentina's most profitable automobile manufacturers, makers of the famous Jeep-like "Cowboy Cars" that were the rage in Latin America in the 1960s and '70s. The son walked across the room to see the eighty-nine-year-old man who was suffering in the latter stages of bone cancer.

"Papa—" The younger man felt suddenly lost in pain and grief, unable to speak to the spectral, eighty-pound figure on the bed. "Papa, Elisabeth and the children send their love." Tears blurred his vision and he could barely see his father's lips move as the old man struggled to reply. The son's Spanish, untouched by any regional accent, very much like his elegant manners and stylish clothing, was the product of an international education—boarding schools in Switzerland and Spain, university in Cambridge, England, graduate studies at Harvard—that had cost the father a substantial fortune. Arturo had been an only child, the blessing and burden of his life, and when his mother had died in his teen years, he had been drawn even closer to his father. In this moment all the highs and lows were leveled as he beheld a helpless husk of a once-powerful man who had made the sun rise through the force of his will.

"You will bring them to see me soon—tomorrow?" the dying man said.

"Yes. The only reason they are not here today is school. And I know it hurts them to see you so . . . sick. Papa, what can I do for you?"

The elder Wilderotter lifted his bony hand with skin that looked like tissue paper. The son touched his father's hand. "You have done so much, been a good son to me and your mama. I still miss her very much." The old man struggled to breathe and to form words. The younger man saw that his lips were as dry as sawdust. "She was a true saint of God."

"Yes, I know."

"I am not . . . a saint. I am . . . a terrible sinner—you must know this—the truth—about me."

"You do not have to speak. I know."

"You cannot—I have not told—"

Father Julio Parrada suddenly and silently materialized at Arturo's side. The pallid, obese priest brought the Eucharist to Señor Wilderotter each day, heard his confession, brought news and gossip from the outside world. He was moderator of the local chapter of Evangelium Christi, an active group of more than six hundred souls, one of the largest local cells in the world. He whispered a hello to Arturo, asked if he wished to take the sacrament of Holy Communion along with his father.

"No, thank you, Padre. I received at mass this morning."

He went outside the sick room for a while to smoke a cigarette. It was torture to see his father like this. When would it end? When would God take him? He fought against the impulse to pray for his own father's death, but he thought it unjustifiable to allow a good man to suffer so. Why must it be this way? His wife and kids came away from visits physically ill themselves; they could barely manage five minutes with the pitiful pile of bones that had once so dominated their lives. Miguel David was a sullen seventeen, Elena Beatrice a wide-eyed fifteen, their mother Elisabeth a trim forty-two with the temperament of a neurotic puppy. As much and as unexpressively as he loved them, Arturo was relieved that they were not here today. Tomorrow would be difficult, but perhaps the last time.

He dragged on the powerful, acrid cigarette, needing it and hating it at the same time. Elisabeth was always nagging at him to quit, and he would one day . . . just not today.

Again with chilling ghostly silence, Padre Julio was there in the hallway beneath a Velasquez portrait of a Spanish cardinal who seemed to be having a bad day. His teeth—the priest's, not the old cardinal's—were yellow and crooked, and Arturo wanted to kill him as he stood with his hands folded expectantly. Why? Parrada was a good and faithful man, a model Evangelium adherent with no whisper of fault or misbehavior of any kind. Perhaps it is because he irritates the hell out of me with his ugliness and desperate need for approval, Wilderotter-Mendez considered. He tried to erase the uncharitable thought from his consciousness.

"We thank you for coming, Padre, for being so good to our family," he said.

"It is my duty and what I want to do. After all that your father has done—" The tears welled in Parrada's pinched eyes. He slowly removed a tattered gray handkerchief from the pocket of his black cassock and put it to his nose. Arturo turned away as he blew. Then he said, "Your father has instructed me, since I am his confessor, to give you this." There was more than a little pride and superiority in the priest's voice, and he passed a small white envelope to the dying man's son.

"What is it?" There was a small flat object inside. It felt like a key.

"I don't know, for Señor Wilderotter did not tell me. Only to give it to you."

"Thank you, Father. He has always trusted you."

"I am honored. I hope that I may be of service to you in some way, señor."

"There may be something I need one day soon."

"Anything. At any time. Call on me." Julio Parrada bowed slightly and waddled blackly down the hallway. His words and the sickly-sweet scent of his breath hung like smoke where he had been.

Arturo returned to his father's sickroom. The old man was receiving a fresh dose of morphine and would soon be relieved of pain for a while. The doses were more frequent and more debilitating, and the son knew that tomorrow might very well be the last day for his wife and children to have any chance to communicate with him. After a few more minutes watching his father fall asleep, Arturo left. He forgot about the envelope until he got to his room. When he opened it he found a key, as he had guessed, and a brief letter in his father's hand.

Dear Son,

With this key I entrust to you my life, my history, my reputation—my soul. No doubt you have heard many of the rumors about my past that plagued me long ago, from before you were born. Ever since I came to Argentina from my native Austria after the war I have built, brick by brick, a life which I hoped would make you

*proud of me, proud to be my son. I did my best to de-
stroy the evil of the past, to turn rumor-mongers and
journalists away from the truth. Once, I even paid off a
government official to deflect possible prosecution and de-
portation from my adopted land. I did this for you, Arturo, so that you might have a good life free of scandal
from an evil time. I committed some misdeeds, some sins
for which I am prepared to pay in the next life. I accept
God's judgment. I fear yours. Perhaps I ought not to do
so, for I know that you love me. But I am willing that
you should know who your father is—even though I
could not face you man-to-man with this truth. You are
strong enough, intelligent enough, and worthy of my
complete trust in this matter. You are my beloved son
and bearer of my name. Do with this information what
you will.*

> *Your loving father,*
> *H.H.W.*

Beneath the signature was scrawled a twelve-digit account
number. A plastic tag was attached to the key. The safe deposit
box was in New York at a branch of the National Bank of Argentina.

That was nine months ago. Hans Hermann Wilderotter had
died a few days later. Immediately after the funeral, Arturo Sebastian Wilderotter-Mendez had returned to New York for a few
days, collected the documents his father had wanted him to see,
brought them home and put them in his personal safe. He had
decided he would destroy them eventually but had changed his
mind a hundred times. . . .

Arturo wrested his attention back to the present, wished his
dinner guests good night. He had declined their invitation to a
gentlemen's club for cigars and female entertainment, for he was
in no mood this night for pleasure, much less the vulgar public
displays in such a venue. By training and instinct he was much
more private in his pursuit of sexual gratification. There would
be ample time for such pursuits, if God spared his life. He re-

turned to his East Side luxury co-op apartment and went to bed. But he could not sleep. He rose and squinted at the digital display of the clock on his bedside table. One forty-nine A.M. He stumbled through the dark rooms, found a fresh bottle of brandy and a snifter, slid into his favorite leather chair with a full glass of the pungent liquor. He drained half of it and sat back with his eyes closed.

His father had been a well-regarded middle-level bureaucrat in Albert Speer's Ministry of Arms and Munitions and for eighteen months the general manager of a Panzer tank factory in southeastern Germany with the power of life and death over a slave-labor force of two thousand men, women, and children. Hans Hermann Braum—his real name (Wilderotter was his mother's maiden name)—had also been an active member of the National Socialist Party from the early 1930s through the war years. Arturo possessed the proof of all in the form of journals, letters, state and party documents, photographs, and a yellowed ledger with entries in his father's distinct hand.

He had read through the papers thirty or forty times, and the words were imprinted on his brain, never to be erased. He drained the remainder of the brandy and placed the snifter on the floor beside the chair in the dark, silent room. Why? He cursed his father with every fragment of energy he could summon, for now *he* was the possessor of this terrible legacy. What was he supposed to do with this information? Bury it? Publish it? The simplest answer was to destroy it. But his father had not done so. Why? He had wanted his son and heir to know the truth. Because, he had claimed, he loved him. Arturo could not remember any more what it was like to sleep through an entire night. It was as if this dark knowledge were a child in the next room who demanded attention every hour without ceasing.

Prayer did not help; he had lost the desire to pray, had almost forgotten how. Elisabeth would not understand, could not be trusted with such information. A friend? A priest? He could think of no one with whom to share his anguish. He groped in the dark for the bottle, found it and unscrewed the cap, poured another glassful. He hated the taste but drank it. The living room clock chimed twice. Even time had betrayed him. Would it never end? Is this what hell would be like for the eternally damned, such as himself? There was someone, after all, whom he could call, to whom he might unburden himself.

He pushed himself from the chair and stumbled over to the telephone on the bar. He pushed a speed dial button. When the other lifted the receiver he blurted, "Hello. It is I. I need you." There was an almost inaudible reply. "May I come see you?" Arturo begged.

Location unknown, October 27, 1945
From the diary of Hans Hermann Braum.

I will not record my present whereabouts in these pages. I should not be keeping a diary in any case, but I will go insane if I do not write down what has happened to me, even when I ultimately destroy these pages, if it becomes necessary to do so. My actions are designed to ensure self-preservation, for it is my duty to survive. I am being hunted like a criminal. Perhaps that is what I am in the eyes of man, though I do not believe it in my heart, and only God can finally judge the truth. Yes, just as I performed my duty as I saw fit to do it, I am willing to accept His judgment.

It is night, and I write by candlelight in a cell—not a prison cell, but a monk's room in an isolated mountain monastery. There is another fugitive here. I do not know his name, do not recognize his face. He possesses the carriage and looks of a Waffen SS officer—how can I tell? The uniform jacket, though stripped of all insignia, betrays a high rank in an elite unit. Though lined and completely haggard, his facial features are that of a man well born, used to command, to instilling fear in others. I am afraid of him myself. I am not a military man, though I served for two years in the German Army before the overt hostilities of September 1939. Perhaps I should have volunteered for active service in the later months of the war, but I did not; I stayed at my assigned post. I got soft, I think. If I or anyone—monks, abbot, kitchen help—were to stand in the way of the strange officer's escape, I have no doubt he would kill without hesitation. Am I also capable of that?

I have killed, in self-defense, and it was in wartime. I have seen men and women die. I cannot say that any of them deserved death. Was I responsible? I supervised the production of military vehicles needed for the defense of our nation. There were more than two thousand workers under my authority for the last two years of the war. This was my duty under the command of Reichs-minister Albert Speer, a man whom I love and respect, a man who is in no way a criminal. I hope he has survived the terrible Bolshevik Red Army carnage in Berlin. We will need men like him to rebuild Germany.

As for me, I hope to escape to another place and start a new life. I cannot face the onslaught of Godless Communism. I will oppose them until I die. But from another country. The Reich will be made impotent again by the communists and the so-called United Nations. How could the United States join with Stalin, the Devil himself? I admit that I am politically unsophisticated, but the Americans have made a tragic error for which they will pay dearly in the years to come. Hitler's alliance was not that at all, rather a ploy to lure the Bolsheviks into complacency. Would that our men had been properly supplied and led, they certainly would have conquered the beast Stalin and liberated the Russians, who are no more than slaves to his evil atheistic tyranny.

The Führer is dead, the nation occupied by barbarian-slaves from the East, the dream of my people ended. I will acknowledge that we were wrong to make war on so many nations, that we overreached our capacity and our true mission, which was to build a greater, stronger nation for the Germanic people and to smash the Communist war machine.

I remember the day I knew for certain that the war was lost. It was January. I sat in my cold office studying the production ledger for the prior year. A single lightbulb hung from the ceiling above my desk.

My deputy manager, Schmidtlein, a trustworthy but unedu-cated man from the forest country of Bavaria, came to me in a frightful panic. "The workers have declared a strike! They refuse to work," he said breathlessly. "You must do something, Herr Braum."

"They cannot do this," I replied simply. "They have no rights in this matter. They are under the command of the army and the government. They know this."

"But they have heard a rumor that the war is over, that Germany has surrendered."

"Not true! It cannot be. I have received no such communication from our ministry in Berlin."

"I don't know what they have heard, or how. They believe it."

"You must simply order them to return to their work. They will pay a heavy price for any further defiance of such a legitimate order." I was firm—naïve and stupid, too. I had never heard of such a thing. Purposely, I had kept myself apart from the laborers so as not to develop any sympathy with them whatsoever. They "belonged" to me and would do what I required of them. I had been successful up to this point.

Schmidtlein came back about a half hour later. "They will not obey me, Herr Braum. Their leaders wish to speak to you."

"I have nothing to say to them except to get back to work."

"Sir, they will not. I brought them here—"

"Very well, I shall speak to them. But let them know that they will regret this action for the rest of their lives—which shall probably not be very long."

He went out and brought two men into my already cramped office. I lived in there as well as worked: A cot and a washstand filled one corner, along with a trunk containing my few clothes, a chamber pot that should have been emptied, and a few books, including a Bible. I existed on a level above, but only barely, these creatures who stood before me.

They were ragged and thin, unshaven, and they twitched like nervous hens. They made me nervous, as well.

As firmly and loudly as I could, I demanded an answer to this supposed strike. "You have no legal rights in this factory. You are prisoners of war and laborers being fed and sustained by the government of the Third Reich. What do you have to say to me that I should hear?"

I could not tell their ages. Twenties? Thirties? The one who spoke was obviously educated. He spoke German with a Polish accent. I listened.

"You have allowed us to keep our families together, for which we are grateful. We thank you for this. But the conditions of our work and our living are worse than appalling, like the concentration camps of the Jews. We hear about these places where women and children die of starvation and beatings. Their bodies are burned and their bones buried in mass graves. No one should suffer in this way. Our people here—yes, some of them are Jews, most of them good Catholic Poles and a few Czechs, some nuns and priests—they are not animals to be whipped and deprived of rest. The women—"

"Be silent. I have heard enough lies and accusations."

"Two women died last night. They had given their food rations to their children and continued to work on the assembly line. They collapsed. Both of them—dead. This must cease. We need an increased food ration for the children. It will not go well for you when the war ends and the Americans come—or worse yet, the Russians."

"Do not threaten me. All of us, workers and supervisors alike, are hungry. I take only half rations myself." It was true. I had not had a full meal in months.

The second man, smaller and worse-smelling, then spoke. He had very few remaining teeth. He said, "We do not feel sorry for you in the least. We do not care whether you live or die. Our children need food." His black eyes carried a feeble but real threat that I could not ignore.

"If I had it to give, I certainly would, but I do not. I have asked my ministry for more. There are shortages everywhere." What I did not say was that the two women who died were two fewer mouths to feed. "If you work, you will be fed. If you do not work, I have no choice but to withhold your rations."

Suddenly, without another word, the second man brought a crude knife out of his soiled shirt and lunged at me. He cut my arm. I fought back, grabbed his wrist, neutralizing the knife. Blood from my arm spattered the papers on my desk.

I pushed the man to the floor, still holding his wrist, twisting it, trying to force the knife from his hand. Schmidtlein and the other laborer froze in horror and amazement for several seconds as I struggled. It took every ounce of strength and determination that I had to fight this man; he was very strong, despite being undernourished, determined to kill me. Then the taller worker jumped into the battle, trying to pull me from the other. As he pulled at me I clung to the attacker, and the knife wavered between us, glinting crudely in the weak light. With every bit of strength I possessed, I pushed at the knife hand and saw the blade pierce his neck. His grip relaxed and I plunged the knife deeper, slicing into his windpipe. I let go, then rolled away, carrying the other man with me. The dusty floor groaned beneath our combined weight. Schmidtlein finally came to his senses and helped me to subdue the taller man. He was too weak to fight any further.

As God is my witness, I wanted to kill this man too, but as I looked at the twisted, bleeding thing on the floor I got violently sick and threw up on the desk, my vomit mixing with the blood and work papers there. Schmidtlein quickly pushed the man out of the office and called to the guards—such as they were, never where they were needed—to take him into custody. Then he went for a doctor, leaving me there with the corpse, the blood, and the vomit.

Two days later, I presided at a summary trial of the worker-leader; his name was Dietmar David Koch. He was, in fact, half Jewish. (I forget the name of the toothless man I killed.) I sentenced him to die by firing squad. He was executed by the guards the next morning before sunup. They were prompt and efficient in this task. Before noon that same day we received a fresh shipment of rations and medical supplies from Berlin. There were now even fewer mouths to feed.

I asked one of the worker-priests to give a funeral for both men. I did not attend the service. I fasted that day.

What is justice? Did I perform my duty or seek personal vengeance? Who shall judge me for my actions? In time of war, is it wrong to kill one or two for the greater good and benefit of many? Were the laborers who attacked me criminals or soldiers?

Or simply men who could not act otherwise? I must live with my conscience in these matters.

I called the workers together to speak to them all. They stood along the assembly line of the main building of the factory. The soldiers were positioned in nests above, armed with automatic rifles and machine guns. I wore a pistol, which felt odd, unfamiliar. But I told myself I would become used to it. I said, "You have suffered greatly in service to the Reich, as have I and my own family. All of us have sacrificed too much. But there is more sacrifice ahead of us. It will be better if you obey, work hard, and—"

"My husband is dead!" a woman shrieked. I did not know where she was, but as I turned toward the sound of her voice I saw movement to my left and slightly behind me. She burst through the line of men, her hands flailing, rushing at me. No one else moved. There was silence. She was the widow of one of the dead workers. "Murderer! Murderer!" she shouted. She attacked me. Because she was so weak, I was able to throw her off. She fell to the dirty concrete floor. I drew the machine pistol from the oiled leather holster on my belt.

"Murder . . . murder . . . murder . . ." A chant arose from the hundreds of workers assembled. Their dirty faces mouthed the words. It was like a low chant in church. All that was lacking was the incense. I could not believe my ears! Me—a murderer? No! I did not, could never believe such a thing. Yet, my blood boiled and I smelled death all around me. I wanted to kill, needed to kill—to stop them.

The next hour is lost to me in a kind of blackout. I ordered the soldiers to shoot. I emptied the auto-pistol in my hand. I looked at it. It was hot and smoky. Several people—about fifteen, I think—lay dead on the cold, grimy floor of the factory. I walked away. They had stopped their unholy chanting. Now there was a silence that pierced my ears, my very soul.

But I know that this time I did not get sick.

I stayed in my office, doubled the guard, and did not see daylight or breathe fresh air for weeks on end. We did not produce anything, but the workers went through the motions. I did not care any more. I was afraid of nothing, not even death. Every day there were fewer mouths to feed than the day before. That was a fact.

Three months later the American army approached from the west. Overnight the laborers melted away as if they had never been there. The same with the guards, who had proved worse than useless, for they conspired with the workers. I had no power to compel them to stay. I do not know why I was not killed during my sleep. I burned as much of the factory records as I could manage. Schmidtlein and I fled south. We parted two days later. I do not expect ever to see him again. I hope he will be able to return to his family in Bavaria. As for me, I sought sanctuary in a country church. The priest was good to me, did not ask my name or situation. He could see that I was desperate and arranged for passage over the border to this place. I am told that I will be removed from here in another few days.

I am not married and have no children, though one day I hope to have a large, happy family. It is reason enough to live. I will live. I will survive and escape from this living hell in Europe. I know that I shall never see my parents or my sister again. The underground system has proven effective enough to date, and I pray that these good monks will see me safely to a port on the Adriatic, thence by sea to South America.

As I write, the dawn creeps through the small window of this cell. Today I will take another step on my journey to freedom, if God so wills it. My life is in His hands. Of course, it always has been.

CHAPTER FOUR

Rome, January 27, 2003

For Mulrennan, it was a strange experience in the morning: shaving the pope's face, combing the pope's hair, evacuating the pope's bladder. An Albanian nun who stood about four-feet-six trimmed his hair and expertly massaged his scalp and shoulders every two weeks. Tim Mulrennan did not ask her where she had picked up these skills. But he did practice his Italian on her, a fellow foreigner in the heart of the ancient Latin empire. She spoke a grammatically flawless, by-the-book Italian and corrected him sternly, without compunction. She did not laugh easily at his jokes—his awkward attempts at humor in a language that still partially eluded him. Perhaps, he thought wryly as he pulled the disposable razor across his stubbly cheek, she has no sense of humor. I should appoint her to the Curia!

She reminded him of the late Mother Teresa of Calcutta, the same diminutive, gnarled, black-eyed saintliness and laserlike—some said ruthless—focus on the unpleasant task at hand, whatever it might be. But Mother had exhibited an occasional impishness, loved to tweak the privileged visitors to her famous mission to the poorest of the poor.

"You are a healthy man and a holy man," she had said to Mulrennan when he met with her in India in 1993. "Which comes first, I wonder?" She smiled at him, a curved slash in the hard, nut-brown face of a saint. She lifted a crooked finger and touched his breast. "Gifts of God. Gifts to share. I am happy that you are here, dear Cardinal, to share what He has given you."

Cardinal Timothy Mulrennan had spent a long month working among her community, the Missionaries of Charity, at a local hospice in an atmosphere of unadulterated sacrifice, prayer, and unimaginable suffering. He experienced firsthand the witness of Mother Teresa and these sisters, and he had never forgotten it, nor the sights and smells of death and dying for days without end. He had corresponded with Mother regularly until her own passing.

Within forty-eight hours of his election, the new pope had received a telephone call from the President of the United States, a well-known Protestant Christian, whom he had met a few times before: once when his father had been in the White House and twice when he had been Governor of Texas. He had been impressed with the president's frank, friendly eye contact, which seemed genuine and reciprocal, rather than needy and calculating as his predecessor's had been. And in the months since his firm response to the terror attacks in 2001, he had earned the nation's respect and affection—and political support; his poll numbers were still very high. It had thrilled Timothy Mulrennan to take the call; he had spoken to precious few fellow Americans in the aftermath of his election, surrounded as he had been by secretaries, security men, and curial watchdogs. A hundred world leaders had sent messages with their congratulations and greetings, especially heads of state who were Catholics, such as His Majesty the King of Spain, Juan Carlos. The American president had personally phoned his countryman from Camp David and reached him when the pope was having an after-dinner cappuccino.

"Good evening, Your Holiness," the president said, jocularly.

"Hello, Mr. President. Thanks so much for calling."

"We are so happy for you and for the Church, proud that an American has gotten elected as Holy Father. You had to get two-thirds of the vote, right?"

"That's right, sir. But they had to count it twice."

"Been there." The president chuckled. "I'm gonna get at least fifty-one per cent next time, fair and square, believe you me. Your sister sends her regards, too. Spoke with her earlier today. She's doing valuable work in the Office of Homeland Security, with Director Tom Ridge. He's a Catholic, too, you know."

"Thank you for that, Mr. President. I got to chat with her

just a bit. It's kind of lonely out here. I already miss my family and my friends back in New Jersey." The pontiff avoided comment on the religiosity of the ex-governor of Pennsylvania.

"Think you'll be able to come back to the U.S. any time soon?"

"I hope within about six or eight months, Mr. President. There's a heck of a lot to do here, believe me, and they keep a pretty tight leash on the pope."

"I know the feeling, Your Holiness. I can't take a—that is, go to the bathroom these days without a full Secret Service alert."

"For me it's little people in black robes, everywhere I turn, nuns and priests—God bless them, they work hard and do a very good job—the care and feeding of a pope can't be easy."

The pontiff heard another voice in the background. "My wife, Laura, sends her love and best regards, too."

"Please tell her I will continue to pray for her husband and our country." The pontiff felt a twinge of that deep loneliness and homesickness at the thought of the First Couple in a cozy room at the presidential retreat at Camp David. Was it unseasonably warm and rainy in Washington, as it was in Rome? And in Newark, in the Branch Brook Park neighborhood where the grand Basilica of the Sacred Heart stood as a gothic sentinel guarding the centuries-old faith of his fathers . . . were the people out strolling and playing ball in defiance of the breezes and cool temperatures of the pre-spring season? Nearly a year and a half after the terror attacks and military strikes of 2001, there had returned some semblance of normal life in the U.S., though it would never be completely the same ever again.

"I'll do that, my friend. I hope we may talk often. I'd like to be able to consult with you—and to pick your brain on some things now and then."

"Call any time, please, Mr. President. And I'll ring you every once in a while, I promise."

"One thing I want to know is how to win New Jersey next time around."

Now the Roman pontiff laughed. "First of all, register as a Democrat," he said. "That will help."

"Good night, Holy Father," the president said.

"Good night and God bless you, Mr. President," Celestine replied. He had sipped his drink and licked the sweet foam from his upper lip. Perhaps I should grow a beard, he had thought idly, like Lincoln after his election—or Al Gore after his defeat. But he had then dismissed the idea.

No, that would distract others—the insatiable press, the Curia, the curious—from the real business at hand, God's own business. He could not afford delays and distractions in the crucial days ahead. But neither could he stop the human and downright silly meanderings of mind that often took him away from the immediate reality—and absurdity—of his position. As the sovereign of a tiny city-state in the middle of this capital city he was incredibly privileged and painfully constricted in his every move; he remembered the attempts Pope John XXIII had made to break out of the Vatican. The warm-hearted John had found it almost impossible, so he had invited streams of visitors in to see him. And it had worked! Much to the continued frustration of his handlers . . .

Since his last walk through the streets of Rome with his dear friend, the woman he had fallen in love with long ago, Rachel Séredi, just before he entered the conclave in July, he had not been outside the Apostolic Palace on foot, except for a brief retreat at Castel Gandolfo in early September. No wonder John Paul II was so blessedly peripatetic, he thought: What normal person could exist in such an ecclesiastical hot house for days and weeks on end, without a break, without some contact with people who did not wear cassocks or nun's habits—a virtual prisoner as some of his less illustrious predecessors had been during difficult political times of invasion or civil unrest among the citizens of Rome itself? But Celestine, who had once hiked half the length of the Appalachian Trail, was determined to break out one day soon.

Nor had he been able to steal any time to indulge in the guilty pleasures of grisly crime stories and espionage tales. His bedtime reading consisted mainly of curial correspondence, episcopal reports from throughout the world, and Vatican II documents.

Timothy Mulrennan considered it his undoubted primary re-

sponsibility to incorporate the lessons of the past forty years, in the Church and in his own ministry as "Peter," to set the course for the Body of Christ in the next generation. The council would be his tool and his platform for such a step forward. No, he would not call it a leap, but a careful, logical step.

Around him, so close he could literally smell it, evil and death lurked: not just personal, physical danger to himself, but the powerful destructive force that had cut down Jaime De Guzman and, he felt, somehow caused the brutal Christmas Eve murder of the Swiss Guard commandant. Investigators did not yet know whether or how the killing of Colonel Schulhafer and the suicide (if that is what it was) of the younger guard were tied in to the council—though the pope intuitively knew that it was, had to be, even though the muck-mongers were at work to fan the flames of sexual scandal. He believed that there were no accidents among the events of the past several months since the death of the pope, nor in the nature of the opposition to his planned council. In fact, he feared more violence, more clandestine activity, perhaps even more killing. Certainly, there were daily reports of terrorist plans and threats. Those closest to the pope were in great danger, even more, perhaps, than the pontiff himself.

So, this was the vise in which he was trapped. Any way out? Call off the council? Pull in the troops behind the high walls of the Vatican? No, there would be no retreat at this juncture in the battle. No change of course, no trimming of sails. He could only pray with every fiber of his being that he might discover and expose the enemy who was doing the work of the Evil One.

He remembered the shock and disappointment he and others had felt in the January conclave when Georg Markus Cardinal Zimmerman, the front-runner for election, had collapsed and died the first night of confinement within the Vatican. The autopsy had confirmed that he had died of a brain embolism, a blood clot that may have formed in his leg and traveled up through the bloodstream to its deadly target. Had it been "encouraged" by an outside source? Mulrennan did not think so, at this late date, a year later. Yet, Zimmerman, a moderate bridge-builder and intellectual, had been reviled by some of the very conservative cardinals

as a flaming progressive throwback to the worst days of Vatican
II when, as they saw it, the guardians of the faith were railroaded
by the "liberals" in cahoots with the "proto-communist" Pope
John XXIII. As Tim Mulrennan saw it, it was both simpler and
more complex than that: In fact, he had been there, as a young
secretary, freshly ordained and full of awe and respect for the
council fathers, whatever their political persuasion. He had not
been aware of the horse-trading and compromises that even the
"good guys" had engaged in to move the agenda forward. The
fact remained, the agenda—and the Church herself—moved forward into the modern world in ways no one could have known
or suspected. Still, the opponents of change had inexorably gathered strength since those heady days of Vatican II.

"Don't let them get inside your shorts," Calabrese had advised
one day when the pontiff confided his frustrations and suspicions
to his trusted secretary. "They will—only if you let them."

North Auburn, New Jersey, Pentecost Sunday 1971

The telephone by his bedside rang harshly. Father Tim Mulrennan
sat up, fully dressed, checked his watch: three twenty-nine. It was
late afternoon! He must have drifted off for an hour; he shook
his head and rubbed his eyes. There was a high-pitched keening
sound in his head that he could not shake. The phone rang again,
insistently. "Hello," he managed to growl into the receiver.

"Father Mulrennan?"

"Yes, this is he." In the background the priest heard the wail
of sirens, then realized that he was hearing them in the neighborhood, through the open windows, and over the telephone. He had
been semiconscious of the sound in the last several minutes of
sleep.

"This is Sam Blume of the rescue squad. There's a fire in the
Cottage House Apartments on Auburn Avenue. It's pretty bad,
and the fire department has called in help from the other towns.
If you could come down here, I think the firemen and the tenants
would appreciate it."

"Is anyone hurt?"

"Yeah, we're treating a few for smoke and minor burns. We're not sure if everyone got out. Some of the firefighters are in the building now, checking to see if anyone is still inside. But it looks pretty bad to me—pretty intense fire, Father. Mike Hendricks asked me to call you specifically." There was a crackle on the telephone line and shouting. "I'm calling from a pay phone across the street, gotta get back. Please come if you can, Father." The line went dead.

Tim Mulrennan grabbed his "little black bag," the portable sacramental kit that he carried to hospitals and homes and emergencies such as this. Inside were the items needed for the Last Sacrament: stole, holy water, oil for anointing. He rushed into the sanctuary of the church, genuflected before the tabernacle, and removed a few hosts, put them in the container, placed them in the kit, and ran outside. The apartment building was only four blocks away, on the main avenue that bisected the town of North Auburn.

He had walked and biked these green residential streets hundreds, perhaps thousands of times as a boy and a young man: to and from church and school and the town center; several friends lived along this short route. He immediately smelled smoke from the fire, saw residents coming out of their homes, curious, alarmed, as he ran past. Some of them called out to him, but he did not stop to answer.

Mulrennan rounded a corner and sprinted the final block, sweating and heaving, realizing that he was out of shape, had not exercised for months, really, since he had been appointed pastor of Our Lady of Mercies. The job had filled up the short hours of the short days and weeks, which grew even shorter as time accelerated and his pastoral responsibilities expanded. As much as he had wanted, one day, to be a pastor, it had come upon him suddenly and with no time to prepare mentally for the drastic change. The archdiocese and neighboring pastors gave him support, certainly, but he had been more or less thrown into the deep end and expected to swim, period. Thank you very much. He pulled up short a half-block from the fire that now raged furiously, white-orange tongues spitting out of the second-story windows. It was worse than he had thought.

Crews from all three of the town's fire trucks scrambled in front of the building. The hoses were trained now on the two next-door structures, to prevent the fire from spreading; there seemed to be little hope for the apartment building itself, ablaze from within.

Tim ran to the fire department chief, a cousin on his late mother's side of the family, Paul Connolly. "What happened here?" the priest shouted, to be heard among the din of fire, hoses, and sirens. The June breeze from the east sent smoke billowing from the blaze into the faces of the firefighters, police, and volunteer rescue squad members.

"Don't know yet. Possibly a gas main. It only started about forty minutes ago, but you can see it's going to take the building down. I've got one man unaccounted for, Father Tim—Mike Hendricks. He went in the back way about fifteen minutes ago, but no one has seen him come out. I'm scared shitless. We can't lose Mike, of all people. God . . ."

An icy fear seized Mulrennan. Of all people . . . dear God, please don't let him be hurt. The words of prayer dried up, couldn't come, as the priest tried to deny even the possibility of such an event. He turned to the ambulances, went over to attend to the apartment residents who had escaped. In the chaos of the moment, no one could be sure who among the two dozen tenants had been inside and who had not. The landlord, a local merchant and town councilman, had just arrived on the scene with a list. Several tenants were speaking with him; some cats were afoot, seeking their owners, perhaps; two elderly people lay on gurneys with oxygen masks strapped to their soot-streaked faces.

The young rescue volunteer, Sam Blume, who had called Tim was attending to a young woman who cried loudly. The priest walked among the victims and chatted briefly with each; a few were his parishioners, others familiar from the town. All the while he pushed out of his mind any thought of his friend Mike Hendricks being in trouble. He half-listened to the firemen calling to each other as they manhandled the hoses. Nothing, however, lessened the intensity of the fire itself. The heat rolled from the building in waves.

Suddenly two more fire trucks, from nearby towns, pulled up and swung around to gain access to pumps. The town utilities department truck also arrived and two men jumped into a manhole in the middle of the street. They were tasked to check for a gas leak; the gas company truck arrived a few minutes later. Cops had already cordoned off the street, stopping any automobile traffic, but local people gathered to watch the disaster from across the street.

The sun shone down on the scene as it had for the entire day, from a metallic, cloudless sky. Timothy Mulrennan wished now that it would rain, that God Himself might wash the fire away. More fire trucks arrived; he counted a total of nine. Still the fire roared out of control. He saw the North Auburn fire department chief slumped against the back of a truck, walkie-talkie in hand, wiping his grime-caked face.

Father Mulrennan approached Connolly with dread. He overheard the chief talking, then listening to the response.

"I've got a man inside, goddamn it," he spat. "We need at least two more ambulances, and we've got to put the burn unit at College Hospital on alert. We've been goddamned lucky so far—except for Hendricks. Call the hospital and get me those ambulances!" He switched off the walkie-talkie and dropped it into the pocket of his coat.

Sweat poured down Connolly's face, streaking the black smoke soot, mixing with his tears. He saw the priest coming. "Father," he said, sobbing, "we lost him—Mike—gone—in the fire. He's dead, Father. One of my best guys, the sonofabitch shouldn't have gone in. I wanna kill him. . . ."

Tim felt a vise of despair and sadness squeeze his heart to bursting. Sonofabitch . . . Just a few hours ago he had spoken to his old friend, Mike, and his wife and kids—those girls, including poor little Marie who clung to his neck like a jungle vine, choking him, delighting him.

Gone. Killed in the line of duty. Needlessly. His family—their husband and father dead, just like that. On the most beautiful day in God's creation. Why? What possible reason could be advanced for the death of a thirty-three-year-old man who had only done good in the world? Little "Marie-see" . . . who would ever love her as her father had?

When the firemen and rescue squad brought out the still-smoldering body on a stretcher and covered it with a canvas tarp, Tim blessed Mike Hendricks, his own vision blurred to blindness by tears. The chief left the scene to place a call to the family. Tim lingered for another hour, helpless but not wanting to leave.

The fire of this Pentecost day . . . death by fire, life by fire. Back in the kitchen of the rectory after sunset, the exquisiteness of the paradox was lost on Father Tim Mulrennan, pastor and friend of the dead, as he placed a late call to Patty Hendricks, the new widow. Then he poured himself another, taller drink to bring sleep.

The day had begun with such brightness and promise.

Earlier, Father Tim Mulrennan had stood just outside the stone-arched front doorway of Our Lady of Mercies Church, greeting parishioners in the breezy, brilliant June sunshine on this climactic day of the liturgical season of Easter. Rain had washed northern New Jersey for the previous five days, giving much-needed moisture to the earth but flooding out several nearby, low-lying towns. The tall, slender young pastor was a striking figure in the bright red chasuble that marked the day of commemoration of the Holy Spirit's dramatic appearance in tongues of flame over the gathered apostles in Jerusalem.

He had been an ordained priest for only eight years but was the newly appointed pastor of this Catholic parish of two thousand families. His predecessor and mentor, Monsignor Robert Froeschel, had suffered a severe stroke and been incapacitated. The archbishop, himself aging and nearing the end of his long tenure as the shepherd of the Archdiocese of Newark, had named Mulrennan over the heads, and hopes, of some senior priests who were in line for pastorships. In Timothy Mulrennan he saw the priest of the future, the post–Vatican II style of modern pastoral leadership: open, energetic, able to speak the everyday language of his people, among whom he had grown up. In fact, Our Lady of Mercies was the parish "next door" to his own family's long-time church, where he had received the sacraments of youth and spent years as a faithfully serving altar boy.

During his few years as an associate pastor under old Bob Froeschel and among other veteran priests, Mulrennan had received the training that would stand him in good stead now that he was ultimately responsible for the administration of this not insignificant parochial unit in suburban New Jersey, in an area that was experiencing a profound change in its economic and demographic composition. Tim's own father had been a white-collar worker in Newark, commuting back and forth for years; many in the community worked in New York City, others in neighboring industrial towns such as Elizabeth and Harrison. The race riots that had torn Newark apart in 1967 were vivid, frightful memories to the people of North Auburn and throughout Essex County; the "white flight" had accelerated thereafter, and the once-thriving city was now a shuttered shell of its former glory.

But it was difficult for anyone to be gloomy about the state of the world on this sun-blasted day of celebration. Mulrennan extended his hand to an elderly couple who tottered toward him. They stopped to accept his greeting.

"Mrs. Lombardo," the pastor said, taking her gnarled and freckled hand in his; it was surprisingly delicate, the skin like wrinkled paper. "Hope you and Mr. Lombardo are having a good morning on this beautiful Sunday."

"Yes, we're just fine," the husband said, briefly and roughly pumping Tim's hand. His was the grip of a laborer, retired now but still iron-hard. He was a long-time usher, Holy Name Society member, and Knight of Columbus. "Thank you, nice sermon today, Father."

"I'm grateful that you are here, Mr. Lombardo. If there's anything I can do for you and your family, you'll let me know?"

"We're doing fine, Father. Eight grandchildren—so far. That's pretty good. All of them healthy, thank God." The seventy-year-old grew several inches in height as he spoke, or else his feet were lifted from the ground. He turned to his wife. She took his arm and beamed up at the tall priest.

"God bless them all," Tim Mulrennan said, then turned to the next in the line that had begun to clog the exit.

His heart sank as he saw one of his oldest friends, Mike Hendricks, approach with his wife and family in tow. In his arms, Mike held his third and youngest daughter, Marie, a four-year-old Down's syndrome child. Mulrennan almost mechanically forced himself to reach out to Mike and the girl, to take her from her father into his own arms. She was light but fidgety, her pale, chubby legs kicking up a storm. She squealed, and Tim could not tell whether in delight or fear.

"Hey, little girl, come here," the pastor said. "What have you been up to? Are you a good girl for your daddy and mommy?" He gazed into her pinched face, trying to make a connection with her, but failing. She struggled against his hug.

"Hi, Father Tim," Mike said. "She's a handful all right. You want to take her for a while?"

"Mike!" Patty Hendricks stood beside her husband, her own hands full with the two other girls, Cindy, age eight, and Karen, six. The older girls tugged at their mother's hands and skirt and danced like little dervishes around her. Patty punched Mike's shoulder with a white-gloved hand. She wore a white veiled hat and a crisp white and yellow summer suit. Not a particularly pretty girl—though Tim Mulrennan had never commented about that—she was a bright and lively young woman when Mike Hendricks had dated, then married her a decade before. "Don't say that," she whispered urgently in his ear.

"I'd love to keep Marie—and the other girls, too," Tim said brightly, meaning it but knowing that it was a silly impossibility, merely expected priestly small talk on such occasions.

He hugged the little retarded girl, gave her back to Mike and tried to greet the two whirling sisters, but he could not quite make contact with them, either.

"Will you talk to Mike, please, Father," Patty said in mock exasperation, but at least half seriously. "He's working so hard lately, I'm afraid he'll collapse one day—and then what would we do? He even has to work today." Her anxiety was real, as was her love for her young family.

Father Mulrennan had watched his classmates and peers grow

up and marry and start families, buy homes, establish careers. Sometimes he felt a bit left behind, a parish priest in his own hometown with people he had known all his life . . . but he could always call on the memories, good and bad, of some remarkable times and places that he had experienced: two years at Yale, the seminary, army service in Berlin and Seoul, the Vatican Council where he had served for two years, three months in Vietnam, the early, difficult years in the parish.

He had nothing to complain or be embarrassed about, though sometimes he thought that God had given him so much and he had returned so very little; he wondered what God might have in store for him in the years ahead. All well and good, he chastised himself, but look at where your feet are planted right now, this very instant in time: That is where you are supposed to be. He remembered the prayer from his seminary days: "Lord help me want to be what you want me to be." And the variation that applied to his priesthood: "Lord help me to be what you have called me to be."

He turned to Mike Hendricks. "Is she right?" he asked.

"Father, she's always right. One thing I've learned after ten years of marriage to this woman." He grinned like a boy who had gotten away with cheating on a spelling test. "I never realized it as a kid, about my own father and mother. I talked to him the other day. It's a secret that nobody tells you before you get married: She's *always* right. Can't fight it. Just accept it and life is a hundred times easier." He put his free arm around his wife. "Right, honey?"

"What are you saying?" She remained distracted with the shrieking undersize ballerinas.

"Mike, you should listen to her about this. You can work yourself to an early grave. It's been known to happen."

"Sure, Tim, I hear you. But you wouldn't believe what it costs these days just to keep up with the mortgage and car payments and put food on the table. And Marie here—" His eyes instantly misted as he said her name. "She needs extra special care, you know. My little Marie-see." He nuzzled her neck and she squealed and locked her arms around his neck.

Hendricks was a town fireman and part-time painter and carpenter in his father's local contracting firm. He had spent several summers as a roofer, always working, always saving money to buy a car, to rent a weekend house down the Jersey Shore, to buy gifts for his girlfriend. Now he worked and saved for his young family. Tim offered a silent prayer that his friend would, in fact, make the right decisions and be able to provide for his wife and little ones. Mike had a good heart—a great and generous heart—always had.

The parishioners continued to stream by the pastor, calling out their good mornings and shaking his hand and complimenting him on his homily about the Pentecost story and the Holy Spirit. He often wondered whether they even listened to his painstakingly crafted messages, which he wrote out and edited and rewrote and memorized from Thursday through Saturday in his office in the rectory. Did anyone really care about his theological expertise, the finer points about the *Filioque* controversies of centuries past? He, on the other hand, wished he had been able to spend more time during his seminary days studying Church history: the popes and councils and theological movements that shaped and defined the institution he served.

"Lighten up, Father," one of his own younger associate pastors had jokingly advised him recently, when Tim had been agonizing over the Easter liturgy and the decoration of the church and the needed financial boost that the season promised when so many bodies filled the pews to bursting—and wondering, where were the people during the rest of the year? Yes, he needed to lighten up, loosen up, enjoy the gifts and challenges of his pastoral responsibilities. Appreciate the people who *did* show up for mass on Sundays and holy days: people like these who were right now stepping out from the cool shadows of the church vestibule into the glaring white sunlight of God's new day. These were, after all, God's people, whom He had chosen to be His own, until the end of time.

"Father! Father!" Tim adjusted his sunglasses, looked around for the source of the call. It was Josh Renner, who dashed toward him, waving his hand. "Father, hey! What's happening?"

"Come over here, Josh," Mulrennan said to the twelve-year-old black kid who was a sixth grader at the parish elementary school—in fact, the only colored kid in the entire student body. "You tell me—what's happening with you?" He lifted his hand, palm out, and received an enthusiastic slap.

"Nothing much. Just wanted to say hi. Hi."

"Hi to you. Where's your mom and dad?"

"They're over there." He pointed to the tall shrubs at the corner of the sandstone church structure. They were deep into a conversation with another black parishioner. "Donnie's home sick, he didn't feel well this morning. I think he was faking it just to get out of going to mass." Donnie was Josh's little brother, who attended the public kindergarten.

"Well, I don't know. Maybe he really is under the weather," the priest suggested. "I don't think he would deliberately miss church."

"Oh, he'd deliberately do a lot of things, Father. Believe me. Mom doesn't know half of what he does, even when I try to tell her. He's a pain in the a—I mean, a real bad kid sometimes." The boy smiled up benignly, even angelically, at the tall man in the red vestments.

"If you say so, Josh. But that's really for your mother and father—and God—to decide. Not you."

"Yeah, like I say, they don't know half of it. I think he even tries to fool God sometimes—you know, do bad stuff secretly, like a sneak. He tries to get me in trouble sometimes. Mom falls for it."

"I'll bet she knows more than you think she does."

That caused Josh Renner to pause significantly and ponder the implications of Father Tim's statement. "More than God even?" the boy asked.

"No. No one knows more than God. Not even moms—or teachers—though it seems as though they do."

"Sister Ann Elizabeth knows everything, can't get away with a thing in her class. She even knows how many runs my team scores in Little League and stuff like that. Amazing."

The sixth-grade teacher was a legendary disciplinarian and feared classroom tyrant in her black and white habit, one of three sisters in the school—a dwindling religious presence. That was another of Tim's nagging concerns as a pastor, keeping the school viable, with as many top-notch Catholic lay teachers as was possible on a tightly managed budget. It was a problem in every parish that had a grammar school—and some were closing.

"Yes, she's pretty amazing. So are your mom and dad."

"Well, I better go. We have baseball practice today. Got to be ready for that. Gonna smack the ball a mile." Josh's great white smile lit up the world with nearly as much intensity as the sun. "Bye, Father."

"See you, Josh," Mulrennan said with a wave as the boy dashed back to his parents.

The noon mass was over and the crush of pastoral greeting finished; a few people remained, chatting in familiar clusters of friends and relatives. Tim often felt a mental letdown when the buzz of Sunday morning activity faded to a hum, then to silence, and the parishioners went back to their homes and families and dinners. He had his own family plans—with his father and stepmother, often with his sisters and their kids.

His young brother Stephen was a teenager who attended Seton Hall Preparatory School on the university campus; even though he was a shy kid, he was awash in his own busy world of the track team and drama society, with a few close friends who hung out at the Mulrennan house on Fairlawn Avenue day and night. Stephen was a great kid who worshipped his priestly half brother. Tim would see him that evening and catch up on all the latest at Sunday dinner.

He walked back into the church, closing the heavy wooden front doors behind him. He did not lock the doors; some people drifted in during the afternoon to pray quietly or meditate in the presence of the Blessed Sacrament in the tabernacle. Since Vatican II there were fewer parishioners who held to the rather musty but familiar old devotions and rituals; Tim Mulrennan had to tread the fine line between preservation of the old ways of the Tridentine Church and implementation of the frequent and dramatic changes decreed by the Council.

Archbishop Thomas A. Boland of Newark, Mulrennan's

bishop and spiritual shepherd, oversaw such mandated changes in his archdiocese with a keen sense of duty but little personal enthusiasm. Now seventy-five years of age, Boland had been the metropolitan ordinary since 1953, and under his leadership, the number of students in Catholic schools had nearly doubled and Catholic college enrollment increased by more than fifty percent. He had engineered an archdiocesan capital campaign for $30 million (which had come up short, though the promised money was already spent on diocesan high schools). He felt a special concern for refugees from communist countries such as Cuba and Hungary and initiated programs to help them. He had also introduced two new religious orders into northern New Jersey, with special focus on the needs of Hispanic Catholics: the Vocationist Fathers and the Augustinian Recollects.

For Archbishop Boland, the Second Vatican Council was an unwelcome obligation, but also an opportunity to be with peers among the episcopate and near the Holy Father; his personal friends among the council fathers had included Alfredo Cardinal Ottaviani, the archconservative curial lion who had headed the theological commission prior to the opening session of the historic council. The native New Jerseyan was comfortable in the dark-paneled chancery drawing rooms and at the altar of his own private chapel, which still faced the wall, but less at ease with the clergy or among the flock of his urban-suburban diocese. He was formal and somewhat severe, though he showed a dry, pungent sense of humor to those close to him. Mulrennan could not claim to be one of these confidants. But he had been singled out for some reason by Boland, perhaps in remembrance of Tim's service to the Bishops' Study Committee, chaired by the Archbishop of Newark, which prepared daily digests of the council in English for the American prelates, or for his work in Newark during and after the riots. Who could know the mind of an archbishop? Certainly not a mere parish priest!

Father Mulrennan felt cooler and lighter as he removed the vestments of the mass: the chasuble, alb, stole, maniple, and cincture. He rarely obsessed about archbishops and ecumenical councils, but the thoughts buzzed through his head on this bright, hopeful June day as he put the outward signs of his pastoral duties aside. What is a pastor, really? he asked himself, thinking of himself standing among the colorful, riotous aftermath of the mass as families young and old streamed from the old church into the daylight. What is an apostle? The men who had been touched by tongues of flame some nineteen hundred years before; who then went out as messengers to the whole world alive with the fire of faith.

He hung the red chasuble on a wide wooden hanger, locked the vesting room, and returned to the rectory. A handwritten phone message awaited him, Scotch-taped to the telephone in the front hallway. He went into the kitchen and poured himself a short drink of whiskey, then dialed the phone number. His sister Theresa answered. "Hi, it's Tim," he said. Theresa was his elder by a few years, married for twelve years now and the mother of four children. He had always looked to her for strength and guidance in the times of their mother's illness—and after her death, when Tim was fourteen.

Theresa had filled the roles of sister and quasi-parent, helped their father and younger siblings, as well, until she had married and started a family of her own; and even then she was always available, always reliable, seemingly always "together" in the face of countless demands upon her.

But today she was upset. Tim could hear it in her voice: "Rosemary is not feeling well and had to cancel dinner at Dad's house. I can't have it here because there's too much going on with the kids—so I guess we're all on our own today."

"Are you okay?"

"Oh, I don't know what to say, Tim. Dad is at a loss, but I really can't help him at the moment. Rosemary just came down with this bug—I don't think it's too serious. My dear husband is leaving tomorrow morning on business, for a week. Kids have school . . . so I don't have a second to breathe."

"Why don't you try it? Breathing, I mean. Just take a moment for yourself. Have a cup of tea or go out in the backyard for five minutes. You're working awfully hard, kid."

"Thanks, but—I mean, I've got so much to do."

"Look, I'll pick up some take-out Chinese or something and bring it by around four. That'll give me a chance to talk to Dad and Rosemary, see how Stephen is doing. You just try to relax and stop worrying."

"I'll try, Tim. Not sure how to do it, though."

"Do like I said: Take a five-minute break."

After he hung up he called his father. Jim Mulrennan was nursing his wife, Tim's stepmother, through what sounded like a severe cold. "I'll stop by later, Dad," he promised. "How's Stephen doing?"

"He's studying for final exams at the Prep. Locked in his room. I guess it's for the best that we don't have all of you kids coming over today."

Mulrennan said a quick prayer for his stepmom and sister, for the whole family: Please, God, keep them in Your loving care this day. Then he sat back in the comfortable kitchen chair and looked out the window above the sink at the green trees on the back lawn of the rectory. This was a rare thing on a Sunday afternoon: He did not have to be anywhere for a few hours; he could take his own advice and breathe a little more easily, enjoy the beautiful day, maybe read a little bit or rest up before he picked up dinner for Theresa's family. His fellow priests were out, and he had the quiet rectory to himself for a change. . . .

CHAPTER FIVE

Oak Wood, New Jersey, January 30, 2003

The clock-radio alarm blasted Jim Wiezevich awake. He always set it for 4:55 A.M., at maximum volume, alongside an old wind-up clock that clanged at about 4:58. Between the two of them, he was sufficiently startled from a fitful, uncomfortable near-coma state to a feet-on-the-floor position by 5:05. He considered that a minor miracle in itself. From there he put his knees to the cold uncarpeted floor at the side of the bed for a brief "God help me" plea. Then he struggled to his feet, knees creaking from cold and long-ago pounding on hardwood and asphalt during his undistinguished basketball career. "God help me," he whispered with hard breath as he maneuvered through the dark bedroom to the bathroom. He flipped on the light switch in the shower stall so that his eyes could adjust with indirect light. His shadowy image in the mirror over the sink looked more ghostly and threatening than usual. He splashed some cold water on his eyes, swished some mouthwash around and spat it out, let the faucet run to bring up some hot water so that he could shave, slowly began to awaken to a new day as pastor of St. Margaret's Church and the as-yet-unknown challenges that this day would bring.

James Paul Wiezevich felt closer to sixty than to forty-two, and he renewed his promise to himself to work out, to get some regular form of exercise to relieve the intense stress of parish responsibilities, to reduce the white spare tire that weighed him down in the middle, to be good to himself and increase his life expectancy. But when? How? Maybe if he could get out of bed at *four* o'clock, or commit to an hour three days a week at the nearby health club, or take a walk in the evening after dinner . . .

it seemed more complicated than it should be. Maybe he just didn't want to do it, didn't like to exercise, couldn't accept that he was really over forty and needed to change. Perhaps today he would write it down in his daily planner (nor could he bring himself to use a Palm Pilot or other computerized organizer) and it would simply happen so that he could check it off neatly. He liked to check off items in his planner, made him feel he had actually accomplished something. Always with pencil. Things change, after all.

Then he made a decision. Before he could think too deeply about it, he pulled on a T-shirt and a sweatshirt, two pairs of socks, longjohns, jeans, and high-top rubber hunting boots. After a frantic search he found his glasses, which had fallen from the night table to the floor under his bed. Downstairs, he took his down jacket, scarf, gloves, and a battered baseball cap from the hallway closet. Thus prematurely bundled, he stopped in the kitchen to put a twelve-cup pot of coffee brewing. He then plunged into the subzero wind chill and hard-packed snow and ice of the still-dark morning.

Another two inches were supposed to fall during this morning's rush hour. He would consult with the principal, Sister Mary Jean Dwyer, about the school; he always felt it was better to err on the side of caution for the kids, many of whom rode the bus several miles from Newark to St. Maggie's grammar school on the Unionfield-Oak Wood border. The pastor would call Sister Mary Jean before six A.M. to make their decision and activate the parent-to-parent "snow chain" calls.

He walked down the curving asphalt driveway that would need another shoveling today; the dusting of snow felt very cold and very reassuring beneath the rubber soles of his boots. Like the school kids, he too enjoyed a snowy day once in a while, a change in routine and scenery. He turned toward the tree-lined suburban neighborhood to the west of the parish property. He stepped into the freshly sanded street. The higher tax base of Oak Wood made it much more municipal-service oriented than the poorer enclave of Unionfield, where streets were usually cleared by sheer traffic volume. His natural preference was to walk in the

more comfortable, quieter residential streets of the suburb where
very few of his parishioners lived.

It did not used to be that way. As recently as a decade ago
there were hundreds of families—you could legitimately call them
"old families"—who supported St. Maggie's. They populated the
pews on Sunday, kept the coffers filled with contributions, made
the Columbus Day and St. Patrick's Day dinners successful annual
events, sent their children to the school, were baptized, confirmed,
and married here. But in the 1990s the bottom fell out: Through
death and desertion by the old families and a tidal wave of new-
comers, most of them less affluent, non-Catholic immigrants, the
parish finances nearly dried up. The school was underpopulated,
and many of the kids were non-Catholics from the inner city; the
dwindling number of qualified teachers subsisted on sacrificially
low salaries. The church building itself, still a vital center for the
community of the faithful, began to feel the stress and strain of
the years, and minor maintenance problems mushroomed into
major repair bills. And he had lost one associate pastor, leaving
him with two priests, one old and ailing and near retirement, the
other newly ordained, wet behind the ears but wonderfully teach-
able and enthusiastic. These were Jim Wiezevich's problems and
blessings.

He had memorized this passage from the Book of Job which
reverberated through his head now: "Human life is like forced
army service, like a life of hard manual labor, like a slave longing
for cool shade, like a worker waiting to be paid. Month after
month I have nothing to live for; night after night brings me grief.
When I lie down to sleep, the hours drag; I toss all night and long
for dawn." He had to smile at his own self-pity. It wasn't *that*
bad. *Was it?*

He glanced at his watch and picked up the pace. He tried to
pray but found it difficult to concentrate, what with the cold and
the overwhelming number of issues that he found himself facing
today. Sometimes he felt envious of the people who lived in these
rambling old homes with multiple fireplaces and book-lined li-
braries and swimming pools . . . he had forsworn the comforts of
family and financial security for the sometimes less tangible re-

wards of the priesthood, a sacrifice freely given but difficult to sustain for a lifetime. Thank God for his mother: He called her nearly every day, saw her at least once a week. She helped him handle the loneliness that overwhelmed him at times. Selfishly, he prayed for her health and long life.

The steady, whipping wind forced the cold through his skin to his bones and shocked him fully awake. "Half in love with easeful sleep . . ." kept looping through his head. He wondered if he showed symptoms of depression, whether there was something wrong that was causing him to feel so sluggish, so blue. He didn't drink or do drugs, thank the Lord, had never been tempted by those means of escape. His diet was not great, and he got too little exercise—these very occasional morning walks were about all. But who had time to go to a doctor? Besides, he was half afraid of what the diagnosis might be. Probably I have cancer in several major organs, he said to himself, causing a sardonic smile. He dabbed with a facial tissue at the tear that formed in his right eye, caused by the intense cold.

He felt his legs and upper body begin to loosen and to warm up. He swung his arms and pumped his fists to force circulation and life to those extremities. What must it be like to freeze to death . . . another morbid thought! He shook his head in disgust and tried to empty his mind of any thought other than God. He invited God to fill him with gratitude and love and hope, to squeeze out the negative impulses and infuse him with His grace.

Father Jim Wiezevich looked up through the bare swaying branches of the trees that majestically sheltered the street. Some of them had to be fifty or sixty years old, for the majority of the houses in this section were at least that, built just prior to or after World War II. The black branches scored the flat, slate-colored predawn sky. In the absence of color was the presence of line and shape and pattern created by an unseen hand, an artist who blended the simplicity of line with the complexity of life itself, for each branch continued to change and grow—or die. Even as he looked now, as he walked, as the wind blew, the branches shifted subtly, never the same for as much as a second.

Yes, God is here: in the blood of my veins and in the sap that, now dormant, will run to the tip of every bud on every branch, pushing life out to the extreme unknowable end a million times or more just on this one neighborhood street. The God of the inner journey and the God of the cosmos in its trillion-times-trillion manifestations of light and dark, death and life. He is here, securely within and untouchable without.

The new pope had called for an ecumenical council of the Church next year. The announcement had rocked American Catholics especially, since the pontiff was one of their own, the first ever elected to lead the Roman Church. For Father Jim Wiezevich, a besieged pastor of an embattled American parish, the call was a welcome one. Anything that might bring more unity to the Church, might further confirm the modernization begun by Vatican II, both locally and worldwide, was a move he supported. Anything that might address the scandals and lapses within the clergy. And he was personally thrilled that this pope, the very man who had appointed him pastor of St. Maggie's, was taking such a historic step.

He remembered young Father Tim Mulrennan as basketball coach for the opposing Our Lady of Mercies teams—which were anything but merciful to Wiezevich's own ragtag Sacred Heart grammar bunch in their faded green uniforms with numbers peeling off the back. Still, he played his heart out, as did the other boys, and they had fun, built a close-knit team. They won a few games, lost a hell of a lot more. Jim was good enough to make the freshman team at Pius IX Catholic High School in Unionfield. No big deal, for it was the mid-1970s and nonchalance was the attitude required among teens. He was plagued with pimples and terrible shyness, eyeglasses at fourteen, a talent for drawing cartoons and caricatures of classmates and teachers.

Mulrennan had become the pastor of Our Lady of Mercies Church in nearby North Auburn by the time Jim Wiezevich entered college. Several years later, after his formation at the local seminary and his ordination, Wiezevich embarked upon his own pastoral career; Mulrennan came back to the archdiocese several years after that—as archbishop.

Surely God had ordained that his path would cross with Mulrennan's; surely there was a purpose, wasn't there?

Wiezevich pushed himself to turn another corner, walk another block, theological ramblings be damned. He was beginning to feel alive and awake and aware of the world. Maybe, just maybe, he would be able to cope for one more day as priest and pastor to a flock who needed him—whether they knew it or not.

A few lights were now on in the upper-story windows of some of the homes. He slowed as he walked past one of his favorites, a long redbrick Georgian with steep slate roofs and gables and tall white pillars and smoke stealthily escaping from the chimney. The snow-carpeted lawn was divided in half by a wide macadam walkway that led to the front door. To one side were wide-paned picture windows covered by curtains. He kept walking, glanced back at the long, plant-filled sunporch that occupied the other side of the house. He did not know who lived there—they certainly did not belong to his parish—and often wondered who they were, how they could afford such a big slab of house and property in this high-tax suburban town. It all looked so neat and proper and well-maintained. What was life really like behind those perfect brick walls? Nothing like his own, he could be certain of that.

Two nights ago he had received a message in his voice mail, a voice from his days in Rome as a seminarian . . . a young woman he had known then. Demetra Matoulis was her name. He had not yet called her back.

Again he consulted his watch, still barely able to discern the face, guessed that he had about a fourteen-minute return walk, and turned back toward the rectory. The coffee would be ready by now and his colleagues likely astir. And he must phone Sister Mary Jean. Perhaps today he would return Demetra's call. He was curious—and moved by the sound of her voice.

This wealthy neighborhood was only about ten miles from where he had grown up—a straight shot north-to-south on the Garden State Parkway—but it might as well be another continent for the vast separation he had felt from the first day of his assignment to St. Maggie's. Well, perhaps that was an exaggeration. There were pockets of great affluence throughout both Essex and Union counties, as well as some of the bitterest poverty and urban decay. But the cultural and psychic gulf remained extreme, with very little crossover from one to the other, and usually a bad result from any such contact. His brother was a case in point, and his sister—he still did not comprehend what had happened to her. And to be honest, he did not miss the old neighborhood in the least and wished Mom and Dad would move to a more comfortable community somewhere along the Jersey Shore.

As a kid Jim Wiezevich had never known hunger or been without adequate clothing (often hand-me-downs from his big brother Chuck) or a place to sleep, but he had always felt a *wanting* for something different and better. His dad, Charles M. Wiezevich, Sr., was breadwinner and enforcer and chauffeur and couch-potato-in-chief and never-miss-a-Sunday-except-for-two-weeks'-summer-vacation usher at the nine o'clock mass. Roberta Marie O'Donnell Wiezevich held the fort at home when her husband was supervising the maintenance department at the Ballantine Biscuit Company plant; she became a mainstay of the Rosary Society and Helping Hands Ministry, to which she remained devoted thirty years later. They had a few close friends, among other parish families and Dad's coworkers, a few aunts and cousins that drifted in and out of their lives.

Charles Jr., Jim's elder brother, and Barbara, their kid sister, were always on the move, it seemed. Chuck, dark and quick and muscular, played several sports until he discovered booze and pills in high school, and then he started hanging out with the "hoods" on weekends. Barbie, two years younger than Jim, was skinny and red-haired and popular among her gang of friends. She never had a steady boyfriend that Jim could remember, but there were always boys and girls calling her and ringing the doorbell; she was a good student, always well-liked by her teachers; she adored her older brothers, and they hovered over her like Huey helicopters, ready to strike at any threat with deadly force.

They were both gone now, Chuck and Barbie, leaving two gaping holes in the fabric of the family. It was still very difficult for Jim to believe—that he was the only one left, that his parents lived with the empty feeling in their souls just like he did. He did not blame himself any more, but only after years of haphazard therapy and prayer and trying to forget. The forgetting came hard. Barbie with her bouncy attitude, always cheerful and concerned about others. Chuck, searching for something—only God knew what—with drugs and girlfriends and petty crime. How had it happened? Why had God allowed such pain and grief, especially for his parents?

Chuck had come home drunk and high one night, a lot earlier than his usual two or three A.M. It was only about ten o'clock, and Mom and Dad were still up, in the living room watching TV, and Jim and Barbara were in the dining room doing homework. It must have been 1977, as best he could remember: a cold night in early spring.

As he looked back, Jim Wiezevich marveled at how the five of them could even fit into the three-bedroom row house in the working-class neighborhood: He and Chuck shared the largest room, Barbara had her own, and the parents slept in a cramped ten-by-fourteen space—without comment or complaint. The small kitchen opened onto a very modest dining room that could seat seven or eight in a pinch (and it did for Thanksgiving and other special occasions). The living room was a generous fifteen-by-sixteen and held a sofa and two stuffed chairs and an "entertainment unit," that is, a color TV and old-style phonograph. The front window looked out directly onto the street where cars were parked and double-parked twenty-four hours a day. A metal awning hung over the front door and the concrete stoop that stood two steps above sidewalk level. So when Chuck, age nineteen and drunk and home early from his adventures, burst into the door he practically fell into his mother's lap as she watched the channel five news.

"What the hell?" Chuck Senior growled, rousing from a half-sleep and shifting his weight on the sofa. "Where you been?"

"I'm gonna crash," Chuck announced, fumbling to relock the door.

"Answer your father, son," Roberta chimed in, worry and fear scoring her face.

"Fuck him—and fuck you," Chuck Wiezevich growled, his voice disembodied.

"By God, you won't talk to your mother like that!" the elder man shouted. "Take your filthy language out of here."

"I just want to crash, damn it. Leave me alone. I haven't done nothing to you." He looked at Roberta, bleary-eyed and wobbly. He had smoked pot with the boys, his regular street-corner crew, and he was feeling paranoid, unmellow. "Sorry, Mom. Just real tired."

"Have you had anything to eat?" she asked.

"Not hungry." He pulled a pack of cigarettes from the pocket of his New York Jets windbreaker, managed to get one in his mouth and searched for a lighter.

Jim and Barbara remained frozen in the dining room, their books and papers strewn on the table. It wasn't the first time they had witnessed this type of confrontation, but somehow it seemed new and different. They watched their father grow angrier.

Chuck Wiezevich, Sr., usually too tired and burnt out to notice what was going on in the house after dinner and three hours of mindless TV, was wound tight and ready to spring. He watched his eldest child like an old wolf. Young Chuck's behavior of late had disgusted him, but he did not know how to cope with it. He saw the effects of the alcohol and the drugs. What was he supposed to say?

"I don't want a bum in my house. You're not going to school. You don't have a job. What the hell are you doing with your life?"

Chuck smiled demonically. "I'm still finding myself, Pop. I'm part of the Me Generation, remember." He had managed to light the cigarette, and it dangled from his lips. He looked like an advertisement for teenage delinquency with his unkempt, nearly shoulder-length hair and scraggly sideburns, his shirttail hanging out and jeans soiled and torn.

"Please don't talk smart to your father," Roberta Wiezevich pleaded. She rose from her chair to stand between the two. "Let me fix you something to eat."

"I said I'm not hungry." He flipped cigarette ash onto the living-room rug.

Charles Wiezevich moved with the quickness he thought he

had left behind on the high school football fields of his youth. He slapped the cigarette from his son's lips and stood toe-to-toe with him, glaring into the drug-veiled eyes. "If you can't respect your mother you will get the hell out of this house. Do you hear me?"

"Oh, I hear you. I've heard you all my life, man. I respect Mom. It's the others I'm not so sure about." The smoke and beer on his breath blew sourly in his father's face.

The older man lifted his hand and formed a fist. But he hesitated and, before he could strike, Chuck waltzed past him and headed for his bedroom. "Come back here!" the father shouted. No reply other than the slamming door.

"Charles, sit down. Dear—" His wife's first impulse was to smooth things over, to make everyone feel better, to put a Band-Aid on the situation. But this would be difficult, for Charles Wiezevich, Sr., was shaking with rage, his fist hovering in the empty air without a target.

"Dad . . ." Jim got up from his place in the dining room, leaving Barbara there with tears in her eyes. He stood before his father, reached for the uplifted, threatening hand. As he touched his father's wrist, Jim felt the anger pulsing through the man's being. He did not know what to do or say to relieve the tension, to bring his dad back to earth, to the rest of the family.

"I work so goddamned hard to provide—to give you kids everything you need. What more can I do?" He stood with shoulders slumped, defeated. "What the hell more can I do? I give up." He walked—almost stumbled—to his own room, pushed the door closed.

"They'll talk in the morning," Roberta said optimistically. "It'll be okay after they get some sleep. They're both so tired."

"Mom, it's way beyond that," Barbie said. She stood beside Jim. "You've got to make Chuck get a job and straighten up. Or else maybe he should go live somewhere else."

Jim said, "I don't know about kicking him out, but you and Dad have got to do something."

It did not get any better after that night. Within a few months Chuck was gone, living on his own in a cheap apartment in town, still hanging around the bars and street corners working a few odd jobs and dealing drugs to keep himself in beer and coke. . . .

Father Jim Wiezevich went to the back door of the residence, wiping snow and ice from his boots.

The rectory kitchen was a large eat-in space with tiled floors and quaint, old appliances. It was warm and welcoming on this bitterly cold morning. Father Jim felt at home there; it was a place where the priests and the part-time housekeeper and the parish workers congregated during the day for coffee and kibbitzing. He encouraged them, to relieve the otherwise heavy load that they all shared. The coffee was brewed, filled his nostrils with sweet aroma as he poured the first cup. He made the telephone call that had been nagging at his mind, agreeing to close the school for the day.

Before his second sip of the scalding black coffee, he looked up to see Father Mark Vallely, bundled and booted and armed with a snow shovel, nonetheless wearing the solemn, scholarly face that impressed many and intimidated most parishioners. Father Mark was willing to labor as hard—or harder—than any man Jim Wiezevich had ever teamed with during his years of parish ministry. He liked the younger man, and liked to tease him.

"Oh, I've already shoveled the driveway," he volunteered casually.

For a moment the serious young priest was baffled, stopped in his purposeful tracks. Then it dawned on him that his boss, the pastor, was joking with him. "Good morning, Father. You've been waiting for me, I see."

"I'm grateful, Mark. With my hernia and this back I can barely lift a shovel any more. You're on your own—unless a neighborhood volunteer materializes."

"Father John said he would help, as soon as he gets dressed."

John Dennis MacBrian was seventy and in marginal health, with high blood pressure and a history of heart problems. Vallely was unaware of all the details, so he had taken MacBrian's offer at face value. John MacBrian was in no condition to shovel even a spoonful of snow. Wiezevich gently corrected the inexperienced man.

"He really shouldn't be allowed to do any manual work in his condition."

Father John MacBrian appeared behind Mark Vallely. "You mean 'at his age.' Well, I'm not dead yet," he said emphatically, perhaps a bit angrily.

"John, you know I didn't mean that," Wiezevich said. "But I have to insist that you not take any risks. There are plenty of other things that you can help with." The pastor scrambled mentally to think of something. "We've decided to close the school and day care today, but I'm sure we'll get a few stragglers who don't receive the message. You can direct them back home when they drive in." It was a nonjob, like a crossing-guard assignment.

MacBrian turned away and went back to his room without further comment. It was clear he had been wounded—and not for the first time. Vallely went outside to begin shoveling. The pastor cradled his coffee cup and wondered how to salve the older man's hurt feelings. That was how he spent much of his time these days: smoothing over ruffled sensitivities, among both staff and parishioners. He went to his study to read and pray for a few minutes and then to look at messages and organize his return telephone calls left over from the previous day. There was correspondence from the archdiocese, accounts payable, scheduling issues, notes and requests from parishioners. He lost himself in the mind-numbing routine of work . . . until a shout broke into his consciousness. It sounded like Father Mark.

The rookie priest burst into the pastor's study. "It's Father John! He collapsed! We've got to call a doctor—Father Wiezevich, I think he's had a heart attack or something."

"You make the call—911 for an ambulance. Where is he?"

"Out in the driveway. He started to scrape off his car and just fell—"

Jim Wiezevich ran outside. He found Father John MacBrian lying on his side, clutching his breast, his head on the cold, icy asphalt of the rectory driveway. He said an urgent silent prayer as he knelt beside the aged priest. MacBrian's eyes were closed, his breathing ragged and irregular. When Wiezevich touched him, his legs twitched and his eyelids fluttered open.

"Jim . . ." he breathed, "what happened?"

"You fell down, Father. How do you feel?"

"It hurts—my arm and chest. It's like the last time . . ."

"Lie still. Mark is calling the rescue squad. They'll be here in a couple of minutes. Just hang on, relax the best you can."

"I'm sorry, Father. I didn't mean—I was just cleaning off the car. I don't want to cause any more trouble for you. I've already—" Tears fell from his glassy, barely focused eyes. "Pray for me."

"I'm right here. I'll go to the hospital with you, John." He took the old priest's gloved hand in his own. A harsh wind whipped the snow around his head and face, but he barely felt the cold. Wiezevich knelt by his colleague and gingerly lifted his head from the hard surface of the driveway.

Father Vallely came out of the rectory with a blanket, which they threw over the fallen priest. Within just a few minutes Jim Wiezevich heard the wail of an approaching siren.

This day was going to be very different than the one he had planned. He looked at the gently sloping driveway, one half of which had been scraped clear of snow. A light coating of new-fallen flakes already covered the shoveled part. The work of man . . . obscured by the sometimes terrible power of nature. As the ambulance pulled into the drive, he prayed silently.

Wiezevich looked again at the fallen priest and in him saw the image of his own brother, Chuck, who had lain in a street not very far from this spot about twenty years ago.

Jim, a college kid at the time, had received a call from the police that day; a cop had found Chuck strung out, literally foaming at the mouth, and discovered Jim's phone number on a scrap of paper in the elder brother's pocket. There was no other ID, no wallet, no money. Chuck Wiezevich was ninety pounds and barefoot and just a few blocks from his own rat-infested apartment . . . dead of an overdose of cocaine or PCP or heroin. The autopsy would later reveal significant amounts of those drugs and alcohol in the young man's body. Jim had gotten word at school and made it to the scene before the ambulance took Chuck away. He touched his older brother's body and felt the cold absence of life. How would Mom handle this? he thought. Why should she have to? And Barbie—and Dad? Already their family had been torn apart by Chuck's behavior, and now this . . . dead of an overdose.

"God has a sense of humor," his fellow seminarians sometimes quipped when something went awry. But this was far from
funny. In fact Jim Wiezevich's entire world clouded over in that
hour. That it was a scorchingly bright June day did not faze him
in the least. . . .

The ambulance pulled into the icy driveway of the rectory,
and Father Wiezevich focused his mind on the present—old Father John still lay in his arms and was still alive. Within a few
minutes the emergency medical personnel had lifted the stricken
priest into the high-tech warmth of the ambulance; they stopped
briefly to check with Wiezevich and Vallely, then sped away with
their cargo, headed for the nearest emergency room in Unionfield.

"Stay here and take care of things, call the chancery to inform
the archbishop. I'll stay with John at the hospital for as long as
he needs me."

The car heater at first blew cold air as Wiezevich backed out
of the slick driveway and onto the street. The windshield wipers
ticked softly as they pushed the wet snowflakes off the glass, back
and forth, back and forth. Slowly the interior of the car warmed,
fogging the glass. He cracked the driver's-side window and inhaled the cold, moist winter air. His mind drifted again to memories—this time of his little sister.

Was it possible that within God's ordered universe a beautiful
young creature like Barbara Wiezevich could disappear without a
trace, vanish like smoke from a chimney, yet be always and ever
present in her absence to her parents and brother? If this was
possible—and he knew that it was, indeed—then what evil was
not possible to be visited upon men and women of good will such
as Charles and Roberta Wiezevich? This was purely hell on earth
for them, each and every day of their lives.

City and county police had exhausted every lead and called
in first the New Jersey State Police, then the FBI. Last seen alive
at the Unionfield bus terminal on November 17, 1982 . . . no witness could say for certain which bus she boarded, if any . . . no
bus driver remembered her as a passenger . . . there had been no
telephone call, no message, no physical trace left behind . . . she
had left her parents' home that morning, headed for Newark,

where she was to pick up a uniform for her work as a radiology technician . . . she had completed her training with honors in the spring and found a permanent position at a health clinic in Oak Wood a few weeks earlier . . . her folks had been so proud of her, and her brother was going to take her out for dinner that night— when she came home . . . he could have driven her downtown himself, if only she had asked him, if only he had just offered her a ride. . . .

The investigation dragged on interminably—for three years. Officially, the case was still open more than twenty years later.

James Wiezevich entered the hospital parking lot and pulled into a space designated for clergy. As he sat in the car, gripping the wheel, the wipers whished to and fro, but they could not wipe away the mist that obscured his vision. For Father John, for his sister and brother and parents, for his beleaguered staff and parishioners and their children and all who looked to Jim Wiezevich for pastoral leadership, for the Church of Christ in which he believed so deeply—and for himself—he wept.

sters from this mountain village just twenty or so kilometers from the border with Croatia. Her next stop would be an interview with the archbishop in Sarajevo, whose thankless job it would be to put a lid on this matter and try to prevent chaos and charismatic outbursts among the native faithful.

The journalist held up her palm-sized tape recorder to capture the girl's words, as well as the translator's—and then spoke into the microphone herself, in English: "Alongside a gray mountain in the republic of Bosnia-Herzegovina, which has known more than its share of political and military upheaval in the turbulent years since the wars in the region, this young woman, whose name is Mirjana Jandisevic, claims that Mary, the Virgin Mother of Jesus, has spoken to her at least six times since Christmas Day. Just what is Mary's message? And does the Blessed Mother speak to the entire world? This teenage girl cannot, or will not say—at least to me."

Never had she experienced such a wet, bone-chilling cold as here in the bleak mountains of this godforsaken country. Or was it truly godforsaken? If what the girl said was true. If . . .

The cardinal-archbishop of Vrhbosna, Sarajevo, met his visitor with a warm handclasp and invited her to his study, a smallish, carpeted and book-lined room without windows that smelled of Turkish cigarettes and inexpensive sherry. Demetra Matoulis sat in one overstuffed chair, Marko Ivan Cardinal Vulharic in another, with a spindly reading lamp and table between them. The prelate placed a packet of cigarettes and a lighter on the table, next to a large clean ashtray, but he kept his frankly appreciative focus on the woman. He was broad-shouldered, built like a wrestler, with small, neat hands.

She held a notebook and pen in one hand, reached into her bag for the cassette tape recorder.

"May I record our conversation, Your Eminence?" she asked.

"I would prefer you did not," Vulharic said. "It is not that I have anything to hide—but I think it is far better that I speak to you on background only, to help you to be factual and correct. The truth serves us both in this matter, does it not?"

CHAPTER SIX

In the Dinaric Alps, Bosnia-Herzegovina, March 8, 2003

You have seen the Blessed Virgin Mary with your own eyes?" the American reporter asked the fourteen-year-old girl. Demetra Matoulis spoke in the language of her parents, Greek, through a translator and waited for the girl's answer. She looked from the translator to the girl to the girl's mother, who scowled fearfully and skeptically at the whole scene.

Demetra sat across from the girl in the front room of the house, a twelve-by-twelve room with three chairs and a table, two windows, decorated with icons and crucifixes and family photographs on the walls. The dingy lace curtains hung like shrouds over the windows, had probably hung there for decades. The journalist used the table as a desk, placing her tape recorder and notepad there, scribbling first the date atop a blank page, then punching the record button on the machine.

"Tell me, Mirjana, what did she look like?"

"It was difficult to look at her face because it was so bright, with light from inside. There was no sun. It was going to rain, and it was cold."

"What did she say to you?"

"She spoke to me like a daughter, like I am her daughter . . . and Jesus is my brother."

Matoulis had come from Rome, where she was a news magazine bureau chief—at thirty-five—in search of a story that might tie in to the pope's recent announcement of the new ecumenical council: an appearance of the Mother of Christ to a peasant of mixed Bosnian-Croat heritage—actually a series of apparitions, some of which had been corroborated by the other local young-

At forty-eight, Vulharic was the youngest member of the Sacred College of Cardinals and had been the youngest elector in the conclaves of the previous year—by ten years, at least. The cardinal wore stylish eyeglasses accented by large brown eyebrows; his abundant wavy hair framed a solid, squarish head that sat atop a rather thick neck. He was of average height and moved with ease, seeming comfortable in and with himself. His smile was granted quickly and often, but his words formed a solid wall, which he challenged Demetra to climb.

"The truth shall set you free? Is that what you mean?"

"I only mean, Miss Matoulis, that no one will benefit from misinformation."

"I have interviewed the girl, spent several hours with her. I think she is very sincere and very credible. I believe that she has seen . . . something powerful—a vision, if you will. Do you think she has been visited by the Virgin Mary? Have you read her testimony? Do you believe her?"

Vulharic's eyes slid from the journalist's face to her notepad, then to the cigarettes on the table. He did not ask her consent to smoke but clearly wanted to. Instead, he sighed and pushed his head back against his own chair. He looked up at the ceiling as he spoke. "No, I have not read the girl's testimony, but I have sent an investigator to study her claim. It is important that we do so—that we not dismiss it without full and fair examination. Her testimony and others' will be weighed, the truth of the matter will be determined. I trust my man, an auxiliary bishop who grew up out there and knows the people. He will report to me within a few weeks from now."

"But what about you—yourself? From what you know, as of right now—what do *you* think?"

"It is really not important what I think. I am interested primarily in a thorough investigation. Let me tell you that I believe God, the Mother of God, the angels—all are capable of revealing themselves to such individuals, and they have, through history. The patriarchs and prophets experienced such direct contact; the apostles walked with Jesus before and after His death—you cannot see God more personally than that. Saints and mystics, too,

have known the Blessed Virgin and her Son through private revelation. Although His public revelation of the Word is closed since
the apostolic age, the Holy Spirit is always with us, always speaking to us in the Church. It is up to the bishops and the people to
discern the intent of the Holy Spirit in our everyday lives, of
course. That is my job, as they say.

"This is what I believe, what has been handed down to us
from the apostles themselves. When the Blessed Mother then
chooses to reveal herself again, as she seems to have done very
often in the last one hundred fifty years or so, we must be open
to her, not turn our backs upon her. Why does she choose these
children and teenagers, often the very poor and in remote places?
Well, because she loves them especially. She has a great heart, a
great capacity for love, being without sin, you see. I realize that
I have not given you a direct answer."

"No, Your Eminence, and it would help me a great deal if
you would be more specific and concrete. I have agreed not to
quote you directly—to keep this all on background."

"Yes, well . . . let me put it in this way: Our region of the
world has been especially troubled for a very long time. Therefore
it is not surprising to me that one so full of compassion as the
Mother of Jesus would want to touch and comfort her children
here who are so devout and who love her so much. Do you not
see how this is so?"

"I have seen a lot. More than I expected," Demetra replied.
As she scribbled her notes, she added, "This girl has been through
a traumatic situation. I believe she needs help—her family, too.
Can you provide some support, perhaps counseling, let her know
that she is not alone in this? Her mother fears some kind of punishment, and that attitude has rubbed off on the daughter. You
are a distant, somewhat threatening figure to them."

"They said this to you? I am saddened that they feel this way.
I would never wish them harm—to the contrary, they are of my
flock, and I am charged with their care and well-being. Perhaps I
should contact the girl and her family myself—but I fear that such
direct involvement by the archbishop would be misinterpreted by
the outside world, especially by the press. Pardon me for saying

this, but it is what I feel. She and her family might then be exploited by the wrong people. I fear this could happen very easily."

"Your reticence could also be interpreted as lack of support, lack of belief in her testimony."

"This is the harsh reality of my position. Yet it would be good, perhaps, to err on the side of compassion. Christ admonished his followers to minister to the poor and outcast, the very least. And it may be that His mother is also calling upon us to do this with the poor people in that mountain village."

"I think I've overstepped a bit, making suggestions as to how you should do your job," Demetra said, somewhat sheepishly.

"What more do you want to know from me—on background?" the prelate said. He wore a black suit with the pectoral cross of his office tucked into the breast pocket of his jacket.

"Eminence, when will the Church declare the visitation authentic, or dispute it? What will it take to earn the Church's 'stamp of approval'?"

"Frankly, this process may take years. In Medugorje, which is perhaps a similar situation, it seemed that the original witnesses and the pilgrims all appeared overnight. That was not the case, however, and the Church officials still monitor activities there, still study the testimony and the experience. The issue of personal revelation is a difficult one. . . . It is not a true-false test, but the phenomenon, if it is to be judged authentic, must conform to the doctrines of faith and revelation. There is no temporal guideline, if you will, except to record the witnesses' experiences while they are alive. The Church neither delays nor rushes into these things— but addresses the situation as quickly as humanly possible, without reaching any conclusions prematurely."

"With all deliberate speed, as we say in the United States."

"From your Supreme Court, yes?"

She was surprised that he knew the provenance of the phrase. He spoke English as if he had spent time in the United States. She must research his background to find out. "Yes, you're right," she said.

He is fencing with me, she thought. Even off the record—like a secretive CEO who wants to put only the most positive spin on his company's performance. But she had gotten used to this style of communication from her long experience reporting on the Roman Curia: The cardinals and staff there were notoriously, expertly opaque in their answers to journalists' questions. Why do we even bother to ask? she sometimes wondered. Because there was nearly always a grain of truth, or a lead, or some useful clue in even the most tight-lipped response. Sometimes a gesture or the inclination of an eyebrow might serve as a punctuation mark to change the meaning of a sentence, to point the way out of a linguistic labyrinth. She had grown to expect the feints, parries, and thrusts of cardinalitial doublespeak, so Vulharic's unrevealing answers did not dissuade her from pressing forward.

"Have there been any claims of miraculous intervention by the Blessed Virgin—healings or messages? What do you expect will happen at the site of the apparitions?"

"There are miracles every day of the week that we may attribute to our Holy Mother. Healings and visions. Changed lives. All of these things are really quite commonplace as God acts in our lives, fills us with His grace and power. Already there have been some rumors of special cures, perhaps attributable to her. But there has been no documentation, to my knowledge, of any miracles at Banja Vinco that merit undue consideration by the Church. As to what will happen—who knows? In fact, we do not yet know for certain what *has* happened, only what the girl has said. We do not know the quality of her mind, nor the state of her soul—do we?"

"I think she is of above-average intelligence, but that she is not clever enough to create such detailed fantasies. That is based on my time with her over the past few days. She is sincere, very attached to her family and friends, and frankly scared to death. She hasn't a clue about the implications of all this—other than the effect on her family."

"She is the child of God, in His generous hands. She is in no danger, nor her family, as long as we are at peace. A fragile condition at best."

"Do you plan to meet her?"

"If she were to visit Sarajevo I would be happy to receive her.

But I do not plan to travel to Banja Vinco any time soon. The auxiliary bishop has the matter well in hand."

Oak Wood, New Jersey, March 10, 2003

Philip Calabrese had briefly flirted with the idea of specializing in canon law but found it too dense and dry for his taste. Instead, he had chosen to focus on systematics, the theological discipline that attempts to pull together the various religious truths and other elements of doctrine into coherent systems of thought. One such dogma would be the Trinity, and systematic theology would ask—and answer—thorny questions such as, who or what is the Trinity and how do we know of it? Why do Catholics believe in it? What is the Scriptural and Traditional foundation for this doctrine? What proof or argument may be put against its existence and role in the life of the faith?

Calabrese surprised himself by his enthusiasm for this field of study. For one thing, it put him in the intellectual company of the greatest minds of twentieth-century Catholic theology: giants like Karl Rahner, Yves Congar, Hans Urs von Balthasar, and the American Jesuit, Avery Cardinal Dulles. These were some of the thinkers who influenced the doctrinal formulations of the Second Vatican Council and the debates thereafter. He received his licentiate in systematic theology from the Pontifical Gregorian University in Rome at the comparatively young age of twenty-six. He returned to his home diocese to teach and to assist in a suburban parish—and pursue another advanced degree—and found his life as full as he could have ever hoped. What had he expected when he decided to pursue his vocation as a priest? His family had not been happy with the decision, but they had come to accept it because it was clear that he was happy; and despite times of doubt and loneliness when he questioned his choice to answer the call, he always came back to the same place: acceptance and gratitude. Was he just lucky? he often asked himself. Or blessed beyond his own merit? Well, certainly that was the case, he knew.

His association with Cardinal Mulrennan on the staff of the

archdiocese, starting in the mid 1990s, had only been further evidence of a benign Providence, he sometimes joked. In reality, Mulrennan had driven him harder, required more hours, tested and taught him more than any boss he had ever worked for—and now the twin tasks of papacy and council would require every ounce of energy and intellect Calabrese possessed. Was he up to it?

He and Wiezevich had been friends since their years at the North American College, but the former had seemed always to be on the clerical fast track, while Jim was a more plodding and steady performer who seemed content to be a good pastor. But their surface distinctions belied the close fraternal bond beneath . . .

While Wiezevich had spent a minimal three years studying in Rome, Calabrese on the other hand had taken his doctorate there, as well as the licentiate, and had worked in the Curia, the Church's multilayered, far-reaching bureaucracy, in the Congregation for Bishops under Cardinal Tim Mulrennan about ten years before. The Jersey City native had impressed not only the American cardinal but other prelates and fellow workers with his wit and willingness to roll up his sleeves and do the demanding work of the dicastery.

Jim Wiezevich, meanwhile, rarely strayed very far from the place where he had grown up, putting his apprenticeship in local parishes for three- or four-year stints, until his appointment as pastor of St. Maggie's. Sometimes he wondered whether he and Calabrese served the same organization, so different did Phil's job description read to him. Yet, admitting a certain restlessness, even disappointment, at his more mundane parish assignments, Wiezevich admitted that this is what he had signed on for: a commitment to the ministry of the priesthood, of serving the members of the Body of Christ, of presiding over the Eucharist within a certain community that was, no mistaking it, attached to that larger Body in faith and in the sacraments. So, yes, he and Phil Calabrese served the same God, the same Church, just in distinct ways.

The more he allowed himself to obssess over the differences, the more trifling they became. So Father Jim stopped himself when he sensed he might be going off the deep end into unfair career comparisons. "What if" too often became a mental game of "why not," which then degenerated into the circular and self-recriminating flagellation: "poor me." Did Phil play the same head games, possess regrets of his own? It was only human. That was the common denominator: humanness, imperfection, sin, the promise of salvation to any and all who were baptized in the name of the Father, the Son, and the Holy Spirit. No saints need apply, one of his seminary professors had once suggested.

Every once in a while one would call the other. Wiezevich was surprised—startled, really—to receive a message from Calabrese on his email: "Call me collect as soon as possible." The Rome-based monsignor included his office and home telephone numbers, which Wiezevich already had—which indicated the urgency behind the request. Wiezevich tried a few times before getting through to his friend—at the office, six P.M. New Jersey time, which was midnight in Rome. He had never made nor received so many calls to and from Rome before in his life as he had in those few days!

When he had returned from the hospital after Father MacBrian's attack, he had remembered the surprise phone message from another person from his past: Demetra Matoulis, now a journalist. But he had not returned her call immediately.

"Well, Father, thank you for trying so hard to get back to me. I received all your messages on this creaky old answering tape."

"You wanted me to call 'asap,' remember?"

"Sure, though I'm used to taking that imperative onto everything nowadays, with this council thing going on. You wouldn't believe—no, of course you *would* believe every absurd and exhilarating minute of it. Nothing like it in the world."

"How's the Holy Father holding up?"

"More than holding up. He puts up with me and with all of these knuckleheaded cardinals and archbishops—hope this phone line isn't bugged—it probably is—so, what the hell, just telling it like it is. You would get a charge out of it, Jim, old boy. You really would."

"I'm sure . . ." Wiezevich replied, skeptically. "So what's so important? And why are you at your office so late?"

"This is nothing. I have a cot here and a change of underwear handy, always. I never know from one day to the next what's going to happen. Sometimes I even forget to shave—then one of the cardinals will remind me. . . . Here's what I was thinking, Jim. How would you like to be a part of the team here, for the council preparation? We have several committees, a lot of coordinating to do in a very short time—"

"That's an understatement. An ecumenical council in less than a year from now? What was your boss thinking?"

"God only knows—and I mean that literally."

"What would you want me to do? And to who?"

"Ever think of stand-up comedy, Father? The serious answer to your question is, work with a committee of bishops on the agenda, seek input from other bishops from around the world, sort through the bullshit items—and we're certain there will be plenty of those. Actually, not very glamorous stuff."

"My Italian is real rusty, Phil."

"Oh, it'll come back in a few weeks, once you're here."

Calabrese was the one the women watched as he moved athletically across a room in his black suit; they clucked and cooed and wished silently that he was available. He was the one the hierarchy had "tapped," as if for a special secret society, early on—but Wiezevich knew that such favor was not based strictly on Phil's handsome exterior or smooth manner. There was substance, keen intelligence, accomplishment, as well as potential in the package. Nor did such favor come without a price. Jim heard it in his friend's voice: exhaustion and stress, responsibility, ambition, and the ability to stick his neck out and brave the executioner's axe.

"I need you, buddy. That's another reason," Phil said.

"What about the parish? It's not a pretty picture right now. And the archbishop? I can't just tell him I've been called to Rome."

"Don't worry about him. The Holy Father has already told him we're gonna poach a few men—people we can trust. He asked me who I'd recommend, so I thought of you right off, naturally."

"Naturally. A charity case, I suppose." He had to smile as he said it.

"I always said you were a better, more gifted theologian than I was."

"Well, we can argue about that some other time. The new archbishop agreed?"

"What do you expect him to do?"

"I get your point." It was happening too fast for him to absorb—all of it: Demetra's call, Calabrese's invitation, Father John's crisis. "Well, I have to think about it, Phil. I can't just pick up and book the next flight out."

"I'll call you back in a couple of days—but we can't extend beyond that point, Jim. This is important, an opportunity of a lifetime. You're smart enough to know that. And it's a very special way to serve the Church, in ways that can't even be described or quantified. But you know all this. From my point of view, I'd love to have you here, to work closely with you. I really mean it when I say we'd be a team. And, remember, the coach is the pope!"

"He was a good coach in the old days. I played against him."

"See, there you go. Now he wants to make a trade—bring you on board the winning franchise."

"Enough, already, Phil. I've got work here. I'm down one priest and—well, the whole damned parish is going to hell in a handbasket, if you want to know the honest-to-God's truth."

"Nothing but, my friend—honest to God, is right."

"Good-bye."

"Think about it, seriously."

"Good-bye."

"Think about it. I will call you back."

"I'm sure you will, *friend*. Good-bye." He replaced the receiver, not even listening for Calabrese's smart-ass last word. He sat back in his chair, ran his hand through his hair and took a couple of big, lung-expanding breaths. I'm going to have to work out on a regular basis if I'm going to get through this, he warned himself. No way can I drag this physical wreck of a body through the next several months, wherever I am—here or in Rome.

Rome, March 12, 2003

Perhaps it's time to start fishing, Demetra told herself, recalling her father's and brother's great outdoor passion. She had gone with them only rarely, being too impatient to sit quietly for hours waiting for a nibble . . . yet as a reporter and bureau chief she had discovered unexpectedly deep reservoirs of patience within herself. When she was chasing a story she could be as tenacious as a politician in pursuit of a vote. It was a gift. She surprised herself. In college she had discovered an innate intellectual curiosity; in grad school and in her first few newspaper stints she learned to meld smarts and a capacity for hard work. At first she liked it, the thrill of the hunt for a story. Then she needed it, like a drug.

Demetra remembered how she had played the part of the more sophisticated, worldly one in their relationship. Yet she had never felt superior to Jim Wiezevich; she had respected his intellect and his commitment to his faith. In fact, she had loved him more than any other man in her life . . . loved him enough to let him go. Yet she had never told him this—and now, she knew, it was too late, even pointless, to reveal her true feelings.

For a dozen years, through wars and disasters and political upheavals—through other relationships, only one of which was long-term—she had pushed the memories aside, chosen not to think of him, consciously purged him from her heart. Why, then, had she decided to call him, to reestablish contact even fleetingly? If the question had an answer, she did not pursue it. Rather, she simply followed her instinct in the same way she followed a story: like the girl in Bosnia or the terrorist cell in Turkey or any one of a hundred leads that might point to a major news break. For in the end, and always, Demetra Matoulis was a reporter; her own life qualified as a story as much as any pope's or prime minister's. And no one was better equipped to analyze the story than herself.

Winter had not yet released its frigid grip on southern Europe. A wet gray pall lay over Rome. Tourists, pilgrims, and residents wore scarves and hats against the cold and carried umbrellas against the cold, pricking rain. Taxis and omnibuses skidded around the traffic circles, oblivious to hazard, horns blaring defiantly. Demetra Matoulis hailed a vehicle outside her apartment building in the Via Veneto, a still-fashionable section of the city. She clutched her briefcase with both hands and closed her eyes as the driver threaded through the busy streets at near supersonic speed. If she survived this trip, she mused, it must be because God had some important plan for her life.

She laughed and opened her eyes to catch the driver watching her in his rearview mirror. "Can't you go any faster?" she said in English. He must have understood because, though he did not reply, he refocused his attention on the street and whipped his car across three lanes toward the next intersection. Her body swayed and jolted, and she considered the seat belt but did not put it on. Even though it had been several years since the gruesome death by misadventure of Princess Diana, the dark fantasy of her own end in similar circumstances still frequently played across her mind.

Once at the office she forgot about the dank weather and the insane traffic: There she became the hunter-in-chief for the news story that might rock the world beyond the crumbling and chaotic city that she had called home for so long. She entered the professional zone that sustained and stimulated her every day.

As bureau chief, Demetra existed farther up the food chain than many journalists and was on most social, political, and diplomatic A-lists in Rome, including the Vatican. However, she had long since shed any illusions that hers was a glamorous lot. Her routine was anything but: early to rise, early to the office, late to parties, late to the office again to file the day's stories and edit others' copy, then late to bed and early to rise so she could do the same thing all over again. Her sister was amazed and appalled when Demetra described her life as it really was—and worried that her career had sucked dry too much of her life, that there would be no time for marriage and children. Demetra, too, worried that existence in this numbing nonstop world would be her fate unless someone or something intervened before it was too late. Unless it was too late already.

Melina, her younger sister, had four kids and a husband who

was employed and appeared to be faithful, was an involved father. Demetra didn't like the brother-in-law very much, but neither did she make a big deal about her feelings. Was it any of her business, after all? As long as the guy put bread on the table and wasn't a fullblown creep. She dug the children: three nieces and one nephew, spoiled rotten. Melina lived in Vero Beach, where there was a Greek enclave among the retired folks from up north. The husband, George, operated a local restaurant for his father and uncle—and one day it wold be his and his son's. (That was George's plan, anyhow.) Their house, a three-bedroom ranch, lay within a few blocks of all the in-laws' condos—convenient for baby-sitting and hell on privacy. But Melina took it all in stride, thrived, in fact, on the close-knit extended family scenario. What a mensch she was, Demetra thought, applying her NYU-learned vocabulary.

The two women spoke at least once every week and emailed each other almost daily. The big-shot bureau chief and world-renowned journalist had to know about little Paul's every sniffle and all the girls' parties and Girl Scout events and school projects. Made her feel connected—and *alive*!

Her direct line rang and she picked up, expecting to hear her sister's voice. "Matoulis here," she said.

"Demetra. It's Jim Wiezevich." Strangely intimate, yet hesitant and unfamiliar at the same time. As she caught her breath he went on: "I'm coming to Rome—totally unexpected. Will you—that is, can I see you?"

"Jim—wow! Sure, it'll be wonderful to see you again. I can't believe it. Seems weird that I called you before. I had no idea—"

"Neither did I. Last thing I ever expected. I guess it pays to have connections. My friend Phil Calabrese insisted that I come to help with preparations for the council. He's in it up to his neck."

"I've met him," Demetra said. "Impressive guy."

"He was my mentor when I was in Rome—before. When I first met you."

"Yes, I remember. You used to talk about him often."

"I told him about us, Demetra," Wiezevich said.

She paused, closed her eyes, recalled when she had last seen Jim Wiezevich face-to-face, thirteen years before. "We did not do anything wrong, Jim. We were in love. And it was before you took your vows. Excuse me, 'sacred promises,' as you once corrected me. I remember everything, believe me."

"So do I," he said. "I've never thought we were wrong." That was not quite the whole truth because Wiezevich had known frequent and intense doubts at the time they had been together and after. He had come to accept—and to treasure—their past relationship, even as he grew to value the spirituality of the celibate life ever more over the ensuing years. The calculation of time and distance between them played in his mind, a thought he had not had for more than a decade. It was a strange, new sensation with echoes of the past—he welcomed the feeling even as it raised alarm within him.

"If you hadn't we might still be together," she said—and quickly added, "but we'll never know for sure. Listen, I really want to see you when you get here. How long will you be around?"

"No idea. I think I'll be a general go-fer and theological backstop. That's another path not taken—academics. I used to be good at it, until I settled into parish administration. I'll have to dust off the cobwebs in my tired brain."

"So what do you think of this whole council thing?"

"To be honest, I don't have an opinion—yet. Sounded off-the-wall to me at first. Then, as I got used to the idea it grew on me. Why not? It's definitely not a good thing to wait a hundred years—or three hundred, as they did between Trent and Vatican I. Time moves much too swiftly now. The Church can't afford to fall into irrelevance ever again."

"So, you think it is still relevant today? Do you think it is still holy?"

She was taunting him, probing. He did not bite. "I'll let you be the judge of that. I've just got to show up every day—in case it is."

Demetra Matoulis laughed. "So, when can we have dinner?"

"How about next week—Wednesday. Unless they keep me locked down, I'll plan to meet you."

She flipped through her day planner, confirmed the gaping blank in her schedule for that evening. "I'll juggle several other engagements just to fit you in," she teased.

"Thanks. The only thing that might stand in our way is a call from the Holy Father himself."

"You know, Jim—I might ask you to be a source for me. 'Officials close to the pope confirmed . . .' That sort of thing. For old times' sake. I'd never abuse the privilege."

"We'll see," he replied tentatively. "But I'm buying dinner." He suddenly felt awkward, dreaded the silence, kept talking. "What happened with the little girl in Bosnia? Is there a story in it for you?"

"Oh, there's a great story. She's for real—not such a little girl—a teenager. She's very credible, at least to me and to the local people. The cardinal has his doubts."

"Cardinals are paid extra to have such doubts."

"Very funny. I find it rather disingenuous—as if the girl's experience is a threat to his position. I suppose it's the way it always has been, Joan of Arc and voices and visions and all that. Don't get me wrong, he seems like a perfectly nice, professional person. But what do I know, a Greek Orthodox kid from the good old U.S. of A.?"

"I find myself qualifying many of my answers these days—just as you're doing. More with kids than adults, believe it or not."

"Yes, I believe you. I've got three nieces and a little nephew who are full of curiosity and challenge. My sister's kids."

"Melina? Is that her name? She was in college when—"

"You remember. Yes, Melina. Housewife and mother of four. I, on the other hand, have changed all of two or three diapers in my entire life."

"Don't sell yourself short, Demetra. You never know what God has in store for you. I don't mean to sound glib—I really believe that."

"We'll talk more next week. Call when you arrive."

"I will. Good-bye," he said.

"Good-bye, Jim." She softly pushed the button to disconnect. For a few minutes she sat quietly, thinking of him—of what had been and what might have been. She felt no emotion. Why had she never told him what she had done? A chill penetrated her numbness. She had not told him because he would have persuaded her not to go through with it; she would never tell him because he would hate her and worse, hate himself for the rest of his life. She was certain that she knew him better than he knew himself (even after so much time had passed). He would never admit it, but for the rest of his life he would blame himself, hate himself. *How can I know what he would or would not do, what he would think or say? I never gave him a chance to love me or to know his child.* . . . Yet now she had reopened the door—by her call to him in January. She had been thrilled that he had called her, that he was coming to Rome—that she would see him again!

After a staff meeting and lunch, Demetra returned to her office and shut the door in order to concentrate fully on her notes for the story of Mirjana's encounters with the Blessed Virgin Mary. She reviewed the transcripts of her interviews with the girl and other family members. All were consistent in their faith and their astonishment that this should happen to them, in their little nowhere village in the mountains. War and rape and ethnic cleansing in their backyard they could understand: It had been that way for hundreds, if not a thousand years. But a miracle of light and goodness and innocence was much more difficult to comprehend.

"My daughter, she is very naïve. We even thought she was simple when she was young," the mother admitted. "She was always praying, never missed mass on Sundays, sometimes even walked many miles to the nearest town that had daily mass. We are not all that religious, understand—my husband and me. Yes, we believe in God and go to church . . . don't tell the archbishop I said that. He might not like us then and try to hurt our girl. Nothing must hurt her—she is special in the eyes of God. You can see that in her, no?"

Why had these people not lain down and died when they had been the victims of some of the most grotesque, fratricidal vio-

lence in a grotesquely violent and inhumane century? What had
kept them alive? How did they retain their faith through it all?
Why did they still believe in God—and in the Mother of God?

Demetra reviewed the transcripts and her notes: She had spent
more than thirty hours with Mirjana Jandisevic and her family
and neighbors. Something had pulled her there and kept her there,
and now she wanted to go back—to relive the powerful effect of
the supernatural on the lives of ordinary people, and on her own.
She flipped ahead to the second day of the interview with the girl
and read over a section that she remembered well.

INTERVIEWER: When did Mary first appear to you, and
what did she say?

SUBJECT: On May 1, 1999 she first came to me. I was just
eleven years old. It was right out there [points to south-
facing window] on that hillside. I was walking by myself
and praying. I stopped and looked up and saw light—
like three flashes of light. There she was—she stood there
looking beautiful and gentle. I have never seen anyone
so beautiful. . . . She stood on a cloud, I think, and she
wore a beautiful blue robe and a white veil. She always
has a crown of stars over head. And the first thing she
said to me was, "Praise be to Lord Jesus, Our Savior."
I said, "I love Our Lord Jesus." She said, "I am the
Blessed Virgin Mary. I am your Mother, and I come to
witness to the whole world. God exists, and He is calling
you to be with Him in peace. All people must return to
Him." My father called the police—but they didn't know
what to do about it. . . .

INTERVIEWER: As you speak about her you seem changed.
Does she have this effect on you?

SUBJECT: Yes. I am a different person since she began
speaking to me. I feel—well, different sometimes, like
one of her angels. Sometimes angels are with her—two
of them.

INTERVIEWER: What does her voice sound like?

SUBJECT: I don't really hear her voice, just her beautiful words. She speaks in my own language. I think she is very smart.

INTERVIEWER: Did you go back—after the first time? Did you ask her to come back?

SUBJECT: No. She told me she would be back. I did not ask. I was kind of frightened, anyway. She told me to pray—always to pray. So, sometimes when I pray, she comes to me.

INTERVIEWER: Do you know what "ecstasy" is?

SUBJECT: Yes. I have learned about it. I think it happens to me. Sometimes I feel like I'm floating above the ground— like Mary on her cloud. And I feel like I've been away somewhere, even though I know I haven't left here. No one else can hear her when she speaks—only me. And they cannot hear me when I talk to her, even though my lips move. Once when I was having a vision near our house a man came up and pricked me with a needle, twice—but I never felt a thing, and afterward I wondered why my blouse was bloody.

INTERVIEWER: I heard that doctors and scientists have tested you.

SUBJECT: They say I am normal and healthy. My mother worried that I was crazy, but the doctors say I'm not. Now I worry that my mother will go crazy because of all that has happened to me!

INTERVIEWER: When was the last time you saw Mary?

SUBJECT: During the first week of Advent, last year. That is when she revealed her secrets to me . . . ten secrets.

INTERVIEWER: Ten secrets? What are they?

SUBJECT: I can't tell you. I can't tell anyone until she says so.

INTERVIEWER: Okay. Tell me, Mirjana, are you happy?

SUBJECT: Oh, yes! I have seen my heavenly Mother, and she has spoken to me. I will be able to tell my own children—if it pleases God—of this wonderful thing that has

happened to our family. It is for everyone, not just me—
but it happened to me. I don't know why. Maybe it's
because I love Jesus so much. Do you think so? Do you
love Jesus, too?

CHAPTER SEVEN

New York City, March 30, 2003

Arturo had never before seen Henry Martin Cardinal Vennholme "out of uniform." The Roman Catholic prelate wore an open-necked white dress shirt, unbelted black trousers, dark silk socks, and leather slippers; he did not wear the familiar glasses that were tinted to protect his sensitive eyesight, but a pair of bifocals for reading. It was apparent that he had dressed hastily to receive his visitor at this most ungodly hour: three A.M. The two men sat opposite each other in the living room of Cardinal Vennholme's two-bedroom suite at the Sherry-Netherlander Hotel. Wilderotter smoked a cigarette, with the cardinal's permission. A brace of broad windows overlooked the extreme southeastern corner of Central Park, with a view of Sherman's statue and the Plaza Hotel as well. The swanky rooms were courtesy of an old friend of the cardinal's: the retired American Catholic "BBQ King" and philanthropist, Francis Xavier Darragh. It was a private arrangement between two staunch Evangelium Christi members. . . .

"My son," Vennholme said, "what would you have me do for you? Anything within my limited powers—"

The businessman from Argentina had spilled out his anguish in a torrent of words, as if he were confessing his own misdeeds instead of those of another man. The once-powerful, now semi-retired—in fact, unofficially exiled—prince of the Church leaned forward and extended his right hand so that his fingers touched Arturo's knee. He tried to make a connection with the Argentine, to display his sympathy and understanding as best he could. Vennholme, a French-Canadian who had served the Church in various important diplomatic and administrative posts for forty years, was at a loss as to what he could do to comfort Arturo Wilderotter. Perhaps all he could do in this moment was listen— and pray.

For several minutes the cardinal spoke words of supplication and blessing. Arturo shifted uneasily in the chair as he allowed the words to wash over him, to penetrate his brain and his soul. He had never experienced such spiritual and emotional pain in his life—such blinding, soul-searing agony. As Vennholme prayed, Arturo Wilderotter-Mendez felt his anger and sorrow lift. He had loved his father and still loved his father—and he would continue to follow his own conscience in these difficult days. Still, to know that his own father had also made such life-and-death choices somehow rattled him deep within. History repeating it- self . . .

Vennholme rose from the chair and stood at his full height— only five-six—before the Argentine diplomat and businessman. He extended his smallish, pale hands, just touching the hair on the younger man's head. The yellow-white glow from a nearby table lamp, the only light in the room, lit this quasi-sacramental tableau. Images of Old Testament kings, priests, and prophets flashed through Vennholme's mind, and his hands felt strangely warm.

"I call down upon you the blessing of the God of our fathers and their fathers before them. Hear the cries of your servant Ar- turo, O Lord, that he may find in You a comfort and a refuge from the storm-tossed seas of his life."

Henry Vennholme was not the most pastoral of Christ's min- isters, yet in this moment he felt a connection with his brother priests and the faithful throughout the world. He felt a strong and sure connection with the men who had taught and shaped him as a priest—including the popes he had served for most of his career. Was this renewed sense of vocation what the current pontiff, the American whom Vennholme had opposed in the two conclaves of the past year, had intended as the result of his demotion and banishment of the seventy-four-year-old Canadian cardinal? Were Vennholme's ambitions and sins forgiven, or being lifted from his soul? Many, many times he had confessed those errors that had brought him into conflict with his peers in the Sacred College of Cardinals, those fellow "hinges of the Church," so-called from the historical usage of a millennium. Now he existed in a virtual limbo, without portfolio or purpose except as he discerned for himself. Like Wilderotter, however, he was not persuaded that his actions, as controversial and even violent as they may be, were in the end wrong. No. Someone must take responsibility for the difficult decisions, unpleasant as they were, that protected the True Faith from its enemies. He was convinced of this, in his bones.

Never in his life, even in the cold days of his youth, spent in a Montreal orphanage, had he felt so lonely.

To be sure, his commitment to the worldwide mission of Evangelium Christi had continued unabated through the scandal-tainted months following the second papal election in July. He had faced his erstwhile adversary, Timothy Mulrennan, now the Bishop of Rome, and swallowed the bitter medicine the pope and his allies had prescribed. He had remained silent, at least publicly, about his role in the conclaves that had elected Innocent, then Celestine. In the past several months he had remained in near-seclusion in New York, seeing only friends from the Evangelium movement, who financed his luxurious living situation. He said mass daily in a small nearby parish church and sometimes helped the pastor on Sundays and holy days. He had visited the new cardinal-archbishop of New York only once—a courtesy call that had been marked by a chill in the air of the chancery that was not created by the air-conditioning system. (One could not blame Con Edison for everything.) During the terrible days of terror in the city he had quietly offered his services as needed for the spate of funerals for police, firemen, and civilians lost in the attacks.

Of what use is a busted-down cardinal who had once been an ecclesiastical power to be reckoned with, a would-be great elector? Well, he could answer a need such as that of Arturo Wilderotter-Mendez . . . he was, after all, an ordained priest and bishop who fully possessed and exercised the charisms of his sacred office. Perhaps, he thought, I could be of help to other diplomats or Church workers in crisis. Or, I might be able to minister to fellow priests, or to seminarians, possibly to lecture at univer-

sities and seminaries as a visiting scholar. . . . The list was nearly
endless, but he had done none of these things—yet. He had, instead, nursed his psychic wounds and lain low for these several
painful months.

Now, with the summons by Pope Celestine for a new ecumenical council, Henry Vennholme heard the bugle call (the angel's trumpet?) and, like a thoroughbred race horse, mentally
trotted toward the starting gate. Would he be allowed to compete
in the Celestial Derby? Would he, one of the few active and sen-
tient churchmen who had participated significantly in the Second
Vatican Council, be permitted to follow his blood to place he had
been born and bred to run? His Church needed him.

As Cardinal Vennholme prayed over him, Arturo felt the
weight of his problems lifting, yet he also felt small and petty for
having assumed that his was the largest and most difficult burden
to bear. After all, he had no control over what any other human
being thought or did. Nor, he believed, had his father sought to
lay a heavy stone on his back, but simply to reveal the full truth
of his life to his son and heir. The sins of the fathers . . . no—
Arturo Wilderotter would assume no guilt for any misdeeds that
he himself had not committed. That was not God's will for him,
he believed—nor for any man. His own catalogue of sins was
quite enough. *But were they sins? Or were they necessary acts of
love in the Name of God?*

"Your Eminence," he began, as Vennholme concluded his
lengthy benediction, "thank you for your blessing. I am so sorry
I disturbed you at this hour. Sometimes I feel like a scared child—
that is, I felt that way when I called. Now, after your prayers—
my difficulties and uncertainties do not seem so very insurmount-
able."

"I have done nothing for you, my friend, just said some
words. God has healed you, as He always does the righteous
man."

The righteous man. Wilderotter nearly laughed aloud. Oh, he
put up a superb façade to the world, a handsome and sincere face
that inspired trust and confidence in most who encountered him.
Did anyone know of the dark thoughts that haunted him, the base

impulses that drove him? No, they could not see it in his unlined visage, perhaps, but surely others could read his heart—blotted, as it were, by the black ink of his sins. St. Augustine had been right, after all, and this man was condemned to a lingering hellfire for eternity—despite the multitude of "good works" he so assiduously performed for his Church through the Evangelium movement.

"Our friend and leader Frank Darragh went on a year-long spiritual retreat after the election of the current Holy Father," Vennholme said. "He has remained incommunicado, more or less—an occasional email. No doubt he is well aware of everything that is going on with regard to the council. The Evangelium movement has been working quietly, behind the scenes, to lobby bishops throughout North America and ask for their support to prevent a catastrophe." The Canadian prelate, semiretired now but still pulling strings behind the scenes, smiled with foxlike resignation. He was well used to setbacks by now, to the unknowable ways of God. And despite his own declining health, he felt that he was fit for this, the latest battle in a long war to reclaim the soul of the one, holy, Catholic and apostolic Church of Jesus Christ.

His protégé, Arturo Wilderotter, drank in the words like wine. "We cannot afford to take a holiday at this time, Your Eminence. There is too much work to be done."

"Yes, my son, that is true. For you and I there is no break in the action, as they say. Actually, I think our friend Mr. Darragh, too, is not on holiday—merely using his time in a different way, for prayer and contemplation, a prelude and preparation for activity. In fact—and you may find this ironic—he has authorized his foundation to make a large donation to the Holy See for the physical conversion of the basilica floor and the accommodations for the bishops. The Americans are very practical, 'hands on' in their participation in such affairs, don't you think?"

"I think he is brilliant. It is fortunate he is on our side." Did Vennholme know that Darragh had been in contact, through his intermediary, Father Ciccone, with Wilderotter? That Wilderotter had, in fact, been dispatched to perform covert actions in defense of the True Faith and to check the insane ambitions of the "Holy Father" himself? These were men who lived, unknown to others, in shadows. . . .

"On God's side, Arturo. Let us not forget that."

"No, I shall never forget that, Eminence." Wilderotter sat at attention, as if in the presence of his commander-in-chief. He remembered the American army and intelligence officers who staffed the School of the Americas, who taught him and hundreds of other Central and South American soldiers the security and interrogation techniques that were put to use by governments and anti-left-wing organizations in the 1970s and '80s. He had also made solid business contacts there, which paid off in later years. These days he often felt that God had abandoned the Argentine economy, and was not sure whose side He was on.

That intense military-police-espionage training had stood him in good stead as a young, fiercely ambitious army officer during the mid to late seventies, when both government and economy were unstable in his native country. He had found his footing—career-wise and ideologically—during those difficult years; he had met his wife then and married her in a crisp but sumptuous military ceremony, presided over by the Catholic military ordinary. His father had been very proud of him . . . a son who had chosen well in his work and his wife. Despite the bleak political landscape of Argentina, Arturo Wilderotter, who rose to the rank of captain in the national guard, felt sanguine about his own life and prospects for his family. The self-assurance—even cockiness—of youth. He looked back now from the tempering perspective of approaching middle age and a quarter-century of hard experience.

"I have a good memory and a strong heart," Wilderotter said.

"Yes you do," Vennholme commented. "I know you well by now and have learned to love you and trust you as I would my very own son."

Those words gave the Argentine diplomat a hard lump in his throat as he sat opposite this once-powerful churchman. Next to his late father, there was no one whose approval he sought more than Cardinal Vennholme. It was like God Himself endorsing his actions. Could any man hope for more? He fought back tears and met the cardinal's stern but loving eyes straight on. "I am indebted to you beyond my ability to express it," he said. "Since my father's death . . ." He swallowed hard and willed himself not to cry, silently cursing his human weakness. "You are the only one I can talk to, as a friend, as a . . . father."

"Our brothers and sisters of Evangelium Christi will one day know of your sacrifices for them, for the Church of Christ. But for now, your work will remain completely top-secret."

So he did know! "That is as it should be. I do not want any recognition for myself. Only that my family might be taken care of should anything—anything unfortunate happen to me."

"Yes, your wife and children are in my prayers always, and I pledge to you on my honor that they shall not ever want for anything, as long as I live and beyond. I have made provisions for you and for them in my will."

"Your Eminence! That is too good, much too generous of you." Wilderotter slid from the chair and knelt before the diminutive seated figure of the neat, bespectacled cardinal from Montreal.

Yet he did not confess his darkest doubts to his friend the cardinal, could not find it within himself to open that hidden door. He said, "You have done more than I can say. I know that God works through you." And where would Vennholme find forgiveness for the monumental blunders of his life and career? Would his long-term commitment to Evangelium Christi counterbalance those now very public errors? Would the new pope find it possible to forgive Vennholme's personal and political trespasses? Or would the cardinal find the strength to continue his principled opposition to this so-called pope who was a danger to the Church?

Vennholme touched the head of the kneeling man, then strode over to the ornate fireplace that gaped coldly on this midwinter night. He looked less like a cardinal of the Holy Roman Church right now, than a tired, haggard, haunted man of the world. But even the hastily donned shirt was perfectly starched and pressed and he even wore gold cufflinks; he simply did not know the meaning of the word "casual," had not kept anywhere near current with men's fashion trends. The Argentine found himself assessing these insignificant details, perhaps to divert his own troubled thoughts. Vennholme spoke in a near whisper, causing Wilderotter to lean toward him in order to capture the disgraced prelate's words.

"Look beyond the man, my son—every man, especially myself. I am such an unworthy messenger of the Word. My beliefs have not changed one iota in the past year, despite what has happened to me. No—the truth of God is immutable, the deposit of faith unchanging. I am deeply critical of the man who would dare to assume the teaching authority of the Petrine See without an undying commitment to this truth; I see a betrayal of the apostolic succession in such a man."

"As do I, Eminence," Wilderotter affirmed.

"So, what can we do about it? What *must* we do about it as faithful Christians? How can we protect Holy Mother Church from such a danger?" The Canadian who had bitterly opposed the man who now sat upon the Throne of St. Peter paused and looked down at the floor, collecting his thoughts. He then raised his eyes to meet Arturo's, to look into the soul of the other man. "Because we are sinful, this does not mean that we are not, cannot be righteous. The Lord, through the Holy Spirit, has granted us the gift of clarity; we see things that other men cannot see or that they choose not to see. Let us then put aside ego and personal agendas and focus only on the work of the Lord Jesus Christ. If we have faith, if we continue to ask for His forgiveness, if we are willing to labor unceasingly in the vineyard, if we seek always to discern His will for us—we cannot fail to serve Him. He will not allow us to fail. This I believe with my entire being. I do not yet know what He has in store for us. Only time will remove the veil from our eyes."

"What will you do, then, about this so-called council?"

"I will obey the Holy Father and do whatever he asks of me— or do nothing if that is what he requires. I do not think he will exclude me from participating. I am a bishop of the Church— nothing, no human power can change that. Therefore I shall remain an obedient servant of the Lord. I await His call, through the Holy Father."

Arturo Wilderotter smiled for the first time in days. "I am relieved to hear this, sir. Your voice will be heard crying out in the wilderness."

"Nothing so dramatic, I think." Vennholme again sat across from his visitor. "And I am far from alone in my commitment to the True Faith contained in the revealed Word. There are many others in the worldwide college of bishops, the vast number of whom were named by the saintly, if sometimes too 'progressive,' John Paul II, who are likewise irrevocably committed. With the Holy Spirit moving among us, as He did among the apostles and the early Church fathers, we shall be guided on the right road. Remember Peter and Paul, my son, apostles and martyrs who showed us the way."

"I am grateful that we have your wisdom to sustain us in this hour, Eminence." Arturo heard himself speak these words, and in his own ears they sounded pompous and false, yet he sincerely meant this statement—he had faith in Vennholme's grasp of the issues at stake in the coming council. He only feared that the cardinal himself would be marginalized in the debates that lay ahead.

"You have been very kind to remain my friend, Arturo. You and Francis Darragh and a few others who did not desert me. I feel less like an old man when I am with you, more like a fighter in the arena."

"And that is just where we need you—in the arena."

"Well, as I said, that depends on the Holy Father himself. I will not disobey him, even when I disagree with him."

"The other cardinals and bishops who think as you do—what about them?"

"Oh, they have spoken to me—quietly, privately—including Cardinal Tyrone. They have assured me that they wish me to be a full participant in the council. What they will do or say publicly . . . that I cannot predict, of course."

"You are in the best position of anyone. You have the support of our movement and influential men such as Mr. Darragh, their financial support, their prayers."

"Don't forget that your work has been crucial, too. All of us are soldiers in the Lord's army these days, like it or not. I may use words, for well or ill, while you employ direct action against the enemies of truth. We each do what we can on the battlefield."

Did Vennholme truly know the full extent of his activities? Wilderotter wondered. He said, "There is much more work to be done."

"I agree. There are several of our friends who are developing new theological arguments that will put the Holy Father on the defensive. I support them but must keep a somewhat low profile. More shall be revealed, in time."

The younger man rose, cleared his throat. "I must go now. I have overstayed your generous welcome, Your Eminence. At this hour . . ."

"You know, I don't sleep very much these days. And when I do it is with one eye open—out of fear, perhaps—yes, fear of the Evil One."

"Please do not be afraid. You must ask God for courage in the battle ahead. With His help you will vanquish the Evil One of whom you speak."

Vennholme laughed drily. He regarded this young Argentine who had so much to offer the world and the Church: such an attractive, vital man. Did he have a woman friend in New York? Was he faithful to his wife when he was apart from her? A picture of Arturo Wilderotter naked, copulating with an anonymous woman, flashed through Vennholme's mind, and he tried without success to erase the erotic image. He did not want to conclude their meeting in this way, but it was time to call it quits—to continue beyond this point would only be to belabor the issues.

The men shook hands. "Good-bye, Arturo. God be with you."

"Thank you for your blessing—and your friendship, dear Henry."

Buenos Aires, September 18, 1951

Special Agent James Charles Cornell stood out among the café-goers on the busy sun-splashed street, wearing the regulation blue suit, white shirt, and wine-colored tie, with creased and cuffed trousers that just touched his polished black shoes; he wore a pair of dark green sunglasses that concealed his actively probing eyes. An OSS veteran who had chased Nazis across Europe in the latter days and aftermath of the war, he had then joined Mr. Hoover's bureau almost immediately upon his return to the States. He liberated a Chesterfield cigarette from a soft paper pack and put it to his lips, lit it, held the battered steel-cased Zippo lighter in his hand and looked at it: the sonofabitch had been with him longer than his wife had—through four long years of war and another six chasing criminals of various stripes throughout the world.

His wife had recently left him, returned to her mother in Mobile, Alabama, where living was easy . . . easier than life with an FBI agent who rarely knew where—or whether—he might wake up the next morning. They were calling this the "Cold War," perhaps ironically, since U.S. soldiers were being shot at on the Korean Peninsula. His home, such as it was, was in a Virginia suburb of Washington, D.C., a short motor ride from bureau headquarters. Too short, according to his estranged wife: "You might as well live there with Mr. Hoover and the others, for all the time you spend with them."

Her words echoed now through his mind as he inhaled deeply on the fresh cigarette and blew smoke from his nostrils, lifted the demitasse cup to his lips. All the while his eyes investigated his immediate surroundings from behind the shield of the dark glasses that also cut the sun glare and allowed him to discern details of human features.

Buenos Aires . . . one of the world's "fun capitals," if a man liked that kind of thing. Under the Perón regime, immediately after World War II, which was propped up by various foreign governments (including Cornell's own benevolent U.S.), diplomats, intelligence agents, international businessmen, and flesh peddlers moved among the elite social stratum otherwise peopled by descendants of Spanish nobility, war profiteers, Perónist-fascist sympathizers, and corrupt politicians. Catholic clergy moved with impunity among all these factions, like earth-bound, black-robed angels. Cornell cared not a lick for any of these folks; they were foreign and repulsive to him, a product of a God-fearing Richmond clan whose men kept their noses clean and left their business at the office. Here, good and bad were out in the open, on display like some gruesome Hieronymous Bosch painting for all to see and partake in. Sometimes it made him sick when he wrote his reports to Mr. Hoover in Washington, but he put it all down, included every detail, because that is what the director required of his field agents. This case in particular, this war crimes matter, turned his stomach . . . and he wanted to get this particular interview over with so that he could fly home and put Argentina behind him, at least for a while.

Hans Hermann Braum sat quietly, almost primly at the round-topped table across from the investigator, fingering the rim of his cup. Special Agent Cornell observed the Austrian's face and movements, which seemed studied and subdued. He betrayed nothing. What was the man withholding? He certainly was not going to volunteer any information, and his answers to the American agent's probing questions were guarded, deliberately limited.

CORNELL: Were you responsible for the supervision of slave laborers in your plant?

BRAUM: I was responsible for production and for the general management of the plant. There were no slave laborers—some prisoners of war, some workers who supported their families, even on the very small pay that we could afford. No one under my supervision was ever mistreated or held against his will, except those under military guard as POWs.

CORNELL: Did you ever punish any of the workers for infractions such as theft or insubordination?

BRAUM: No. The military guard were responsible for discipline among the prisoners; I do not know whether they inflicted punishments. The civilian workers were never punished, as you describe, during my time there.

CORNELL: Did you ever order an execution of a worker?

BRAUM: No, never.

CORNELL: Did you provide for the care and safety of the

workers and their families before you left the plant?

BRAUM: Every provision possible was made, including food and shelter within the building itself for those who had nowhere else to stay.

CORNELL: There were barracks on the plant property, very much like those at the death camps that the Allies liberated at war's end. I saw one of them, Monthausen, myself.

BRAUM: To my knowledge, these were military barracks, primarily for the soldiers and the prisoners.

CORNELL: Did you ever enter one of these barracks?

BRAUM: No, never.

Buenos Aires, April 2, 2003

Arturo Wilderrotter obsessively pored over the correspondence and the report of the investigation, reading the transcription of his father's responses to the FBI's questions, admiring how the old man had avoided sharing specific, potentially incriminating material. The investigators had pursued Herr Braum to Argentina . . . but then, there were hundreds of senior Nazis, as well as military officers of all levels, from lieutenant to field marshal, who had sought haven in Buenos Aires and nearby communities. Braum had been small potatoes, compared to others—and Austrian rather than German, which drew not quite as much attention to him as to some of the Berlin high command. Still, in their thorough, bulldoggish way, the blue-suited agents tracked down every lead, every suspected war criminal, and created voluminous files for later follow-up. Now what would be *his* response to this knowledge about his father? That is what he had wanted to ask Vennholme in January but had been unable to bring himself to do. Not so much guilt or shame about Braum's past as about the events of the immediate present and his own clandestine activities that he hoped would stop this pope from bringing ruin upon the Holy Church of God.

Arturo Wilderotter had led a double life during his university days in Buenos Aires, as a military trainee as well as a student. During those years, the Dirty War had claimed hundreds of victims, the *desaparecidos*, or "disappeareds," who had spoken or acted against the military junta that ruled Argentina: They had come from all strata of Argentine society, poor laborers, university leftists, disillusioned Perónists, religious men and women, middle class white-collar workers. How did they come to disappear? Arturo, and a corps of others sworn to secrecy, knew the answer but could not tell, on pain of instant execution by their commanders and comrades. The skills he had developed there came in handy as the unrest of the seventies became the all-out war of the eighties in Central and South America. El Salvador, Guatemala, Peru, Mexico, Brazil—in these places revolution and repression were the twin handmaids of violence. And men like Arturo Wilderotter, trained and tested, loyal beyond question, were valuable currency that was exchanged between military leaders of various governments in the region. He and others like him saw action in numerous countries during a decade rife with public street clashes, guerilla movements, massacres, and secret reprisals.

Arturo hated the term "death squad." That is not how he viewed his assignment during the difficult times. Also, he always kept a full-time job and saw his political activities as a duty and an avocation, not the definition of who he was. He was driven by faith and an unshakable political ideology. He was a soldier, prepared to lay his own life on the line, if necessary, in this war, as clandestine and dirty as any other he had ever experienced.

Like his father, he knew that he must divorce the acts of his past from the duty of the present: duty to family and Church. But the memory and the current reality blended like a volatile chemical concoction in his soul, ready to explode if ignited. . . .

He knew how to kill, cleanly and efficiently, how to make someone disappear, if that was necessary. He had been alerted to the need to eliminate the commandant of the Swiss Guard last December. The Evangelium Christi network was vast and deep, very well connected. He knew that somehow—whether through indirect financing, intelligence, or direct support with arms and personnel—the society he revered had removed the Filipino pope a year ago. How did he know? He was plugged into the secret action arm of the Evangelium organization, which is how he had received the Schulhafer assignment. The organization had known about the immoral sexual affair between the two men, and the scenario involving Wilderotter as a supposed contract killer had been put in motion by someone highly placed within the Vatican. More than that he did not know, and would not seek to know. He had received his instructions in a coded email message, and he had turned over the money that had been extorted from Schulhafer to his anonymous contact via a dead-drop system that had never yet failed, in his experience.

He smiled when he thought of how effectively his career had served as a cover for his Evangelium work. Business and diplomatic travel gave him wide latitude and allowed him to account for his time—to his wife, especially—as he chose. And to his father . . . he had never revealed his covert activities, fearing that Hans Hermann Braum, as he now knew him, would not have approved. He regretted that these days, wished he could have confided in the old man and sought his advice and counsel—his consolation.

He did not smile when he remembered the first man he had killed in defense of the Holy Name of Jesus, but he still thought back to that event with a sense of satisfaction that he had done his duty. It was important to him, always, to do his duty. . . .

Eight years after the attempted assassination of Pope John Paul II by a young Turk who had been a pawn of communist intelligence agencies, and before the demise of the Soviet Union and its Eastern bloc, other threats had arisen: against the pope, against other Church leaders, against Vatican City itself. Arturo Wilderotter, who had just begun his U.N. assignment, had been approached by an American priest whom he knew to be an Evangelium member. He knew the priest only as Father George, and assumed it was a pseudonym, played along without probing too deeply; in fact, he preferred a cellular or need-to-know type operation for his own and his family's protection.

He met a smallish, pale man in Madison Square Park, then a dilapidated, drug-ridden, but lushly green pocket on lower Fifth

Avenue in New York City, across from the Flatiron Building. It had been a cold and sunny October day, and he had been a much younger man. Even so, his Dirty War experience was already more than a decade behind him, as were dreams of blood and screaming and the smell of a disappeared person's bowels evacuated on low-flying aircraft before a forced, final leap into the sea . . . or would it ever be fully and finally behind him? The man in the park spoke only a few sentences to him, in Spanish, with clipped syllables, which Arturo strained to hear amid the midday din of barking dogs and honking taxicabs. He was conscious, too, of small-time drug deals happening along the asphalt pathway near the bench where he sat. The smell of marijuana smoke tainted the air beneath the trees.

"Our people are unhappy with this situation and require a resolution, swiftly and finally. Can you do it?"

"Yes," Wilderotter stated confidently, though inside he was much less so. No need for the stranger to know that.

The man did not use a name nor exchange anything on paper. He described the assignment in some more detail. A Mexican bishop from the state of Chiapas was the target, and the time frame was given as six weeks. More information would be forwarded to the executioner in two days, via U.S. mail to his residence in New York. After that point there would be no further contact made by either party; if the job could be accomplished, the result would be self-evident. If it could not be done, the target would still be alive in six weeks. Simple, straightforward, not easy, but Wilderotter was confident that he could handle it. All of this was communicated between the two men on the park bench in a matter of a few minutes, with a minimum of words. Arturo was instructed to leave and not look back and not return to the park for at least one year. . . .

A month later, Arturo Wilderotter traveled to Mexico City and took a room in a favorite five-star hotel. He had worked out his plan, set his schedule, with a week to accomplish his mission and fly back to New York.

According to his research, based on materials supplied by Evangelium Christi sources, Bishop Juan Nicolás Manrique, had been collaborating for years with the antigovernment forces in southern Mexico, in Chiapas, Tabasco, and Campeche. He celebrated mass for the rebels, ministered to their spiritual needs, saw that they received food and money, and allegedly helped smuggle arms to them under cover of his Christian mission. His sermons were legendary, inflammatory, Marxist-leaning. There was no question in Wilderotter's mind that this man must be eliminated if the work of Christ and the True Faith were to be protected, which was the stated goal of the Evangelium.

Contacts from his past life as an undercover operative enabled him to work efficiently and quickly once he got to Mexico City on Monday. A man from Guatemala, whom he knew to be a CIA-trained officer of the secret police, provided the ready-made car bomb. The bishop was expected to visit the cardinal—presumably for an official reprimand for his noncanonical activities and Marxist-infected theological teachings, prior to formal disciplinary action—in three days, on Thursday. There would be a private mass, prayer, more talk, perhaps dinner. The visit was scheduled to end on Friday and the bishop to return home to the south.

That day was clear and crisp, unusually so, with only the thinnest blanket of smog over the sprawling chaos that was Mexico City. Arturo set out early from his hotel, one travel bag packed, airline tickets purchased, seat reserved on an evening flight to JFK airport in New York. He did not plan to stick around to admire his handiwork.

He met his Guatemalan contact at a garage, saw for himself that the bomb had been installed in a limousine, an old blue Lincoln that was ready for the scrap heap as it was. The bomb would be activated by remote radio signal, not by the ignition. Wilderotter inspected and approved. He paid the Guatemalan the agreed-upon price for his services, then both took a taxicab to the airport. There they awaited the incoming flight with Bishop Manrique, due at about eleven A.M. It was a good plan, he thought. He had a sense of satisfaction, accomplishment, rightness about it. The small remote device fit in his palm like a pack of cards ready to be shuffled and dealt.

When the time came he pushed the button, then walked away. The explosion rocked the driveway and the terminal, but he did not look back.

There had been unforeseen collateral damage: the driver, another bishop, and two religious sisters. The driver was killed along with the bishops, the two nuns were seriously wounded and eventually fully recovered, and Manrique himself was injured most gravely of all, not killed but confined to a wheelchair ever after. Although the primary target lived, the mission was counted as a success by Wilderotter's superiors, for the second prelate had been just as bad as Manrique, or worse, they said.

PART II

Keeper of the Keys

CHAPTER EIGHT

Rome, May 11, 2003

Nights were often very difficult for the transplanted American prelate. Although over the years Mulrennan had gotten well used to spartan living and sleeping conditions, as a priest and a bishop, he keenly felt displaced, in unfamiliar territory, in the papal bedchamber. The bed itself was neither too hard nor too soft, but not quite long enough for his height. White linen sheets and a thin cotton blanket were usually more than enough covering. Even after a full day—and hours every evening of reading, writing, prayer, and meetings—he craved a bit of private reading time before sleep.

Around midnight he sought the quiet comfort of bed and a book, facing the open window of his room, to read for a half hour or more: current popular fiction, some history and biography, and, a new passion, the works of G. K. Chesterton, which had suddenly risen to his consciousness in a new way. It began when he reread the classic biography of St. Thomas Aquinas, in a little paperback edition that had somehow traveled with him among the papers and personal effects that he received from Newark. He experienced a renewal of interest not only in the Angelic Doctor, but in the mind of the great twentieth-century defender and explainer of the Catholic faith, Chesterton. The books—fiction, essays, biographies—were as tasty as candy but far more nourishing and challenging; they helped him, he thought, become a better, clearer writer himself—not that he considered himself anywhere near an author. But the great Englishman's facility with words and ideas was infectious, and the pope especially enjoyed such Chestertonian chestnuts as *Orthodoxy* and *The Everlasting*

Man. Tonight he would crack open a collection of Father Brown stories, which lulled him near to sleep.

As a young priest, Timothy Mulrennan had stolen time as often as he could to read Church history and contemporary theology, to learn whence the Body of Christ had come and where it was going along the continuum of world history. In his very first parish assignment after service at the Vatican Council, in his hometown of North Auburn, New Jersey, the recently ordained Mulrennan had been blessed with the example of Monsignor Robert Froeschel, a grizzled veteran of the parish and the archdiocese who, without explicitly sitting him in a classroom, had furthered the younger man's practical education as a priest, and he knew something about being a pastor. Tim was a rookie and ambitious to boot, so he drank in everything Froeschel said and did, like an eager grad student. He learned that ambition, in itself, did not count for much at all, either in the eyes of his fellow priests or of God. He also questioned just what he was aiming *for*: Clerical advancement? A plum assignment? Fame? To be loved by parishioners? Time and experience tempered his hopes and tamped his ego, appropriately.

In the diocesan seminary, at Darlington, New Jersey, he had not yet sharpened the spear of ambition; rather he had cultivated his spiritual and intellectual inclinations in a near-monastic atmosphere. He learned to enjoy and appreciate the daily disciplines of prayer, learning, and pastoral service. He liked being with the other guys who, like himself, were sincerely trying to find their way in God's world on this difficult pathway to salvation—for themselves and others. Amid the study of dogma, Scripture, rubrics, and Latin there was little horseplay (none sanctioned) but a lot of laughter and sympathy and companionship.

Those seemingly innocent times were long gone. Today Tim Mulrennan, Pope Celestine, faced a world remade by terrorism and war—not "saved" by technology and science, as some had predicted. . . .

This night, after dinner, the pontiff changed into a black pullover sweatshirt and black Dockers and put on his walking shoes and slipped out of the residence with a bodyguard following at a discrete ten or twelve meters. His back had been bothering him, and he hoped that a walk would cure the ache. Earlier, to Cardinals Biagi and Tyrone and the other dinner guests he had said simply and enigmatically, "I wish to pray with the others."

Biagi, at least, knew what Pope Celestine meant: a late-night trip to the sacred places beneath the great basilica.

The *scavi* are the excavations begun by Pope Pius XII on the eve of World War II and carried on in secret throughout the conflict that nearly spelled the end of European Christendom. A visit to the street of tombs, the ancient Roman necropolis beneath the high altar of St. Peter's, is a privilege granted to very few, mostly scholars, archaeologists, selected clergy, and wealthy Catholic pilgrims—with occasional tours for regular folks. The pope, when he first descended the steps at the Arco delle Campane entrance that led beneath the Vatican grottoes, the subterranean chapel where many of his predecessors were entombed, thought he had stepped back in time to the city of the emperors and martyrs— and, in fact, he had. He felt an immediate visceral and spiritual connection to St. Peter, to Pius XII, to all the two hundred sixty-three other men who had been called Bishop of Rome.

In this place, really a narrow, dusty Roman street between somber brick walls and doorways, which had seen no sunlight or open air for sixteen centuries, the Supreme Pontiff of the Holy Roman Catholic Church could barely breathe. Not for lack of oxygen, but for a surfeit of *presence* of the Other World—ghosts, perhaps, or pagan bones, or the Holy Spirit . . . a presence that robbed his lungs of their capacity to function and quickened his heartbeat. Tonight, accompanied only by a single unarmed guard, he somberly entered the roadway and gazed at the painted chambers where dead Romans still lay in sarcophagi or in urns. Above him stood the magnificent basilica—the most recognizable monument of Christendom—and layer upon layer of building and destruction that had begun with Constantine and ended with Bramante and Michelangelo: directly over his head was the high altar of Clement VIII where he had said mass on the eve of Christmas, before his historic announcement at the Lateran. Always, always he was drawn back here, to this place of death and history and dust and life.

The ancient street upon which he stood had run from the

brown river to the heights of the Vatican Hill, tracing a route that more or less corresponded to the modern Via della Conciliazione, Mussolini's mad, modern fascist slash of a street that brought foot and automobile traffic to St. Peter's Square at ground level.

There was very little opportunity for true solitude. Timothy Mulrennan the man had privately vowed to himself to see that Celestine the pope had the chance—at least occasionally—to be away from the papal office, to seek quiet renewal of his spirit. This little trip into the past filled him up, energized and focused him. It was a reminder of the "Romanness" of his position—in the Church and in the world.

Beneath the red wall, so called because of the bright red— though long since faded—plaster facing on once side of the brick wall itself, the excavators had discovered, more than sixty years ago, the human bones that were thought to be (indeed, hoped to be) those of St. Peter himself. On the night of this discovery the reigning pope himself had been summoned to the site of the dig.

The pontiff, a scholarly, bespectacled Pius XII in his spotless white cassock (on other visits, it was reported, he wore white overalls and a white protective helmet), gave permission for the archaeologists to proceed and sat in a chair on the marble pavement near the pit. For hours he watched as bones were unearthed and carefully deposited before him. Human hands and brushes and trowels were employed in the delicate task. The pope was silent. The skull did not appear (it was, of course, claimed by the Cathedral of St. John Lateran, preserved in the reliquary above the altar of the pope's parish church: verified in 1804 to contain a portion of cranium, part of a jawbone, and more than a handful of dust)—but vertebrae, ribs, fingers, toes, legs, arms, and pieces of breast bone and shoulder blade were raised. In the end more than two hundred fifty fragments and whole bones lay in three lead boxes at the pope's feet.

Pius blessed and thanked the archaeologists; the boxes were sealed and transported to the Apostolic Palace where, over the next several months, they were examined by medical men. These experts confirmed that the bones had belonged to a powerfully built man in his sixties. Were these, in truth, the bones of the first Bishop of Rome?

Over the next decades a small army of researchers examined evidence from the *scavi* itself, as well as texts and artifacts such as the Samagher Casket in the Lateran Museum, which contains a reproduction of the shrine of St. Peter as it must have first appeared . . . linguistic, forensic, graffiti, historical, and other physical evidence was sifted and marshaled to reach the astounding conclusion that the Tropaion (as the shrine itself was called) was not just a grave marker, but a large "chapel" with an altar in the center and the probable focus of worship, baptism, and Eucharistic celebration by large gatherings: perhaps as many as three or four score persons.

It is possible that the apostle's grave site was purposely hidden—among pagan tombs, some of them for prominent Roman citizens—and eventually buried beneath the rubble of subsequent cathedrals to ensure that his bones remained safely deposited, undisturbed by persecutors and invaders, in the dust of the imperial city. If Pope Pius XII had not authorized the work that made room for his predecessor in the Vatican grottoes, perhaps the bones might still lay peacefully in that place where—the popes and the faithful wish to think—the followers of Peter and earliest members of the Church had carefully and lovingly interred their martyred leader. The man to whom Christ had directly entrusted the keys of His kingdom on earth . . .

Pope Celestine, the sixth of that name, stood with his hands clenched, his breathing labored. There was little doubt in his mind that he was allergic to this ancient dust, but he could not stay away. He stepped closer to the bronze grillwork gate installed by Pope Paul VI in 1968—when the pontiff had finally announced to the world the "fact" of St. Peter's remains—and peered through the bars toward the so-called graffiti wall where a glassed-in niche held two Plexiglas boxes of leg and skull bones, visible to the eyes of men and women some sixteen centuries after Constantine and twenty centuries after Peter's death. What had brought the big fisherman to Rome in the first place? Surely he had known what lay in store for him at the hands of the madman Nero. The words of his Savior and the breath of the spirit had led him here to do the Father's will—to nurture His people of the New Covenant. Tim Mulrennan of New Jersey sniffled and coughed in the presence of Simon Peter of Galilee, his predecessor of seventy generations.

The pope blew his nose in a wad of tissue that he had carried with him; like the good Boy Scout he had once been, he was prepared. He closed his eyes and prayed for a few minutes, asking for Peter's guidance and God's blessing. Surely it was no accident that the American stood here at this place and this time in history. He prayed, too, for clarity of mind and purity of motive: Was this council the right thing to do, or was he driven to prove himself somehow with a grand historical gesture? Was it really necessary? The power of his office—which he had accepted, but which he had not sought—pressed monumentally upon his broad shoulders, seemingly the size and weight of the very cathedral that loomed above him at this moment: a burden, a joy, a marble and granite vessel of sorrow.

This man who had been variously called Simon and Cephas and Petrus—St. Peter, the first Bishop of Rome, had thrice betrayed his Lord just as Jesus predicted at the Last Supper. Yet, in his hands had been placed the keys, and from his lips had come the words that defined the rule of faith, the *Word* that had been inspired by the Holy Spirit. Along with his fellow apostles, Peter sowed the seeds of this true church of Christ, which took root throughout the Mediterranean world and beyond; by their authority the Eucharist and the episcopacy had been established, the deposit of faith passed to the generations through tradition, eventually to be written down as Scripture. This man Peter, in whose presence his latest successor now stood, had borne on human shoulders the mighty weight of supernatural authority; yet God had made the burden light and called His servant unto His throne when the Galilean's task was done. Just as Tim Mulrennan would one day be summoned to account—just as every man would.

Since his election, the pope had not experienced any of the strange visions that had punctuated his time in the conclaves of the previous year. Yet he felt ever more closely connected with each of his predecessors, from Peter through Innocent, as the days passed inexorably—and the seasons changed from summer to autumn to winter. What would the new spring hold for him and for the Church? The seasons of Lent, Easter, and Pentecost would unfold as they had for two thousand years; in addition to the liturgical cycles, preparations for the council would occupy the prayers and deliberations of the Servant of the Servants of God in each waking minute. Even if he had not *seen* the spectral images of the men who had been pope before him, Mulrennan held them closely in his heart. The low, heavy table beside his papal bed in the spacious apartment where he slept was piled high with biographies of John XXIII and Paul VI, with the documents of Vatican II and other ecumenical councils dating back to Nicea I. All of the popes and Church fathers were more alive to him than any momentary apparitions.

Indeed, his prayer life had intensified, of necessity, over the past several months—starting from the moment he awoke in the morning, continuing sporadically through the day, including a full hour before supper, and concluding with a full recitation of the rosary at bedtime. He slept for five or six hours on average each night. He tried, too, to squeeze in time for exercise at least three days a week—and he found that the time on the treadmill was also an excellent opportunity to pray, to mix sweat with supplication. Prayer had sustained him through sixty-four years of life. As a baptized Christian and confirmed Catholic and daily communicant for as long as he could remember, the words of the creed and the liturgical formulas of the Holy Mass had become as natural and necessary to him as his skin. He could not even imagine a life that did not include the gifts of Word and Spirit— and when he prayed he asked God that these gifts might be available to all who had not been so blessed as he to know the presence of Christ and His message of salvation.

How close he was, then, in time and space, to the Redeemer: in this dusty cavern of a necropolis now buried beneath the most majestic cathedral in all of the Christian world. Here lay the bones, the beloved relics, of one who had walked with Him, had heard from His own lips the life-giving truth. These very molecules of earth and air might have touched His human form; and some of these monuments may have stood since the first century of His era. Yet, even with this palpable, physical thrill of proximity to an apostle of Christ, was he now closer to the real presence of Jesus than when he held the consecrated host or drank the Savior's blood in the outward form of wine? No—in the sacrament of the Eucharist, which he celebrated every day, the body and blood of the Lord mingled with his own in profound mystery and gift of faith, in the exercise of his sacred office of priesthood. "Do this in memory of Me," Jesus had instructed Peter and the other apostles. And they had—and they had transmitted the memory of the act itself in the rite of the mass . . . and the teaching authority of the bishop from one to another down through the ages.

Rome, January 12, 2003

The former Archbishop of Portland, Oregon lay dying in a Roman hospital, awaiting a visit from his old friend and colleague, the pope. Joseph James Johnson closed his eyes and recovered a stark image from his childhood: the vast Bay of Mobile that shimmered like a sheet of steel as it stretched toward the horizon as if to sever the earth from the sky. This disease of the liver was doing the same to Archbishop Johnson—cutting off his physical life—but in an ugly, agonizing way. He clung to the vivid memories, replayed those long-gone days in Alabama as if they were hourly news updates on television (which he never watched any more). Dying of hepatitis and shame, resulting from his once-secret addiction to booze and drugs, he waited for his friend and for release from bondage to this earth.

He was beyond discomfort, beyond pain, on the threshold of acceptance, of meeting God face to face, and he was not afraid to die. He was afraid to live.

Joe Johnson, a bishop of the Roman Catholic Church and as such a successor to the apostles, recalled what was sure to be characterized in his obituary as "humble origins," the small house that sheltered a large family near the bay of memory. The house where he had been born and slept and ate for nearly twenty years, before college and seminary. The house where he had played and cried and loved and grown into a man. It still stood, and his mother still lived there and her grandchildren visited her there. Joe, the youngest boy, had given her no grandchildren—and that was a distinct disappointment to her, he knew. But he had tried to compensate for that lack in the best way he knew how: by achieving a measure of earthly success in the service of a supernatural Master. Thank God she did not know of his utter failure and depravity, largely hidden from the world.

He stared, dry-eyed, at the white-painted plaster of the ceiling of his hospital room. The smudged window admitted the light of a cold sun.

The newly opened hospital wing provided hospice care in a gleaming white, hushed environment—oddly juxtaposed to the bustling urban medical center. It was named after St. Peter and the staff joked that, as this was "heaven's waiting room," that is who the patients would see next. Archbishop Johnson, in room 10A, enjoyed a window that provided a western view, including a patch of green in an otherwise concrete and brick landscape. He was having one of his good days—that is, he could sit up and listen to his beloved jazz without too much physical agony.

A gentle knock on the half-open door was followed by a query in the familiar voice of his old friend, the new pope: "Joe?" Mulrennan stuck his head into the hospice room. He swallowed a cry of shock and sadness at the sight of the skeletal form of the former Archbishop of Portland. J. J. Johnson had been a college basketball standout in the early 1970s; he had held his own as a small center against such athletes as Bob Lanier and Artis Gilmore, though his team had posted mediocre won-lost records. Now he was a shrunken, sallow shadow of that young man.

"Come in, Holiness," Johnson rasped in his strongest voice. His face lit up at the sight of Tim Mulrennan entering the room, an apparition in white. "For a minute there, I thought I was getting a visit from the Klan—glad it's only you."

"Only me, is right. Just the Successor of St. Peter."

"Not the real thing, thank the Lord."

"Nowhere near." The pope came to him and embraced him. Johnson felt as insubstantial as a scarecrow—he must have weighed about 120 pounds, to look at him, about half his normal weight. "You seem to be your old, incorrigible self today—God help us."

"I'm doing the best I can, under these rather difficult circumstances. . . ."

"I know you are, Joe," the pontiff said sincerely. "And you know I pray for you every single day—even mention you at mass. It doesn't get any better than that." He attempted a jocular smile but succeeded only in a false, pained one.

"My soul needs all the help it can get, for sure. I royally screwed up, Tim—I mean, Holy Father. Nothing is going to change that."

"You have confessed your sins and received absolution, my friend. You don't have a thing to regret or be ashamed of, since God has forgiven you. You are required now to forgive yourself and put your burden down. Leave that for the rest of us. That is our struggle. Yours is—" He caught himself, heard his own words. His old friend had been in recovery from his alcoholism and drug addiction for about a dozen years, and it had not been easy, he knew. "Yours is nearly finished," he said.

Archbishop Joe Johnson looked away from Pope Celestine, out the window that admitted a thin shaft of afternoon light. *Nearly finished.* It was a harsh thing to hear, though intended as just the opposite. A wave of pain emanating from his gut washed over him, but he did not flinch or show any outward sign of the searing inner agony that he felt. *What good would it do to bring this good man down to my level?* he thought. *He has his own supreme cares and responsibilities—more than enough for any single human being—enough, literally, to cripple or kill most men.*

"Thank you for coming," Johnson said, his eyes rheumy.

"I'm glad to be with you—and away from the office."

Mulrennan stood by the bed and looked around the room: It was comfortably appointed with visitors' chairs and a tea table, a CD player and a small TV set situated on a four-foot bookcase that held a few random bestsellers in Italian and English. An undistinguished modern painting of the Roman Forum hung on one wall, opposite the single window, portraying the landscape of ruins as colorfully as a Western omelet. Beside the bed was a tall, sculpted lamp that softened the harsh fluorescent light from the panel above the patient's head. A slender crucifix hung unobtrusively, almost apologetically nearby. Here was an imperfect blend of homeyness and medical necessity. The wraith that had been a distinguished prelate of the Roman Catholic Church lay in silent witness to human mortality amid the evidences of man's denial of the inevitable. Johnson observed his friend taking in the details with which he had lived for several weeks—and would endure for several more, God willing.

"Not terrible for a hospital room. God knows I've visited the sick and dying in unspeakable places. 'If you have done this for the least of mine . . .' " He smiled hopefully, trying to put the visitor in the white cassock and zucchetto at ease.

"Look, Joe," the pontiff said, "you don't need to be concerned with my feelings. I'm here because you're a good priest—and a good friend. I hate to lose you. It feels so very wrong and unjust. I'm not blaming God, you understand, but I want to curse at something."

"You've got bigger fish to fry now. Believe me, I don't feel neglected. I know you're paying for all this." Johnson waved his bony black hands to indicate the room. "And for my family to be here. They told me. I can't tell you how grateful I am. And how sorry, Holy Father."

"We're brothers. I know you'd do the same for me if the tables were turned—and I truly wish they were, that I could trade places with you."

"Well, I don't. I'm just an alcoholic and a junkie—garden variety screw-up. That was God's will for me. I think that the bishop thing was an accident—even that I lived long enough for it to happen. The price I paid to keep my secret . . . oh, I functioned, but the things I did . . . Each and every day of the last twelve years—since I've been clean and sober—has been a miracle of the highest magnitude. *One* day would have been as powerful a sign to me as Lazarus or the lepers." He paused to catch his breath, gulped a lungful of air. "Not that I need proof of His love beyond my birth and baptism. But so much more was manifested in my life, even at the very bottom—even now in this illness. I thank Him each day for this exercise in humility and powerlessness."

"Let's pray together for a while," Mulrennan said.

"Sure—pull up a chair," Johnson said with the same game, grimace-smile.

As the pope pulled one of the chairs over toward the bed, a policeman stuck his head into the room—alerted by the noise. "We're fine—*bene, bene*—just the chair," Mulrennan assured him, then sat at the bishop's bedside.

The two men clasped hands and prayed silently, intently together for fifteen minutes. Through Mulrennan's mind, pictures flashed in a nostalgic slide show: images of Joe Johnson as a healthy, charismatic young priest and seminary teacher; as a bishop-elect receiving the signs and authority of his office from the hands of the Archbishop of San Francisco, with Tim Mulrennan of Newark as a co-presider; as a mature Church leader serving his diocese and the national conference of fellow bishops, earning their admiration for his compassion and eloquence. What a man—what a bishop!

The two men in the hospice room ended their prayers. Mulrennan, the Bishop of Rome, released the somewhat clammy hand of his brother bishop who was dying of liver cancer. Joseph Johnson had a month, perhaps six weeks at the outside, left—an acutely unpleasant prospect. The pain was not yet totally debilitating, but soon he would be on a constant morphine drip and begin to drift away from reality. There was no turning back now, no hope except for a swift passing.

"You know what I regret most of all?" Johnson said. "Missing the main event—this council of yours."

"What do you think, Joe? I mean, do you think it is the right thing to do? I expected some flak. I don't think I could do anything that's not controversial—goes with the job. But the utterly virulent opposition from the Evangelium Christi folks . . . I guess I was surprised by the swiftness of it. I guess they were ready for me. Thanks to our pal Cardinal Vennholme."

"Is he still lurking in the bushes? He nearly destroyed you a year ago."

"Now I'm a bigger target."

"Be careful. Even I have heard of threats and the possibility of some kind disruption, so you must know they're out there. And this bizarre conciliarist argument—that the council will sit in judgment of the pope and have ultimate authority over him, over you, that is. It's like something out of a science fiction novel." Johnson turned to face Mulrennan squarely. "You do realize the dangers you face?"

"I suppose I do. But I can't let it handcuff me. My personal security is not an issue—not since they blew poor De Guzman away. No midnight rambles or Sunday picnics for yours truly."

"You asked me what I think about the council, Holiness. I think it is truly the right thing to do—at the right time. With terror and unbelief out in the world and opposition from some of our own—the next ten years may be the most crucial in the history of the Church, at least since the Roman emperors' persecutions. The faith will endure such an assault—unimaginable, even to those who remember the Second World War."

"That's what Il Santo Papa said to me before he died—almost exactly . . . oh, I'm sorry, Joe, I didn't mean—" Mulrennan looked crestfallen, felt as if he had slugged his friend in the belly. He hadn't meant to speak so coldly to him.

"Forget it. We both know I'm dying. But you have to live a long time to see this through. I'm counting on you to do just that. A lot of people are. You know, the nurses and staff here are so impressed that I know you. 'He's a great man,' they say. *Il Americano*, they call you. And these are hard-bitten Romans, understand. They've seen popes come and seen them go."

"No doubt, they'll see me do both—and realize that I'm no great man."

"You are to me, my friend. Always will be."

Again Tim Mulrennan, Pope Celestine, took the ailing bishop in his arms. For a brief, searing moment he remembered his mother's death—now a half-century ago—and the yawning hole that her loss had left in him, and the deep sadness and deeper ambivalence he had felt then. She too had been an alcoholic, but never sober. Her gift to him had been life and her most profound legacy, empathy with the suffering of another.

This man was teaching him new lessons, prophesying new dreams: In his suffering Joe Johnson fulfilled some kind of strange, salvific destiny that even he was not sure of. For Mulrennan it was a mottled mirror in which he might behold a partial, obscured version of himself, a pathway down which he might walk, albeit from a different point of origin. To the same place in the end? Who knew?

"You have no basis to say that, Joe. Only your own limited perspective, only what I have allowed you to see."

"Don't give yourself so much credit, man—or sell me short. I know you're as screwed up as the rest of us. Yet you keep putting one foot in front of the other. As often as you've wanted to quit—and sometimes you have, like when you tried to drop out of sight after the first conclave last year. What I'm trying to say is, I gain strength by knowing you are here, that you are standing up to *them*."

"Who is 'them'?" Mulrennan was both amused and troubled.

"The ones in the Curia who must control everything—the ones who do not trust God to the people of God but must keep Him in a jeweled box in a vault in the dark. You are going to open the window and let in the light on them. And they don't like it in the least—do they, Holy Father?"

"You are imagining a lot of things, my son."

"Don't pull your papal rank on me." The emaciated black man poked his bony finger into the space between their faces. Mulrennan noticed the purple smudges beneath his glittery brown eyes. "I am not playing. I don't have time for that. I'm telling the truth, and you know it."

"I suppose I do. But that doesn't mean I have to accept it."

"No, just like I don't have to accept the truth of my dying— which does not change the fact of it."

"Joe, what are you saying to me?"

"Open your ears, Timothy. That's the last time I'll call you by your given name." Johnson slid down into his pillows, exhausted by the sustained effort he had expended in this meeting with his friend and ecclesiastical father, his fellow shepherd. "I trust you, know that you'll act with the Spirit. Already you have answered His call. Now you will lead His people into the light of truth." He lay still for a moment, his breathing labored. The pontiff placed a hand on the man's forehead, felt the moist warmth there but coldness beneath. "Open your eyes, Holiness, and see for yourself—as well as for me. When I am gone you'll have few left who will tell you the whole truth."

The pontiff helped his friend get comfortable in the bed and blessed him, held his hands upon the man's head. He felt a twinge of pain in his own lower back, must have strained it without being aware. In a few moments, when Archbishop Johnson had fallen asleep, the Bishop of Rome in his finely tailored white cassock left the hospice room. He called to mind a refrain from that psalm, sometimes recited in the liturgy of the Word at mass: *Shepherd me, O God, beyond my wants, beyond my fears, from death into life*. Shepherd Your son Joseph, he prayed.

CHAPTER NINE

Rome, May 29, 2003

Demetra smiled even as she fidgeted, glanced at her watch, swept the dining room with an amused, penetrating eye. Jim Wiezevich had chosen the premier Chinese restaurant in Rome, the Jade Lion, as their meeting place. Unusual, to say the least, and she had enjoyed the humor of it. But now he was ten minutes late—she had been about ten minutes early—and she was beginning to worry that he wouldn't show up. Perhaps something had kept him, a new assignment or command appearance at the Apostolic Palace. These men from New Jersey, she mused, considering the provenance of the pope and several of his inner circle, had suddenly found themselves at the center of the universe (at least their own universe, the Church). So, what in God's name were they supposed to do? It would be like Demetra Matoulis waking up as chief executive of the largest news organization on the planet with the power to shape billions' knowledge of the world and the crushing responsibility for the lives of uncounted employees and consumers.

She munched on some dry but tasty deep-fried noodles and sipped hot tea, doodled on a scrap of paper with a cheap, leaky pen. Wish I had brought a book or magazine or something, she thought, hating to waste even a passing moment such as this, seemingly unable to relax and enjoy the deeply comfortable chair and enticing aroma from the kitchen.

Perhaps it was a symptom of her discomfort with the whole idea of being with Jim again—after all these years of silence and separation. There was little room in her life for friendship, let alone a relationship with a man, let alone a *complicated* relationship with a man. . . .

The very first time she had seen him, thirteen years ago, he was among a throng of tourists at the Vatican museums in the courtyard, sitting on a stone bench resting his feet, contemplating the outsized head of the Emperor Constantine. She had been there many times before but frequently came back to see the art and the history of the city—and the world. She was just establishing herself in journalism, as a copy editor and occasional rewrite maven, and she always kept her eyes peeled for the story that would take her up the next rung on the ladder. She could tell he was an American, from his demeanor and his utilitarian clothing; she liked his square shoulders and large pale ears, for reasons even she did not quite understand. He looked like a guy who might be nice to talk to—so she did, approaching him directly and frankly.

"Hi. You're an American?" She hedged her bet, phrased it as a question instead of a statement.

Jim Wiezevich was startled. He had been absorbed in the scope and majesty of the place, and of the giant imperial image of the man who had singlehandedly transformed the Christian Church from a troublesome sect to a state religion, overturning forever the far more ancient pagan tradition of his own nation. He looked up and into her face as she stood there and said, "Yeah, American. From New Jersey. Born and raised. Here as a student. You?"

She smiled. "Florida and New York."

"Usually it's the other way around."

"There's more. Family from Greece. I was actually born there."

"Well, sit down if you're going to tell me your whole life story," he said, moving to one side to make room for her on the cool stone. It was midafternoon, bright but still a bit chilly for spring, and the shadows fell in dark slashes like wounds on the grass and walkway. "Or if I'm going to tell you mine."

Demetra liked his smile. It seemed easily obtainable, welcoming. She wanted to know more, to tell more, so she sat. "Graduate student, I presume?" she said.

"Yes—seminary. Studying at the North American College."

"Oh, I've always wondered about that. Sounds very austere, important, Ivy League-ish."

Wiezevich laughed. "Of course it's none of those things, really. I find it a grind mostly. Not that I'm not grateful to be here, to see—this—" He swung his head around to indicate the courtyard and the museums and the Vatican grounds. "Today I'm playing hooky, had to take a break and come here to breathe in all this history and beauty."

"Me too—I mean I felt I had to come here today, to get my 'fix.' Culture and antiquity. Put some balance in my life, which is sorely lacking at the moment. I work full-time for the *International Herald-Tribune*, Rome bureau. Big-shot reporter."

"I can tell," he said, gladly playing along. "What might your name be? I'll look for your byline."

"Demetra Matoulis." Her small hand appeared, available.

"I'm Jim Wiezevich. Pleased to meet you." He took her hand and gave it a sincere pump, businesslike yet friendly. There was no mistaking the current he felt pass from her to him and back, and he let go and regarded her with more interest even than he had shown the old emperor. "Very pleased. If you don't mind my asking, are you recently out of college—graduated, I mean?"

"Two years out. I've been in Rome for almost the whole time."

"I got here two Januarys ago. I don't ever want to leave."

"Me neither. There's a reason it was the capital of a world empire," she said.

"So, you think he was wrong?" Jim pointed toward the stubborn-jawed, big-lipped Constantine.

"Yes. In more ways than one."

The seminarian appraised this good-looking young woman who had suddenly appeared, as if she were a museum nymph who revealed herself to lovers of art and antiquities. Bemused, he shifted his butt on the cold bench, turned to face her full-on. He very much liked what he saw: a lovely oval face with high cheekbones and sea-gray eyes, light, straight brown hair touched by the sun, wonderful lips that curled easily in a smile. But it was not so much the physical appearance as the bright spirit that touched him. She seemed to be reaching inside him, even in their inconsequential banter, to pull something—some part of him—out.

"What do you mean?"

"There's definitely an element of corruption, death, an odor of criminality that pervades the city. At least that's what I see. Another way to describe it might be the sins of the past. I think we never truly escape our past, so . . ."

"So we are prisoners of it. I assume you include the Church in that description?"

"Yes. Sorry if that offends you, but it is how I see it."

"No offense. I am curious, though, why a Greek girl from Florida would choose to be here—given all the corruption and crime—instead of someplace more inviting, like Paris."

"Well, I studied Italian instead of French, and it's closer to Greece. I've been over there a few times to visit family and see the old home place. And I think there's something irresistible about Rome, once you've got the bug—not sure what it is, really. Faded glory . . . promise of resurrection . . . the pure, raw history that you see everywhere. But—look—why are we talking about this? I don't even know you."

"Not yet. You accosted me, remember."

"That's a nice word, 'accosted.' Sounds more than vaguely criminal."

"Didn't mean it that way, I—"

"I know. Just kidding. I have a warped sense of humor. I guess you know me pretty well by now. How about you tell me about yourself. We could get a cup of coffee or something."

His head was spinning like a gyroscope. Was she asking him out on a date? He had not been with a woman since early in his college years, had avoided the occasion of temptation since he had accepted the fact of his vocation. Or, was he reading too much into her simple invitation? Perhaps she saw him as a curiosity, a semi-interesting adjunct to the larger story of the Vatican, the American Church—an entré into the world of priests and prelates. But the immediate question was, should he continue the conversation?

"Sure," he said easily—at least he hoped it came out that way. "I've done the circuit here today." He mentally toted up the number of times he had taken the full tour: at least seven or eight, maybe more. He stood.

"Great. I know a place close by." Demetra led the way back

into and then through the maze of hallways to the easiest exit, one Jim had not seen before. Outside, she walked purposefully along the narrow sidewalk clogged with beggars and souvenir stands. He moderated his long strides to match her shorter ones, was close enough to breathe in the warmth of her body but did not touch her.

"Where do you live?" he asked when they had settled at a small table near the front window of the café.

"Not far, short taxi ride or long walk from here." She lit a cigarette, did not offer him one. "Oh, do you mind if I smoke?" she asked belatedly.

"Well, I guess not." He felt prudish and straight, thought that she was trying to put him in that position, to test him. "It's no good for you."

"I know, but I like it. Helps pass the time, and everybody does it. They're not so uptight here about health and pollution and all that. In other words, they don't give a damn."

"So where did you go to school?"

"We're getting totally boring here," she replied. "Where do I live? Where did I go to school? What did I have for breakfast?"

"Look, I sincerely want to know. Besides, what else do you want to talk about? The Super Bowl?"

Demetra Matoulis laughed. "God, anything but that! I always hated American football, and now I sometimes cover the Italian football matches here. They're fanatical, crazy. I think it's much worse in Europe—riots and hooliganism. My kind of sporting event, not boring Dallas Cowboys with pads and plastic helmets playing on plastic grass."

"I'm a big Giants fan," Wiezevich said ruefully, almost ashamed to admit something so culturally mundane.

"Hey, guys are different. It's in the blood or the genes. I don't claim to understand it—don't want to. All I know is I was bored silly many a Friday night in high school trying to follow the grunting and hitting of all the biggest, dumbest guys in town. Never thought of it as fun."

"Well, that brings me back to my question. Where'd you go to college?"

"If you must know, Florida State for one year, then transferred to Barnard in New York City. Best thing that ever happened to me. Other than meeting you today, of course."

Again, Jim Wiezevich laughed. She had a wonderful way of slicing through the bullshit and pointing out the existential absurdity of the immediate situation; meanwhile, he felt reduced to his own appropriate size and station.

"Glad to know it. You've changed my life, too."

"Oh, how so?"

"Next time a woman approaches me at a museum I'll wear a Roman collar—or pretend I'm a deaf mute."

Her laughter crashed over him like an ocean wave on a white beach. He was drowning and did not quite realize it in the hot glare of the sun, in the shock and dreamlike quality of her presence. How the hell had it happened? He had known her for less than an hour and he could not imagine loving anyone or anything as much as he loved her in this moment. Then, suddenly, he was afraid of losing her—never having possessed her. A pang of confusion and guilt pinned him in the chair.

She said, "I'll learn sign language."

It was his turn to laugh, and it relaxed him, eased his overworked conscience. Damn, she was funny and smart and gorgeous and unavailable to a seminarian who was twelve months from ordination as a Roman Catholic priest. Now how do I wiggle out of this situation? he asked himself, wanting to remain forever just like this, to move nary a muscle, to make her laugh—always.

"Probably I should get back to the College. I've got tons of work to do. I was really playing hooky today. Let me pick up the check, please."

"Why should I do that?" Demetra said. "I invited you—and we haven't finished this conversation yet. You know *everything* about me, but you didn't tell me a thing about yourself. So start spilling your guts, right now."

"Don't know what to say."

"Birthdate. Where you grew up. Where you went to school, which you seem to think is so important. Why this priest thing. You know: what you tell all the girls."

"That's the point, of course—girls aren't a part of the biography. Born thirty years ago. Grew up in Northern New Jersey. Normal screwed-up family, lost both my older brother and younger sister, parents still alive. They're out of it—thank God. Not sick or senile or anything, just in total denial, go to church and play cards and putter around the house. My dad will retire very soon." Jim looked at his watch. "Another year or two. Sorry—just trying to remember what day and month it is."

"That's a start," she encouraged. Demetra felt comfortable and challenged at the same time with this guy. She was not sure what she expected from him—or herself—but she was willing to stick with it, follow through with him to discover whatever there was to discover at the other end of the day. "Don't quit now."

"You want to know why I decided to be a priest."

"Something like that."

"Well, I don't know—that is, it wasn't really a decision as such, more something I learned along the way and accepted at one point as a fact. I believe the call comes from God and it is up to the individual to hear it, to answer Him."

He turned his cup, watched the coffee dregs move blackly at the bottom of the cup, held the cup's handle for dear life, wanted to crawl into that cup and be drunk into oblivion by some unseen giant and disappear in the silence. Damn, she made him uncomfortable with himself! He thought only his mother or worst teacher could make him feel so small and vulnerable. Perhaps it was any woman whom he allowed to get close to him. . . . There had not been that many over thirty years. He replaced the cup in its saucer and looked at her lovely, open face.

"Usually I can articulate it much better than I am now. For some reason I feel intimidated by you. I don't want to—but I do."

She reached across the table and put her hand on his wrist. "I don't mean to make you feel that way. I'm sorry. I just wanted to know, to hear you say it. I like you, thought it might be fun to spend a little time together. Maybe I should have left well enough alone and not bothered you back there at the museum."

He wanted to agree, to end it here and now, pay the bill and go home. But he heard himself speaking words that had never escaped his mouth before. "I'm glad you did—approach me, that is. I had seen you, wanted to talk to you myself but was too scared. I hope you don't think you've hurt or offended me in any way because you haven't. It's just—I want to spend time with you too, get to know you a little. We can be friends, can't we?"

"Yes, we can. I hope we will. But I should tell you that I'm not easy to know. As much as I pry and press with you, I'm that private about my own life. You'll have to do some of the work. I don't know if you want to. I wouldn't, necessarily, if I were you."

Jim Wiezevich laughed. "You're not, I'm happy to report. And I don't know how much work I'm capable of, Demetra. I mean, my life is full and complicated already. To have a—friend—like you—it isn't something I've been looking for."

"Well I have. I want to have a guy in my life, to know somebody I can respect. You're older than me but you don't seem so—I don't know . . . like other men who are so sure they're right all the time and don't want to listen to a twenty-three-year-old girl."

Wiezevich had returned to his room at the North American College, collected his notebook and some texts, and planted himself in the reading room of the library.

It was difficult to study. Thoughts of the young woman crowded out nearly every other fact or consideration in his mind. Is this what love was all about? He was a stranger to these kind of thoughts; he had not even had a crush on a girl since high school, and then only a passing fantasy of the most gauzy, insubstantial kind. Since he had known of his vocation to the priesthood, he had prayed for—and received—relief from lustful and covetous impulses. This had been a gift from God, beyond his deserving and not taken for granted. Nor was it easy. He had been grateful as he renewed his prayers and his commitment to the Father to live a chaste life in His service. Sometimes it struck him as cruel or absurd, this requirement of celibacy for priests of the Latin rite; after all, it was not true of every Christian church, east or west, nor had it always been true throughout the history

of the Catholic Church. But he did not dwell on it. Jim Wiezevich
offered his doubts and difficulties up to God, who took him, with
all warts and sins, into His heavenly care. So simple . . . and yet
so damned difficult now that he had met *her*.

He had not received the sacrament of holy orders, nor yet
taken the sacred promises of chastity and obedience required of
a diocesan priest. That final, irrevocable step was about a year
away. If his teachers and his bishop found him worthy, he would
be ordained next May in the Cathedral of the Sacred Heart in
Newark, New Jersey.

Later that night—after failing to penetrate the academic material before him—he took a walk, which he was fond of doing,
especially in Rome: to breathe and think. It wasn't easy. He
pushed those thoughts of Demetra Matoulis as far to the side as
he could manage. He had to be realistic—and true to himself and
what he knew to be right. What, then, lay ahead for Jim Wiezevich? More studies. A year as transitional deacon and some hands-
on pastoral experience in a local parish. Finally, ordination . . . if
the Lord allowed him the privilege, if the heavens did not collapse
upon his head. There was no room in his future life for a
woman—even one who ignited his senses and his intellect as Demetra did.

But what about the here and now? What about this one
chance in a million to be with such an unbelievably attractive
creature who really liked and respected him, who did not care
where he came from, only what was in his soul and his mind right
now? How many men ever have that chance? How could God be
angry at him for grabbing this beautiful prize—even for a moment? Could He be that cruel, as some bitter secular skeptics
supposed?

He stood on the Bridge of Angels that spanned the Tiber in
the neighborhood of Hadrian's Tomb. The spring night was
warm, redolent of blossoming trees and flowers. Where was *she*
tonight? Perhaps traveling on assignment, or working hard to
meet a filing deadline. He felt somewhat less than adequate in her
presence and because of it, he wondered what she could see in
him, a plodding seminarian who would rather daydream or play

touch football than hit the books any day of the week.

Demetra Matoulis . . . the name itself seemed so exotic to him, so foreign to anything he had ever known in his life. Their meeting was seared into his memory and always would be. He had, difficult as it was to admit, fallen in love with her at that moment—forever. He returned to the North American College and sought out his mentor.

"You look miserable. What's the matter?" Phil Calabrese said to the younger man who had appeared at his door. "Let's have some coffee."

"I'm not miserable, just not sure what to do right now."

"About what?"

"I can't talk about it."

"Oh yes you can—and you will," Calabrese insisted. "I would be the world's lousiest friend if I let you walk around like this without at least trying to help."

"What do I look like to you? I feel fine. I have my share of problems—but I'm really happy deep down inside. Hard to explain."

"Please try. I mean it, Jim. There's something bugging you, and even if it isn't a problem at the moment, it might become one."

Jim Wiezevich stared into the cup of coffee as if it were a pool into which he could dive to escape Calabrese and everything else that was holding him back. "Phil, I feel like a prisoner—remember that old movie, *The Great Escape*? Steve McQueen kept trying, kept digging. He had to get out. He did, finally. Well, I don't mean to say that I'm being made to do anything against my will, but I feel the walls closing in, the barbed wire being strung around me. I . . . I'm not sure I can stick it out, even for another week. I've never felt like this—I mean, since I knew about my vocation. I'm not sure—I guess I've lost that conviction, that sense of *knowing* that I'm doing the right thing here, that I will be a priest—and a good one."

"You're not telling me what's at the bottom of this, just the surface. You're uncomfortable, not sure. You even feel trapped, with no escape. We all go through that at some point, Jim. But there's something more here that you're not saying."

Wiezevich looked directly at Calabrese. Although he was only a few years older than Wiezevich, the priest already had streaks of gray in his hair that gave him an aura of maturity that was belied by his wide smile and mischievous brown eyes. Calabrese was studying for his licentiate in systematic theology at the Gregorian University. He made it look easy to his fellow Americans, but he did not wear his erudition and accomplishments like a badge. Instead, he was very much "one of the boys" in every way, including pickup football games on the otherwise quiet quadrangle of the North American College.

Calabrese went on, "If you don't want to talk to me, talk to somebody. I've learned that much. You can't keep shit inside. It's dangerous. If you need to go to confession, I would be willing to hear you. Whatever you like—but talk it out."

It was very difficult for Jim Wiezevich to share with his friend what was hurting him, tearing him apart inside. One conversation, one cup of coffee with a woman. A beautiful, stimulating, intelligent young woman. He had never known a person like her before. It was a once-in-a-lifetime convergence of forces—some kind of providential, astrological, mystical, celestial happening . . . how else to explain what he was experiencing? How could Calabrese understand? Wiezevich himself was baffled, unsure of the answer—any answer—and afraid to hear what the priest might say.

"It's tough for me. I'm not used to spilling my guts, Phil. I've held it in for years—at home, at work, at the seminary. I've always felt I had to be 'together,' stronger than anybody else, for my family especially, after all they've been through."

"I really think you've got to start somewhere, with someone."

"Well, I'll just say it. I think I'm in love, Phil. This girl—Demetra—God, I haven't even said her name out loud before now. She probably doesn't even know how I feel."

"You haven't told her?"

"Hell no. I've only seen her once."

"Don't you think you might have gone off the deep end, Jim? Your mind is taking you places you have no business going. Not very mature—and not fair to her, either."

Wiezevich lifted the porcelain cup to his lips; the coffee was cold. It had sat untouched for a half hour as he had held this nonconversation with Calabrese. He took a gulp of the black liquid. *I don't know who I am or what the hell I'm doing*, he said to himself. Aloud, he said to the priest: "Fair? It's not fair that she's so damned attractive and—*alive*. There's nothing fair about these feelings and doubts. She wants to see me again, but I should probably just call it off—put the whole thing behind me."

"You may be surprised to hear me say this, but I think that's the exact wrong thing to do. You should face her, talk about your feelings—and pray your ass off. There's too much at stake here to just put her on the shelf. Forget about what's fair. Think about yourself and your own sanity, your commitment to the priesthood, everything you've invested of yourself for the past several years. Maybe she'll surprise you. How long did you spend with her, for God's sake? A couple of hours? You can't know until you talk to her."

"I think I'll surprise *her*," Wiezevich said, sitting back in his chair, looking up at the ceiling of the college dining room. Having confessed to Calabrese the cause of his spiritual discomfort, he felt immensely relieved, almost human again. He had been carrying around these unspoken feelings for days, and the inner pain had only gotten worse with time. In fact, whenever he saw her now he felt as if he was being put through some extreme, exquisite form of physical and mental torture. *This is love?* He wondered.

"Maybe—maybe not. Women usually sense these things before we do."

"So, you seem to know a lot about women."

"I have four sisters—and, in all modesty, I must admit that I was considered quite the ladies' man in high school. I even went steady a few times. The joys of coeducation!"

"Well, we're not talking about a teenage romance here."

"I realize that. And I'm not minimizing the seriousness of your feelings—and what a relationship like this means for your vocation." Father Calabrese reached over the table and touched Wiezevich's arm. "I believe that God wants us to be happy right here on earth—none of this waiting for heaven stuff. His kingdom is here and now. The banquet is laid before us and we are invited to partake. Yes, He requires sacrifice, and yes, there is sin and pain and uncertainty every day of our lives. But we make the choices as to how we deal with the pain—whether we go it alone or ask for His help. I'm willing to help, Jim, without condition or judgment. Just let me help you."

The air escaped Wiezevich's lungs—and his entire body—as he heard and accepted the words spoken by his friend. "All right," he said, "then here's what I'll do. I'll see her, tell her up front about my feelings. I won't have any expectations one way or the other. Whatever happens . . ."

"*Que sera sera*," Calabrese teased. Then he became serious again. "Understand that I'm not saying whether this is right or wrong. Only that you've got to be honest with her—and with God. And most importantly with yourself. One more word of priestly advice: Pray. Then pray some more."

"I'm scared, Phil."

"Nothing wrong with that."

Fear propelled him through that day and into the next. He called her, and she was happy to hear from him, eager to see him. They made a date for dinner. He showed up in civilian clothes, a sport shirt and blazer. Demetra Matoulis wore a loose-fitting blue pullover sweater and black slacks. She looked utterly gorgeous, he thought.

When they had sat down and ordered a bottle of wine, the tension that had been building within him for days suddenly melted away. She was neither the goddess of his dreams nor the she-devil of his nightmares as she sat across from him and smiled and entwined her fingers with his. He felt right, at ease in his own skin. Although it was really just a first date, it seemed oddly familiar.

"I've thought about you over the last few days," she said.

"And I've missed you."

"I'm afraid to explore that too deeply." Her eyes, he saw as he looked into them, were gray-blue and the color shifted ever so slightly from one to the other, depending on the light or time of day. She wore a frosty pink lipstick that highlighted the curves and fullness of her lips. With a smile, she said: "Tell me all your thoughts, Jim, I want to know."

"Do you, really?" he asked. She gazed at him, unblinking. "I'm falling in love with you, Demetra. That's the bottom line, as they say." He had said it—heard his own words as he spoke them—and the sky had not fallen—not yet.

Demetra gently squeezed his hand. The waiter brought the wine and poured it, but the glasses remained untouched, the meal unordered. The restaurant was a hole-in-the-wall on a narrow side street. Now it seemed not to exist: the surrounding bustle of waiters and laughter of the other diners was muted as they concentrated solely on each other.

They left without eating, hailed a taxi, which took them to her small, neat apartment in a modern building near the Colosseum. Wiezevich overpaid the taxi driver even more than usual, this time by several thousand lira. Demetra clasped his hand and led him into her building and onto an old-fashioned steel-cage lift that carried them to the fourth story. Hers was one of four flats on that level. They entered, and she bolted the door behind them. She took his arm and caused him to pause and turn; they were only a few steps inside, in the small, shadowed foyer. They said nothing, but kissed.

Jim's mouth fused with hers. He had never experienced anything as purely sensual as this in his life. He would have laughed aloud but he couldn't even breathe or move or think. She pulled him into herself—all of him. Before he knew it, they were standing by her bed, as if they had been transported there.

Demetra folded herself into Jim's arms, pressed herself against his body. He held her tightly to himself, breathed in the scent of her hair and skin. His arms encircled her, pulled her into him as they kissed. He felt her hands reaching upward, to his neck, her fingers there as she stroked his hair.

"God, no," he said after he tore his mouth from hers.

"Yes, Jim. It's all right. It's all right." Demetra stood on tiptoe and lifted her face, hungrily kissing him once again. Her tongue darted into his mouth, surprising him, melting his resistance.

He responded, matching her urgent probing, his hands moving down her lithe body to take in every inch of her. Never had he experienced such an intensely overpowering need to be with another human being, a woman. He gave himself over to her.

Demetra Matoulis took what he offered. She slowly undressed him and pulled him onto the bed. Then, with his inexpert help, she removed her dress and underwear and lay beside him. Wiezevich drank in her nakedness, and she smiled as she revealed herself to him. She reached over and traced her fingers over his pale chest.

"How do you feel?"

"I'm not sure. I mean, you're beautiful. I've never seen a woman like this, never been with a woman before, Demetra. You know that, don't you?"

"Yes. I know you very well. I knew all about you when we met in the courtyard with ugly old Constantine staring at us."

"I haven't been back to the museums since that day."

"Neither have I. I've been a lazy slug, haven't done anything. I haven't eaten anything since then, either, until tonight."

"That's not good." He took her hand in his, enlaced his fingers in hers.

"I've only been hungry for you," she said in a husky whisper. She reached down to touch his manhood, gently held it. "How do you feel now?"

He gulped and felt a shiver of pure desire. "Just fine," he lied.

"You really are, you know. Just fine. Don't think, Jim. Just be with me now, here, let me show you the way."

At the Jade Lion, Demetra was relieved to see her date walking toward the table. James Wiezevich approached in his rather shambling gait, aware that she was watching his every step.

"Hello there," she said.

"Better late than never, I hope," he offered.

"Never would be a girl's worst nightmare."

"I'm hungry. Will you order for me, please?"

"Gladly," she said sincerely. She kissed him on the cheek. "Now you just sit down and tell me all about it."

CHAPTER TEN

Rome, June 7, 2003

The council was only ten months away. Early on in the planning discussions, the pope had said that he wished to allow within the council structure the opportunity for lay participation and involvement of all Christian churches, Jewish and Muslim representatives, and input from other major religious traditions from around the world. After all, he was writing the rules, as Pope John XXIII had done before him. He realized this was a tall order and would prove controversial among many Catholics and non-Catholics alike. Some commentators had long ago suggested that it was viable to hold ecumenical councils every twenty-five years or so, in order to make the council a more regular instrument of governance in the ongoing life of the Church, and to give each generation of bishops a chance to meet and act as a universal body for the good of the whole Church.

Against that thinking were any number of officials in the Roman Curia and a substantial number of diocesan bishops who thought that they were governing just fine, thank you very much, and that a council would be a distraction and an interference with their prerogatives and powers. A few important prelates, however, were beginning—in this precouncil phase—to float another idea, based on the decree from the fifteenth century Council of Constance, *Sacrosancta*, that affirmed the juridical and doctrinal authority of a general council over the pope himself, similar to the practice of the eastern churches. This idea of conciliar supremacy had lost support in the west over the previous five centuries as the papacy again became more monarchical, the power within the Church more centralized. Vatican II, in fact, encouraged collegiality (along a modified model of the primitive Church) of decision-making among the College of Bishops and expanded roles for laity in Church affairs; but still there was a strain of opposition within the Roman Curia and among some bishops to the reforms that opened those doors of government to wider participation—by anyone. John Paul II and the Curia of his era had methodically reduced the real powers of regional and national episcopal conferences. So the new pope now faced opposition on at least two fronts: from those who would revive a form of "conciliarism" to limit his powers, and those who decried any significant return to the ancient idea of collegiality or any lay or non-Catholic participation in the council to come.

"There are more than four thousand bishops, including several hundred retired, throughout the world. Must all of them be invited? Who might be willing to support my agenda in the committees and in the floor debates?"

"You cannot know that for certain until we convene the first session, Holy Father," Cardinal Biagi said. "Remember what happened at Vatican II when the bishops rejected the Curia's attempt to force their agenda on the council. Now *that* was a moment when the Spirit was at work!"

"You haven't had time to appoint very many bishops who are personally loyal to you," Calabrese cautioned the pontiff.

"I hope they are all loyal to Christ, whoever appointed them," the pope said. "This is not Jersey City patronage politics, you know."

"Maybe more than you think," the American monsignor came back—then added deferentially, "Your Holiness."

Biagi said, "There has been politics in the Church since the council at Jerusalem—since Christ and Pontius Pilate, even."

Pope Celestine, Cardinal Biagi, Archbishop Ignatius Min of Taipei, and Monsignor Calabrese had met for ever-longer hours throughout the spring, plotting out the organizational strategy for the council. Each man had read all of the available literature on the Second Vatican Council, focusing on the preparatory period, which had lasted about three years, from 1959 to 1962. The pontiff had ordained that the preparations for Vatican III should be condensed to twelve months and asked every bishop in the world to send in suggestions for agenda items of local and universal concern. Already the office of the preparatory commission had been flooded with e-mail, faxes, and bulky manuscripts, some evidently prepared months or even years before. Clearly some of the bishops were excited about the prospect of such a council; to most, Vatican II was the watershed event of their long-ago youth, and they had little or no memory of the Church before the *aggiornamento* of that remarkable period. And nearly all had come into maturity as priests and been consecrated as bishops during the pontificate of John Paul II. The Polish pope, the fifth-longest serving pontiff in the history of the Church, had undoubtedly put his stamp on the episcopacy as few others ever had. Mulrennan, the new pope, wondered whether he would, or could, have anywhere near the impact that John Paul and his predecessors, Paul VI and John XXIII, had—for good or ill. And he sincerely prayed that his pontificate would be a positive, even progressive one. Yet he knew enough about the world and the ecclesiastical milieu that he would not dare to predict or hope for a particular outcome to all this intensive planning.

What he wanted most—and he had to guard against wanting it so much that it became a matter of unwonted pride—was to foster a deeper appreciation of the sacred and a new and lasting unity within the one, true, holy and apostolic Church of which he had been elected the earthly head. Was this the right way to achieve such unity?

Calabrese intruded on the pope's silent brooding, bringing Mulrennan back into the conversation that he had departed several minutes earlier. The planning group sat around a large wooden table in a small, brightly lit office in the Apostolic Palace that had been dedicated to these special meetings.

"Here are the official letters of appointment to the presidency of the council. Do you wish to sign them so that I can send them out today?"

The pope had already asked three men to be copresidents of the council: Cardinals Biagi and Tyrone, and Archbishop Min. Each had good language and management skills and could be trusted to be firm as well as fair in any necessary parliamentary-style rulings. And Tyrone, as a curial heavyweight—currently the prefect of the Congregation for the Doctrine of the Faith, formerly known as the Holy Office, or the Inquisition (in the bad old days)—would be the strongest and most conservative of the three.

He glanced at the letters. "I think I'll speak to Cardinal Tyrone face-to-face. In fact, would you please call him now to find out if he is available to see me first thing in the morning and join our planning meeting tomorrow."

"Sure. He'll be surprised."

"I doubt that anything the Holy Father does now will surprise our Irish friend," Biagi said, beginning to think several moves ahead in the eternal chess game that was Vatican politics. "Although I imagine he will be temporarily put off balance. Not a bad thing."

"Allo, stop your Florentine political machinations. He'll be pleased to be of service, I'm certain," the pope said. He shifted uncomfortably in his chair: That damn back was still giving him trouble.

Calabrese picked up his cell phone and dialed Tyrone's office number—which he had memorized along with a few dozen other key phone numbers.

Pope Celestine regarded these three men who now sat with him: Biagi, Calabrese, and Min. Three good minds and dedicated churchmen, each from a different milieu and very different background; but they—and he—were limited by personal and cultural experiences. Whereas the Church herself was a universal institution that must encompass so much humanity that lay beyond their immediate, direct understanding. That was at least one reason why, Pope Celestine realized, the indefatigable John Paul the Great had traveled so frequently and widely; he had thereby immersed himself deeply in the life of the Church through the lives of its vastly varied peoples and local churches.

"I suppose politics is simply another word for humanity. We cannot condemn it, even when we disagree with the ends that others pursue—or else we are condemning ourselves, too." Timothy Mulrennan felt confident that he knew at least that much about the imperfect nature of man. In fact, he knew himself.

"When will you surrender your idealism, my friend?" Leandro Biagi asked.

Calabrese winced. The New Jersey-born priest sometimes could not stop himself from interjecting his irreverent point of view. "For God's sake, don't we want a spiritually idealistic pope? Of all people . . ."

The Chinese archbishop, no stranger to political maneuverings from his long years as an underground Christian and priest on the mainland and as a bishop on the Nationalist-controlled island of Taiwan, absorbed the information and opinion before him before speaking his own mind. Just forty-nine—very young for an archbishop—he projected an aura of espionage, perhaps as a matter of learned self-preservation. Earlier in the meeting, during the discussion of the survey of bishops, he had announced, "We have so far received responses from more than one thousand bishops, Your Holiness. These will take weeks to sort through and distill for your information. We shall highlight a number of them for your reading, in English translation when necessary; the rest will be presented to you in digest form." Ever the Confucian bureaucrat.

A dozen years previously, Father Min had come to Mulrennan's attention during the latter's service as prefect of the Congregation for Bishops, as he culled through résumés and recommendations for candidates for the episcopacy. Min had descended from a line of Christians that extended back nearly two hundred years, from the age of the missionary in the interior of the vast, ancient empire. The Jesuits, of course, had converted the ancestors, peasant-farmers and merchants of Canton province; and the faith had passed uninterrupted down to the present day.

Ignatius Min had the soft, creamy skin of a child, pale in contrast to his dark brown eyes and dense black hair that he wore in a modified U.S. Marine-style buzz cut. He smiled only rarely, but evinced a warmth and intelligence with his few, well-chosen words.

The Chinese prelate now spoke up in his quiet, perfectly modulated voice: "The Holy Father must be practical enough to accept the best possible product of human effort, but spiritual enough to require that all of us be open to the guidance of the Holy Spirit. These are not contradictory, but complementary aspects of our life in the Church." His words were invested with the authority of one who had directly suffered state persecution of his faith—and who had survived to be a witness to others of his own country and the world.

"I appreciate what each of you has said—believe me—and each is right. There has to be a blend of hard-headed realism along with Christian principles in all of our preparation for this council. And there is another element: Trust. We must trust each other and God, who will lead us to the correct result."

Early the following morning, Bernard John Tyrone—the one-time Archbishop of Armagh and Primate of All Ireland, and as such by hoary tradition a successor to St. Patrick himself—strode purposefully through the ornate corridors of the Apostolic Palace toward his meeting with Pope Celestine. Six feet, seven inches tall, at about 280 pounds of Irish bone, flesh, sinew and stubbornness, Cardinal Tyrone majestically filled out his black soutane with its bright scarlet piping, buttons, and wide sash, and carried his huge frame with surprising quickness in a place accustomed to a more deliberate diplomatic and ecclesiastical pace. Covering his scarlet zucchetto, he also wore a priest's black biretta of watered silk with a small silk tuft at top—an unusual, even incorrect accouterment for a man of his rank, which sometimes raised eyebrows among the cognoscenti on matters of protocol—and his large pectoral cross swung on its gold chain across his chest like a golden pendulum with each giant step he took. His dark reddish hair and bristly eyebrows, each barely tinged with gray, belied his age, seventy-four, as did the youthful energy of his stride.

Beneath the vaulted Renaissance ceilings of the Vatican, where he had worked and resided for the past few years, this lion of the Roman Curia cut a classic and intimidating figure that caused other, lesser priests and prelates in his path to give way before his approach. In his wake he left the heavy scent of cigar smoke that permeated his clothing; his curial office was notorious for the clouds of smoke that emanated from and hung over the cardinal as he tore through piles of paperwork on his custom-built, over-size desk. Some wag had once said, "The Censor is a censer," and another had called him "a human thurible," both comments which stuck and were continually whispered in gossip-filled conversations about the Holy See's inquisitor-in-chief.

Next year, before the projected opening of the ecumenical council, Bernard Cardinal Tyrone would celebrate his golden jubilee as a priest: fifty years of service to Christ as a minister of the Gospel. After lengthy years of study at Maynooth and Rome during those seemingly ancient days as an awkward, gangly youth on fire with his holy vocation, he spent two decades as a curate and pastor of churches in the rural northern counties of his native land. Then he was plucked from pastoral obscurity to be secretary to the Archbishop of Armagh, a distant maternal relative, setting him on a swift course of clerical advancement that made him bishop at forty-six, archbishop at fifty-five, cardinal at sixty-two. Four years ago he had been brought to the Vatican as head of the senior papal dicastery, the *Congregatio pro Doctrina Fidei*, which had been led, famously, by Cardinal Ratzinger for nearly twenty years, and by Cardinal La Spina after that. Tyrone was the first Irishman ever in that position and one of two in top curial posts; at present, only twenty percent of prefects of congregations were Italians down from more than ninety percent forty years before.

The congregation itself had been founded in 1542 in response to the Reformation, and it was called the Universal Inquisition; three to five cardinals were charged to root out heresy and heterodoxy, which they did, to an extreme, even scandalous degree. Later, Pope St. Pius X renamed the congregation the Holy Office, and sixty years after that, Paul VI further reorganized the Roman Curia, restricting the work of the congregation to the promotion of the Gospel and theological clarity—with a firm but loving hand. Pope Paul also gave the present name to the congregation. In all matters concerning the faith, the congregation is heard when a doctrinal question becomes a matter for analysis by the Holy See, the bishops, and the clergy and laity at large.

The Curia, like the Church herself, was changing yet again. Thus, all of the political and administrative and theological skills of Tyrone's forty-nine priestly years were called into play every single day. At an age when most western European men were long retired, Cardinal Tyrone was reaching the peak of his power and influence in a worldwide institution that touched more than a billion human lives.

He had originally been chosen for his prefecture due to his orthodoxy and oratorical skills; the pope needed a credible, loyal face for this most sensitive congregation that drew most of the critical attention awarded to the Curia. Regularly, the skeptics within and without the Church pounced on the doctrinal decrees of the congregation with venom and glee, and the "separated brethren" of the Orthodox and Protestant churches similarly parsed and debated each new pronouncement, as did religionists of nearly every tradition. So, the job required a man of iron constitution and quick feet—both of which Tyrone could rightly claim. Those feet, shod in worn black oxfords in need of a polish, now took him through the marble-sculpted, chandelier-lit hallways to the papal chambers.

The pontiff, this American from New Jersey who had been elected just a year previously, had summoned Cardinal Tyrone the previous day to this early-morning meeting over coffee. It was very much like Pope Celestine to add a distinctive element of informality to such a meeting—rare as it was thus far in his pontificate—with his senior curial prefect. The two men had not been friends during Tim Mulrennan's prior career, three years of which he had spent in the Vatican with the Congregation for Bishops; nor could they be called "enemies," for neither bothered to tag opponents with that pejorative. It was true, relevant or not, that Tyrone had voted only and always for Cardinal La Spina in both recent conclaves. And he had made no secret of it.

Moments later, after he had greeted his pontiff and accepted a cup of hot, black coffee, Tyrone did not hesitate to speak his mind in plain terms: "Holy Father, you must know that I oppose this council of yours. I believe it may cause harm to the Church in these unsettled times. We are still working through the implications of Vatican II. Surely you are aware of all this—any good Catholic is. I mean no disrespect to you or your office, of course, when I state my position."

"I understand, Your Eminence," the pope said. "And I appreciate your frankness. I realize that there are many among the Curia who would rather this not happen any time soon—in fact, who wish that *I* had not happened at all. I don't blame them." Mulrennan smiled ironically at the big beefy Irishman who sat stiffly before him. He observed Tyrone's hands, the large red gnarled hands of a laborer. He respected this man's mind, however much he might disagree with his position on the council; he was also in a position to command obedience from curial officials such as Cardinal Tyrone, or accept their resignations. From his knowledge of this man, however, he had every reason to expect cooperation—up to a point.

"There are murmurings of a new conciliarism, Holy Father. Some who might wish to shift the balance of power from the pope to the council itself in order to check any potential for change or innovation. And even before your election some of my more rabidly orthodox brethren had floated the idea of a new council—for reasons very different than yours."

"Yes, and there are some who have whispered that my election itself was illegitimate because I was not wearing the scarlet choir robes during the last conclave! I expect opposition, even outright chicanery, from many sources. I am also making preparations for extraordinary security measures to protect the council itself—unfortunately necessary in the face of potential outside threats." The pontiff searched Tyrone's face for clues, some insight into the cardinal's soul. "Tell me, Bernard, as a brother bishop and theologian, why do you oppose me?"

"Since you ask so forthrightly, I shall tell you. You are wrong, Holy Father, to encourage open discussion and debate about controversial issues within the Church at this time. Our late Holy Father, John Paul II, issued more encyclicals and declarations on doctrine than practically any other pope in two thousand years. He, of course, was a skilled philosopher and theologian of the caliber who rarely rises to such an exalted level in the Church—in fact, I am certain that one day soon he shall be not only canonized a saint but named a doctor of the church.

"In any case, he knew that we were still living in the age of the Second Vatican Council, all of the implications of which will take at least one hundred years to be fully absorbed by the world-wide Body of Christ. We must allow the Holy Spirit to complete His work. We are far from that place. Now, to convene another general council only forty years later—it is premature, ill-advised, dangerous, even foolish. Pardon me, Holy Father, for speaking so frankly—but this is what I believe."

"Yet, if I set you to the task, you will help me to organize this 'foolish' council in record time? And you shall preside over it?" Pope Celestine said with the sardonic American smile that so infuriated his opponents.

"You are the Supreme Pontiff and Bishop of Rome, successor to St. Peter. Upon your shoulders rests the weight of the true Church of Christ. You are my brother priest and shepherd. I cannot tell you that I will give up my convictions, but I can say that I will obey my bishop as I vowed to do forty-nine years ago at the sacrament of holy orders. In other words, you have me by my blessed balls, Holiness."

"That is the last thing I want, Bernard. Sincerely, even if I cannot convince you of the rightness of this course, I will trust that the Holy Spirit will work on you. And practically, knowing your heart and mind are set against my decision, I would rather have you very close to me so that I may keep an eye on you!"

At that, Bernard John Cardinal Tyrone barked loudly with laughter. His large head tilted back and his mouth hung open; he slapped his giant hands onto his knees. The golden cross at his breast, an ancient Celtic-Christian symbol beloved by so many Irish throughout the world, trembled from the gale force of his roar. He wiped a tear from his eye and addressed the pope: "You have me by your side—and from there I can watch you, too. I shan't let you step out of line, Holy Father."

"Sounds like an equitable arrangement," Mulrennan said.

"May I have your blessing, then?" Tyrone requested, shifting his bulky, black-robed frame from the comfortable visitor's chair onto the floor, kneeling before the chair of the Servant of the Servants of God. The pontiff remained seated and placed his hands gently on the Irishman's head. Tyrone clasped his own hands tightly in prayer.

"O Father, look upon your servant Bernard with favor that he may be a strong and honest and loving shepherd of Your people, as he goes about the holy work of Your Church. I ask this blessing in Your name and the name of the Son and the Holy Ghost. Amen."

"Holy Ghost, eh?" Cardinal Tyrone rose to his full height and stood before Christ's vicar on earth.

"Sometimes it still slips out," the pontiff admitted. "But don't let the cat out of the bag, will you?"

"I won't. See what I mean about Vatican II?"

"Your Eminence, in addition to copresident of the council, I am going to appoint you chairman of the Committee on Theology."

"Now you know why I voted for Cardinal La Spina."

"Oh, he'll be a vice president of the council. But don't tell him. I want to have that conversation with him myself."

"He'll be—surprised."

"The Holy Ghost—I mean Holy Spirit—is full of surprises, Bernard." Pope Celestine escorted his guest to the door of his study. "That's what gets me out of bed each day. I am so anxious to know what He has in store for me."

"I think He has His hands full with you, Your Holiness."

"Perhaps. And with you too, I think, my friend."

"That's what my dear departed mother used to say to me."

"I'll remember her in my prayers, though she is no doubt standing in the glory of God's presence as we speak."

"There is no doubt of that at all." Tyrone turned at the doorway and took the pope's hand in his, enveloping the American's long fingers in a slab of flesh. "I will pray for you, my friend—and I will continue to speak my own mind to you, as well."

"I would ask nothing less of you. And I shall see you within the hour at the meeting of the preparatory committee."

Afterward, Mulrennan asked his secretary to raise Cardinal La Spina of Turin on the telephone. This was going to be another interesting conversation, he was certain.

La Spina was a blunt prelate of peasant stock, sort of an anti-Roncalli, the pleasant, intelligent, doughy-faced saint who became

Pope John XXIII and changed the course of Church history forever. La Spina came across as a harsh reactionary with words spewing rapidly from his hatchet-shaped head in great volume, sometimes in ungrammatical jumbles, when in fact he had several academic degrees and excellent administrative skills—and a solid, if stolid, theological mind. Physically and intellectually, he was as immovable as Gibraltar. And when Timothy Mulrennan, Pope Celestine, considered these things and looked back at the two conclaves of the previous year, he realized that La Spina would have been a perfectly fine pope, as long as he could remain independent of Cardinal Vennholme's Evangelium-fueled influence. Was that even a remote possibility, however? It was something no one now would ever know for certain. That ubiquitous Holy Spirit at work again, Mulrennan mused. These things are not for me to know . . . only to waste precious time speculating about.

La Spina, after some modest blustering, agreed to serve as vice president of the council, if that was the Holy Father's wish. Next step, then, was to call Cardinal Ibanga of Nigeria, which he would do in the evening after supper, to ask the same question. Mulrennan rose slowly, painfully, from his chair—his back had been plaguing him recently. He stretched and walked to the committee meeting.

The pope entered and all stood. He waved them back into their seats. He saw that Monsignor Calabrese was briefing the group, which now included Tyrone, and he signaled to the priest to continue.

"Still debated after forty years is the question: Did Vatican II leave unfinished business? This does not address the qualitative issue, if you will, of whether they did *what* they did correctly. In fact, it is too late to turn back the clock on the reforms of that great council—as some have undoubtedly tried to do. But the council really did not face square-on the severe problems of the Roman Catholic priesthood and its future, not did it resolve adequately the important issue of episcopal collegiality versus centralized bureaucracy.

"Perhaps the most troubling issue—crisis, really—facing the Church today is the priesthood. Not since the Council of Trent four hundred fifty years ago, which instituted sweeping reforms of the priesthood, has there been such an urgent need to examine the roles and responsibilities of this sacred institution. The most obvious area to examine, at least in the West, is celibacy and sexuality: Should priests be allowed to marry? How should pederasts and sexual abusers be screened, identified, and ultimately dealt with? How should victims be helped by the Church? Should openly homosexual men be Catholic priests? How are we to deal with gay priests currently serving in the sacred ministry? Of course, these questions do not address the ever-growing support within the Church—especially in the United States—for the ordination of women as priests and bishops. Should the dialogue that was effectively closed in 1994 by Pope John Paul II be reopened by a new council of the Church?

"Granted, these 'hot-button' questions are not on the minds of all Catholics in Rwanda or China or Brazil. In those places and others the issue of true evangelization and acculturation are paramount. Why are the evangelical churches meeting the needs of Christian people? Why is the Catholic Church losing converts and credibility in these areas of the world? How is the Church dealing with persecutions and human rights abuses in remote, poor, repressive countries?"

Msgr. Philip Calabrese was clearly in his element as he prepared to deliver his Powerpoint presentation on council planning to the Holy Father and the preparatory committee. This, of course, was only the tip of the iceberg, so to speak—or "top line," in corporate-speak—of the preparation activities, focusing on the theological rather than practical issues that would face the council fathers.

A trim forty-two-year-old, with an attractively unruly thatch of gray hair and dark, intense eyes, the priest from Jersey City— the urban badlands—could have as easily stood before the Joint Chiefs of Staff at the Pentagon or the board of directors of General Electric as a group of celibate men in the See of St. Peter. He had been fortunate—and he had worked hard—to find an appropriate professional niche where he could demonstrate his skills as writer, communicator, and strategic thinker. But what were the odds, he sometimes wondered, of a kid from the mean streets of Hudson County ending up as a communications director for the Supreme Pontiff of the Holy Roman Catholic Church? Very, very long indeed . . .

The pontiff himself opened the meeting with a prayer for the inspiration and guidance of the Holy Spirit in their endeavors. "This will be the only such meeting that I will attend," Pope Celestine said. "That does not mean that I'm not interested in *everything* that is discussed here—but it is *your* job, as my chosen representatives, and as spokesmen for the Church on matters of doctrine and governance, to make this council process work as God intends it to work. My role will be similar to that of a modern corporate chairman—but, more importantly, based on the models of my predecessors, John XXIII and Paul VI. I will remain in the background even as I review and approve every step we take along the way. The copresidents of the council will assume the 'up-front' positions, here in the planning phase and at the council itself. The theological commission also will perform much of the difficult preconciliar work by writing the proposed schemas on all of the agenda items that will be debated in the first session.

"Note that I said *first* session," the pope added, looking around the broad, gleaming table at the dozen committee members' faces.

With the exception of Tyrone, each man affected a neutral-to-positive demeanor, awaiting potential bombshells from their unpredictable pontiff. The cardinal from Armagh, the ancient traditional see of St. Patrick, looked like a sphinx with indigestion, part lion, part god—every massive inch the monument to orthodoxy. Tyrone's eyes of dark fire never wavered from the speaker.

"It is my hope and expectation that we can accomplish the business of the council in one session of less than two months. If we limit our focus to no more than five or six topics and stick to the agreed-upon agenda—and if God cooperates with our plan— we can do it. I hope that all of you agree."

Several heads bobbed up and down, others showed inscrutable smiles, but Tyrone, not unexpectedly, reddened and looked as if he were about to explode into a billion Celtic molecules.

Timothy Mulrennan asked, sympathetically, "Eminence, are you okay?" He knew the answer and braced himself to hear it.

Cardinal Tyrone rose to his full majestic height. "Your Holiness," he stated with all propriety, his jowls aquiver, "you ask more of us than we are perhaps capable of, even with the Holy Spirit to sustain our effort. And why the hurry? The Second Vatican Council was three years in the preparation phase and unfolded over another three years, long, difficult years at that. You want us to do it all in less than two? Is it worth turning the entire hierarchy on its head to accomplish this—I don't know what to call it?"

"*Council*, dear cardinal," the pope said simply. He regretted it immediately: The Irish prelate stood mutely, flummoxed—angry and humiliated. "I am sorry, Tyrone—I didn't mean to be flip. Please forgive me. On all counts, in fact. I do realize that I am asking for a lot—perhaps the impossible."

The other men remained silent, awaited Tyrone's response. As the pope sat quietly, a few pages of handwritten notes on the table before him, he stiffened with a painful spasm in his lower back. It felt all too familiar—he had experienced back problems on and off for years and been a sporadic chiropractic patient—yet somehow different, perhaps in the specific location of the pain, near the base of his spine. It was as if a sharp kitchen knife had been inserted there by a malevolent, unseen hand. Mulrennan looked at the others to see if they had noticed him wince, but they had not; they were focused on Tyrone, who was speaking again in his authoritative, animated manner.

"Certainly we are in the business of performing the impossible," the cardinal allowed. "We are the guardians of the greatest miracle in the history of mankind: the revelation of God Himself in the Word. Yet—we are only human. I believe in the sincerity of your intentions, Holy Father, but as I have tried to suggest to you, the spiritual and theological foundation for wise actions by a proposed council does not—in my opinion—exist in the Church at this time. And it may take years to build such a foundation."

The pontiff winced as he shifted in his chair, but did not otherwise acknowledge the stabbing pain in his back. He said, "Eminence, do you not trust the Holy Spirit to do His part in this? Has He ever failed the Church of Christ in its hour of need? It is important to remember that we are not really 'in charge'—He is. We are temporary, temporal servants who execute His will, to the best of our imperfect abilities."

"Yes, Your Holiness, I do understand that. But my point is: We should not act precipitously or prematurely—which may result in harm to the Church we love so much."

"Your sensible objections are noted, Cardinal Tyrone." Pope Celestine's tone was direct and authoritative but not unkind. "I insist nonetheless that the planning and conversation go forward, to wherever they may lead. I have no intention of allowing a free-for-all or unstructured debate. I have no wish to abrogate my appropriate authority, nor yours, in matters of doctrine and morals. That would simply be wrong. But in the spirit of the Second Vatican Council and the twenty general councils before—the bishops will come together intellectually prepared and spiritually fit to address the crises that threaten our Church today. This is what we are called to do."

He turned to each man as he answered Tyrone, to ensure that each received his message. "Actually, I believe that Vatican II prepared us very well, that the past forty years have been not only a postconciliar phase, absorbing and implementing the modernization process begun in 1962, but also a period of preparation and anticipation of this next step by the Church into the future."

Now the Holy Father stood, in part to relieve the pressure he felt in his spine. "There will be a diversity of opinion within the Body of Christ about this council—I anticipate and accept that. Yet, by coming together in council, some more willingly than others, we will achieve the unity that we desperately need in order to survive another decade, let alone another century. We must face ourselves—the good and the bad—in the harsh light of truth. Then let the debates and decisions come on. And they *will* come, God knows. And let us listen to the Spirit as He reveals His heart in our own. Is there ever any harm in listening, dear brothers?"

The two men, Mulrennan and Tyrone, stood facing each other across the polished table—the pope in his white cassock, the cardinal in his black cassock with red sash and wafer of white in his black Roman collar. The tension between the two men was visible and felt by all in the room—yet there was also a keen sense of brotherly, familial love that reassured everyone present.

Monsignor Calabrese continued: "A substantial percentage of the bishops, who cite the concerns of the laity and their clergy, insist that we address Catholic-Jewish issues." He could see that his listeners—at least some of them—were made uncomfortable by this assertion. A survey of the bishops throughout the world had been conducted with the assistance of a British market research and polling firm. "They acknowledge that Vatican II went a very long way to correct and heal this troubled relationship, and that the late Holy Father, John Paul II, went further than anyone in the history of the Church to address faults and injustices head-on. However, there is a consensus—based on our survey data—that more work must be done. The council cannot ignore or minimize the bishops' expressed desire on this sensitive subject."

"But *why*?" Tyrone blurted. "Haven't we beaten this thing to death? I admired the late Holy Father's deep commitment to justice and repentance regarding the Jews. How many times need we apologize and flog ourselves publicly for the sins of others?"

"I leave our current Holy Father and the council to answer that question, Eminence," Calabrese replied. "I am reporting to you what the bishops have said. There is no room—spiritually or statistically—to doubt their sincerity on this. They feel that anti-Semitism is of gravest concern, historically and in the here and now." The American priest shifted gears. "On the subject of ecumenism and Christian unity: not as much interest as you might have expected. There is a sense that we are making progress through dialogue with our separated Christian brethren—at least among the Protestants. Yes, there is little tangible progress with the Eastern Orthodox community. But it is clear that, as long as there is some form of dialogue, we can keep ecumenical matters on the back burner, so to speak." Calabrese manipulated the laptop computer as he spoke, and the supporting text and numbers flashed on the screen before the assembled committee. The pope followed his presentation carefully.

"There is a new, or relatively new issue that is on the minds of many bishops—I would call it a significant minority. That is Catholic-Muslim relations. Migration to the West and a high number of conversions have increased the Muslim presence in Europe and North America over the last twenty-five to thirty years. There is little formal dialogue under way, which raises concerns in the minds of some: Should this issue be brought to the front burner? Apart from the events of September 11, 2001, of special concern is the ongoing perception that Pope Innocent was assassinated by Muslims for religious reasons. We know that the investigation has revealed the flow of money from the West into the hands of the terrorists who actually killed him; there is speculation that the plotters exploited the volatile political and religious climate of the Philippines to cover up their involvement. So, more than thirteen centuries of antagonism and suspicion continue to this day. The question is, should the council confront this controversy? Or at least acknowledge it in some way?"

CHAPTER ELEVEN

Rome, June 18, 2003

The pope cursorily scanned *The New York Times*, then the *Wall Street Journal* as he awaited the doctor's arrival; he had been awake and busy for three hours, following the routine that had sustained him for a year as Supreme Pontiff of the Roman Catholic Church.

The United States economy was unexpectedly sluggish, the politics just beginning to heat up for next year's presidential election cycle as the war on terrorism had receded from the front page. The editorials in the American newspapers decried the Congress for lack of activity to stimulate the economy (*Times*) and too much meddling in military affairs (*Journal*), but both praised the president for staying focused on international matters and out of the way domestically, allowing (they hoped) the market to right itself and still-seesawing technology stocks to find their ever-lower bottom. Otherwise, murders, natural disasters, and corporate mergers dominated the news pages. Timothy Mulrennan found it remarkable how little had really changed in the States during the past two years, despite constantly heightened security concerns: It had been a relative roller coaster ride for most Americans—neither too high nor too low—which was just as well, because American casualties were beginning to add up, quietly but steadily. The international scene had been different, however. Castro was finally dead of natural causes and Saddam Hussein assassinated by his own people, and China was still experiencing drought and famine; every other month one regime in central Africa fell and another rose, and disease and genocidal wars continued unabated. Europe was flying high at the moment: Germany boomed, Britain was getting fat, the Balkans seemed to be napping, the Middle East was still a bloody mess, and Italy remained relatively stable and prosperous. South and Central America, however, roiled with political unrest, a kind of post-Marxist native consciousness movement that echoed the liberation struggles of the early nineteenth century. Korea and the Philippines remained flashpoints, but Japan was a model of recovery after some very scary and very lean years. . . .

Mulrennan felt powerless over so much—but wished he could be a healer and constructive player in the many crises on the world scene, especially in the Americas where Catholicism was the dominant—if nominal—religion among the teeming, impoverished populations. Yet he could not insert himself in any of them without being asked. Through back channels and his own papal diplomatic corps, he could exert limited positive influence and help to speed humanitarian efforts in some cases—but far too few.

He solved several lines of the *Time*'s daily crossword. How long had it been since he had finished one? Some years—and certainly not since his election as pope. But today he needed a distraction, at least until his physician arrived. Instinctively, he knew it would be bad news, and he prayed that he would be able to handle whatever the doctor had to say. His old friend Archbishop Johnson had died in May. He had turned sixty-five a couple of months ago. Was it his own turn already?

Dr. Sebastiano Laghi arrived at nine sharp, the appointed time. He was a thin, balding man of average height, in his forties, with a dark brown goatee and a pleasant, professional demeanor. Laghi's father had regularly examined and treated Pope Paul VI for several years during the 1960s; and there were doctors in the family going back many generations before that. Two brothers and a sister were doctors, as well. He spoke a combination of Italian and English, hoping to put his patient at ease as much as possible—but he got straight to the point of his visit, in a calm, matter-of-fact tone.

"Holiness, the MRI scan of two days ago shows that you have a tumor at the base of your spine. X rays confirm the diagnosis.

We do not know whether it is cancerous. I advise immediate exploratory surgery so that we may take a sample for biopsy. I cannot be certain, but I estimate that the tumor has been there for several months to a year. You must have lived with terrible pain for most of that time." The pope did not comment. "I also do not yet know whether it is attached directly to the spine or not. Again, only a direct look via surgery will tell me that. Do you have any questions?"

"About a million—but I'm too stunned to ask."

"That's not unusual, Your Holiness. Par for the course, as my American physician friends say."

The pope laughed. "They would. First question, then—what do you mean when you say 'immediate' surgery?"

"Tomorrow morning would be most advisable. Day after at the latest." Laghi smiled wanly as he spoke, hoping to soften the harsh impact of his words. He showed the pope his X rays and MRI results, answering specific questions for twenty minutes. "So, shall I schedule the surgery?" he asked, pressing the patient as hard as he dared.

"I'll have to consult with my staff and various senior people, but let's go ahead with the day after. I need some time to—to make the proper preparations."

Dr. Laghi replaced the charts and X rays in his bag and stood to leave. "Holy Father," he said, "may I have your blessing—not only for myself, but for my family and medical colleagues?"

"Of course," Pope Celestine replied. "I will keep your knife-wielding partners, especially, in my prayers over the next forty-eight hours."

When the doctor left, Celestine closed his eyes and took a few quiet breaths; he reflected back on the previous six or eight months of back pain and discomfort, the mornings he had struggled to get out of bed and walk across his room to the lavatory, the countless times he had sat in meetings or with visitors gritting his teeth for the pain. He had kept the problem to himself all that time, choosing to bear it on his own and with God's help. He knew what his sisters would say about that—and he'd hear it when he called them later. His stepbrother Stephen in New York would ride him, too. He supposed he deserved their criticism, but he hoped they would understand and forgive his stupidity and male stubbornness.

He met with Biagi, Calabrese, and Jean-Yves de Taillon, the chief press spokesman, at noon and gave them the news, withholding nothing. At first the three were shocked to silence, then de Taillon blurted what was on each man's mind: "Holy Father, this is an unpleasant surprise—the entire world will be so sad to learn of your illness. They will—we will—pray for you, that the tumor is benign."

"Thank you, Jean-Yves. I want you to issue a detailed release with all the relevant facts. Hold nothing back, please."

"But, Your Holiness, should we—must we be so frank? There is no harm in a little discretion, I think." Cardinal Biagi said this with a pained, pinched look on his face. Mulrennan was a close friend as well as his pastor and fellow bishop. Biagi had invested himself in the success of his pontificate.

"Leandro, we cannot return to the old days of secrecy about the pope's health. Better to have full and complete disclosure than allow rumors and half-truths to tell the story. And you must see that a living will and the proper paperwork on disability are on my desk by this evening. *That* needn't be in Jean-Yves's press release, but it must be taken care of as soon as possible."

"I understand," the cardinal said. "And I agree."

"You haven't said anything yet, Phil," the pope said, looking at his aide. Calabrese was stunned, ashen. Mulrennan smiled, just as Dr. Laghi had when sharing the bad news earlier—unconvincingly.

"I don't know what to say," Calabrese responded. "I had no idea—can't really believe that you're—not well." The normally articulate New Jerseyan could barely put two words together. He had grown to love and respect this man so much, to see potential greatness in him and his pontificate. *Why, God, why?* "I know you will be fine. I must believe that. Whatever you want me to do. Just say the word, Holy Father." His eyes misted.

"Business as usual." The pope put a hand on his younger friend's shoulder. "If all goes according to plan, I'll be out of the hospital in two or three days. There may be treatments after that, some physical therapy. We just don't know yet. It's all in God's hands."

The four men put together an action plan for the next two days, including a series of informational meetings within the Vatican—especially with key Curia members and council planners—as well as an upbeat statement from the pontiff himself. Dinner tonight with Biagi, Tyrone, and a few others—followed by calls to the Mulrennan clan. He would say an extra mass at ten o'clock tomorrow morning at St. John Lateran and preach a brief homily that would surely be covered by the press. There would be legal documents to sign, some blood work and other preop tests before checking into the hospital in the evening. A seemingly endless list of details—things to have accomplished, just in case . . . In case what? Death and disability were the unspoken assumptions behind nearly every task they outlined.

"Gentlemen, enough," the pontiff said finally. He stood and gingerly touched the small of his back. There he felt a surprisingly slight ache—nothing very painful at all. "Let me know later what else I need to do. I'll keep this afternoon's schedule, until dinner. Leandro, see you then. Jean-Yves and Philip, you have your marching orders."

Outwardly he remained brisk, upbeat, commanding—though inside lived a scared boy. He saw them to the door of his study, then retreated through a private exit and slipped quietly into the nearby Sistine Chapel. It happened to be closed to tourists, so he was able to sit there in quiet solitude for a while as thoughts and memories cascaded through his mind. The security men left him alone. So much remaining to do—so little time—how much, he was not given to know.

What do we *know*, in any case? he asked silently. All of knowledge—all of life—is like Plato's cave: shadows upon the wall. With the important difference of God's love in action, His choice to reveal the reality of Himself and His love through His only begotten Son. After that, the fulfillment of an ancient covenant, all knowledge ended—or began . . . and, like Adam, each man faced his own free choice. For Timothy Mulrennan, it was a choice renewed each day of his life: to discern and follow, to the best of his limited, human ability, the will of the Father.

In this great chapel—a Renaissance shoebox, really, albeit a gorgeously decorated one—so much of his own life had been exposed and played out. He had faced his own judgment right here in this close, high-walled chamber. Looking up at the astounding images of Michelangelo's version of the Last Judgment, behind the small altar that held six spindly candlesticks, he saw more than a shadow play on the wall. From the brush strokes of the master who had lived in the world of Lorenzo, Julius, Machiavelli, da Vinci, Bramante, an adumbration of eternal life was emitted—in light and color rather than words, yet reflective of the Word. And Mulrennan, the 264th Bishop of Rome, asked to understand the Word as expressed so truly by Michelangelo in centuries-old pigment. He found himself in the same conundrum when he visited the Vatican Library and Archives and examined old manuscripts, some written by saintly scholars, others penned by rascals in service of the Kingdom of God on earth. He felt the same way when he wandered among the remains of Romans and martyrs in the excavated tombs beneath the basilica's altar: that he could touch the history of the Christian era and breath it in, that it was a physical as much as a spiritual experience. The Word lived in the traditions and works and sacraments of the community of believers, passed on to new generations from the old. Through symbol and image and object, as well as by proclaiming the Gospel and respecting the supremely simple commandments of the New Covenant . . . through *Church*, the working out in history of the salvific mission of Jesus. And through it all, in the hearts of the people of faith, He lived as the Eternal Word.

There was comfort for Pope Celestine in this knowledge—yes, *knowledge*. Faith had revealed it, intellect had illuminated it, and the free gift of grace had elevated it beyond his human grasp. Perhaps after all, knowledge of God, the knowledge of Plato and Aquinas and the apostles and mystics, existed as the ultimate end: the Alpha and the Omega of every man's striving.

Calabrese's face was an ashen mask and his hair seemed a bit grayer than it had the day before as he stood beside the pope's hospital bed at five A.M. Rome time. He had not shaved, which only emphasized his haggard mien, and the smell of cigarette smoke clung to him like a closely fitted pall. The timing couldn't be worse, he thought. The pope, Timothy Mulrennan, had fasted from noon the previous day and was being prepped for surgery; the anesthesiologist hovered impatiently behind the American monsignor, medical chart in hand. Phil Calabrese struggled to breathe before he spoke.

Pope Celestine saw the look of pain and panic on his secretary's face. "What is it, Phil?" he prompted. "Must be pretty bad to bring you here at this ungodly time. They're getting ready to slice and dice me."

"I called Cardinal Biagi—and he's also on his way over. He said he'd meet me here. He has been in direct communication with the Chinese embassy in Rome."

"I think you better start from the beginning. Chinese embassy?"

As if on cue, the tall Florentine prelate, the Vatican Secretary of State, appeared and came toward the pontiff's bedside, pushing the waiting physician farther from his patient. He mumbled a hasty apology, then stepped beside Calabrese and bent to kiss the Fisherman's Ring, which would not be removed from Celestine's finger during surgery, at the pope's request. Biagi, too, appeared uncharacteristically somber and distracted.

"Holy Father . . ." he began—but did not complete the thought, seemed lost for an agonizing moment.

"Well, you have my attention—both of you—that's for sure," the pope said, shifting himself upward by his elbows so that he could better see and speak to them. "I assume it's bad news."

"The very worst, Holiness," Biagi admitted. "Archbishop Min called Monsignor Calabrese and me this morning. He is in Taiwan, as you know. He has heard—unofficially—some very disturbing reports out of Beijing. He's checking them through his sources on the mainland, as are we—and I've contacted the Chinese ambassador in Rome."

"Now you're telling me what I already know, Allo. Get to the point." Weak as he was from lack of nourishment and sleep, as well as anxiety over the dangerous surgery that was only an hour

away, the pope felt anger and impatience and was close to a rare
loss of temper. He had no time for Biagi's diplomatic two-step,
however—and the cardinal knew it.

"I must emphasize, Holy Father, that the reports are not yet
fully confirmed—and we are receiving more details minute by
minute. But it appears there has been a horrible massacre just
outside the city of Beijing—possibly as many as two hundred
Catholics, men and women—we don't yet know if any children
were killed. We think there was one priest with them, but that
has not been confirmed either."

"Who—who did this?" Mulrennan asked, now sitting upright, aghast.

Phil Calabrese said, "We think it was a local police unit—but
it's very unlikely that they would initiate something like this on
their own. Again, the reports we've got so far are sketchy—we're
not even sure the news organizations are onto this story yet."

"They will—and they should be," the pope said. He shook
his head. "Dear God in heaven . . . Is there any chance that this
is a false report—a hoax, maybe?"

"I sincerely doubt it," Biagi said. "I'm so sorry—I—"

"You have nothing to apologize for, my friend. Go back to
your office and monitor the situation, please. Report to me every
hour—whether you know anything new or not."

"But you will be in surgery for several hours—and unconscious for more after that. This could not have happened at a
worse time."

"I agree, Allo. But I cannot continue with the surgery now."

"Holy Father," Calabrese interjected, "you can't call it off
now—it's too late. The doctors are here—the documents are
signed—and the risk to your health at this stage—"

Pope Celestine raised his hand to silence Phil Calabrese's objection. "It is necessary to postpone the surgery. Perhaps for a
matter of days. We can't know right now—and it's not that important." He turned to the waiting anesthesiologist. "Would you
call Dr. Laghi in to see me, please, Doctor?"

With a bow, the flustered physician left. The pope looked at
his two friends, a wan smile of acceptance on his lean face.

"Listen, there is a purpose to this. You and I do not know at this moment what it is, but we must accept it on faith." He shifted position again, to be fully upright, and reached for their hands; for just a moment he held them and looked into their eyes. "Let us pray together before we do or say anything else." He bowed his head.

When the pontiff had finished, the three men solemnly made the sign of the cross. Dr. Sebastiano Laghi appeared in the doorway and paused out of respect for the pope and his advisers. When he saw that they had finished, he stepped forward, dressed in blue-green scrubs, minus cap and mask.

"Holy Father, what do I hear? You cannot cancel this surgery. We have assembled a team of doctors who came especially for your operation—and it is imperative that we move forward—today!"

"Doctor, you must understand—and I hope you and your colleagues will forgive me."

"The tumor on your spine may not be so forgiving, Holiness. It wants to kill you—and it might do just that if we do not remove it promptly cancerous or not." Laghi smiled sadly but indulgently. "Believe me, I do understand—there is a crisis you must deal with. Yet, do you not wish to be as fully capable to handle it as you can be? And after it is over—what then? If you postpone the surgery, you delay your recovery—and any treatment regime that will be necessary. And in this case, because the tumor appears to be growing, such a delay could mean death."

"I do understand, Doctor Laghi, fully and completely. But we cannot proceed today; I can't risk being incapacitated, even for a short time, until we know for certain how bad the situation in China is. It's as simple as that."

"Simple and potentially fatal, Holy Father. I am obligated to tell you this frankly. I do not like to speak to you so sternly, but I must."

"Yes, yes, you are doing your job—just as I am doing mine." As he shifted his weight in the bed, the pontiff felt the familiar stabbing pain in his lower back. He attempted to disguise his reaction but could not—the knife-pain was too intense, and his body was weakened from fasting. "May I have some water?" he rasped with difficulty.

Calabrese poured a glass of water as Biagi and Laghi looked on. The assisting physician stood just inside the doorway and witnessed the pope's agony along with the others. Their faces betrayed their own pain and horror as they watched Celestine gulp down the water greedily, as if he were a desiccated desert wanderer about to die of thirst. They held their breath and waited for him to recover and speak to them.

Finally, he regained his focus as the pain subsided. He looked at each of them in turn, saw the sympathetic, tortured expressions on their faces.

"Gentlemen, I thank you and God for your charity and concern. But my decision stands. No surgery today. We will reschedule as soon as possible, perhaps in a week. Dr. Laghi, please pass my regrets and deepest apologies to your surgical team—I realize I have already disrupted their lives. It gives me no pleasure to do this, be assured."

"Can I somehow beg you to reconsider," Laghi persisted. "Holiness—"

"No. Go now and tell your colleagues." The pope turned to Biagi. "You must contact the Chinese ambassador first, then the foreign minister; and I will expect those updates starting at six. You're going to have a busy day, Eminenza." His smile was forced, but not insincere. "And Philip," he said to Calabrese, "help me find my clothes and get out of here, then alert our press office to what's happening, if they don't already know. I have visions of an American breakfast in my study, in front of the TV, watching news bulletins all day. What did the popes do before, without CNN, I wonder?"

That evening the pope sat in the dining room for supper, at the same table, he recalled, where his predecessors had hosted him numerous times. He was alone. Calabrese, Biagi, and others were still working the crisis-management shift and would be at it through the night, no doubt. He received hourly updates. No guests had been invited, because the pope had been scheduled for surgery. The waiter, a Vatican employee of thirty years' service, quietly placed a bowl of tomato soup before the pontiff and handed him a napkin to place over his white cassock-front like a bib. Timothy Mulrennan smiled and muttered his thanks.

He stuffed the napkin into his collar and spread it over his breast, began to spoon the delicious, mildly spiced soup to his lips. The waiter slipped into the kitchen, leaving the pope in complete solitude. It was a situation unfamiliar to him ever since his election; always there were prelates and assistants and bodyguards hovering, managing, directing, watching him. The feeling was delicious and depressing at the same time. He needed people, family, friends, colleagues. He was by nature a social being, albeit a quiet person, not a back-slapper. He missed Joe Johnson, the priests and people of his home diocese, his sisters and their families, his brother and stepmother. Never in his life had he experienced the loneliness that suddenly descended upon him in this moment. He heard the clink of spoon against soup bowl, observed his own movements as if from an out-of-body place somewhere else in the room.

The pain in his lower back and abdomen had subsided, perhaps numbed by the adrenaline rush that had set his heart racing ever since he had heard the news from China. He finished the soup and attacked a plate of broiled herbed chicken and rice, barely tasting the finely prepared food.

He received several telephone calls in the hour after supper, and then he placed one of his own: to New York City.

"This is Cardinal Vennholme," came the greeting—no secretary or voice mail screening.

The pontiff was at first taken aback, then grateful that there would be no dance before making the direct contact he sought. "Henry, this is Tim Mulrennan calling."

A pause, loudly silent, was followed by, "Your Holiness. I am more than surprised to hear from you." The voice was subdued yet redolent of authority; it was without a doubt the same man who had nearly destroyed Mulrennan himself, man and priest, at the conclave of fourteen months before. But Vennholme had been through his own doubts and difficulties, as well.

"I'm equally surprised to be calling, but I think you may be able to help me, Henry—if you'd be willing to do so."

"Of course, Your Holiness. Anything you ask of me—anything . . ."

Timothy Mulrennan, now the canonically elected successor of Pope Innocent XIV, Jaime De Guzman of the Philippines, had long wondered about (suspected, even) Vennholme's involvement in or knowledge of the brutal assassination of the pope in Manila. During the past nine months the international investigation had dragged on, with no conclusion in sight, following numerous cold leads and sketchy evidence of a terrorist conspiracy among Filipino rebels, Arab militants and malcontents, IRA splinter factions, North American moneymen, and possibly even a subgroup of the Evangelium Christi movement—which was still officially endorsed by the Holy See. Mulrennan had not yet acted to change the relationship between the controversial lay organization and himself; in this, he would move very slowly and deliberately, not wanting to alienate the society—which had, in the person of Cardinal Vennholme, opposed his election. *Keep your friends close, your enemies even closer. . . .*

"I appreciate your willingness to be of service—and I never doubted it, by the way. How is your health these days?"

"Excellent, as a matter of fact. I had a full check-up recently, completely clean, blood pressure under control." Vennholme had collapsed during the July conclave of the previous year and been in self-imposed semiexile in New York City ever since. Evidently, pure nervous exhaustion had brought on the collapse—and a simple, quiet regime of diet and exercise had restored him. He had, of course, learned of the pontiff's pending operation from the news media—and knew about some of the more intimate details from his long-cultivated sources within the Vatican itself.

"How are you feeling?" Vennholme asked. "I understand that you've had to postpone your surgery because of this terrible news from China. I hope your doctors aren't too upset. I know how they can be."

"Thanks for your concern. They're learning to cope with me— the doctors, that is. I'll probably reschedule in a week or two.

They have found a tumor on my spine. We don't yet know whether it is malignant or not. I know I shouldn't have put it off even another minute, but—" Mulrennan found himself sharing honestly and easily with his mortal adversary. Had Henry Martin Vennholme changed—or had Timothy Mulrennan? He took a long drink of water, suddenly feeling parched. He continued: "Meanwhile, the Chinese situation is even worse than the news reports indicate. We are certain that at least two hundred Christians were gunned down—simply because they were gathered illegally for mass. We know now that one priest was murdered, and there may have been more clergy present. Archbishop Min is sending us information as best he can. But he cannot enter the mainland—he would probably be arrested on the spot. Would you consider being my emissary to the Chinese government, Henry?"

"Have you spoken to Cardinal Biagi and the Secretariat of State about this?" Vennholme asked.

"No. I'd like to hear from you first, then present it to Leandro and the others. I need your diplomatic skills and experience—and if I tell them to put you to work, they will."

"The advantage of being pope, I suppose."

"There are some." Celestine VI smiled to himself, amazed that he was even having this conversation with the man he had known for nearly forty years, since he had been a young priest and the Canadian a young monsignor. Oceans and rivers of time and experience separated these two men from each other—and from their younger selves. "I am learning to leverage the resources at my disposal," he added.

"Spoken like an American corporate chief," Vennholme said. "I learned the hard way about your talents and your resilience, you know." He spoke respectfully, if a bit begrudgingly, to the man who was now the vicar of Christ on earth.

"And I have come to value what you have to offer to our Church, Henry."

"Holy Father, I want to, of course, but I—"

"Please think about it and call me back as soon as you can. We have no time to waste." The words came out sounding harsher than Mulrennan intended. There were a few seconds of silence on the other end of the line. He filled the gap: "I know this is very unfair of me, unfriendly even. But it is a matter of the highest urgency to the Holy See, to all Catholics."

"Yes, that is obvious. What is not so obvious is what exactly I could do."

"Talk to the Chinese government. We have been in continuous secret negotiations with them for years, as you know—a meeting of the world's two oldest and most intransigent bureaucracies. Ask them for justice in this case and for an end to further persecution. They must stop it—and only they are capable of doing so. Though they don't have much motivation to change their ways; the world keeps turning no matter what atrocities they might commit."

"I will do what I can, Your Holiness, you know that. Please have a word with Biagi. I do not want to cause any trouble for him or to have any conflict with him."

"He's too busy juggling a thousand balls, Henry. I'm sure he'll be glad to learn that you're available." Even as he spoke them, the pope did not believe his own words. The enmity between Biagi and Vennholme ran very deep, as a result of their opposition to each other during both conclaves, as well as their fundamental political differences; and Vennholme had bargained to become Vatican Secretary of State, the position Biagi now held, as a price of his support for the losing *papàbile*. It would take more than a mere papal fiat for the breach to be healed.

"Ever the optimist," Vennholme said.

"Naïve, I think you used to say," the pope corrected. "If memory serves."

"I think you have a perfectly adequate memory, much to my chagrin, I might add."

"Henry, we cannot afford ill feelings between us now. There are no rivalries, no competing interests any more."

"We have not talked about your council, Holy Father. That is something I have grave doubts about."

"I'm not surprised. Let's discuss it—when you return from China. Good-bye, Henry. God be with you."

"Wait—I must say, Holy Father, that I believe you are moving much too quickly and in the wrong direction with this ecumenical council—it is too soon after Vatican II." Venholme heard the bitterness and skepticism in his own voice. "Please forgive me for expressing my negative thoughts, Holiness. But since you opened the door, I felt compelled to walk through. Despite my reservations, I will participate fully and prayerfully in your council."

"*Our* council, Henry. No one man should take on either credit or blame. The Holy Spirit is working through us—you and me included."

"You must know that there are some who would use the occasion to revive the old theory of conciliar supremacy over the pope. I have heard such talk."

"No doubt you would," Pope Celestine said. For the past several months he had kept the Canadian prelate at arm's length, in a state of forced semiretirement; but he had not forgotten Vennholme's use of personally destructive tactics against him, actions that had nearly driven Tim Mulrennan from the priesthood he cherished so much. Yet with the passage of time and the surprising turn of events that had propelled him onto the Petrine Throne, he looked at Vennholme—at all men—through different eyes. Now he was their shepherd, and he was obliged to care for them—each and every person, friend or enemy—with equal and unconditional love.

"Henry, we don't have to agree on everything—and I know we simply never will. But it is important that we are seen to work together. I would be foolish and wrong not to take full advantage of your skills in service to the Church. If I accomplish anything in this job, I hope it is to bring about some healing and unity among those who are at odds within the Church."

"A very ambitious goal, Your Holiness."

"I am made ambitious by the Holy Spirit—and for Him. I really believe, deep down in my soul, that you and I are called to holiness, Henry. Despite ourselves and what we have done in the past—we are called to reform and renew this old institution, to do our little part in the short time we are allotted."

"I'm afraid that you are far ahead of me, Holiness. I fear that we are falling backwards, into darkness and heresy. I suppose I am a natural pessimist—my northern upbringing, perhaps."

"Don't sell yourself short, my friend. I value your blunt counsel and honest criticism. Of course, I'd like nothing better than to prove you wrong!"

"Having severely underestimated you before, I shall not do so again," Vennholme said. "In the meantime, you have my talents, meager as they may be, at your disposal. I will prepare to travel to China immediately."

"Thank you, Your Eminence. I'll see that you have everything you need to make your mission a success." After he hung up he turned to Phil Calabrese. "Get me Jack Rath, please."

CHAPTER TWELVE

New York City, February 26, 2003

Jack Rath placed his drink on the polished bar surface and said, "I haven't been to church in ages—you might say since the Middle Ages."

His younger brother Chris, a fellow product of Fordham University and a Jesuit priest, just laughed. "Even when you used to go, you weren't really there. We'll have to invent a new term: 'Lapsed Catholic' doesn't begin to cover the vast, empty theological turf you occupy."

"Don't get Jesuitical with me, fella. I have not yet begun to fight."

"And what the hell does that have to do with anything?"

"For me to know and you to find out."

Christopher Rath, S.J., threw his hands up and laughed with bitter irony. His brother was in one of his "moods," and there was no reaching him on the spiritual level, so he focused on the pure business aspect of the proposal.

"Are you interested or not? I know you've been approached by the Olympic Committee to work on the 2004 summer games, and that's potentially a longer-term situation for your firm. But this is one of those once-in-a-lifetime gigs that could really increase your profile and lead to future work."

"It could also blow up in my face. A meeting of all the Catholic bishops from all over the world—can you imagine telling them to keep their heads down? Vatican security, Roman traffic cops, carabinieri, Interpol, CIA . . . a regular tea party. There are real and potential terrorist threats, internal shit going on that I have no clue about, and the assassination of the last guy in the

Philippines is still officially unresolved." The elder Rath, ex-
NYPD and veteran of the last days of the long-ago Vietnam conflict, shook his head and regarded his Jack Daniels rocks through
the expensive cut-crystal tumbler.

Over a decade Rath had built up a successful private security
firm, drawing on his fourteen years on the police force specializing
in crowd coordination at major events (including papal and presidential visits) and a stint as NYPD–United Nations liaison (sometimes carrying drunken diplomats to their front doors), exploiting
his State Department and intelligence-agency contacts, and kissing
more than one man's share of political butt. This churchy stuff
did not appeal to him in the least . . . though the fat paycheck
certainly did.

"The timing is off," he went on, ticking off the negatives,
thinking out loud. He and his priest brother sat on plush, high-
backed stools in the Hunt Room of the Palace Hotel. It was past
nine P.M., and each of them had worked late, agreed to meet for
dinner, which had been mixed nuts and three cocktails apiece on
the expense account—whose was yet to be determined.

"At least they're going to stay in the Vatican. Very easy to
secure in itself from any ground-based attack. It would take a
small army to blast its way in there, but we'll have to import
most of the electronic security—the latest gadgetry, for show if
nothing else. And I've worked with the Swiss Guards before. Too
bad about the guy who was offed, he was a decent officer. In
recent years some of your cardinals tried to beef up the Vatican
security operation. Didn't stop the pope from getting blown away
in Manila. And the new guy is an American—what a target for
every disgruntled Western-hating bin Laden clone. Then the bishops: Each of them will bring his own entourage and political
baggage—from Africa and China and South America . . . four
thousand of them? Jesus Christ, it's a mess!"

Christopher Rath smiled evilly—the way he used to as the
younger brother of the Bishop Molloy High School 1970 athlete
of the year when he wanted to stir up trouble during dinner-table
political debates that pitted their staunch Queens County Democrat dad against the pro-war, pro-Nixon Jack. And Chris knew

how to do it, all right. Then he would sit back and watch the fireworks. Now he said, with mock resignation. "Too big a mess, maybe."

Jack Rath was blind in his left eye, after a pipe bomb explosion on Wall Street in 1992 that killed two other cops and the terrorists themselves. A series of surgeries had at least saved the other functions and the eyeball itself, useless as it was, so that he was not horribly disfigured. At the same time his wife had finally left him, which she had threatened to do for years, and took the teenage children, a daughter and a son, out to Long Island where her parents lived. He retired early with commendations and a disability pension, but couldn't remain idle, living on his own, for very long. In 1993 he founded his own security consulting business in partnership with a former city fire commissioner and a retired FBI buddy. They had zero capital but parlayed their contacts into a million-dollar gross in the first year, five times that the following year. Rath felt reborn, energized and validated; he even reestablished contact with the kids, in their later high school and early college years, making himself available to them as he had not been during the round-the-clock grind of his NYPD career. He had dated a few women, too, in the meantime, but not seriously—at least in his own mind.

"You make a good devil's advocate," he said to his brother. Are you sure you're on the right team?"

Chris Rath laughed. "I'm on your team," he said, flicking a cigarette ash into the old-fashioned, oversize glass tray, the kind that was so rare these days. He was the only one in the bar— possibly the entire hotel—smoking. "And I mean it, Jack—I think you should consider this very seriously, on a strictly business basis. Besides, I think you'll like him, the Holy Father, I mean. He's our kind of people."

"Well, I should hope so. I'd hate to see him corrupted by all those Italian politicians and bureaucrats."

"He used to work there. He knows the score."

"I can't figure you guys," Jack went on. "What does it benefit a man if he should gain his soul but lose the whole world? It's all we've got."

"There's where you and I differ, brother. And I don't believe that you really believe that. Deep down you're as much a Catholic as I am. It's in our blood, not just a Sunday thing—even less than that in your case. What I'm saying is, I'd like you to do this, for me, for the Church, but mostly for yourself. You'll get more out of it than you can know at this moment."

"I will think about it. Could be lucrative. Talk to my partners." Rath sipped his drink, grown lukewarm and a bit watery, cutting into the smoky flavor of the aged bourbon.

"I think they'll go for it. Hope they do, anyway."

Three days later, Jack Rath was on the telephone with Monsignor Philip Calabrese, the pope's special assistant for council planning. His partners and other colleagues in the security field told him he would be nuts if he did not explore this prospect: to create and supervise the security arrangements for one of the most important events in contemporary world history . . . there could not be any greater professional opportunity. Others were going to grab for it if he did not. His brother Chris had been only too pleased to give him Calabrese's direct line at the Vatican.

"Do this for me," Calabrese said. "Work up a brief planning document and fly over here to present it to the Holy Father—no middlemen or red tape. If he likes it—and if Cardinal Biagi likes it, which is at least as important—you're good to go. How long will it take you?"

"I'll fly out from JFK tonight," Rath replied. "I've already begun to sketch out my ideas. I can be prepared to talk about it day after tomorrow. How about nine A.M. local time?"

"Fine. Your brother told me he wasn't sure . . ."

"He's made a career out of being cautious. Me, I've erred on the other side, when it comes to my own safety. On the other hand, I haven't lost a single world leader yet!"

With yellow legal pad and laptop computer in tow, Rath flew to Rome that evening, presented to the pope twenty-four hours after his arrival, then called his partners to give them the good news: He had won the contract for his firm. He estimated it would be worth about ten million dollars over the one-year span of planning and execution. And it would take his personal, full-time attention for the duration. Calabrese would now arrange for office space in the Apostolic Palace for the Vatican's soon-to-be-formed Independent Security Unit, under the jurisdiction of the Secretariat of State. On the return flight, Jack Rath thought to himself: Chris really nailed you to the wall on this one, chum. Again . . .

Rome, July 7, 2003

Jane Thaler-Fitzrobinson swept into the papal library with breathless purpose, as if she were late for a lecture before two hundred undergraduates at Boston University. Amid the imposing baroque moldings and gilt-framed pontifical portraiture, the impossibly rich leather-bound volumes of official Vatican history and diplomacy, beneath crystal chandeliers hanging from the thirty-foot mahogany-paneled ceiling, the American prelate who had been plucked from Newark, New Jersey to occupy the chair of the primatial see of all Christendom awaited her. She plunged across the plush Persian carpeting that absorbed her bounding steps in absolute silence. The Belgian-born, Irish-wed professor of theology was a diminutive figure in a loose-fitting gray suit and primly buttoned cream silk blouse, unadorned with jewelry of any kind except her wedding band. Her black square-toed shoes were nearly lost amid the swirling blue, gold, and red patterns of the carpet. The pope stepped forward, a bit tentatively, to arrest her progress and put out both hands to take hers. Startled, as if facing an oncoming bus, Thaler-Fitzrobinson halted a few feet from the tall man in a white cassock. Her gray-brown hair, a chaotic crown above her pale face, flopped over her eyes; she combed it back with stubby fingers and met a friendly pastoral gaze that disarmed her—for a few seconds.

"Your Holiness," she breathed, properly, taking his proffered hands in her own. "You are very good to see me today."

"How could I not, Jane. Your letter intrigued me—and alarmed the papal household and colleagues in the Curia."

"I hope you are feeling better," she said, noting that his handshake was weaker than normal, his palms clammy, and that he looked haggard—from the chemotherapy regime, no doubt.

"Yes, I am, with the help of a lot of prayers and good doctors." It had been only a week since the delayed biopsy that had confirmed the tumor on his spine to be malignant.

"Good," she replied simply, not knowing what else to say. "Now, about my letter—"

In fact, the letter from the most prominent feminist theologian in the world had turned the Apostolic Palace on its ear: She had demanded an audience with Pope Celestine to set him straight before it was too late on the matter of the ordination of women as Roman Catholic priests. It had been nearly a decade since Pope John Paul II's definitive proscription against further discussion of this issue. Now, however, a couple of popes down the line, the feminists' banner had been raised again, higher and brighter than ever before; and with a full-fledged ecumenical council in the offing, there was no way Professor Thaler-Fitzrobinson and her peers would allow the issue to be swept under a priceless, handcrafted Vatican carpet such as she stood on in this moment of moments.

There was nothing surprising in her letter, but the pope had been impressed with her directness and her high-flown rhetoric:

> *The oppressive hand of the patriarchal church shall not,*
> *indeed cannot stay the legitimate aspirations of the*
> *women called to ministry in our age, as Mary Magdalene*
> *and Prisca and others were in the primitive, apostolic era.*
> *We will not hold our tongues, God-given means of*
> *prophecy and protest, any longer—for we are called to*
> *proclaim the rightful place of all women, not only those*
> *of priestly potential, within the living Body of Christ that*
> *was borne within a woman, nurtured and brought forth*
> *to all the world as the Savior of men and women for all*
> *time.*

He knew, too, that there would be no shutting down the debate this time around. Here was Pandora come to claim ownership of her box and all its contents.

"You know, I have read all your books, even taught from

some of them in a course on contemporary theology at the seminary."

"To an exclusively male student body."

"Actually, no. There were several women. Representative of the full Body of Christ, nonetheless. All of us stand to be educated to the best of our abilities. You have opened many minds, Madame Professor."

"But enough? Enough minds opened, enough minds changed? Your Holiness may be the lone—albeit most important—exception to the rule of ignorance and bias."

"I cannot claim that much credit. You will understand that I must give as much weight to each of my predecessors' declarations as to the most brilliant theology."

"I feel that you are leading me on, Holy Father. Neither I nor my colleagues will be patronized or put off—not by you or by four thousand bishops—or four million bishops. The prophetic feminine voice is informed and lifted up by the Holy Spirit herself. We seek the genderless Kingdom of God that the Gospels have promised since the first century of our era."

"Professor—Jane, I am familiar with the arguments from Tradition and Scripture regarding women in the ministry of Christ, the arguments on both sides. I hope you realize the fact that you are standing here is a revolution in itself, whatever may or may not happen from this point on."

For the first time since her arrival, Thaler-Fitzrobinson's face took on a spot of color and flexed with a smile. "I do, Holiness. Indeed, I do." She reached over to touch his arm. "You will not see me prostrate on the floor with gratitude, but understand that my heart is very full in this moment—my cup runneth over."

Mulrennan sat and gestured for his visitor to do the same. Recovery from the exploratory surgery was hard-bought. Dr. Laghi had discovered that the tumor was wrapped tightly to his lower spine. So, he had begun every-other-week chemotherapy treatments that sapped him for days. Still, the tumor had not yet shrunk a millimeter. His face betrayed the pain and fatigue that he felt constantly. Yet he kept a grueling schedule of meetings and audiences on the days when he was not flat on his back.

"I have read your latest book with great interest, Jane. It might even be a best-seller—it's that good." Her new tome—several hundred pages' worth—traced the role of women in the Church from the time of Jesus through the end of the first millennium. While some historians and theologians had criticized it for being far-fetched in places (putting it kindly), the research that had gone into the book and the narrative power of the writing were undeniable. Jane Thaler-Fitzrobinson was undoubtedly stirring the pot of feminist debate in a timely and persuasive fashion. Her mission was to ensure that a new council would take up the subject of her life's work: feminist theology and women as priests.

Already voices had been raised both for and against female *periti*, expert advisers who would be assigned to the committees tasked with drafting council documents. As with Vatican II, many such assignments would be controversial to one group or another. But this pope was determined to invite such diverse voices into the discussion—despite the critics. He listened to Professor Thaler-Fitzrobinson for nearly thirty minutes.

The next audience was difficult for Celestine and everyone else in attendance.

The gruesomely maimed and twisted form of Bishop Juan Nicolás Manrique was folded into a wheelchair powered by a battery pack and controlled by his own gnarled brown fingers—the ones remaining; he had more use of his right hand than his left. Manrique, from Chiapas, had survived a car bombing in Mexico City in 1988; surgery and physical therapy had recovered many of his important body functions, but he remained a paraplegic (on good days) and sometimes a near-quadraplegic. He required twenty-four-hour care, as well as constant security, reluctantly provided by the Mexican federal government. Amazingly, the fifty-two-year-old bishop said mass almost daily, usually twice on Sunday, and traveled throughout his diocese nearly as frequently as he had before the devastating injury.

His face, a gaunt but animated mask, was carefully shaved each day by a faithful attendant, his hair, now starkly white, brushed meticulously back from his high, scarred forehead. He wore protective tinted glasses, and black bushy brows bristled above the eyes that captured everything within their scope, as if to miss even the slightest movement or nuance would deprive the viewer of life itself. The bishop could move his head only slightly, painfully to the left or right, and he had very little hearing in his right ear.

"I thank God for what He has given me, for what He has taken away, and for what He has left me. He chose to allow me to live, and I do not question His infinitely good purpose for me," the bishop had written in his recently published memoir of physical and spiritual struggle. A prolific scholar-writer before the terrorist attack, Manrique had been known for many years as a defender of orthodoxy and the magisterium under Cardinal Ratzinger in the 1980s and '90s. But when he had been appointed bishop of the southernmost and rebellious area of Mexico, far from the academic and political establishments in Mexico City, he had changed: turned from very conservative to near radical, embracing much of the theology of liberation as defined by Gutierrez, the radical theologian who had posited the "preferential option for the poor" as the basis of true Christianity and ecclesiology, especially in the former colonial countries of Central and South America.

Manrique's direct exposure to poverty and the spirit of revolution had affected him deeply and as his own theological position evolved he angered the powers in Mexico City and the Vatican, as well as local landowners. He had become known as the "pink bishop" and thus a target of right-wing assassins; the irony was that the Chiapist rebels were slow to accept his conversion to their agenda. Only after the brutal car-bombing, in which a fellow bishop was killed and the driver and two nuns injured, did Bishop Manrique earn the unqualified confidence of the left-wing guerrilla factions. And he became a world-recognized figure and symbol of the struggle he had adopted as his own.

"We seek a classless society and a classless Church that nurtures all of God's people in the way Christ intended," he preached, echoing the intent of liberation theologians who had been silenced by the Congregation for the Doctrine of the Faith over the previous two decades. "Did not Jesus live and teach among the poorest people, and did He not promise to them the kingdom as the fruits of their labor? Did he not work as a carpenter Himself and cast nets with fishermen and walk the roads without a roof over His own head? Whom did He prefer, the rich who found it difficult to follow Him or the poor who had nothing to lose, for they had nothing in the first place?"

These words, which grew more strident and challenging as the years went on, caused great discomfort within the Vatican. Subtle communications, asking the bishop to moderate his language, became more direct and critical, eventually threatening to strip Manrique's episcopal and ordinary authority if he did not cease his radical rhetoric. But Bishop Juan Nicolás Manrique, a doctor of theology who had studied at some of the most prestigious institutions in the Catholic world, stayed the course, intensifying his prophetic message even as he gradually lost control of the physical being in which he found himself imprisoned.

Pope Celestine VI understood that his predecessor, Innocent XIV, who had also been the victim of terrorist violence, had deferred any action against the Mexican bishop, hoping that Manrique might respond to the Filipino pontiff, who was himself a fellow product of Spanish colonial heritage, in a different way than to the previous pope's powerful, increasingly orthodox—some even said quasi-reactionary—magisterium.

Timothy Mulrennan knew Manrique well from his time as prefect of the Congregation for Bishops, before the Mexican prelate had been so gravely wounded. He had always respected Manrique's intellect and stamina and his commitment to the flock of Christ in the remote mountains and jungle terrain of southern Mexico. It must have been a tremendous shock for the urbane academic who had studied in Paris and Rome, as well as at the ancient university in Mexico City, to be thrust among the native and mestizo population as their bishop. Yet he had handled it with aplomb, soon adopting simpler, coarser, and more casual everyday attire as well as less elaborate vestments at high liturgical occasions.

So, both outwardly and inwardly, the brilliant bishop had

changed, evolved, become focused on something other than his own ecclesiastical career: He had become a true shepherd. Now, with the new council on the horizon, Manrique would have a larger role, on a wider international stage. How would he play it?

The new pope invited him to the Vatican within a few months of his installation as Supreme Pontiff. He knew that Jaime De Guzman, Pope Innocent, had planned to spend several days in Mexico City and to visit with Manrique and all the Mexican bishops there before returning to Rome from his homecoming trip to the Philippines last summer. That had not happened. . . . All of the bishops of Latin America had been devastated by the pope's assassination, none more so than Juan Manrique. The Bishop of Chiapas had fervently hoped that a fellow minister of the Gospel from a poverty-ridden nation would be more sympathetic to the theology of liberation than a European. He would never know, would never have the conversation with De Guzman that he had dreamed of.

Celestine and Manrique sat together in the pope's private study off the elaborate library-salon where he met high-ranking visitors and pilgrims to the Holy See. Father Phil Calabrese, Cardinal Tyrone, and Manrique's auxiliary bishop and his personal assistant, a young mixed-blood priest, were also present for the meeting. Coffee and light refreshments were served, but no one touched his out of deference to the crippled bishop who could not eat anything without help. The ailing pope felt humbled in the Mexican's presence, as he had with a number of holy men he had known, including the previous two Bishops of Rome. But it was time for frankness, not deference.

"Bishop Juan Nicolás," Mulrennan began, "we are so pleased that you were able to respond to our invitation. I know it was a hardship for you to travel so far, that you do not like to be away from your diocese. Certainly your people miss you already and cannot await your return."

"It gave me the opportunity to visit with the cardinal in Mexico City and to see some of my old university colleagues." His voice came out in breathy rasps, with painful pauses between words. He seemed not to be self-conscious about it and attempted to put others at ease. "Your Holiness knows what it is like to be away from home, from familiar surroundings and friends. Though I can see that you have made new friends here, such as Cardinal Tyrone. *Eminenza*, you honor me by your concern for my health which you have expressed so many times very recently."

Tyrone had, in fact, written Manrique several letters of caution and near-reprimand (reserving any such punitive action for the pontiff, not overstepping his extensive but not final authority). He considered the bishop a dangerous and difficult person who was gaining more of a following as time went on, and who would be more difficult to bring to account with each passing year. Manrique had nearly achieved the status of Archbishop Oscar Romero of El Salvador, who had been shot to death while celebrating mass in his cathedral in 1980—the handiwork of a death squad not unlike the group that had made the attempt on the liberal Mexican. So Tyrone's Congregation for the Doctrine of the Faith, the chief doctrinal watchdog agency and guardian of the ancient deposit of faith, must tread carefully in its dealings with the now-legendary popular cleric.

Tyrone interjected: "The honor and pleasure are ours, Your Excellency. We meet face-to-face for the first time, you and I."

"What face I have left," Manrique quipped, with a wince that substituted for a smile.

"Are you getting adequate care, Juan? I have thought of transferring you back to Mexico City, or here to Rome, so that your condition doesn't deteriorate." Pope Celestine was sincerely concerned, and at the same time he would not mind if Manrique were closer, easier to keep tabs on. He saw Tyrone flinch at the suggestion, but the visiting bishop did not react visibly.

"I am very well cared for, Holy Father. I doubt even the finest facility in Rome could see to my needs as well as the dear people of my own diocese. True, there are not many physicians in my part of the world, but the ones who are there are angels of God— they sacrifice all to serve His people, and they do it with great skill and commitment. Myself included. I am in excellent hands. I thank you, my brother."

The next morning, Timothy Mulrennan again sat on the Petrine throne, this time on the stage of the Paul VI Audience Hall, looking out upon the assembly of several thousand people in the modern auditorium that had seen so much Church history over the past few decades, including papal audiences, musical performances, and consistories such as this. A mild painkiller made him somewhat groggy but did not impair his awareness of what was going on.

The pope had convoked an ordinary consistory of the Sacred College of Cardinals, the first in more than two years—since the deaths of both predecessors had cancelled previously planned sessions. As provided in the Code of Canon Law, specifically Canon 353, the pontiff may call to an *ordinary* consistory the cardinals present in Rome or all the cardinals, and he usually installs new cardinals at such meetings; to an *extraordinary* consistory he calls all the cardinals of the world, when, according to the code, "the special needs of the Church or the conducting of more serious affairs suggests that it should be held." Pope John Paul II held a number of extraordinary consistories throughout his pontificate to consult with his body of his most senior advisers, the last in spring 2001. The new pope, Celestine, intended the Ecumenical Council to serve the "needs of the Church" for a long time to come but needed to replenish the Sacred College with new blood, get it up to strength and reward some deserving men for their faithful service to the Bride of Christ.

"The Holy Father has created twelve new cardinals of the Holy Roman Church," the Vatican news office had announced six weeks before. It was a thrilling proclamation for some, controversial to others, but it was clear that the world took notice.

Arrayed in a human fan at the foot of the altar were the red-robed cardinal-designates, a dozen men from ten nations and four continents. From his chair Mulrennan scanned their faces during the Scripture reading; he knew some of them very well, others not so intimately, and soon they would all be members of his "cabinet" and "senate" with unique status and prestige within the Church. To these men the pope looked for advice and counsel in managing his custody of the Keys of the Kingdom of Christ. He had been one among them, a colleague and peer; now he was first among equals.

Who were these men called to receive the red hat this day?

Frederick Paul Misener was Archbishop of Kansas City, Kansas. In all there were a half-million Catholics, including a substantial number of Native Americans on reservations, under his jurisdiction. Twenty years earlier Tim Mulrennan had been bishop of a neighboring diocese in Missouri, and he had known Misener as a younger priest, recommended him for the post of auxiliary bishop to the then-archbishop who had died six years ago. Fred Misener had impressed Mulrennan, now Pope Celestine, with his zeal and open Midwesterner's style; he was especially effective with young people and with the terribly poor Indians throughout the diocese, making them his special apostolate for nearly a quarter-century.

He was a tall, spare figure, tanned and toughened by the time he spent outdoors, traveling to and working with his people. He had been known to wield a hammer in the building of new churches and with Habitat for Humanity, which he actively encouraged among his two hundred scattered rural parishes. Now fifty-four, he would be among the younger group of cardinals who would serve well into the first decades of the new century, the twenty-first of the Christian era. And Mulrennan held him in special regard for his honesty and lack of pretention. This elevation of a relatively obscure archbishop to cardinalitial rank was considered unusual by most observers, was certainly unprecedented for the Kansas archdiocese.

Misener caught the pope's eye during the lengthy reading in Latin and smiled, receiving a papal wink in return.

In contrast to the rurally focused American was the Austrian who had replaced the late Cardinal Zimmerman—a front-runner for election to the papacy who had died in the conclave of the previous year. Alfons Maria Stalnaker, Archbishop of Vienna, an urbane prelate with distinctively military bearing who claimed Hapsburg ancestry, sat at attention and looked straight ahead at the altar and listened intently to the words that echoed through the vast basilica in the ancient language of Rome. Here was an old-style Prince of the Church, with noble blood, no less, who looked the part and carried himself with a natural aristocratic demeanor. He was fifty-eight years old, also a comparatively young man to receive the red hat.

Alfons Stalnaker had developed a reputation during his thirty years as a priest for intelligent ecumenical dialogue, savvy secular political instincts, and a fervent commitment to the conservative Evangelium Christi movement. He was, in the current pope's mind, a mixed bag but too valuable a "hinge" to withhold recognition as a cardinal. His father, Claus von Stalnaker, had been an Austrian diplomat, and his mother a Jew who had converted to Catholicism in order to marry, during the height of the war that claimed nearly all of her extended family. She still lived in a suburb of Vienna, and her son visited her as often as he could; he considered her a saint who had miraculously survived the horror of the Shoah, and he was secretly as proud of his Jewish roots as of his imperial bloodline, though he never spoke of it publicly.

Mulrennan found him somewhat stiff and forbidding as a personality, but engaging and challenging as an intellect—and a more than capable administrator of a hugely important European see. Recently a series of scandals had erupted in Austria, revelations of sexual abuse of young men by priests and by one bishop. Stalnaker had dealt with the abusers swiftly and severely, comforted and aided the victims and their families just as swiftly. The response from press and public was overwhelmingly positive, softening and humanizing the image of the stern, precise archbishop. The pope valued such actions and today rewarded the man responsible.

Stalnaker looked the part of a corporate chief or military commander with rimless spectacles, Prussian-style haircut, square shoulders, and mouth closed in a serious, even severe straight line. His six-two height only emphasized the imperial impression.

The others who were to receive the red biretta of office sat straight-backed, hands folded, in the formal choir dress of such a significant occasion; they would receive their scarlet skull caps as well as the birettas in lieu of the now-outdated floppy-brimmed and tasseled hats of the Renaissance era. There were a few Italians, inevitably, among the elect, one Frenchman, two Africans, three Asians (where the Church was growing and facing persecution, especially in the People's Republic of China), and an elderly American monsignor who had taught Church history and theology at Notre Dame for fifty years; it was a papal privilege to name such a man cardinal as a signal of gratitude and favor. Nine of the twelve were under the age of eighty, which meant they were eligible to vote in a papal conclave, when the next one occurred at the death of the pope. This brought the total number of eligible electors to 128, eight over the canonical maximum—but the pope had the discretionary power to name as many as he chose, as had John Paul II in the historic consistory of February 2001.

After the Gospel reading from St. John, the pontiff remained standing and delivered a brief homily that highlighted each man and his accomplishments as priest or bishop. The pope said, "And now Christ calls each of you to this ecclesiastical rank and lays upon your shoulders the important responsibility to 'preach to all nations' of His love, and His Father's love, and the inspiration of the Holy Spirit. In addition, you shall advise me, the new and unworthy successor of St. Peter, in my role as brother bishop and overseer of the Church of Rome. Today you receive title to some of the churches of this diocese, the traditional function of the earliest cardinals who were, in reality, the local pastors who elected their presider in Rome."

Over the past few years Tim Mulrennan had read up on the Sacred College and its role in the Church's stormy history; he had researched conclaves and councils of ages past. As pompous, corrupt, and even silly as some of the old cardinals had been—which drew the often justified censure of reformers and critics—they had been the instruments of the Holy Spirit working within the community of believers, as the hierarchy of the Christ-ordained Church. Was it too high and mighty for words? Yes, sometimes—in the worst of times of inquisition and schism and deadly politics. Were those abuses now consigned to history? He sincerely hoped and prayed it was so. As pope, the Servant of the Servants of God was committed to pulling the College of Cardinals into relevance in the modern world, cleansing their hearts and focusing their minds on the nearly impossible task of ecclesiastical reform that he envisioned—in effect, completing the work of the Second Vatican Ecumenical Council. These handpicked men, with whom he had major differences, would lead the bishops of the world in the council. Were they up to it? Was he?

CHAPTER THIRTEEN

Rome, July 9, 2003

Demetra Matoulis slid carefully out of bed so as not to disturb the man who lay there, his mouth agape, dead asleep. She slipped into an oversize U of Penn T-shirt that covered her slender figure like a tent. Barefoot, she padded into the cramped Roman kitchen to make coffee, then sat at the small table there and lit a cigarette. Her hair, tousled after a night of lovemaking and fretful sleep, looked like a thatched roof after a violent windstorm. She ran her fingers through the tangle, to no avail; she inhaled a pungent lungful of smoke and blew it out vigorously through her nostrils. For a woman in love, she felt like crap this morning.

The rising sun struggled to penetrate the smudged east windows of her fourth-floor flat, casting a diffuse glow into the cluttered enclosure where Demetra sat. She watched the blue-white smoke of her cigarette swirl into the half-light and escape through a crack in the window. The cigarette tasted terrible and she stabbed it into the already overflowing ashtray.

Soon the strong black coffee was ready. She rinsed her face in the kitchen sink and poured a cup of the hot liquid stimulant, hoping to jump-start her body into wakefulness. It didn't quite work that way: She did experience a buzz, but a surge of anxiety and guilt, as well.

There he lay—her friend and lover, James Wiezevich, a priest of the Roman Catholic Church. What in hell was she thinking when she had taken him into her bed last night? It was a replay of their affair of a dozen years before. Is that what she wanted? Was it fair to him? She took a sip of the scalding black coffee and felt it burn her throat, seep into her gut. She liked this guy—a lot. He had been on her mind for months, and she was so glad he was here. It was almost like a miracle, like the vision of the girl in Bosnia . . . but there was also something very wrong about it. He was a priest, after all, and she was causing him to violate his sacred promise of chastity. To what end? She cursed herself.

Although she had been determined to sleep with him again, the previous night had started off innocently enough. They had agreed to meet for dinner to have an off-the-record discussion of the council preparations. Jim had already plunged neck-deep into the process under Phil Calabrese's direction and had been working twelve-hour days; his Italian had come back easily, and he was prattling on with waiters and taxicab drivers almost like a native Roman. He delighted in the excitement and seemed to be getting out of himself and putting his personal troubles aside. She could see that it was good for him to be busy with this very demanding job.

At dinner they spoke about their lives and dreams, their families, their careers. The restaurant was busy and noisy, but they had a semisecluded table and a conveniently inattentive waiter. They sipped the house wine and a bottle of water, devoured a large plate of antipasto, and ate every bread stick as they talked, nearly oblivious to their surroundings.

"Glad you're here," Demetra said, raising her wine glass.

"Not half as glad as I am," Wiezevich replied, clinking his glass against hers. "Even though I miss my parish—and worry about old Father John and young Father Mark. We made quite a trio." He smiled, genuinely moved and amused by the memories of just a few weeks before. As difficult as it was, being a pastor and brother priest to these men, it filled his life with purpose and made him feel useful in a unique and powerful way. "I suppose they'll get along without me."

"They're probably crying right now, missing you."

"I sincerely doubt that. They have their hands full with the parishioners. The archbishop has brought in a new man to be the administrator and keep an eye on Father John, probably push him to retire to an assisted-living residence. I didn't think he was going to make it after that last attack. Scared the living daylights out of me."

"You love them, don't you? Your fellow priests, I mean."

"Yeah, they're good people—trying to *do* good and be ministers of the Gospel. Not easy these days. Never has been, I guess—but they get so little support now. They don't get the respect that priests used to take for granted."

"Well, you've got to admit there are reasons for that. There have been so many cases of abuse and misconduct—at least reported cases. God knows how much had been going on for all those years. And when a priest fucks up it really makes headlines. Then the Church—in its great wisdom—has tried to cover up and deny these terrible problems. Secret trials run by the Vatican. Blame the victim, move the priest out of town, pay off the local officials—and then hope it doesn't happen again. But it usually does, only worse. It's a vicious cycle, Jim; at least that's how it looks from the outside, like you can't get your act together."

Wiezevich sighed and gazed into his wine glass. "This sounds stupid, I know, but—it's not that simple. The bishops really are addressing these issues, especially after the last years. Not enough, and not quickly enough, I grant you."

"What about the bishops who themselves abuse young men? I've personally reported three such cases in Europe and know about two or three in the States. I'd guess that's just the tip of the iceberg."

"I think you are leaping to conclusions based on very little evidence. But to be honest, I don't know," he said in reply.

Jim Wiezevich sat back and regarded Demetra across the table. He had never been so attracted to a woman in his life. He had gone out of his way to avoid the occasion of intimacy with women, of course, and his work did not often put him in one-to-one contact—by design. He was listening intently to her words but could not help falling in love with her eyes and mouth as she spoke.

"You don't know, or you don't want to know? I think the Church is in deep denial about the problems in the priesthood." She was fishing now for information about the potential agenda of the council, probing and prodding her "highly placed source"—and getting in a few digs, as well.

"The council will address aspects of the priesthood, for sure.

I don't think it will get into sexual abuse issues—that's not what an ecumenical council is about. But I cannot imagine that the bishops will not mandate some work in this area in places where it's a real problem—like the U.S."

"What—will they order a study, then take years to study the study, formulate recommendations—then hope the whole thing will go away? Even though I'm from the Greek Orthodox tradition, it still matters to me."

Wiezevich remained silent for a long moment. Then he said: "You will be blown away by what this council debates and decides. I guarantee it. I'm not saying you'll like everything you hear, but you—and the whole world—will certainly pay attention."

"Okay, I'll let this one go—for now. But that brings up another subject: security. This is one mother of an event, and there will be both internal and external threats to the safety of the pope, and everyone else. What can we expect to hear—and when—about security plans?"

"Very little, on the twelfth of Never." He watched her face. He loved to watch her face when she was very serious or very angry. It took only a heartbeat for the anger to set in, then pass, and she smiled. She had large white teeth that melted him when she smiled. Wiezevich reached across the tablecloth and touched her hand. "I'm pulling your leg, Demetra. More shall be revealed—but not much more—at the appropriate time."

"You're no help at all, worse than the press office geeks."

"Look, I'm paying for dinner tonight, so I'm calling the shots." His hand lingered over hers, and he felt the body heat there, saw it in her challenging eyes. "I hope you know I'm being facetious—trying to be funny."

"Not succeeding all that well," she said, ceding no ground. "This is one of the biggest stories I'll ever report, and you're making it ten times more difficult than it has to be. I told you everything we talk about is off the record, for background only. I need to develop some leads, some direction—I'm not sitting here for my health, you know."

"That makes me feel real good," he replied, sitting back and regarding her more distantly. "I *am* here for my health and sanity. I thought it would be fun just to spend some time with a smart, beautiful person who doesn't wear a Roman collar or have some theological axe to grind."

"Does my being a woman have anything to do with it?"

"Yes, it does." He felt as if his chest—his entire upper body— was in a huge, powerful vise.

"Of course, in your world a woman can't wear a Roman collar."

"Knock it off. You've already chopped me down to size."

"So you're just chopped meat. Poor old you."

"You can be mean when you want to be. Have you no respect for your elders?"

"Seven years is nothing, my friend. We're both approaching middle age."

"You're hardly a matron, Demetra."

"So when will women be ordained as priests?"

"Expect a press release any minute."

"All right, I give up—for now. I'm starved. Have we ordered our dinner yet?"

"I don't think we have, as a matter of fact."

They laughed and picked up their menus. They had been oblivious to the passage of time, more engaged in their verbal sparring match than their surroundings. Wiezevich caught the errant waiter's attention at last. They belatedly placed their order for dinner and requested another bottle of wine.

"Tell me about what *you* hope to see at this council."

"Well, I hope there will be some discussion of the role of pluralism in our life as a Church. I think this can be achieved, within proper limits, to celebrate the cultural diversity and theological progress that has occurred within the past three or four decades. Remember, the ancient Church was really a collection of churches, and places like Jerusalem, Antioch, Alexandria were as important as Rome; and everybody spoke Greek then, not Latin."

"So, what about women being ordained priests? That's what everyone wants to read about."

"I believe it will be discussed at this council. The structure of the priesthood is one of the major issues that the Holy Father insists be placed before the council fathers. He has not uttered a word about the role of women, whether he thinks they might one day be ordained or not. I honestly think he wants to have this debate. Doesn't mean it will actually happen in our lifetime. I predict one thing, however, that we will have female deacons as a first or interim step. No one has told me that, but it's a feeling I get. It's whispered about, but no one yet has come out for it, except among the feminist theologians."

"Do you know how insanely boring you sound? And I'm actually interested in the subject."

"Sometimes the details get tangled up, I'll admit. I'm sorry if you're bored, Demetra. All I'm saying is that something tangible, but far short of priestly ordination for women, will come out of this council."

"That seems to be a kind of half-measure."

"Yeah, I guess so. But it might be something that a substantial majority of the worldwide bishops can agree on. Not that it wouldn't tick off a large number of them. God knows there will be some reactionary undercurrents at work."

"Aren't there always? Look, Jim, I fear for the pope—and for you—with this council."

"Why?" he asked.

"Because there are those who oppose it so much." She searched his eyes for an answer. "Don't you think it is dangerous? Does God really want a Church council? What does the pope say about the forces lined up against him?"

"He said to me, 'The Holy Spirit is not perturbed—challenged, yes.' That is the pope in a nutshell, equally unperturbed. He's amazing."

"Isn't Cardinal Tyrone still working to stop the council from happening?"

Wiezevich smiled. "I love that old guy. He is like a giant Michelangelo statue, like Moses or something. Yes, he opposes the very idea, but the Holy Father made him a copresident of the council, and he can't very well shut it down in that role. I see him as an Ottaviani figure: fiercely representing the traditional 'old

Church' against the radical changes that will be called for from the floor. And he is necessary in that role. Somebody's got to be an anchor to the past.

"And you know what else I think? Most of the bishops from Asia and Africa will line up on the conservative side of social issues. They will far be more reactionary than the Europeans and South American bishops. Followed closely by a majority of the Americans. With exceptions on all sides, of course. Remember, Pope John Paul II appointed about ninety percent of the current crop, and he made sure to bolster orthodoxy in the ranks, really his first priority."

"I get that. Like my friend in Bosnia, the cardinal. He kept an extremely tight lid on the phenomenon of the girl's visions; I would go so far as to say he opposed the very idea of personal revelation as a possibility. He'll be happy when the whole thing goes away—if it does."

"Religion is busting out all over the place. Hard to keep it from happening."

Their meal came eventually, and they ate a little bit, talked a lot. Neither was particularly hungry by the time it arrived, even though it smelled and tasted delicious. They were feeding off each other, more relaxed and intimate than either had expected. He watched with great pleasure as she ate her pasta. She helped him clean a bit of sauce off his black jacket with soda water, and they laughed.

"How about we don't talk any more about the council tonight?" he suggested as they shared a spumoni for dessert.

"How about we have coffee at my place, after we walk off some of these Roman calories?"

"I definitely need the exercise. I haven't been able to take my regular early-morning hikes since I've been here."

They strolled through the neighborhood for an hour, saying little, until she turned them toward her apartment. A sense of easy familiarity infused them both, and they were comfortable with the silences, did not feel the need to fill the minutes with chatter. Their arms brushed a few times, and each felt the bolt of human electricity when it happened, but said nothing. They eagerly breathed the warm air of the city.

"Here we are," she said as they approached her building. "By the way, thank you for a wonderful dinner."

"You are very welcome. It was years later than it should have been," he said.

"True, but not *too* late." She stopped and touched his arms. "I'm happy and sad at the same time. Honestly, I don't know what I am feeling. Is it too late, Jim?"

"Let's discuss that agenda topic over a cup of your famous coffee," he suggested.

"Famous?"

"You keep talking about it."

Demetra laughed, was still laughing as they entered the lift in the lobby of her apartment building. The elevator swayed and groaned as it transported them to her floor, then rattled before the doors swung open.

"I suggest you walk down when you leave. You don't want to get trapped in this thing."

"My worst nightmare," Wiezevich said. "Maybe I'll never go down, just stay here. I'll be a fugitive from the Church."

"Jim, I know you're joking, but I hope you don't feel that way—that I'm taking you away from your Church, or God."

They stopped at her doorway and kissed. For the first time since those long-ago nights when they had first known each other their bodies melded and they held each other in a fierce, hard tightness. Their lips fused magically, pure touch.

"We better get a room," she teased as she pulled herself from him and fitted the key into the door. She pushed inside, and he followed. "Well, how about this one?"

Her so-called famous coffee was forgotten in the next several blinding minutes of sensual exploration between a man and a woman who wanted nothing but each other, the world and everything in it be damned. . . .

Demetra smiled as she lit a second morning cigarette: The morning after, she thought ironically, isn't it grand? What now? What will he say when he awakens? She started when she heard his voice suddenly.

"Good morning, friend," he said.

He stood near the kitchen table wearing his shorts and a

sleeveless undershirt, looming there like the fifty-foot man from that terrible old science fiction movie. But he was a hell of a lot better looking, and she wanted to take him back to bed and do things to him—keep him in her arms for the rest of the day.

"It is, in fact. Friend."

"Well, we're not family," Jim responded. "Your awful cigarette smoke woke me up."

"It has a tendency to do that. It is terrible, but I love the first one or two or three in the morning."

"I love you in the morning."

"Jim, have we done something wrong? I am so sorry if you feel that we have. I didn't mean—I don't want to hurt you in any way. I just can't help it if—"

"Demetra, I don't have anyone in my life. My parents, yes, but I mean a close friend, someone to love, to trust. My brother and sister are both gone; I have priest friends, but it's not the same. I guess what we did was wrong, if judged by canon law, but not by human law—and I doubt that God is terribly angry that two people spent the night together. I probably won't feel so casual about it tomorrow, but for right now, right here, I'm ready to pay whatever price is required of me." He looked at his watch. "That said, I have to be at work in an hour."

"For someone who doesn't do this very often, you're good at it."

"What do you mean?" He was genuinely baffled.

"I mean making an exit!" she said, with a laugh in her voice and tears in her eyes.

He went to her, brought her into her arms and kissed her brow, her eyes, her cheeks and nose. "I still love you in the morning—this morning."

She felt his arms around her, clung to him. Tears flowed from her eyes—tears of both sadness and joy. "I believe you," she said. "And I love you. I want to be with you, right now. That's all I want."

Jim Wiezevich tried to hold his own emotions in check, but felt himself crashing to earth. What have I done? he thought. To her and to myself? God knows I want to be with her—but what price am I willing to pay for that privilege? And what does she really want? Not a failed priest. Not a depressed guy from New Jersey.

Aloud he said: "I'll come back tonight, if you want me to."

"Yes, I do," she said. She relaxed her embrace and stood back, wiping away her tears. "But you can't go till you have a cup of coffee, maybe something to eat?"

"Sure—you had promised me some last night but never delivered."

Demetra Matoulis poured a cupful and placed it on the table. "I always fulfill my promises," she said, "however long it takes."

She opened the small, streaked window to let her cigarette smoke escape and light and air to enter the room. Both of them sat at the kitchen table, and again they shared an unspoken conversation—a poignant communion of two souls drawn together in a place far from home. Yet, where was home, for either of them? Their careers had taken them on solitary journeys and led them away from marriage and family. Neither regretted the chosen course, yet here, after a night together, their paths would take them in separate directions once again unless they stopped at this crossroad to be together. For how long—another day? A month? A year? Eventually it would matter, but for now they would not allow the uncertainty to darken their morning.

Rome, July 19, 2003

The pontiff's sister Kathleen and stepbrother Stephen had flown to Rome. They were concerned about his delayed exploratory surgery and treatment regime, somewhat angry about his stubbornness. He put them up at the Hotel Excelsior, which still retained some of its Old World charms and style—as well as some carpeting and wallpaper that was pre–Vatican Council: the *first* Vatican Council, some joked. But they spent little time there, because the pontiff invited them to be with him during the day at the Apostolic Palace, where they caught up on family business at meals and between papal meetings and audiences. Celestine cel-

ebrated a special mass in his personal chapel for their deceased
mother and father and their aged and Alzheimer-ailing stepmother. The other two Mulrennan sisters, Theresa and Gertrude
Anne, held down the fort with their families in New Jersey.

Kathleen Stanton, a private lawyer in Washington, D.C., was
married to another attorney who, like her, had been active in
Republican politics for many years; he was currently the Under-
secretary of Defense. Stephen was editorial director of a Random
House imprint that published quality nonfiction, and he was co-
writing a book with a female Episcopal priest about gay spirituality and the Christian tradition. "Heavy duty," his brother, the
pope, said. In fact, Timothy Mulrennan was thrilled beyond
words that they were with him, even though he had to endure
their concern and criticism about his decision to postpone the
surgery. They saw, as others could not, that he was in near-
constant pain from the tumor—and they feared that the treatment
might not effect a cure.

"Tim, you cannot play around with this any longer," Kathleen said over luncheon on the second day of their visit. She
looked to Stephen for support; he nodded vociferously. "All of us
agree, and if you don't listen to us we'll kidnap you and make
you do it. The crisis in China is not a legitimate excuse."

"I guess I'll have to summon the Swiss Guards to protect me,"
the pope said, bemused and touched by Katie's unequivocal
words.

"We're not joking about this," Stephen interjected. He smiled
gently at the elder brother who had offered him unconditional
love and support in his own time of crisis two decades before,
when he had lost a lover to AIDS. "We don't want to lose you.
And besides us you have a billion other 'family members' to consider. A lot of people love you, Tim."

"And more than a few would prefer I didn't exist." He
quickly held up his hands to stifle their protest. "I'm just stating
a fact of life that goes with the job. Not arguing with you."

Kathleen, at fifty-two, was the same trim, intense, scholarly
woman that her elder brother had always known. Her glittering
résumé in itself ensured her a high profile in the nation's capital—

let alone the fact of her husband's and brother's positions in the world. Yet she had taken a clearly independent path for herself that did not exploit in any way her famous relations. As a practicing attorney and part-time professor of Constitutional law at Georgetown, Katie—as only her family still called her—was often on the lips of the Great Mentioner for federal-level judicial appointments by conservative administrations. She eschewed the chat-program circuit and wove a mantle of mystery around herself—except for close friends who knew her as a warm, funny, down-to-earth wife, mother, and professional.

Stephen Mulrennan, on the other hand, was an open book in his career milieu and personal life—but it was in a somewhat less public field of endeavor: trade book publishing in New York City. He had toiled for nearly twenty years as an editor at various houses, with a number of successful books to his credit; now he was more or less settled into a mid-level executive position at the largest publishing conglomerate, he had recently marked a ten-year anniversary with his domestic partner, and he felt confident enough to try his hand as an author, albeit in collaboration. He was forty-five and cut a handsome, almost elfish figure in well-chosen, traditionally tailored clothes and stylish eyeglasses.

"Well, I *will* argue with you," Kathleen Stanton said. "I am concerned about your safety as well as your health. After what happened to both your predecessors, it's a very real threat to you or anyone in your position. And I don't think you should take it lightly."

"Ditto from left field," Stephen put in.

"You two are certainly an effective team. I'm just glad Theresa and Gertie Anne aren't here to gang up on me, too."

Stephen said, "I hope you understand that from where we sit, it looks like the world is closing in on you, Tim."

"This China situation especially could become a huge burden for you," Kathleen added, no stranger to high-level diplomacy.

The Bishop of Rome looked from one to the other, admiring and loving them; he was grateful to God that he had his sisters and his brother in his life—despite the demands of a vocation that had kept him apart from them so often. His elder brother,

Kevin, had been killed in Vietnam in 1968. Kevin, a Marine Corps captain, had been young Tim's idol and best friend. His whole world—and the family's—had been irreversibly upended when Kevin had lost his life.

Breaking bread with them, arguing with them, just *being* with them resurrected the acutely painful, still vivid memories of his days as a youngster in North Auburn, New Jersey: the rambling old house, the smell of freshly mown lawns in summer, their mother, Madeline, passed out drunk when he came home from school, the tears and silences that belied the love that was ever-present among them, the pain and sorrow of a mother's early death, the rock-steady presence of a father, James, who always comforted the kids and made wrong things right again, a deep, mysterious faith in God and His Church that swelled like a balloon in his young breast and filled him with grace and peace in difficult times. How to remember and grasp the meaning of those times and hold onto the memories—good and ill—for a lifetime . . . was not this the stuff of all our lives, the gift of our God?

The Supreme Pontiff of the Roman Church was jolted back to reality by a severe, sudden pain in his midsection. He felt the blood drain from his face. In the others' eyes he could see that they knew something had happened, something was terribly wrong with him.

"Tim, what is it?" Kathleen asked, alarmed.

Stephen stood and went to his elder brother. The waiter ran into the kitchen where the pope's bodyguard was eating lunch and brought the man into the dining room. Timothy Mulrennan sat as still as a pillar of salt, his quiet moment of memories and peace shattered. The security man called for Philip Calabrese, then his own superior to request backup and a doctor. The pope felt Stephen's hand on his shoulders like a lead weight keeping him in place. He wanted to stand and shout that he was fine, that there was no reason for worry—but he could not move and no words came from his mouth. He glanced down at his own hands, which looked as white as his papal cassock. Sweat beaded his ashy forehead.

"Steady, Your Holiness," Stephen said. The words sounded

particularly odd from a brother's lips; but the younger man found himself in an exquisitely strange situation, perhaps the strangest in his life: in the dining room of a stricken pope!

After a seeming eternity, Pope Celestine found his voice: "It has passed," he said with a strained rasp. "I'm okay."

"You're far from okay," Kathleen said to him. She stood opposite her stepbrother on the pontiff's left side, a frown of fear and concern embedded on her face. "Don't try to move."

"I need to stand up," he insisted. "Please help me." His hands fluttered, found a grip on the arms of his chair.

As he stood, with Stephen's help, Celestine gasped from the shooting pain that engulfed his entire trunk. He could tell that it centered in the lower back and from there blossomed through his nervous system. His eyes burned and his head swam. He took in a deep breath, which helped ease and steady him.

"I'm surprised," he said, with a rueful, crooked smile.

"We are, too—believe me," Kathleen replied.

Monsignor Philip Calabrese erupted through the kitchen door, followed by two Swiss Guards in civilian clothing. "Holiness!" he exclaimed as he approached the pope. He saw now what the others were alarmed about. "Let's get him into the study," Calabrese suggested. He took one arm, Stephen Mulrennan the other, and they walked the pontiff gingerly to his favorite easy chair, which he had brought to the Apostolic Palace from his Newark chancery. "Now sit—carefully."

The two men gently lowered Timothy Mulrennan into the pliant leather chair. Immediately the pope breathed more easily and some color returned to his face.

Throughout the afternoon and into the evening, the pope's sister and stepbrother stayed nearby in the papal apartments as the emergency techs and doctors came and went. Dr. Laghi was unavailable until the morning—locked into an eighteen-hour surgery schedule. Biagi, Tyrone, and other Curia officials came to be with the Holy Father and to keep him updated, at his insistence, about the Chinese situation and the daily council preparatory meetings. He took a mild sedative at seven P.M. and dozed off. The cardinals melted away, and the others reluctantly left about eight o'clock.

Phil Calabrese accompanied Kathleen and Stephen back to their hotel in a Vatican limousine. Like them, he was afraid and angry, unsettled by this latest episode, anxious to return to the Apostolic Palace but reluctant to confront the pope—again—about his health. There was no question now: another surgery must be scheduled immediately.

Kathleen Stanton was nearly in tears; Stephen held her hand. "I can't believe it," she said. "He is one stubborn sonofabitch, even if he is my brother—and the goddamned pope."

"It's a guy thing," Stephen said, trying to lighten the mood in the car, without success.

"Don't give me that," she spat. The chemo hasn't been working. "He is killing himself, and for no reason—to prove some point? It's not right, and it's certainly not moral. Phil, can't you speak to Dr. Laghi and get Tim onto the table in the morning?"

"It is more complicated than that, Kathleen," Calabrese said. "I have been in touch with Laghi every day, two or three times. He's trying to hold the team together for a second surgical intervention, but he'll lose one, get one back on any given day. He's ready to go any time, but he wants to have the best specialists on hand when he opens him up. He wants to get the entire tumor this time. So do I." He looked out the window into the city night as the black automobile weaved past the gaudily illuminated Victor Emmanuel monument, another outsized Roman tribute to the nation's past glory, which only pointed to its more recent failures.

"You might have to drug his coffee or something," she said, only half joking. "Anything to get him into that operating room."

"We can talk to him again tomorrow," Stephen volunteered. "He has to see how serious it is, after tonight. And Dr. Laghi will work on him—I'm sure of that. He must be pretty well disgusted by now." He removed his glasses and rubbed his eyes.

"Do you think he has taken on more than he should with this council? It's so much, so fast . . ." Kathleen clutched a thin patent leather bag on her lap, looked out the car window. Her words fell like dry autumn leaves into the air of tension and despair the three shared, addressed to no one in particular.

They struggled in silence to express, somehow, the love and

fear they felt for this man: brother, friend, priest, and pope.

At the entrance to the Excelsior all three exited the limo and stood by the front door. Calabrese dismissed the driver. "I'll walk back," he said. "I need the exercise." Without protest, the driver departed, leaving him with Kathleen and Stephen Mulrennan. "It's warm. Maybe I'll sweat off a few pounds." Not that he needed to; he was nearly as thin as Timothy Mulrennan, his ailing boss.

"We'll send a car for you in the morning," the American monsignor said.

"Thanks, Phil," Kathleen said. "I know you're doing everything humanly possible to take care of Tim. We all appreciate it—you must know that."

"Do you want to join us for a drink or something?" Stephen asked. "Before your hike back."

"No—thank you. I want to clear my head and work off this tension." He shook his arms and shoulders, stretched his neck. "I don't get much chance to work out these days."

"They have a nice health club here," Mulrennan's sister volunteered. "I do my three miles on the treadmill every morning." She looked every inch the part of the healthy, high-powered attorney that she was, with a touch of elegance in her subtle choice of jewelry and understated makeup.

"I guess I'm just a lazy slug," Stephen said. "I haven't seen the inside of a gym in years. I love to swim, though."

"You make me sick," Kathleen said. "Look at you—you have the metabolism of an ocelot." She smiled affectionately and pinched his arm. "That's why I hate you."

"So, I'll leave you two to work through your sibling issues," Calabrese said. "See you in the morning, then?"

"Good night," Stephen said.

"Be careful on your walk home. You never know who is out there," Kathleen offered. Then she gave him a quick sisterly hug and a peck on his lined cheek.

Indeed, he began to perspire within a few blocks of the Excelsior as he headed back to the Vatican, but he maintained a relatively quick pace, pausing to cross the busy streets and dodging cars and fellow pedestrians. He felt liberated and alive and

Roman—forgetting for a moment the trials of the day.

He considered what Jim Wiezevich had told him about his early-morning walks back in New Jersey. What would it be like to be a parish priest, a pastor, directly responsible for the spiritual care of a few thousand souls? Calabrese had only briefly and intermittently experienced that aspect of the Catholic priesthood, and he felt occasional pangs of regret about it. Yet . . . he could not—would not—complain about the path he had taken in his career. After all, it had brought him here, to Rome, to the Apostolic Palace itself, to the eve of an ecumenical council of the Church, into the very presence of the Holy Spirit and history. His fear, though, was that the pontificate of the first American pope would be cut short by illness and premature death. Was it God's will for Timothy Mulrennan, Celestine VI, to reign for an even briefer time than John XXIII, the pope of the Second Vatican Council, who, as the elderly Angelo Roncalli, had been elected as a "transitional" figurehead?

Too much for my small brain to comprehend, Calabrese told himself as he walked, breathing in the springtime night air of the city. The smells of automobile exhaust, cooking oils, human beings, dog poop, and blossoming trees filled his head with competing sensual impressions and sparked other thoughts and memories. Philip Calabrese said a quick prayer to his Lord to lighten the burdens on the shoulders of the Holy Father and to keep him in health and safety that he might live to fulfill the task of his life, however long that may take. . . . And, oh, for good measure—give me the strength, Lord, to be of help to him in his work, to advise with wisdom and serve with diligence.

He had already covered more than a kilometer at a brisk clip, felt his lungs and heart getting a good workout. He began to think that a drink would be welcome, after all, perhaps when he got home: a tall vodka and tonic with some lime juice just might knock him out and let him sleep through the night for a change.

Calabrese had grown up in a Jersey City neighborhood of Irish and Italian roughnecks who drank hard and fought hard— among themselves and with the blacks who lived in the adjacent streets. The area continued to change throughout his youth and young manhood, some lamenting its decline as the homes deteriorated and the population grew ever darker; a high-rise housing project for lower income folks loomed over the 'hood and nearby St. Peter's College. His parents were now long dead, and his only sister long gone to Berkley Heights in suburban Morris County. Their old parish, Christ the King, was now primarily Spanish-speaking, with a smattering of Haitan and African congregants who held their own national masses and social gatherings, as well. The priests struggled to keep up with the demands of an ever-changing, and ever-poorer, community. Calabrese had pulled weekend duty there sometimes, and he was always grateful to celebrate mass for the hundreds who showed up faithfully on Sundays and to practice his rusty Spanish in his homilies.

But scholarship had irresistibly drawn him into the "higher" realm of diocesan administration and seminary teaching. And he had to admit that he relished the challenges: working closely with the archbishop, lecturing to the eager seminarians and graduate students on systematic theology, filling his days with reading and writing, rubbing shoulders with local business and political leaders, mentoring a few young men—as he had Jim Wiezevich long ago—in their formation as priests of the Church. He was good at it. The call to Rome had shocked and frightened him at first, but soon he had become used to the frenetic pace of the contemporary papacy, with the incessant demands of household, Curia, residential bishops, media, and the legions of faithful—in Rome and all around the world—who needed to communicate with their pope through countless letters and frequent audiences. It was more vast and complex a "business" than he had ever imagined. No mere chief executive of a multinational corporation, the Roman Pontiff was truly the shepherd of a flock who required his nurturing attention twenty-four hours a day, waking and sleeping, talking and praying, breathing and touching.

Phil Calabrese was thus blessed to be a privileged witness to the inner structures of the living Body of Christ, the complex community of saints and sinners that dated to the visitation of the Holy Spirit upon the apostles in a room in Jerusalem about two thousand years ago. Like those men and women, he believed the Incarnate Word to be risen from the dead and poised to return in judgment at any moment, perhaps even today. Wouldn't that be a mind-blowing experience! He smiled to himself and felt the blood of life pumping in his veins.

His thoughts returned to Pope Celestine. What lay ahead, afterward? When the council was concluded and the pope—God bless him—passed on at an old age . . . when the seed Celestine had planted took root and grew and blossomed as a great tree of faith . . . when the new generation of Church leaders, the younger bishops and cardinals, matured and assumed custody of the keys of the kingdom of God. Unknowable . . .

He could not shake the palpable sense of danger and doom that had pricked at him during the ride with Kathleen Stanton and Stephen Mulrennan. The pope's health, the terrible news from China, opposition within and without to the council—all these things weighed heavily on everyone who was associated with the Holy Father. Grave concerns, any one of which could break or kill a man. He looked around at the others who were walking on the street as he was, fewer now as the time grew later; most people were home or settled into a comfortable seat at a café for supper, tending to their own needs or their families'. So-called normal life, he thought wryly, behind the walls of the city and throughout the world. What concern had any of these people for an ecumenical council of the Roman Catholic Church? What did they know of power politics within the Vatican, or care?

The Evangelium Christi faction had been quiet recently, really ever since the election of Celestine VI; perhaps they were biding their time. The rumors of their involvement in the assassination of Innocent XIV persisted, but investigators had published no proof of any such conspiracy; they had targeted the extremist Islamic rebels based in the Philippines and sought financial and ideological links with Arab terrorists of the Middle East and North Africa, and that avenue of investigation seemed to be paying off—anyhow, that is what they said publicly. Evangelium activity, though definitely anticouncil, was muted these days, on the surface at least. Only some of Cardinal Stalnaker's recent pronouncements indicated what the "party line" might be.

He turned off the main thoroughfare onto a quieter, more dimly lit side street several blocks from the Vatican, taking a familiar shortcut: He often walked about at night. Ahead, he heard a streetcar and knew he was close to home. There were fewer people about, and the city night noises, such as his own footsteps, became amplified in the darkness.

He worried about his friend and protégé, Jim Wiezevich though he was glad to have him in Rome, close by during this crucial precouncil phase. Wiezevich seemed distracted, troubled by something, and he was not sharing his problems with Calabrese, as he had in years past. Phil Calabrese remembered when Wiezevich had been involved with a young woman during his time at the North American College. How long ago? Twelve, no, fourteen years? Time flowed like the muddy Tiber through his memory—ever moving, relentless in its power to wash away the pain of history. What was left was memory as filtered by need, cleaner but less clear in the details. Still, he remembered Wiezevich's painful indecision, the natural, indeed beautiful, lure of the female animal. It had been a close call, and Calabrese now wondered whether the younger man's return to the city of his love had reawakened those old feelings.

I must talk to Jim, he noted on his crowded mental to-do list. Can't allow problems and distractions to erode his effectiveness in the important work we have to accomplish. There was so much work to do . . . and not enough time, not nearly enough.

Despite the crushing, overwhelming notion of impending failure, Philip Calabrese smiled, glad to be alive and at work in the vineyards of his Lord. What a unique and truly historic opportunity for him—for the Church—to be here, *right now*, as the apostolic ministry was poised to reform itself, to conform itself to the will of God as revealed by the Holy Spirit! Was he fooling himself to believe this, to believe that the Holy Father had been called like one of the prophets of old to lead the earthly kingdom to a new place? No, he knew in his mind and in his soul the rightness of Celestine's sacred mission.

We are instruments of God, working in His hands in this time and place: imperfect tools of his perfect, eternal will.

The saga of ecclesiastical history, including twenty-one previous general councils of the Church—which Calabrese and the
pope had studied and discussed at great length many, many
times—would now include the first great gathering of the Church
in this new century, a powerfully symbolic act in a new age of
history yet to be written. It was good sometimes to think of it in
these sweeping terms rather than to get bogged down in the daily
grind of details and disappointments, of human foibles and failures, including his own. Yes, Phil Calabrese thought with a
strange beatific smile that no one saw, we are writing a new chapter in the book of Christ's Church, to be read by generations yet
unborn to us but known intimately in the mind and heart of God.

Footsteps echoed dully in the heavy night-darkness. He
breathed in the ancient yet ever renewed air of the Roman summer and picked up his walking pace. The Holy Father needed him.
He must return to the pope's side this night of all nights, perhaps
to help persuade Celestine to submit immediately to the doctors'
urgings. Everything had been put in order so that the surgery
could proceed. It was now a matter of securing the stubborn pontiff's agreement and cooperation. Not an easy task for any of
them . . . but, at the sincere urging of Mulrennan's sister and
brother, Calabrese would apply his best efforts.

His smile faded as sensed a malevolent presence: the Evil One?
First, he quickly dismissed such a lugubrious, juvenile thought;
then he turned, instinctively protecting his back. He thought he
saw someone else walking in the street, ten yards or so behind
him; but the shadows of the buildings obscured the figure. There
were, however, the unmistakable *tap-taps* of footfalls within his
hearing, keeping pace with his own. He did not stop, and he
turned forward again, took longer strides to quicken his clip. The
next major street was not visible in the serpentine twist of the
narrow byway in which he found himself.

Calabrese turned again, saw the darkling figure—was it a man
or a woman?—in the indirect yellow light of a doorway. Most
definitely, the follower had increased speed and moved with purpose in the American priest's direction. There was nothing

friendly about this would-be encounter, Calabrese knew somehow.

Perversely, against his own better instinct, he stopped and turned to face the other; he braced himself for the encounter. If he was wrong, if the person was not following him, he would simply count himself foolish and embarrassed. It would not be the first time . . .

The figure moved quickly and efficiently toward the stationary Calabrese. The American now saw that it was a man, the face in shadows, about his own height and weight, wearing a dark suit. There was nothing particularly distinguishing or threatening about him. Calabrese did not recognize the face; he clenched and unclenched his fists, held his feet in place, though he wanted to run. What did the stranger want? He stopped about two yards from Calabrese, looked him directly in the face but said nothing. He breathed in the co-mingled odors of cologne and tobacco.

Philip Calabrese said, simply, "Yes?" He awaited an answer, at least some sign that the man had heard him. There was little in his face or eyes that Calabrese could read, except menace. No words were offered.

The stranger took another step forward, then another, until he stood within an arm's length of Calabrese. He lifted a small-caliber automatic pistol in his right hand, planted the barrel in the priest's chest, pushed it into the fabric of the black shirt several inches below the white celluloid strip of the clerical collar. Calabrese looked down, straining to see the gun, surprised, then understanding. The man pumped the trigger twice in quick succession. Two bullets ripped through Calabrese's chest. For an instant in the unknowable continuum of eternity, as he fell to the pavement into his own pooling blood, Philip Calabrese felt only pain and understood within his soul that his life in the earthly realm had ended.

CHAPTER FOURTEEN

The Vatican, August 1, 2003

Biagi and Tyrone met daily for a light breakfast in the Secretary of State's office, along with Cardinal Yenda, the dean of the College of Cardinals, titular of St. Sergius and St. Bacchas, bishop of the ancient suburbicarian diocese of Ostia, and former Archbishop of Kinshasa, Democratic Republic of Congo.

Paul Joseph Yenda, at eighty-seven, had been a cardinal since 1971, and a bishop since 1960; as such, he had attended the Second Vatican Council where he spoke and voted with the progressives and gained a reputation as a supporter of women's rights and an enemy of violent tribalism in African life. He had survived the Mobutu tyranny, when the nation was called Zaire, been exiled twice in the 1970s but returned to his see stronger and more beloved each time. It was his chief disappointment that in the Congo, and throughout central Africa, there had been few periods of peace and no real prosperity for the people during his lifetime; in recent years disease and famine had wiped out more than a quarter of the population, and political unrest had crippled the already feeble economic situation. Yenda had retired from the Kinshasa archdiocese to come to Rome to be near the heart of the Church he loved so much, and to be of service to his Holy Father and fellow cardinals; the pope had elevated him to the Order of Bishops among the cardinalate in 1987. As dean and senior member of the Sacred College, he was often called upon to perform ceremonial duties, which he executed with energy and alacrity that belied his advanced age. He had not been eligible as an elector in the recent conclaves, since he was well over eighty. The Cardinal Dean is the oldest by seniority of the Order of Bishops (not necessarily the oldest in the entire College). He consecrates the newly elected pope in the unlikely event, nowadays, that the pontiff has not already received episcopal consecration.

In this interregnum of papal illness, Yenda was valued for his wisdom, saintly presence—a stooped black figure with a halo of white hair beneath his scarlet zucchetto—and immensely practical, decades-long experience in ecclesiastical administration. He had no obvious agenda, no axes to grind, and there was no one in the Curia who did not respect him, as a survivor if nothing else.

He sat with the others, formidable churchmen in their own right, at a long polished table beneath a wide lead-mullioned window in a small room off the main offices of the Secretariat of State. The window was open to admit the warm air and noises from the piazza below. The three sipped coffee and ate little, as Father James Wiezevich briefed them on the pontiff's condition.

Wiezevich shared a paragraph that had been prepared by the Vatican press office, which would be distributed at ten A.M. Rome time, if the cardinals approved: "The Roman Pontiff is resting as comfortably as can be expected under properly prescribed sedation, feeding intravenously, and aware at most times of his surroundings. His vital signs are all with the normal range for a man of his age who has been in excellent health until recent weeks. The doctors have discussed with the Holy Father and his advisers the treatment options that are available, but no final decision has been reached regarding which course will be pursued. Twice-daily bulletins will continue until further notice."

The American priest was still getting accustomed to his new role, having replaced the late Philip Calabrese as interim secretary to the pope; it was the last thing on earth he had expected when he had come to Rome at Calabrese's insistence in the spring. His friend's murder had stunned him as badly as the losses in his own family had, years before. And it was still a tragic mystery who had killed him and why . . . though there was no doubt in Wiezevich's mind that it was politically motivated, directly related to the council. There had been no such "Vatican murder" for years, until the December killing of the Swiss Guard commandant, and now Calabrese. This, though, was different: the secretary to the pope, an American of sterling character with no skeletons in his closet (none that anyone had yet discovered in the intense, on-going police investigation), gunned down in the streets of Rome, just several hundred meters from the Vatican itself.

There had been no time to react, to mourn properly, to think about the consequences of his friend's death. Within a few days of the funeral, the body had been flown back to the States and the pope had entered the hospital. A pall, both literal and figu-rative, had fallen over the Apostolic Palace with the absence of the two men; Calabrese had been a presence of wit and American-style can-do attitude, as well as a canny, graceful behind-the-scenes operator—perhaps he possessed the same blood that had flowed in the veins of his Democratic Party politician-ancestors. He had been liked and respected by his fellow priests and staff throughout the Vatican. God, what a devastating loss, Wiezevich thought now and then, when he had a moment to breathe and think about anything.

"Father, do you think this is enough information for the hun-gry media today?" Yenda asked, unaware that the younger man's attention was fading in and out of the present moment. "This is virtually the same announcement as yesterday's."

"They want too much," Cardinal Tyrone growled, applying a patina of butter to a piece of bread.

"They need something to chew on," Biagi interjected, ever the diplomat. "I fear that if we do not give them information of sub-stance they will seek out or invent something—anything—to broadcast. They are insatiable."

"Yes, which is why I asked the question," the Cardinal Dean said, regarding Tyrone, the big Irishman, with an arched brow.

Wiezevich said, "To be honest, this is all there is to report. We would be inventing news ourselves if we were to elaborate beyond what is here. Also, the press office has cautioned us all along to limit the daily statements to just what we know. I realize that the Holy Father is big on full disclosure, but we are really doing that, as it is." He shrugged and looked from Yenda to Biagi to Tyrone.

The aged African prelate folded his hands beneath his chin and smiled like a holy gnome. "As long as the Holy Father's wishes are honored, I am satisfied that the Church is being well-served. But we must expect a less than generous, perhaps less than rational response from our brethren in the media."

"Jackals," Tyrone muttered darkly.

Biagi said, "Let the statement stand as it is—for today. But I believe we must formulate a different strategy very soon in anticipation of a backlash, as Cardinal Yenda has wisely suggested. Father Wiezevich, let's you and I meet with the press secretary later this morning, after the release of the statement. We will report back to their Eminences tomorrow morning, perhaps with a suggestion or two regarding this dilemma." He lifted a slice of cantaloupe on his fork. "Our charge is to feed the hungry—whether they be jackals or not." He placed the moist melon slice in his mouth.

As Jim Wiezevich observed the interactions among these three princes of the Church he was both amused and appalled. Is this how great men behaved during crises? How did he expect them to act? What would the Holy Father think if he could see them now? He would be more amused than appalled, Wiezevich thought, answering his own question.

Pope Celestine VI had learned of Monsignor Philip Calabrese's murder within a few hours of the event. The caribinieri had alerted the Swiss Guard, who in turn informed the pope's chief of security, Jack Rath. Then Rath and the new colonel of the Swiss Guard, Joachim Schraeder, awoke the pontiff at 12:47 A.M. to tell him the news.

"Holy Father," Rath had intoned, "your secretary has been murdered." The words that followed were unintelligible to the Roman Pontiff. "Holy Father . . ."

"Yes, Jack. He's dead. I heard that. Tell me again what happened." He then listened impassively to the colonel's recitation of the facts as they were known at the time. After, he did not sleep, but spent the night in prayer and sorrow.

In the morning the Holy Father himself had called Jim Wiezevich into his office, the first one-on-one meeting the priest had

ever had with Timothy Mulrennan—whether as archbishop or as
pope. It was a cool, cloudy day in Rome: There had been a brief
downpour in the very early hours, which had washed the murdered man's blood from the pavement where he had fallen. Jim
was excited and more than a bit awestruck at the summons. He
couldn't wait till he told Phil Calabrese about this! Of course,
Phil probably already knew what this was all about—he antici-
pated the pope's every move, practically his every thought. He
was good at his job. Celestine was fortunate to have a secretary
and adviser as sane and savvy as Calabrese among the political
sharks of the Curia crowd; Phil could give as good as he got—
and still not make many, if any, enemies in the process.

Wiezevich was certain that Calabrese knew all about him and
Demetra Matoulis, even though he had said nothing, not even
hinted at being aware of the affair—if that is what it could
even be called . . . Phil, in fact, made it his duty to know *everything* . . . which made Wiezevich uneasy. He already suffered
from a heavy burden of guilt. Perhaps Calabrese sensed that and
did not want to make it worse for his friend. But did the pope
know—somehow?

God, thank you for a friend like Phil Calabrese, Jim prayed
silently as he awaited his morning audience, and please let the
Holy Father be blind to my sins. No doubt payment would be
extracted from him for his violation of the promise of celibacy.
No need to impose upon the already overburdened pope with one
priest's shortcomings. Besides, he might be packed off back to
New Jersey if the relationship were exposed.

Calabrese had warned him of spies and malcontents in the
Curia Romana who lived for gossip and scandal. Like bureaucracies anywhere in the world, the Curia was a most fertile medium
for the growth of every human failing and foible: It was dark and
secretive and moist with the cold tears of men's sins, both committed and contemplated.

And where is Phil this morning? Wiezevich wondered. Usually
the American monsignor was at his desk before the pope, who
spent a significant time each morning at prayer and study. Off on
some secret mission, Jim Wiezevich surmised with an inner smile.

He was surprised when the pontiff himself appeared and invited him into the inner office. The pope wore an unusually solemn face.

"James, please sit here." Mulrennan indicated a comfortable leather chair that faced a spindly-legged desk of dark mahogany. The priest obeyed. "I wanted to tell you this myself," the pope said by way of explanation, which only confused and concerned Wiezevich even more.

"What is it, Your Holiness?" He looked into the man's eyes and saw the deep, dark pools of sorrow that they had become. Also, Pope Celestine did not look healthy, but drawn and ashen, with purplish blotches beneath his eyes and angles of emaciation on his face. "Is there something wrong? Have I—" His heart sank violently.

"No, Father, it isn't anything about you. In fact, I will need you to be even closer to me now—now that—" Celestine stood before the seated priest, his hands clasped tightly beneath the Celtic pectoral cross that hung on a gathered gold chain. "James, our friend Phil Calabrese was shot last night—killed. I don't know what else, how else to say—"

The shock sliced through Wiezevich's head like a buzz saw. Calabrese? Dead? Shot? How? Where? Why? Dear God, this could not be worse or more hurtful news . . . Phil—dead? Was it possible? "Holy Father, what happened?"

Pope Celestine told Wiezevich the few details that he knew. He painted a dark picture of the death of a man they both loved. Wiezevich could barely comprehend what he was hearing. "A man who lived in the neighborhood found Phil and called the police. Must have been within minutes of the shooting. Two bullets to the heart. Dead instantly. God rest his immortal soul—and damn whoever did this to him." It was a further shock to hear these harsh, condemning words on the lips of the Bishop of Rome. "I was the target, Jim. Calabrese was in the way. He was far easier to get at, but those bullets were really meant for me. They are sending me a message."

"What message, Holy Father? Is your life in danger, too?"

"It is about the council. Phil was instrumental in our preparations. He was doing a brilliant job of pulling the whole thing together. This was his punishment—and mine."

Now Father James Wiezevich faced these three powerful cardinals who were responsible for carrying on the business of the Holy See during the pope's incapacitation. He was still reeling from his friend's murder, yet he found the demands of his job strangely comforting. At least he had something to do every minute of every day. He had seen Demetra only once since Calabrese's death, and it had been an awkward, tense, inconclusive meeting between them. It was two days after the funeral mass, which the pope celebrated in his private chapel for the family and friends of the deceased; then they had flown the body back to New Jersey for a memorial service at the cathedral in Newark and burial in Jersey City.

Demetra had invited him to her apartment for a quiet dinner; when he arrived they made love, passionately, almost violently, and later sat down for a meal, which neither ate. They drank wine. They spoke little.

"What will you do now?" she asked, as he prepared to leave.

"The Holy Father has asked me to serve as his secretary for the interim. He can't really appoint someone permanently until after his surgery. I told him I am willing to stay on for as long as he needs me."

"Then it could become a permanent job for you," the woman said hopefully.

"Unlikely," he replied. "And I'm not sure I'd want to do it if he offered it to me. As much as I have liked being here, or did before Phil died, I don't think it's right for the long term." He had difficulty meeting her eyes, which were trained intently on him. "I just don't know, Demetra."

"Do you know whether you want to be with me?"

He paused for a seemingly long, awkward moment before he answered. "No—that is, I don't know. I'm being honest. I don't want to lie or pretend. I just don't know right now."

"You know that I don't have any expectations. I said that in the beginning. But I do want to know from day to day whether we are—whatever we are." She attempted to smile, but his discomfort stymied her. "I want to be with you, Jim. I like you—and I love you. We are good together. But at the same time I do not want to be a burden, a pain in the ass. I'm not proud of what we have done; I don't want you to give up your priesthood for me—the last thing in the world I would want. But if we're not going to be together, I have to know it."

"I understand," Jim Wiezevich said. "Please be patient. Give me some time to figure out what the hell I'm doing."

"You'll keep me informed? Daily news bulletin from the Vatican maybe?" Now she was able to smile, but felt the tears brimming hotly in her eyes. "Jim, I am so sorry about Phil Calabrese. I can see that it is very difficult for you, that he was a great friend. I'm so sorry for your loss. You need to put me on the shelf for a while, anyway. I accept that." She reached across the narrow table and put her hand on his arm. There were tears in his eyes, too.

The voice of the old African cardinal cut through Jim's remembrance of his last conversation with Demetra. "We must treat the press not as our enemy, but our friend. They can be most helpful to us, to the Church and the Holy Father. I do not advocate that we let them into the pontiff's recovery room, but perhaps we should feed them—selectively—with a bit more information than we have so far. They love their 'sources.' "

"Have you lost your mind, Yenda?" Tyrone blurted.

Wiezevich regarded Yenda quizzically, suddenly feeling very naked. Did he know something? The wily old man certainly had his own well-placed sources throughout the Vatican and the city. Had someone spotted Wiezevich with Demetra? Was he being followed? Then it struck him with the power of a lightning bolt: Had Calabrese been followed, targeted, eliminated with a purpose—as the pope had intimated—rather than randomly erased by a chance encounter with street violence? He had not allowed himself to follow that train of thought before, in sheer denial, he supposed. But Cardinal Yenda's allusion now was surely not coincidental. . . . Was it?

"His Eminence may be right," Jim said, stepping into the trap, if it was that. "We could target one or two reporters, quietly offer more background, perhaps allow them to look at the Holy Father's medical records, not to quote directly but to show them that we trust them with such sensitive material. They would in turn be grateful, perhaps cooperate with more enthusiasm. Is that what you meant, Your Eminence?" He addressed the African and monitored Tyrone's and Biagi's faces at the same time. They betrayed nothing.

"Yes, Father. You have correctly captured my essential point. Win them over to our side, a few at a time." The old man smiled dazzlingly, the white-yellow teeth and pink gums a stark contrast to his inky skin.

"Anyone in particular?" Wiezevich challenged, and he immediately regretted the question.

Biagi said, "This is the expertise of the press office. I shall discuss my Lord Cardinal's suggestion with Signore de Taillon at the earliest possible opportunity, today in fact, as I said before. As long as Cardinal Tyrone has no objection to this public relations tactic. We three must do nothing, take no actions unless we have substantial agreement among ourselves."

"I don't like any of it," the Irishman said, his bile apparent to all. He contemplated a long unlit cigar in his big hand, tapped it against the tabletop. "But you know what you're talking about, you two politicians. I'll go along with your judgment on this."

Wiezevich sat back, relieved, as the three princes decided who would visit the pontiff first. Biagi got the assignment, as he most often did. Both the others would go to the hospital in the afternoon. They did not conduct any business with the recovering man but monitored his condition and gave him some spiritual comfort and assurance. Like any man, he needed the support and presence of friends and colleagues. Wiezevich had seen him only once, and he had been unconscious at the time, several hours after the surgery.

The surgeons had removed more, but could not attack the main body of the tumor because it had more or less fused with the lower spine. When he was stronger the pope would begin a renewed regime of chemotherapy and physical therapy to recover use of the muscles that had been damaged during surgery. Weeks, months of pain and uncertainty lay ahead for the Servant of the Servants of God.

"We shall hear from Cardinal Vennholme today," Biagi added. "He has prepared a report on the situation in China and sent it via a diplomatic courier who will arrive at Aeroporto Leonardo da Vinci soon." He consulted his watch, a huge gold-encrusted marvel that lay between his snow-white formal French cuff and dark brown skin. "Within two hours. Let us reconvene at three P.M. Gentlemen, go with God this day."

The American priest rose, gathered his leather-bound planner and file folder of papers. He faced another full day of meetings and phone calls as the planning for the ecumenical council continued, despite the papal disability. Cardinal Biagi put a firm hand on his arm as he started to leave, indicating that he should stay put. Biagi escorted the two cardinals from his office suite and returned to Wiezevich.

"Father," he said, "do not let Cardinal Yenda or Cardinal Tyrone throw you off balance. I could sense that our most revered dean has more information than he is sharing with us. Do you have the same feeling? Does he in fact know something that would be important for me to know about as well?" His brown gaze penetrated Wiezevich's skull. "My son, I suggest that we have no secrets from each other. We may be able to help one other in some way."

"Yes, Your Eminence, I understand." Wiezevich faced a difficult decision and wished his good friend Philip Calabrese was available to advise him . . . but he was dead. What did the cardinal want? What did he know already? He considered Biagi one of the "good guys," trustworthy and loyal to the pope. But he avoided a direct answer; he would have to consider what to share with the Secretary of State, what to withhold. "I don't know what Cardinal Yenda has in mind. Do you think he has an agenda?"

Biagi laughed, a melodious bark. "The old man always has an agenda. I am not saying it is negative or destructive in any way, but it is his alone. He has perfected his survival techniques over many years. Perhaps he is bluffing. I'll not press you about it, Father Wiezevich. But I am available to you if you wish to share anything or seek advice. I want you to succeed in your work. So does the Holy Father."

In a split-second, James Wiezevich made a decision. Instead

of leaving, he paused, turned, and said to Leandro Biagi: "May I make my confession to you, Eminence?"

"Certainly, my son." But Biagi sensed the import of the moment, saw the uncertainty in the younger priest's eyes. "Are you certain you wish to do this? I will keep the seal of the confessional inviolate, because as a minister of Christ I must. But if this is something you do not wish someone in my—well, in my position, to know . . . if it is politically sensitive, let us say."

"I trust you," Wiezevich said. "I have to trust someone since Phil Calabrese is gone. It seems less important now, but I cannot carry it within myself, alone."

"Come, sit." Cardinal Biagi guided him to a comfortable chair at the far side of the room, beneath a tall, north-facing window that was half open. The cardinal sat in another chair directly facing the penitent. He magically produced a thin purple stole from one of the voluminous pockets of his simar, kissed the gold cross imprinted upon it and placed it around his neck. "I am listening," he said and leaned forward toward Jim Wiezevich.

The priest, who was used to confessing to fellow priests, local friends and colleagues, felt awed and intimidated by the presence of the cardinal-secretary of state but tried to wash those reservations and implications from his mind, to open his heart to God and His only begotten Son. What did it matter who sat in the chair opposite or in the confessional box? It was Jesus to whom the sinner released his sins and secrets, not to a man. The human minister was only the medium through which the sacred transaction, the sacrament of reconciliation, was accomplished.

Biagi closed his eyes and offered a benediction in whispered Latin and made a small sign of the cross over Wiezevich's head with two fingers. He touched his right ear with the same fingers, indicating that Jim should start, his eyes still closed. His bald head smelled faintly of cologne and tobacco, the residual of Cardinal Tyrone's heavy smoking during their meeting.

"Bless me, Father," the American began, "in this confession of sin. It has been about three weeks since my last confession. But at that time I did not tell all of my sins, especially the one that I offer up now to God, begging His forgiveness. Father—Your Eminence—I have broken my sacred promise of chastity."

As he spoke, he felt the weight of his guilt and sorrow melt from him. The burden lifted, but the love for Demetra remained. How could this be? He wondered, as he continued: "I have slept with a woman several times since I came to Rome. She is someone I knew when I was a seminarian here, before I was ordained to the priesthood. I loved her—in fact, I still love her and respect her with all my heart. I—I have needed her. She is a good person, a loving and sincere person. I believe she needed me in her life, perhaps she still does.

"She is a good person, and I think she loves me. She will be very hurt if I end our relationship."

Biagi said, "But you know this is the correct thing—the only thing—to do, to stop being with her. If you were not a priest, it is obvious, it would be different. But we priests are called to sacrifice so much of ourselves to Christ, for His sake."

"I am having difficulty understanding the morality of that sacrifice, Your Eminence. I have lived as a celibate for my entire priesthood, until I came back to Rome. I have thought of only one woman during that time, but I never expected to see her again. Why would God bring her back into my life now, and me into hers, if we are not supposed to be together?"

"These mysteries we are not given to understand. And I do not say that to be glib, Father. We must sometimes simply accept that which befalls us and not be too disappointed when we do not understand why. This is the price of being human—and we priests are human first, ministers second—God Himself made us that way and knows that we will often fail to live up to his hopes and expectations for us."

He heard himself justifying his actions and stopped, refocused on his immediate purpose, to confess his sin. "I knew it was wrong—for both of us—yet I continued. Until Phil's death I fully intended to continue until—until I don't know when." Why am I saying this? Dear God, please take this cup from me and guide me back into Your arms. "For this sin and all the sins of my past life, especially for breaking my sacred vow to God, I am truly sorry."

For a moment Cardinal Biagi was silent, sitting still and expectantly like a flesh-and-blood Rodin, revealing nothing of what he was thinking. He is good at that, Wiezevich thought. The cardinal from Florence, the product of a dozen generations of political and ecclesiastical breeding, was the most comfortable fit with the pope and the Curia imaginable. But was he the one to whom this American parish priest ought to confess his most severe transgressions? Now, having done just that, only time would reveal the rightness of it.

"My son, I have heard your confession of sin and I know that God has heard you, as well. He hears our every breath, tastes our every tear. He has revealed Himself to us in the Word, speaks to us in the Gospel and through the teachings of the Holy Church. You know all this, yet you are as fallible and sinful as any man— as I am. Do you truly grasp the gravity of your sin, James?"

"I do, Your Eminence." He could not yet meet Biagi's gaze directly. "I am sorry and wish to change. This is very difficult for me, however. I love the woman. My feelings are genuine, and hers are too. We are good together. . . ."

"You have a reservation," Biagi said. "You must give it up to God and turn away from sin. Your very priesthood is at stake, and your immortal soul. You must not see her for a time. Do you understand and accept this?"

"I know. I know."

"You must promise," Biagi said, not harshly but firmly.

"Yes, I will give up this sin. I will speak to her, tell her we cannot be together any more. I understand. I am not a child, though I feel like one, a stupid, erring boy."

"You're God's child, but you are not stupid, Father—only human. And I understand how difficult it is. I don't underestimate the pain and hurt you are feeling, believe me."

Biagi asked Wiezevich to make a sincere Act of Contrition. He bowed his head to listen.

"O my God, I am heartily sorry for having offended Thee, and I detest all my sins, because of Thy just punishments, but most of all because they offend Thee, my God, Who art all good and deserving of all my love. I firmly resolve, with the help of Thy grace, to sin no more and to avoid the near occasions of sin. Amen."

How many times had he received those same words from penitents, like himself, from men and women and youngsters who were making their very first act of penance? The words spilled from his mouth, and he listened to himself as he sincerely prayed for forgiveness. He meant every word, and yet the magnitude of his commitment, to himself and to God, crushed him like a huge boulder.

"You are absolved in the name of the Father, the Son, and the Holy Spirit. Go, my son, and sin no more. Trust God and turn from the temptations of the flesh." Biagi again made the sign of the cross over Jim Wiezevich, who, head bowed, touched his forehead, breast, and shoulders in response.

He had sought God's grace in the holy sacrament of penance; he had sought God's forgiveness through this act of expiation and the promise to amend his ways, but he did not truly feel that he had connected with the Father. He did still have a reservation in his pocket, was unwilling to let go completely of his feelings for Demetra . . . but he said nothing.

Cardinal Biagi extended his hand and Father Wiezevich took it, bent to kiss the ring. He felt hypocritical and afraid.

"Dear Father," Biagi said, "know that you have done the right thing in the eyes of God."

Vienna, July 20, 2003

"It is so very good of you to see me on such short notice."

"I was intrigued by your message. I had no idea we were related—and I am pleased to learn of this. You are well known and respected among the leadership of the Evangelium movement, especially by Cardinal Vennholme, who is my dear friend."

"He suggested I meet with you after—that is, when he had departed for China. Did he speak to you, then?"

"The good cardinal and I speak often. And he sent me the documentation of our kinship. He is very thorough, our friend and mentor." Stalnaker smiled: a slash across his narrow face. "He sees farther ahead and more deeply than most of us, do you not agree?"

"He has carried me through some very difficult times of late, shared his insight into my soul and the souls of others. Yes, he has the prophetic gift, I think. It has been frustrated by circumstance, however—and by the Holy Father. Cardinal Vennholme knows that this council, as envisioned by the pope, is a terrible mistake. I cannot but agree with him."

"You are in a unique position, as a layman, to aid those of us who wish to prevent this terrible error from occurring. You understand what I am saying, Arturo?"

"Yes, Your Eminence."

Did Cardinal Stalnaker know the extent of Wilderotter's "aid" and involvement thus far? Should I share *everything* with him? Arturo wondered. He decided to restrain his tongue for now and let the conversation unfold; he did not yet know Stalnaker well enough to trust him fully. God would lead him to the correct decision, as He always did.

"I regret that we do not have Henry's presence at this critical time. The Holy Father is still very ill, but recovering, thanks be to God. I, of course, wish him health and a full recovery. I pray for him, and for our Holy Catholic Church, each day. You have just come from Rome—what did you learn there?"

"I was only there overnight, just for a stopover, really, before coming here. I have been traveling a lot, of late, and hear the same thing everywhere: discontent, dissatisfaction with the pope and his call to council. There is the unspoken hope that he may become too ill to proceed. I hesitate to mention that, but . . ."

"We may be frank with each other," Stalnaker said. "The Evangelium Christi movement is united in its opposition to the council. We help each other in many ways, large and small—just as you and I are doing now. By the way, have you heard that the pope's secretary was killed last night? I heard it on the early news broadcast this morning. It is a shame—probably a street hoodlum—a terrible accident, which could not come at a worse time for the pope himself, ill as he is."

"I know. I heard something about it at the Evangelium Christi house but have not seen the newspaper yet. He was an American?"

"Yes. There are far too many Americans in his office as it is.

I was afraid of this, as were many of the bishops. The cardinals were too easily swayed by Biagi, too sentimental in their choice in the conclave. I suppose we must live with it . . . especially after the shocking assassination of Pope Innocent. The Church cannot afford another such upheaval."

"No, Eminence. We would lose credibility in the eyes of the world, I think, if we lost another pope so soon after—it would be like the Dark Ages all over again. But disease might take him from us instead—prematurely."

"If that is God's will, we must accept it. I will now be one of the electors who will have to choose the next Holy Father. I pray that there will not be another conclave for a while, at least."

"Please, Your Eminence, I look to you for guidance. Tell me what I can do. I am very troubled by what I have learned about my father, as well as what is happening within the Church. Cardinal Vennholme said that he would share my dilemma with you, and that perhaps you would have some direction for me, especially since we now know that we're cousins, blood relations."

"I am not certain what I can do, except listen and be a friend. It may help you to tell me what is in your mind. We can become confidants, if you like. We should spend some time together, get to know each other. Tell me about your family."

Wilderotter was relieved at the change of subject, even though in his mind there were still a lot of blanks to be filled in; he began to sketch the details of his family life and watched his tea grow cold in his lap.

Stalnaker's thin, angular face turned slowly like a satellite dish receiving signals from distant space; from the side, his head seemed wide and flat and gray, his ears large and flat. All the time his dark eyes remained locked like radar on Arturo, even as he sipped his tea and replaced the cup on its saucer.

"My work keeps me away from my wife and children, perhaps half the year. Sometimes my mind strays from them, even when I am about God's work with my Evangelium friends. I am a man with flaws and failings, Eminence, but I want to do right, to serve my Lord and Savior and His people. I just pray that my sins may be accounted against my good works on the day of judgment. I spoke to my family last night, and they are well. I ask God with my whole being for their health and happiness."

"He hears your prayers, my friend, and answers them. This we can know with a certainty, and for this we thank Him," Cardinal Stalnaker said. "I have prepared a statement that calls for an indefinite postponement of the council. So far, I have the endorsement of twenty fellow cardinals and thirty or more bishops. The total numbers are not great, but I have had to limit the distribution of my draft letter for the sake of confidentiality. And I must trust you, Arturo, likewise to remain silent about this—even among our friends in the Evangelium fraternity."

"I shall, Eminence, without question."

"The pope is ill. His secretary is dead. He has not made clear, to my satisfaction and others', the need for a general council at this time. He, in fact, has every right to convoke a council, but the bishops also have the right—and the duty—to express themselves in this matter. The bishops represent the teaching authority of the Church, and the cardinals are the Roman Pontiff's chief advisers and ministers. These sacred colleges, therefore, may guide and correct the pope in a brotherly fashion—for his good and for the welfare of the entire Church."

"What if he does not respond to your corrective effort?"

Stalnaker closed his eyes for a moment, then answered: "God will show him the way, as He always has."

"But God needs our help. We are His soldiers," Wilderotter said, his jaw clenched. What would Hans Hermann Wilderotter, née Braum, think of him now? How would his father judge what he had done and what he was prepared to do as a "soldier" of the Church? He prayed that both his earthly and heavenly fathers would know that in his mind and soul he was a righteous son. "We are His sons, unworthy of His grace."

"My friend—my new friend and cousin," the Austrian cardinal intoned, "I abjure you not to take upon yourself the burden of history. If you are His soldier, then you must learn to be humble and to obey the Lord's captains and generals. Neither you, nor I, nor any one man can reverse the tide of history. We can, and must, each do his part in the great work of preserving the

Gospel and the Holy Church. But you have already done so much as an active lay leader in the Evangelium Christi." Stalnaker grimaced, his face a tortured mask of mingled authority and sympathy. "I ask you only for your prayers, Arturo. Now you must tell me, what do you wish of me?"

CHAPTER FIFTEEN

Rome, August 19, 2003

Timothy John Mulrennan, the Vicar of Christ on Earth and Servant of the Servants of God, sat up in his bed in the papal suite of the Gemelli Hospital and gingerly swung his long legs around so that his bare feet touched the carpeted floor. He winced at the pain in his lower back and felt weak, sapped of physical energy and helpless as a baby. The oxygen mask and the needles in his left arm tugged him back so that he could not rise from his bed, only enjoy briefly this first attempt at independent movement. He knew it was an artificial moment, that within just a few minutes he would be flat on his back again, receiving the ministrations of the nurses and physicians who had brought him this far—quite a remarkable distance—in his recovery. The pain was sometimes so intense that it sharpened his every sense; he would soon be given his morning dose of medication to ease the pain and dull his perceptions. He was immensely grateful for such care but also resentful that he was periodically robbed of his full capacity to think and feel.

His sister Katie and brother Stephen would leave today for the States; he looked forward to seeing them later in the morning. It was still very early in the morning and no one was in the room with him; the nurses were changing shifts and conferring outside the door where the security men stood guard. The rising sun touched the rim of the city and the treetops, slid surreptitiously through the east windows. He reveled in the sight, the hint of God's ever-presence in the world, and bowed his head.

Dear Heavenly Father, he prayed, half aloud, I thank you for the gift of life this day. I am conscious of Your sacred presence, even through the pain and difficulties that I face. Shine the light of Your grace upon me in my sickness and my responsibilities, please be with the people who love Your Word as they go about their duties this day, seeking to obey Your commandments. Help us in our failures and doubts, for we have them in abundance. Be with those who are ill and dying and those who died last night, in this place of healing and throughout the world. Most especially I pray for the repose of the soul of your servant Father Philip Calabrese, my friend and fellow servant of Christ. Bless him and his family and friends; he died for You, too young and full of so much life, blessed with so many gifts and talents. Help me to put aside my anger and suspicion about his death. Father, I pray for my enemies, although I choose no man to be my enemy, that they may know Your love and righteousness, that they may not harm Your Church in their zeal to do right. Amen.

He looked up, took a deep oxygenated breath through the plastic mask. Although he said mass each day, it was difficult, abbreviated, awkward in his condition. Usually just one priest, Father Wiezevich, and a nurse or a doctor were present, concerned primarily that he not overexert himself in the effort.

The pontiff kept some of his Vatican II readings close by his bedside, dipping into them when he was able, rereading the council documents in Latin and English. He also remembered his own role, as a priest and young pastor, in implementing the decrees of the council under the guidance of his archbishop. He remembered that at the time, a commonplace saying among both clergy and laity was "Nothing has changed, even though things will never be the same again." This was true because the movement of "updating" and "renewal" by the council fathers touched upon Scriptural, liturgical, ecclesiastical, and ecumenical issues but the Church's precious and fundamental deposit of faith was not touched or altered, nor had Pope John intended that it be diluted or disturbed in any way.

Had the Church continued to move toward its mission to carry the Gospel message to all nations and to serve the faithful members of the Body of Christ? Had the priests and bishops really become consultors and coservants with the pope in response to

the needs of the faithful and the direction of the Holy Spirit? Were
the faithful throughout the world receiving the attention and
nourishment they required as children of God?

These questions and concerns troubled him deeply. He knew
both directly and from his well-developed intuition that the opposition to his council was a dangerous fault line in the landscape
of the Church that might tear open at any moment and shift the
very ground upon which he trod, already with much difficulty.
Opponents of the council were constantly at work, sub rosa, to
subvert the very legitimacy of the gathering.

Could he classify these who worked against him as enemies
of the Church? No. If there was room for and encouragement of
pluralism of thought and activity within the modern Church, then
anyone was free to express an opinion in contradiction to the
Holy Father on such an issue. Why, then, did he feel the personal
hurt and discouragement at some of the debate that raged even
within his own hearing? From Tyrone, Vennholme, Stalnaker,
and others. He was aware that within Evangelium Christi, the
semisecret lay organization that had been a personal prelature of
a previous pontiff, and which Timothy Mulrennan had opposed
for most of his life as a priest, were men and women actively
working and praying for the council not to happen, for the pope
to fail. Could he fault their motives? They were convinced that
they were right, that the Holy Spirit was directing them to act in
this way as a matter of conscience. How could it be convincingly
demonstrated that they were wrong?

Pope Celestine sat on the edge of his hospital bed, his bare
legs dangling, awaiting the reappearance of a nurse who would
upbraid and fuss over him. He felt very much like a boy who was
home sick in bed, missing a day of school—which in fact he had
been, a long time ago: nearly sixty years. And he thought of his
mother and how she had cared for him the best way she knew,
even when she struggled with the alcoholism that had eventually
destroyed her and torn apart the family. He had felt her love and
her pain; she had shared both with him, even as a very young boy
on those days when he had a cold or stomachache that kept him
home from school, eating hot soup and taking naps throughout

the seemingly endless day . . . a rare day with his mother, a day like no other in his life. There was no one present to see him smile, as the plastic of the mask bit into his cheeks, no one to see him wince in agony at every slight movement of his body.

He heard their voices through the barely ajar security door that otherwise completely muffled sound from the outside, but he could not make out specific words. His surgeon was due at eight A.M., the oncologist an hour later, the physical therapist an hour after that, then at eleven o'clock there would be a bedside meeting with Biagi, Tyrone, and Min. Perhaps Cardinal Yenda would stop by later. Jim Wiezevich would be in and out all morning with news bulletins and council planning updates and a million small items that the pope wanted to know about, even though there was damn-all he could do about any of it in his current, rather helpless and hopeless position.

Slowly and painfully he pulled his legs back onto the bed and repositioned himself with his head propped up, the intravenous lines more relaxed and dripping properly. He became even more acutely aware of the throbbing pain of his lower back and legs, wanted to cry out for help, for relief, but bit his tongue. Then he felt thirst, a deep, ravaging, sandy-mouth thirst for water or any-thing liquid. The thirst overwhelmed the pain. Thank you, God, he prayed in acknowledgment of the mysterious ways of the hu-man body to cope *in extremis*. He almost laughed at the absurdity of his situation, at the ultimate powerlessness of the human body that he was experiencing at this moment.

But isn't that the way I've always been, the way we all are? he mused. Since those days in my mother's womb, through the chilling hours in Berlin and Vietnam and Newark when my life was worth less than a thimbleful of spit and could have been instantly lost had I made the wrong move at the wrong time with-out knowing it.

Who knows for certain what is the "right time" for any action or decision? Like this surgery that I stubbornly (the other said) postponed for two weeks. Was that the right thing to do, the right time to do it? If we try our best to work with the Holy Spirit, to seek His guidance in all we do, chances are, He will help us master the timing—and other—problems in our lives.

Newark, New Jersey, October 10, 1994

On the day of his installation as the fifth Archbishop of Newark, Timothy John Mulrennan felt as if he were swimming in a lake of inadequacy, with no view of the shore and safety. It was a feeling not unfamiliar to him when he faced a new assignment in the Church, perhaps the equivalent of stage fright, he thought. How many times, since his training as an altar boy some five decades earlier to his first parochial assignment to his elevation to the cardinalate as head of a prefecture of the Roman Curia, only a few years before, had he known this ache of fear and anticipation? Familiar, yes, but this time mixed with the similarly overwhelming notion of a return home, which he had secretly craved but had been certain would never happen . . . so much had conspired to take him away from this place: study, ambition, searching, fate—or Providence, if you will. Now the Holy Father had called him to serve *here*, in this place that Mulrennan had always thought of as a place marked by holiness, set apart by the singular devotion of the Catholic people and others of different faiths. He knew that there was a tincture of pride and self-absorption in such an unhumble view of his hometown and the surrounding counties that comprised the archdiocese. In his heart he had hoped, but never dared express aloud his desire, to return to his birthplace. In fact, it was highly unusual for such an appointment of a native son—unlike the olden days—for usually the pope and his advisers, of whom Tim Mulrennan had been one, eschewed considerations of personal preference and local and priestly sentiment, opting for what was best, in their view, for the Church as a whole.

So, the old man in his inimitable, pontifical way, had surprised Mulrennan, the people of the Church of Newark, and the college of bishops (some of whom had waged fierce sub-rosa efforts—through sponsors and surrogates—to win the prestigious metropolitan see).

Paul Luke Garrison, now aged seventy-eight, three years beyond the mandatory retirement age for bishops—mandatory, that is, to submit one's resignation, discretionary on the part of the Supreme Pontiff whether or when to accept—had finally been granted the reprieve he sought after twenty-one years in the archiepiscopal chair. He had been a dynamic, pastoral, energetic, sometimes controversial archbishop, and he loved the job—but bad health had slowed him recently: Arthritis in both hips and knees occasionally crippled him, kept him bedridden and in horrible pain. He was scheduled for surgery as soon as the new man had taken over, then recovery, therapy, and his first long vacation in more than a quarter century. Still, like nearly any man in such a position of authority, Garrison did not enjoy the idea of relinquishing the pallium of a metropolitan, nor the dignity and prerogatives of an ordinary. He had never expected to live to this age, nor to face retirement, emeritus status.

Paul Garrison sat in a wide, deeply cushioned chair in the archbishop's office in the chancery—his domain for these many years. Tim Mulrennan had been a priest of the diocese, under Garrison's care and supervision, long ago. Now Mulrennan, his successor, sat in a comfortable leather chair and nursed a cup of coffee, under the older man's owlish gaze.

Garrison was five-eleven and two hundred sixty pounds, which only contributed to his physical woes; his priests and fellow bishops chided and encouraged him to lose some of that weight. Archbishop Garrison, however, religiously ate a quart of ice cream at midnight or so every night of the year except during Lent or holy day fasts. It was his great, secret vice—or not so secret, thanks to some of the more gossipy diocesan clergy. His gray eyes blazed, undimmed by age or infirmity, behind thick eyeglasses (now trifocals), and bushy white brows tufted menacingly above the rims. Pinkish jowls quivered above a seemingly too-tight Roman collar, and his massive football-tackle shoulders often seemed to fill an entire room. When he stood he was a great obsidian square topped by a large pink and white ball—his head. Always, Tim had noted decades earlier, his black shoes were immaculate, gleaming, polished, perfectly tied—always. Mulrennan could not remember ever seeing this bear of a bishop in mufti, anything other than black priestly garb, with a starched and pressed, French-cuffed shirt beneath the black, square-cut jacket. His pectoral cross, though, was often slung almost casually into a breast pocket to keep it out of the way of his own darting hands and quick, almost jerky movements when speaking. Subdued now by time, the physical presence of Paul Garrison was nonetheless still quite powerful, even sitting with a porcelain coffee cup and saucer perched daintily on one ham-sized, black-clad thigh.

"We're not in bad shape, you know, financially—not the way we were when I took over. There were accounts payable squirreled away in every desk drawer in the chancery, dating back years. And damn few accounts receivable, I'll tell you, except from deadbeat parishes who borrowed like drunken sailors from the old archbishop. He thought of himself as the Lord's banker, I suppose. Nearly bankrupted the diocese, I'll tell you." He paused and looked at Mulrennan over the tops of his glasses. "I guess I'm the 'old archbishop' now, and one day you'll be telling stories on me, eh?"

"Never, Your Excellency," Tim Mulrennan said.

"Liar. You don't have to be a politician with me, Timothy, my boy. We all do it—we all find our own way of doing things." Garrison laughed, a seal's high-pitched bark. "God only knows what the priests and the auxiliaries say about me now. I tell you I love them—they may not know it, but I love them as my own children."

"I think they know it, Archbishop. How could they not?"

It was true, Garrison had a sterling reputation among his priests and his curia, among the religious and lay staff of the diocese as well. He could be remote at times, even demigodlike, and his volcanic temper was legendary. But if he was wrong or had ill-used anyone, he was quick to realize his error and to apologize—to go to extremes to make up for bad behavior. And with his priests, most especially, he controlled his natural New England sternness with gentleness and compassion. They knew it. They felt it, without question.

"Well, they don't show their love and appreciation all that much," Garrison said. "And they are a decidedly bad-mannered bunch, I'll give them that."

"Now, that gives me something to worry about. Coming in among the barbarians."

"Could be that I'm a stickler for discipline and proper Church protocol," the older man admitted.

"Yes, I've heard that about you." Mulrennan knew that for days after, Garrison would still be grousing about some perceived slight—a door not held open, a casual hello in the archdiocesan offices, a necktie pulled down and shirt opened during working hours. But the old archbishop was less concerned about his person and his own feelings than about the sacred office that he represented. He believed that there was a proper order to things in God's universe, and that an archbishop had a certain status in that scheme that ought to be recognized for what it was.

"Now they won't know what to do with me, being retired and all that. Oh, don't worry, I'll fade away fast—that's my main job now, to stay out of your hair!"

"I'll want to call on you for advice. I hope you'll be available for me."

"Certainly. But I'm under no illusion that you'll actually take any of my advice. You need to make your own judgments, and your own mistakes. That's how you'll learn."

Mulrennan had been bishop of a diocese for nearly ten years, in Jackson City, Missouri, in what seemed like a different age of mankind—and as a different person himself. Before he had been called to Rome to serve in the Curia, he had faced all the horrible headaches and the incalculable rewards of being a bishop, a chief shepherd and teacher among a Christian community out there, a thousand miles away. He clung to memories, good, bad, bittersweet, of those days; and he still missed many of his friends and colleagues from that time and place: he missed his dearest friend, Rachel, though he could conjure her image, her very presence, wherever he went. . . .

He forced himself to push the image and the memories aside, to respond to Garrison. He said, "I hope to surprise you, Your Grace. Not by my mistakes—there'll be plenty of them, I'm sure—but when I come to you for counsel."

"You want some more coffee? I do. Got to stay awake for this hoopla today—we're talking three hours, at least."

It was almost noon, and Tim had already taken an early morning walk before mass, revised and rehearsed his homily, met with visiting ecclesiastical dignitaries, which included four American cardinals and the papal nuncio, and now he felt ready for a nap! He stayed for more coffee and more time with this man whom he so much respected and admired. If he could be half as good—even one quarter—he'd be immensely satisfied with his own performance in the job.

The night before, Garrison had hosted a celebratory dinner for the cardinals—from Boston, Philadelphia, Baltimore, Washington, D.C. (the man from New York had begged off, citing prior commitments)—at which the conversation had ranged from President Clinton's woeful political standing to the upcoming national bishops' conference to the baseball playoffs, just begun. This was an elite group of churchmen: all highly educated, multilingual, politically connected, managerial, and each a genuinely faithful and orthodox priest of God, loyal to the pope and to his policies, or else supremely skilled in blurring any overt differences or disagreements.

Sixty bishops were expected to participate in the installation ceremony, an unusually large number because many were coming in from the Midwest where Mulrennan had been a popular colleague, others from New Jersey, Pennsylvania, New York, Connecticut, even as far away as Maryland and West Virginia. Significantly, Mulrennan was to inherit four auxiliary bishops who had been appointed by Garrison, each with a regional responsibility for one of the four counties of the archdiocese: Essex, Bergen, Union, and Hudson. Newark was geographically the smallest archdiocese in the United States, but easily the most diverse in terms of racial, ethnic, and national categories—though the old-line Irish and Italian groups still dominated the local church, culturally if not numerically. About one third of the Catholic population spoke Spanish, nearly another third some language other than English: Creole, Korean, Polish, Ibo, Chinese, Portuguese, among others. The liturgy of the Eucharist, which would be celebrated on this special occasion, would feature prayers and intercessions in several languages, and the liturgy committee had promised to be creative with the music and other aspects of the installation service. Mulrennan had traditional tastes in liturgy—post–Vatican II, yes, but not too far out . . . so it would be interesting to see what they had cooked up for him today. He had decided not to worry about it—nothing he could do at this point.

"I will offer this gratuitous morsel of advice, if you'll allow," Garrison said when both their coffee cups were refilled and steaming. His lips skinned back for just a second in a fleeting smile, exposing strong white teeth that contrasted to his pink New Englander's face. "Take your priests into your heart, but be a stern father to them. If you don't they'll run you down and wear you out; they're good men, but they need a strong hand to guide them. And there are a hell of a lot more of them than there are of you. If you have the priests doing their jobs well in the parishes and in the schools, the laypeople will follow. If the priests are not unified and reading from the same page, the laity get nervous; even if they don't like what they're hearing in the pulpit, at least it is consistent and true to the faith. As teacher and overseer here, you must get out in front of the band—and stay there."

"You recommend Professor Henry Hill as my model?" Mulrennan interjected. He had, in fact, seen *The Music Man* at least two dozen times in various productions around the country, and he owned a well-used copy of the videotape.

"I don't care if you're liberal, conservative, or communist, just be what you are and be consistent." Garrison ignored Tim's attempt at levity. "The priests and the people crave consistency—they can deal with it, and they respond to it. I tried to be nice, for a while, but not for long."

Before Timothy Mulrennan could reply, the telephone on the archbishop's desk rang. He hesitated, but Garrison said, with relish, "It's all yours now, baby."

"Yes, Mulrennan here," Tim greeted, answering the phone.

Although the story he heard from the speaker was more than a bit convoluted, the bottom line was that the Washington, D.C.–based apostolic nuncio to the United States, Archbishop Aloisio Achille Manzi, the pope's representative at the installation, was nowhere to be found. He had been due at Newark's Pennsylvania Station, where cops had repeatedly scoured the premises. But, so far, no sign of Archbishop Manzi—and thus the formal proceeding of reading and examination of the papal mandate for the archbishop's appointment could not take place. Stunned but also bemused by the turn of events, Mulrennan consulted his watch: two hours before the start time for the ceremony. He needed to be prepped and vested very soon himself; he could not be late and set the wrong tone for his new archiepiscopal administration . . . and over the years he had become a stickler for punctuality in his diocese in Jackson City and his curial office in the Vatican.

He knew Manzi, liked him, wondered where he could be. He said a quick prayer; then, to the retired archbishop: "Paul, we're missing one papal nuncio. Are you hiding him?"

"No, I don't know where the sonofabitch is," Garrison replied gruffly. "Maybe he went AWOL. We can hope."

"Don't say that. He has to install me—otherwise you'll be stuck here forever."

"He'll turn up," the old bishop said. "And if he doesn't, we'll figure out some way to get the job done. I'm retired, remember?" He smiled again, a quick flash of teeth, this time with genuine relief and gratitude.

Just as the lengthy procession was to begin, about thirty minutes before the formal meeting at the doors of the cathedral, where the old archbishop received the new, a taxicab pulled up at the curb a block from the cathedral and out came the papal nuncio, Archbishop Manzi, alone, carrying a garment bag and a briefcase. The security detail scrambled toward him, nearly carrying him up the cathedral steps and around the side of the building where the priests and bishops were lined, awaiting the start of the grand spectacle. They hustled him into the chancery lobby where the new man, fully vested in a white and gold miter, greeted him with open arms and a smile.

"Aloisio, where have you been?"

"Metropark, Your Excellency. My secretary must have purchased the wrong ticket. The conductor removed me from the train, even though I told him I was going all the way to Newark. I didn't know where I was at first, except that I was in New Jersey." He responded to the nervous laughter from the gathered staff. "I am, I hope, aren't I?"

"You are, and you better get vested quickly, we're ready to rock and roll."

"Here," the Italian archbishop said, holding out the taxi receipt. "Where will I receive repayment for this?"

Mulrennan himself laughed at the sight of the somewhat befuddled priest-diplomat presenting the scribbled chit. "I'll see that it is taken care of immediately, Your Excellency." He took the receipt himself and slipped it in his pocket, within the folds of the elaborate vestments that he wore.

Archbishop Garrison said, "He came by himself, by train, to the wrong station—this is one for the history books."

The congregation, which would total about three thousand when all the priests were in place, had begun to gather and take their assigned seats about two hours before the ceremony. The mighty thrum and song of the organ, with voices from the choir loft, filled the cathedral and the hearts of all present. Pious and generous laity mingled with sisters of various orders in white, black, and brown habits, with the Missionaries of Charity in distinctive white, blue-striped veils, who formed clusters of female chastity and prayerfulness. The cathedral itself smelled of wood, stone, flowers, and incense, with crisp drafts of outside air wafting in through open doors on this cool, super-bright October day. The life-size crucifix with a paper-white marble figure of Christ hung above the altar, suspended above the head of the celebrant. The cathedra—the chair of the archbishop—awaited him in marble splendor with plumped red cushions in place.

The procession incorporated all the pomp and pageantry of a medieval royal court: Knights of Columbus, Knights and Dames of St. Peter Claver, and the Sacred Military Constantinian Order of St. George formed the honor guard; then followed the one hundred deacons and five hundred priests of the diocese, then the visiting bishops, archbishops, and auxiliary bishops of Newark, Timothy Mulrennan, the archbishop designate, the apostolic nuncio, fully vested and smiling as if nothing untoward had happened; and the four cardinals brought up the rear, about a half hour after the line had begun. The people watched with awe and amusement, pointing at the Eastern Rite bishops with their jeweled crowns and the plumed knights and dames, waving to their own parish priests and friends, and they applauded when Mulrennan began to walk up the center aisle of the grand gothic cathedral. He waved and bowed as he processed slowly, breathing in the liturgical music and the sacred fragrance of the place. In the front pews of the cathedral his family stood and waved and wept as he passed.

He held back his own tears of awe and gratitude as he negotiated the steps of the sacristy, approached the altar and bent to kiss it, then turned and took his seat across from the cathedra that he would soon possess in the name of the Father, the Son, and the Holy Spirit, for the greater glory of God and His people. . . . Wearing the miter of his hierarchical office, as had bishops for more than a thousand years, he felt a bit awkward and out of time, but also felt in his bones and his soul the connection to those bishops and all the way back to the apostles who had founded this holy community, which had, over so many centuries, spread across the globe like a fire. These outward signs of holiness and authority still moved the people, brought them to the altar, hushed the voices of doubt. But ceremony and sacrament were not enough, nor could a bishop merely preach the faith of the apostles—he must live it! To this life Timothy John Mulrennan had committed himself, in this life he would minister to his people to the very best of his human ability, hoping and praying that God would give him the strength he needed.

After the blessing and welcome from the retired archbishop, who had served during the *sede vacante* as administrator of the diocese, Manzi rose and read the pope's bull, which actually held this pope's signature, and his seal, hence the term "bulla," the Latin for lead seal.

After the assembled consultors briefly examined the document, the chancellor of the archdiocese announced to the assembly: "Let it be known that, in accord with the provisions of Canon

Law, the College of Consultors has duly examined the Apostolic Mandate of His Holiness, Pope John Paul II, by which His Eminence Timothy John Cardinal Mulrennan is appointed Archbishop of Newark."

The vast congregation stood and applauded their new shepherd. Then Archbishop Mulrennan was led by the nuncio and the retired archbishop to the chair and presented with the golden staff, the sign of his pastoral office. Officially, he was now the fifth Archbishop of Newark. He held the crosier in his left hand, raised his right in greeting as the applause continued. He looked down the central aisle of this beautiful cathedral which had been completed less than fifty years before, after nearly fifty years of construction, and he saw the giant roseate stained-glass window at the rear of the building, through which the light of the world streamed in bright primary colors that had been designed and set by craftsmen of another age, another place . . . and there he saw the Light of the World and knew the presence of the Holy Spirit within and among the people, his people, the Lord's people.

After the Scripture readings and before the profession of the ancient faith, the new man delivered his first homily as the metropolitan ordinary of 1.4 million Roman Catholics.

"I begin my time as your shepherd with a prayer and an invitation. A prayer for each of you, in thanksgiving for what God has given us on this day. And an invitation to you to gather at His table for the nourishment that provides us eternal life with Him. I ask of you, that you remember me in your prayers, now and as long as we are together."

He greeted his family and the priests and seminarians of the archdiocese, thanked his brother bishops, spoke about the issues that would be of special concern to him: Catholic education, vocations, life, family, peace, and justice. He acknowledged the many clergy of other faiths and lay community leaders, including the mayor of Newark. He said, "What kind of archbishop will I be? Time will tell, and you will judge. God will be the ultimate judge—that is, right after Archbishop Garrison—" He looked over to his seated, now emeritus predecessor, and waved. Garrison waved back and nodded silently. The people laughed, appreciated the gentle jibe. "I'll not ask you to be gentle, and I know he won't be!" As a matter of fact and long practice, the retired ordinary would fade into obscurity, visit parishes at their invitation, perhaps write his memoirs. The new guy was in charge, fully and completely, and there was no room for the old one in the scenario. Tim Mulrennan possessed the ball, and now he must run with it.

PART III

Vicar of Christ

CHAPTER SIXTEEN

The Vatican, March 1, 2004

For those few who were present at the Second Vatican Council as adult observers or participants—including some four hundred current bishops—the scene was a somewhat familiar one. The Supreme Pastor himself had been a young priest, freshly ordained, from the second through the fourth sessions, working as a secretary to the committee that kept American bishops and theologians updated daily on council goings-on. Those years in Rome were imprinted indelibly on his mind and soul. As he walked at the head of the procession of four thousand bishops from the Apostolic Palace, across the sun-washed piazza, into the recently restored Maderno façade of the basilica, Timothy Mulrennan, now Celestine VI, looked into the faces of those gathered to cheer—and some to jeer—the new council. Security forces had erected barricades that kept the closest spectators nearly fifty yards distant from the huge, slow-moving procession of damask-mitered figures who followed the Holy Father into St. Peter's. The security measures were extraordinary in scope, employing the latest technology and most sophisticated counterterrorist techniques, creating a series of perimeters that increasingly restricted access to the floor of the basilica, the offices and grounds of the Vatican, and the person of the pope himself. The Swiss Guard were out in full force, more for show than papal protection; they were arrayed in medieval splendor—officers in their ceremonial dress uniforms with maroon tunics, red ostrich-plumed stainless steel helmets, white gloves, and sabers; guardsmen in their familiar blousy red, yellow, and blue uniforms, with white gorgets and the same embossed stainless-steel helmets, halberds at the ready. As if in a dream, his feet touching but not feeling the worn stones of the plaza, the pope waved and signed the cross in apostolic blessing.

It was of great significance that the pope led, rather than followed, the procession as called for by ecclesiastical protocol. John XXIII had appeared in 1962 at the end of the procession, carried on the *sedia gestatoria*, the papal chair with an awning that looked like a little box and the occupant like a comic figure with a gaudily jeweled miter atop his large peasant's head. This time, in the early years of the twenty-first century after Christ, the pope walked ahead of his fellow bishops; he wanted to signal his cofraternity and collegiality with them. St. Peter's Square itself had been washed by four days of rain prior to the day of opening. So there was a freshness in the air and on the pavement. He was glad to be walking and would never have countenanced being transported like an Asian despot with ostrich feather fans signifying his primacy and spiritual potency. Of course, it had been nearly forgotten that Pope John dismounted at the door of the basilica and walked up the narrow aisle of the nave in full view of the bishops who had by then taken their seats along the tiers that had been built to accommodate them. Also, the pope of Vatican II had asked for the Gospel to be sung in Arabic and Old Slavonic, as well as Latin and Greek, had placed the triple crown of office on the altar and left it there, and had ordered his chair—a simple chair, not the pontifical throne—be situated on the altar level rather than a spot elevated from the sanctuary floor. Little touches of humility and humanity that were trademarks of the great man. As the opening council mass went on, spectators crowded into the apses grew restless and noisy, even during the most solemn moments when bread and wine were consecrated as the Body and Blood of Christ. Souvenir hawkers jostled through the locals who stood like cattle throughout the hours-long ceremony. After mass, the cardinals, archbishops, and bishops paid homage to the pontiff, greeting him one by one and kissing his ring, knee, or foot, depending on rank, religious order, or individual taste and preference.

For this new council, obviously already dubbed "Vatican III" for consistency and convenience, many things were different, updated, even surprising to some observers. One of the great innovations—of which the pope allowed himself to be particularly proud—was known simply as "the chair" . . . that is, the four thousand chairs that held the council fathers.

Early on in the logistics-planning phase, a Korean priest who was a former U.N. employee had presented a sketch to Philip Calabrese, who had then passed it directly to the Holy Father. It was an idea for a specially designed and fitted chair modeled after a supersophisticated airline seat that would give each bishop in attendance a full menu of communications capability at his fingertips. In effect, each was to be equipped with a computer, television, radio, telephone, Palm Pilot–like memo and email device, and translation equipment, including headphone, that allowed interpreters to give real-time versions of council speeches in dozens of native languages. "I don't want another Cardinal Cushing problem," the pope had said, referring to the Boston archbishop's notorious lack of facility in Latin during the Second Vatican Council (to say nothing of other Americans' unease with the traditionally common language of liturgy and canon law).

Apart from the technological challenges was the issue of manufacturing enough of these devices on time for the opening day of the council. Working thousands of hours of overtime in development and testing, then actual production, a Korean electronics manufacturer (no coincidence: run by an uncle of the priest who proposed the idea) was able to deliver all four thousand chairs on time—more or less; some were still wrapped in plastic as the pontiff and bishops processed into the nave—and in working order, with the translation stations tucked into the apses where restless tourists had stood in 1962. Some of the bishops were aghast at the prospect of these space-age devices, while others welcomed the electronic and translation capabilities as gifts of the Holy Spirit, intended to make the council move more smoothly and efficiently through the debates and decision-making.

At the main door the pope, tall, gray, gaunt, and slightly stooped from the ravages of his disease and the surgeries, stood aside for a few moments to let the stream—river, really—of

white-mitered men pass into the brightly lit basilica. His personal
security team then whisked him away to a special holding room
where he lay for about a half hour, taking a catnap to recoup his
strength before the pontifical mass and homily that lay ahead. He
felt fine, all things considered, though he especially missed his
friend and adviser Phil Calabrese, wondered what the Jersey City
native would be thinking—and no doubt expressing in salty language—at a time like this.

Mulrennan closed his eyes. From beyond the heavily curtained
and bullet-proofed cubicle walls he heard the tolling of bells and
the cheers of the people assembled in the bright square outside.

When he opened his eyes he saw Jack Rath, the council security
chief, hovering above him. On his face a frown of concern hung
like an upside-down moon. The pontiff sat up, straightened his
sleeves, and ran his hands over the side of his closely trimmed
head. He felt fine, if a bit groggy, and reached for a glass of water
near the cot. "Are they all in yet?" he asked Rath.

"Almost, Holy Father." The ex-law enforcement officer said,
"You don't look very good. This is a huge strain on you. No one
would fault you if you returned to the palace. We've prepared a
closed-circuit video hook-up for you to speak from there. I can
get you there in two minutes, if you give us the word."

"Ironic use of the 'word' in these circumstances," Celestine
said. "I am obligated to speak to my brother bishops in person,
and to celebrate mass with them." He took two big swallows of
water, tasting the life as it entered his body. It was then that he
noticed the doctor and ambulance attendants standing at the
other end of the small room, unobtrusive but waiting—they, too,
alert for the "word."

"I'll be ready to move as soon as they are all in and seated.
I've come this far—no turning back now."

"As you wish, Holy Father, but I must present the options to
you. From a security point of view, of course. I will continue to
do so."

"You needn't be so cryptic, Jack. I understand. I do appreciate
what you're doing, what you have done. Everything is going well

so far. We haven't lost any bishops or any popes—yet."

Rath almost smiled. "The day isn't over," he said dryly. He saw a very sick man sitting before him, in far greater danger of death from disease than from a bullet or a bomb. Perhaps his native stubbornness would be the deciding factor, either carrying him through or bringing him to his knees.

"Lighten up," the pope advised. "We've got a council to get to." Other papal aides, including the choir-vested master of ceremonies, awaited the boss's signal. "Help me up, please." He held out his hand and the American pulled him to his feet. Liturgical music swelled from the sanctuary, somehow propelling him to his full height and strength.

Harkening back, again, to Pope John, the current pontiff recalled the effect his illness had wrought on the people of Rome and the Church throughout the world: In those days the press office had never straightforwardly announced that the pontiff was dying of cancer, but issued discreet and optimistic bulletins until the very end, in May 1963. Pope John did not live to see the opening of the second session of his council. The conclave chose Giovanni Batista Cardinal Montini, the archbishop of Milan and a former curial apparatchik and intellectual, to lead Church and council—that is, if he chose to continue the council. He did, to the great joy of some and eternal dismay of others. Mulrennan did not think that he was terminally ill, only set back a few paces, and determined to gut it out through the day's rubrics and tomorrow's first business session. He had prepared two versions of his homily for today: A shorter spoken text, and a longer exhortation to be printed in the official record of the council. He prayed for the physical energy to make it to the altar and through the mass, to give voice to the feelings of his heart and the stirring within his soul on this great occasion. He did not place himself in the same category as the good Pope John, but providence— and politics—had thrust him onto the apostolic throne and he would give to that office everything he had in himself to give.

The four thousand men in the nave, in their high-tech chairs, rose and cheered as the Supreme Pontiff appeared at the entrance to the basilica. He stood tall but leaned a bit on his shepherd's staff, his own gold-flecked miter slightly atilt atop the handsome head, his vestments flowing like the colorful sails of an ancient ship. Indeed, the Roman Catholic Church itself was sometimes called the Bark of Peter, after an old-style sailing ship, and the pope called its captain. The visible links to antiquity were ever-present. Despite the sometimes deadly political and theological conflicts with the now-separated Eastern Christian churches, dating back to the decline and fall of the empire in the West, the Roman church had adopted aspects of the Byzantine style of dress and government that remained to this day. Celestine VI, like it or not, could easily be transported back to Constantinople in the time of Justinian and not seem out of place. As he walked forward through the applauding episcopal ranks he thought sadly of his friend and trusted secretary, Philip Calabrese, who had been viciously eliminated, cut down, before he could witness this scene. His ears absorbed the sounds that spoke to his very soul, his eyes the sight of such an assembly as had only rarely been visible throughout the history of the Church. A pang of doubt seized him and his hand went to his abdomen for a split second. Was it the surgery or the Holy Spirit? He smiled and continued to walk; he lifted his right hand in salute to his brothers.

A wave of affection and hope rose and crashed over him. He knew that many among the tiered prelates did not support the council, calling it "the American's scheme," and did not trust the pope. Yet they were obedient to the call of their pontiff, men of faith and honor. Wait till the first round of procedural voting and debate, Mulrennan cautioned himself, then you'll see what they are made of—and what you are made of. Surely, his predecessors John XXIII and Paul VI had experienced these same thoughts and fears. Surely the council fathers of that time cheered and lauded the pope, even as some of them bitterly opposed every decision he made. It was the way of men, even holy men charged with building God's kingdom on earth.

Conscious of every mortal cell in his body, Pope Celestine VI made his way slowly, like a bride, up the middle aisle, clutching his bishop's crosier tightly, feeling the perspiration on his brow and upper lip. Behind him, the small corps of attendants that trailed him always on such ceremonial occasions; unspoken was their preparedness to catch him if he faltered along the way. The expanse of the basilica had never seemed so vast as it did now to the man recovering from recent surgery. Oddly, in this moment, the pain was lifted from him, the fatigue he had felt now disappeared, and he breathed more easily, gaining strength with each step.

The high altar stood beneath the breathtaking baroque baldachino with its serpentine columns that supported an elaborate, angel-anchored canopy, and beyond, at the head of the apse, the image of the dove shone out over the great assembly. Along the lower rim of the dome above, visible to his right as he approached, the simple words of Scripture spoke to him as never before: "*Tu es Petrus . . .*" He paused before he took the final steps into the transept and looked to his right. There the thirteenth-century statue of Peter upon his cathedra, or throne, the creation of Arnolfo di Cambio from a melted-down statue of Jupiter, was vested, anachronistically, as if the apostle himself were actually in attendance with his successors. Timothy Mulrennan turned and walked to the foot of the statue and touched the blackened bronze where pilgrims over many centuries had kissed the image of Cephas, the Rock, and worn it smooth. Although he had never considered himself particularly mystical or a believer in ancient relics, he experienced a spirit-presence before this statue of one of the greatest and most imperfect of saints. Had not Jesus forgiven Peter's betrayals and doubts and falterings many times over? Had not Peter been given truly superhuman strength of will and character to cofound, with St. Paul, the very community that was represented here today in this council of elders and overseers gathered in the Holy Name of Jesus?

"Upon this rock," he said in a bare whisper that no one else heard amid the crescendo of dying applause and now-rising music.

Within a few minutes, Pope Celestine was seated in the pontifical chair before the altar, listening to the singing of the Gloria, his eyes closed to block out the sensory overload of the scene. The liturgy of the Word was then sung in various languages, culminating in the Gospel reading from the first chapter of John: "The Word became a human being and, full of grace and truth, lived among us. We say His glory, the glory which He received as the Father's only Son."

In various sections of the basilica were representatives of religious denominations, Christian and non-Christian, from every continent of the planet. The world's press, too, was present—print journalists and electronic media voices, in a specially built tribune, or reviewing stand behind the altar—as well as lay and religious Catholic leaders. Special lighting, too, had been installed to combat the natural gloom that sometimes shadowed the outsized nave, making it difficult to read or to see clearly for more than a few yards out. Sprinkled throughout the basilica and positioned above along the interior of the dome of Michelangelo were plainclothes Secret Service personnel and sharpshooters. The pope had been reluctant to allow weapons of any kind into the basilica but had been convinced that not only his safety but that of the thousands of others was at stake.

Such extraordinary security measures were somewhat mitigated by high-tech advances that allowed for less visible methods: electromagnetic weapon- and bomb-detectors, cameras and sensors, ID pins and badges for each official participant and spectator, human intelligence and profiling capabilities. None was a perfect deterrent to any party or parties determined to loose mayhem and havoc upon the assembly, but added together they were the best available means to protect human life. For months, threats had been received, to no one's surprise: bomb threats and biological terror threats. The pontiff himself, always a top security priority, had decided to trust God and Jack Rath to protect his own skin and others'. He would not be crippled by worry over what might happen. He focused on the words of the Evangelist.

"Jesus said, 'Do you believe just because I told you I saw you when you were under the fig tree? You will see much greater things than this!' And He said to them: 'I am telling you the truth—you will see heaven open and God's angels going up and coming down on the Son of Man.' "

The Gospel had been presented in Latin, and now would be

resung in Greek, then Italian, then English. Because of his post-surgical condition, the pontiff remained seated through the liturgy, during which he would normally stand with the rest of the faithful. He was conserving his strength and did not want to appear frail or tentative. The jewel-and-gold-encrusted book was brought to him when the sung readings were completed, and the pontiff kissed the page, then stood.

"Brothers and sisters," the Holy Father began, his voice amplified by concealed microphones, "we have heard the Word of the Lord and the testimony of St. John the Baptist today, just as our mothers and fathers heard it before we were even born, just as the early Christians heard it from the mouths of the apostles themselves, just as the disciples heard it from Christ's own lips when He walked among us in the flesh. What, then, is our response this day, to His call?" He took a step forward from his chair. "Have we come here as His followers, indeed, as apostles, which means messengers of the Word? Do we believe what has been written and spoken to be the self-revelation of God, in love, to every man and woman who have ever lived?

"As Christians, members of the Body of Christ, we so believe. We profess this faith in our liturgy, live this faith every day, honor this faith through prayer and worship. Let us then examine and explain this faith to the entire world as it pertains to the holy mystery of the priesthood and the sacred structure of the Church." He hoped to inspire and educate the council to his purposes, if in fact they were not clear already as to why they had assembled in council. He echoed his predecessors, John XXIII and John Paul II, in his words of admonition and encouragement: "The naysayers and 'prophets of doom' have always been among us, dear brothers and sisters. At each general council, at each crucial moment in the history of the Church of Christ, from its very first days, there have been negative voices who deny the reality and the presence of the Holy Spirit among the people. Remember, we are here to lead and to represent the masses of human beings who profess our faith—those alive today and those as yet unborn." The pontiff paused significantly. "We have been given the authority to gather in the name of Jesus, to accomplish the work of Our Father, under the guidance of the Holy Spirit. And we shall surely accomplish His purposes for His one holy and apostolic Church if we simply listen to the truth that lies within us at His hand.

"Put aside every consideration of national and personal interest. Call upon every teacher you have ever known, from the time of youth and the time in seminary and university, with true humility and gratitude. For through those inspired teachers His work was revealed to you, and through your teaching office to us."

The words of his homily scrolled across the surface of a Tele-PrompTer, so that he would not have to read from a piece of paper. But this required him to hold his mark and not move too far from the chair. His communications advisers had installed the device just a few weeks previously, during the construction of the "bleachers" and camera scaffolding within the basilica. He had rehearsed a few times, until he was almost comfortable with it. But he was able to put aside any nervousness or unease at this moment as he spoke the words he knew would set the tone for the entire council.

At the pope's right hand sat Cardinal Tyrone and Archbishop Min, at his left Cardinal Biagi. The council's copresidents sat with seeming impassivity as the pontiff spoke. He set a historical context for this sacred synod: "The Second Council of the Vatican brought the Catholic Church into the modern world so that we would be better positioned to preach the message of Jesus Christ to all nations, using all available means of communications, in language understandable to contemporary men and women. That historic council elevated the importance of cultural pluralism within to strengthen our unity as a community of the faithful. The seeming paradox of unity amid diversity is a reflection of the mystery of God's love. After all, in the earliest age of the Church, there were significant and beautiful differences among them—though never did they legitimately disagree as to the divinity and oneness of Jesus with the Father and the Spirit. Eventually heresies arose and were condemned. The Church learned and matured, divided and reformed through the ages. We made mistakes but our love of God never diminished one iota. So, where do we stand today? And where are we going? Like the Council of Trent, we come together in a time of controversies and divisions, some would say a time of decline and decay. But we face those difficulties head-on, without either a denial of their existence or a simple answer to each criticism. Like Vatican II, we are not a council of condemnation. There will be no anathemas or excommunications among the decrees of this council."

Tyrone flinched, almost imperceptibly. Mulrennan sensed this subtle reaction to his strong words; he felt his own physical strength returning, the resonance and quality of his voice carrying through the monumental structure.

"As the Blessed John XXIII stated, 'Nowadays, the spouse of Christ prefers to make use of the medicine of mercy rather than of severity. She considers that she meets the needs of the present day by demonstrating the validity of her teaching rather than by condemnations.' We of another Christian generation say, let us put to the task the wonderful, faithful minds of our magisterium, which is you—the college of bishops gathered under the authority of the Holy Spirit. We charge you to bring the light of truth to the world in which you live, to burn brightly with faith, hope, and love for your fellow man of whatever religion, or of none at all. We who possess the ultimate truth must not be so jealous of it that we do not share with the women and men of every nation. At the same time, we remember the Good Pope's admonition that the substance of our doctrine is one thing, its representation to the people another."

The battle lines had already been drawn. Little that Mulrennan said today would make a difference. The twenty-second general council of the Church was under way.

CHAPTER SEVENTEEN

The Vatican, March 20, 2004

Bernard Tyrone himself presented the schema on the priest-hood that had been drafted by his own Theological Commission. He and everyone else considered it "his" commission. There were no surprises—and no openings. It was airtight in its orthodoxy, laden with scriptural, traditional, and canonical concepts supporting a sacred, celibate, exclusively male order of ordained priests and deacons. In effect, the bishops had simply expanded John Paul II's 1994 statement and grafted on some of the less progressive language of *Presbyterorum Ordinis*, the 1965 decree of Vatican II. The Irish cardinal spoke in perfect if dense Latin to a nearly full house of council fathers: Very few had chosen to be absent for the debate on this crucial agenda item. It promised to be the first, and perhaps most controversial, major issue of the council. Tyrone knew what was at stake, and he knew his audience. These four thousand *episcopoi* were among the most traditional, if not downright conservative members of the *ecclesia*—the overseers and guardians of a deposit of faith that, they believed, had remained inviolate since the apostolic age. So, Cardinal Tyrone, the chief enforcer of orthodoxy and voice of the magisterium, droned on confidently; in fact, the votes had been counted in advance.

"We believe, therefore," he stated, arriving at his conclusion an hour after he had begun, "that the priestly office was conceived in the Old Covenant and reformed by Christ Himself in the New Covenant, for this age and forever, shall remain intact and effective in its sacred mission only if we continue to enforce the ancient rule of total obedience to Christ's authority and absolute chasteness in arrangements of living."

The tall, heavily browed copresident of the council surveyed the tall bleacherlike structures that lined either side of the nave. He blinked in the strong artificial light; he was not yet used to these intensely bright lamps that shone on the floor of the basilica so that cameras might better capture the proceedings for the outside world (as well as for the Vatican's own archives).

"From the time of Our Savior, through the days of the Church Fathers and the earliest general councils, from the hard-earned experience of our predecessor priests and bishops over many centuries, and in the wisdom and truths promulgated with supreme authority by apostles, councils, and popes, from time immemorial, we must declare and aver that the Holy Church has not erred in her doctrine of priestly duty, function, and mission."

Leandro Biagi wielded the gavel today, alternating with Cardinal Tyrone and Archbishop Min, his copresidents. The three of them had briefed the pope daily on the housekeeping work of the council and would continue now in more gruesome detail as the agenda was breached and the real theological issues came in play. Biagi braced himself for the debate. Several of the council fathers had previously requested recognition from the chair so he had some idea of who wanted to speak on this topic. By the rules of the council, which had been adopted by a greater than two-thirds vote, each member could speak once on the subject under consideration, for no more than ten minutes. Presentations of the draft decrees could take longer—as long as needed, depending on the document. Thus Tyrone, no stranger to lengthy homilies and countless theological filibusters, had rather succinctly—for him— and convincingly—for him—laid out the material in all required detail. If the debate went as smoothly . . . Leandro Biagi—he of the Machiavellian disposition—could only hope that there would be no blood on the marble floor when this was over. He scanned the computer screen, which electronically indicated those who sought recognition, and swept over the live bodies in the bleachers. He spotted an elderly bishop from Belgium rising from his chair.

Tyrone shuffled and restacked the thirty pages of his speech, clattering at the elegant, microphoned lectern, oblivious to the movement around him and craving a cigar. Biagi patiently allowed his colleague to finish his business before calling on the Belgian. "Your Excellency, the Bishop of Brugge," the Florentine cardinal intoned, "you are recognized for ten minutes."

The old man consumed every second of his allotted time, until he was discreetly gonged and sat down; he rambled on about his own vocation and various priests he had known and the climate and art of his native region, but said nothing about the draft document itself. In fact, the next few speakers had little to say in the way of moral theology, dogma, or ecclesiology, though they too were not reluctant to take all the time that was allowed.

Biagi then recognized a rural Brazilian auxiliary bishop named Roberto Caraciellho, a leather-skinned forty-eight-year-old with a deep, musical voice that rolled in waves over the purple and red skull-capped heads of the assembly. He spoke quietly but clearly, mixing some imperfect Latin with his own more colloquial and less formal Brazilian-flavored Portuguese. "*Ecce homo*," he began in the familiar Latin formulation. "Behold the man who is a priest, who *is* Christ among us, and deny not that he *is* a man, as Our Lord Jesus was, and that he walks the hard earth with bare and dirty feet."

There was a collective intake of breath and adjustment of headsets as the speaker clearly reclaimed some wandering attention. He stood about five-seven, broad-shouldered, brown hands raised, palms inward, in a gesture of sacred supplication. The Brazilian prelate smiled. "However, today, I am wearing shoes!" A wave of laughter rippled over the assembly, and he continued his speech.

"I am not disposed to favor this draft, which excludes consideration of the role of women in the ordained ministries. Do we, as priests, represent the people to God, or God to the people? Well, we know that we do both—but the emphasis in the proposed decree is strictly on the latter, elevating the Catholic priesthood to a class of persons who seem to exist somewhere between the human and divine spheres. I have, my brothers, often reflected on this supposed distinction between myself and fellow human beings and wondered whether the Lord drew such a line between Himself and His earthly disciples, and between those disciples and their successors.

"We have increasingly set ourselves apart from the people of Christ, and above them. The sacred council of the Vatican forty years ago began to open a consideration of the role of priests in the care of the faithful, and the fathers also began to redefine the role and responsibility of the laity of the Church. The council said: 'In virtue of the sacrament of orders, priests of the New Testament exercise the most excellent and necessary office of father and teacher among the People of God and for them. They are nevertheless, together with all of Christ's faithful, disciples of the Lord, made sharers in His kingdom by the grace of God who calls them. For priests are brothers among brothers with all those who have been reborn at the baptismal font. . . . They must work together with the lay faithful and conduct themselves in their midst after the example of their Master, whom among men "has not come to be served but to serve, and to give his life as a ransom for many." '

"What do these words mean? Do we believe them and practice them? I submit to you, my brothers, that we have put aside the true and holy intentions as expressed in the council's decree, and in the document that has been offered to us we propose to retreat further from the heart of the community, the Body of Christ, into a cloister of power and separateness. There was such an uplifting of priests and people in the reality of Vatican II. But as time went on, the number of priests in sacred orders diminished rapidly, and the number of vocations also; it is only in the past few years that we have witnessed a 'bottoming out' of that trend, and perhaps this means a renewal of the priesthood among the Catholic people around the world."

Bishop Caraciellho did not refer to any notes as he articulated his opposition to the draft document on the priesthood, touching upon only a few reasons for his position. Perhaps others would flesh out some of the other points of disagreement. He went on:

"There has been something gravely wrong, you might call it a cancer on our priestly and pastoral community, and we must address this problem with our hearts open to the Holy Spirit and to our own experiences. Pretty language and lip service will not resolve the problems of our priests. Blaming the laity—or even the priests themselves—will not bring us closer to a solution. Instead, let us reexamine the very structure and nature of our Cath-

olic priesthood and seek to reform what has gone awry. We are
obligated as teachers of the faith, in our roles as bishops and
legislators, to correct such problems as may exist within the
Church, not to push them off onto the next generations. It is
possible that if we do not take corrective action now, at this opportunity presented by the Holy Father, we shall risk the death,
by disease from within, of our beloved Church.

"Therefore, I suggest to you, brothers in Christ, that we reject
the draft as presented and attempt to reformulate the definition
of priestly ministry in the contemporary world—which, though it
changes continually, is still God's own world, created and re-
deemed through the life, death and resurrection of His only Son."
Caraciellho's hands fell to his side, and he bowed his head, as if
in prayer. A scattered staccato of applause marked the approval,
by some, of the bishop's remarks. As he returned to his chair, the
applause grew louder and more general.

Cardinal Tyrone looked up from the papers before him at the
president's desk. Biagi, too, swept the chamber with his owl's
gaze. Between them, Archbishop Min sat with seeming impassivity. The favorable demonstration gradually died down, with just
a few bishops standing in their places, clapping steadily and somewhat stubbornly. Cardinal Biagi slowly lifted the giant gavel, then
gently tapped it three times upon the base, prodding the assembly
to silence so that he could recognize another speaker. The big
Irishman glowered silently from his chair as the next man, James
Alexander Hartshorne, the retired Archbishop of San Francisco,
a self-described liberal, began his remarks in fluent Latin, then
switched to English after a few sentences.

"My dear friends and brothers, I rise to add my voice to this
debate, I hope constructively and with soundness of language and
logic. The esteemed brother bishop from Brazil has raised some
valid criticisms that must be examined. Allow me to follow his
critique on the draft decree with my own thoughts, focused on
yet another fatally flawed premise. Although in my life I have
known the wonderful gift that is chastity, and although it was at
some times a struggle to conform to my holy vows, I urge this
historic synod to consider the true history and all too real effects

of priestly celibacy in our sacred community. Let me be as clear as possible, lest my words be misinterpreted: I do not advocate the elimination of the vow of celibacy for priests. We, as a body, are not prepared to 'go there' yet, in my opinion. Instead, I ask that the subject be discussed openly and honestly among us here assembled. Is that too radical a request of you, my brothers?"

The archbishop emeritus, now eighty years old, had nothing to lose at this stage in his career—which had been distinguished by a vigorous pastoral presence and a hugely successful social-services ministry in one of the smaller but more significant arch-dioceses in the United States. Even now Hartshorne retained a full head of sandy-colored hair and a smooth, beatific visage. In the late 1990s the pope had accepted his mandatory retirement at age seventy-five, which signaled the pontiff's—or at least the Curia's—willingness to remove him and make way for a more vocally or-thodox archbishop. San Franciscan Catholics had openly mourned his retirement and given a cool reception to his replace-ment, at least initially. Over time, the new man had worked hard to display personal warmth and charm, even as he wielded his episcopal authority without any apparent reluctance or timidity. He sat next to his predecessor.

"Further—and I know you will think me a bomb-thrower for this, so I beg your forgiveness, dear friends—we must become willing to discuss the practical and theological justifications for ordaining women as permanent deacons of the Catholic Church."

Now there was an audible gasp among the council fathers, punctuated with scattered cheers and applause. The unspoken fears and nightmares of the traditional-to-reactionary wing of the episcopacy was now verbalized, on the table, in play . . . from the mouth of a smiling, well-liked and respected liberal American. Among the curial leaders who were seated in a tight grouping near the altar, Henry Martin Vennholme sat rigidly without ex-pression on his face, among colleagues who felt the weight of history pressing upon their elderly shoulders. Vennholme had not taken the microphone once during the council proceedings, but had held private meetings in his Hotel Columbus suites for like-minded bishops.

Bernard Tyrone rose and began speaking, interrupting Hartshorne's comments and the rising tide of reaction among the other bishops. Biagi whispered something to Min, who tugged at Tyrone's scarlet sleeve. Then Biagi pounded the gavel, this time with some vigor and volume, to quiet the chamber. "There will be order, Fathers, order! Your Eminence, Cardinal Tyrone, please be seated." The words erupted in English, without Biagi's having made a conscious decision. Everyone—except perhaps Tyrone himself—understood exactly what he was saying. The prelatial uproar died significantly but not completely. Again, Biagi tapped the gavel, then pounded it, secretly enjoying the display of some emotion and controversy at last. "Excellencies, please, please! Our brother archbishop has the floor for another seven minutes. Please come to order and give him a respectful hearing. Order! Order!"

Cardinal Tyrone rose swiftly and dramatically, a tower of red—including his beefy face topped by a zucchetto that threatened to tumble off to one side of his head. He had reached the breaking point, seeing the council swing so severely away from him; he thought that the minority of so-called progressives was about to hijack the agenda and lead the fathers out into a theological no man's land of feel-good, multicultural liberalism, from whence there might be no turning back. For the sake of Christ, he would not allow such a potentially heretical turn! He forgot, or ignored, the rules of debate and yanked free one of the table microphones and held it to his mouth.

He spoke before the chair could stop him. "Excellencies, heed the voice of one crying out in the wilderness. You must not, cannot pass the amended statement without causing grave and sinful harm to the constitution of our holy Mother Church. She has survived heresies and schisms before, but in this day when she is under assault from every messenger of the Evil One, throughout the world, we must not admit corrupting forces within our own house."

"Lord Cardinal, you are out of order!" Archbishop Min gaveled the Irishman to silence, but Tyrone remained standing. The assembly erupted in a tumult of protests and cheers, divided for and against the conservative's staunch position.

"I am permitted, brother bishop, to speak as copresident of this council and chairman of the Theological Commission." The cardinal stood adamantly, facing the steep tiers of prelates that lined the vast sanctuary as far as—in fact, farther than—he could see. His octogenarian eyes were not as strong as his lungs. "I speak in the Holy Name of Jesus Christ and the Holy Spirit! I shall not be silenced, Reverend President!"

Now applause rippled down the sacred trough, which had come alive after hearing these uncompromising words.

Jim Wiezevich slipped away from the Apostolic Palace at ten P.M., luckily caught a taxicab, and made it to the trattoria for his dinner date with Demetra within thirty minutes. He arrived before she did, took a table in the back, ordered wine. He needed a drink, needed to sleep tonight, doubted he would get much of the latter.

Throughout the day he had watched the unfolding council debate on a closed-circuit TV monitor in a meeting room just off the papal library, a notebook with the daily agenda and draft documents open on the cluttered table in front of him. The Holy Father had worked through the morning, taken a long nap, then awakened and watched an hour of the debate himself. Wiezevich could not discern the pontiff's frame of mind, only saw him peering intently, with total focus, at the red-robed figures on the screen. Occasionally he shifted his position or stood and moved his legs, not wanting to become a completely sedentary lump. Wiezevich made a mental note to request a treadmill for the room, for the pope's mental and physical health.

On his laptop he was able to call up background on each bishop who spoke in debate. He eagerly read the comprehensiveness of the online database that was available not only to the council members and apostolic staff but to the press and public as well. And just as the pope could watch the council proceedings live from within the Vatican, so people around the world could log in to the Holy See's special Web site and receive the real-time stream of audio and video, courtesy of the press office, which had tripled in size to accommodate this special, historic period called Vaticano Tre, or, somewhat more acidly, Concilio Americano.

Jim Wiezevich was trying desperately to retain a sense of humor amid the carnival atmosphere, and trying more feebly to let go of his infatuation with Demetra Matoulis . . . but he had achieved neither objective. As he awaited her in the comfortably noisy restaurant, where they had met at least thirty times before, he looked around at the other diners, most of whom probably cared less that the third ecumenical council of the Vatican existed, let alone that it had arrived at a crucial and dramatic turning point. It is the way of the world, he knew. Yet it might change the world—in ways as yet unforeseen, as Vatican II had, rippling out through the generations in the life of the Church. He did not begrudge them their good food and drink, their unconcern or even their lack of belief. Who could judge another's inner life? Only God. Not Jim Wiezevich, for sure.

He lit up inside when he saw her at the front door, rose from his chair to wave—unnecessarily, since she had located him instantly. She was that way: aware of her surroundings, drinking in information like oxygen or water. That was why she was such a good reporter. She swiveled and snaked through the table-cluttered room, smiling ruefully as she approached him.

"I'm late, I know," she said. "Filing a big story tonight. 'Women to be Deacons? Council Debates.' You like it?"

The priest pulled free a chair for her and sat, unable to take his eyes from her face. "What's not to like? I can dig deaconesses."

"That's not what they're talking about, and you know it, Mr. Holy Orders. They're talking about women as full-fledged permanent deacons. None of that Old Roman catacomb-type stuff, running around filling men's wine cups and singing hymns."

"Deacon comes from *diakonia*, meaning service or servanthood. The old Roman deacons—all of them men, as far as we know—were in charge of social services, operating community houses and parishes right here where we sit so smugly and securely. The Bible only mentions *deaconesses*, if we're going to be technically correct."

"By all means, let's be technically correct," she said. "Your John Paul the Great declared that the Church 'has no authority whatsoever to confer priestly ordination on women,' and told us to shut up about it. But he didn't say anything about the diaconate. Technical oversight?"

"Look, I'm not defending one position or the other. That's why we're having this little confab called a council. Let the old geezers slug it out on the floor of the basilica. I have read J.P.'s *Sacerdotalis Ordinatio* a dozen times—brilliant, if tortured, theology, poor, indeed terrible timing."

"He was a man for whom time did not exist."

"No, it existed, I think, but in a very different way than for you and me—or any other human being. He existed in a continuum that emcompassed all of human history, and the twentieth century in particular, every murderous millisecond of it. I think when he was hiking with his students or acting in some godawful play on stage that he carried history in his pocket—kind of like Shakespeare, able to accommodate all that was good and evil for all time . . . or something like that. I need some more wine." He filled their goblets from an unlabeled bottle.

"You're good when you want to be."

"It's just that I don't want to be very often—most of the time."

"Finally, it's getting interesting," she said. "Some of the old guys have roused from their slumber."

"We expect it's going to be a slug-fest from here on. Tyrone is very angry because he knows—or thinks—he has the votes to pass the draft virtually intact, but the way the debate has been going, who knows if some of the votes will change."

"I don't think there will be any surprises, in the end."

"Why do you say that? You never know. The entire story of Christianity is one of unexpected things happening."

"Don't try to convert me at this late date, Jim."

"I'm not. Just pointing out the flaw in your argument."

"If you want an argument against the male celibate priesthood, I'll be happy to lay it out for you. The Church has relied on faulty readings of Scripture and purely authoritarian pronouncements, rather than reason, historical experience, or the true needs of the people. I find it appalling that when a few old men finally have the balls to make tepid criticisms of this decrepit old system they are thought to be radicals. There has been a lot of good work done in feminist and liberation theology over the past half-century—much of it dismissed by the Church 'fathers,' but taken seriously by rank-and-file men and women. Your great council will ultimately rubber-stamp the ages-old practices that exclude women and keep the poor and ignorant in their place while elevating and protecting the interests of the ecclesiastical hierarchy."

"Demetra, I am not about to defend the status quo—especially to you. Especially tonight. But, I don't think this council is going to rubber-stamp anything. Nor does the Holy Father."

"Then he is hopelessly naïve, and so are you. Look, none of these guys—not even you—really believes that priests should be allowed to marry, nor that the Catholic Church should ordain women as priests. They wouldn't be in the position they're in, as bishops and cardinals, if they even for a second entertained such an idea. There may be a few who think it would be cute to have lady deacons, but even that might open the door too wide—and the women would surely push through. We're very pushy, you know. John Paul II put the lid on any discussion, real or feigned, pretty firmly in '94, you'll recall."

"I recall the outcry, yes. Although I must say it was not a general clamor. And I don't mean just among men—very few women spoke out loudly at that time."

"I think they were just exhausted, and felt that J.P. wouldn't be around much longer, so they'd ride it out. I disagree that there was little reaction. Among those I spoke to—and there were dozens of women in U.S. and Europe—there was a nearly unanimous dismissal of the papal letter, not dissimilar to the response to Paul VI's encyclical on birth control."

"You just said it—women in the United States and in Europe, educated, wealthy, white women. Are they representative of the women in the Church as a whole?"

"Somebody has to take the lead, to be the apostles, if you like. Do we follow the least educated and most oppressed among us? Jesus lived and worked with women, trusted them, did not set them apart from his ministry. Are we going to continue to marginalize and even ignore those who have so much to offer? We have withheld education and responsibility beyond the household for millennia."

"No, but we minister to them, bring to them the fullness of the gospel and take care of their souls."

"A nice, priestly way of saying, 'keep them in their place.'"

"Bullshit, as Phil Calabrese would say. You are looking at this through an ideological rather than a spiritual lens. That is a trap I cannot and will not fall into. Faith must come first, in the gut, then philosophy and ideology, if at all. Most people—myself included—seek simplicity, a direct relationship with God that religion only facilitates, does not create. It has to come from within, first. Look at me. I am in love with you. For all the good that has done me. But my faith has not changed or diminished. I've just gone insane, that's all."

She regarded him with a strange smile, her face lit more from within than from the soft candle- and lamplight of the trattoria.

"I love you, too, James."

"What are we going to do about it?"

"I have no idea. Marriage seems out of the question."

"Not if the council changes the conditions of my employment."

"And we both know how likely that is." Demetra laughed. "Do you ever feel like you exist out of time, maybe in an alternate dimension or something? Do you know what I mean?"

"Actually, I do. I wouldn't put it exactly that way. I think I'd say it's like experiencing a parallel history, with few points of intersection with other histories. And you and I are in a little capsule or boat within the larger stream."

"It's too stupid to contemplate. Any way you cut it, we don't have a lot of time."

"You need someone who can love you and give you children."

"Where did that come from? Now you're my social adviser? If I had wanted to have kids I would have had kids, married or not."

"Demetra, I know you want to have children, like your sister.

You've told me so yourself. I see it in your eyes and hear it in your voice. I feel it in your body when we—well . . . are together."

"Can't you say it? Can't you say, when we fuck? For God's sake, Jim, talk about parallel—that's how we are living. We can't even really talk about what's going on between us. We can say we love each other, but what the hell does that mean? I feel guilty when I get angry with you. I feel guilty when I want you to be with me, like I'm taking you away from God. It's wrong . . . or maybe I'm wrong, I don't know."

"My mother would drop dead of a heart attack if I said 'fuck.' " They both laughed. "Maybe I would too. I'm still learning about you—about us. I feel guilty and wrong and dirty sometimes. But it's not the worst situation in the world. I don't know either. But I don't think it's an accident or an evil thing. Somehow it's right and good. I can't justify it theologically—"

"Please don't try," she said dryly.

"I am willing to try. To talk about—us. You know I'm not a closed shop. I wouldn't be here with you if I were. We've got to be honest with each other. Sometimes I feel that you're holding something back."

"I'm afraid. Of a lot of things. I try not to be. But I think of what happened to your friend Phil, and I know that it could happen to you, too."

"We need some more wine. I'm feeling a bit high, which is not a bad thing, either. I guess I'll have plenty to confess next time!"

Her cell phone rang, a jarring, unwelcome intrusion. She picked up and listened for a full minute. "Right," she said, then turned it off. "I've got to go. A Roman hospital has reported that a patient has been admitted with a case of smallpox."

"Holy Christ! Are they sure?"

"Only a tentative diagnosis thus far—but rumors are spreading throughout the city."

Wiezevich whispered a quick prayer: God help us all. And he said to Demetra, "This will mean the end of his council."

"I'm so sorry, Jim. I mean it."

"Dinner's on me tonight," he said.

Outside, the sun had set behind St. Peter's Basilica in a serene blast of yellow, with clouds hovering like angels above the soaring cupola. Within, the council fathers, thirty-eight-hundred strong, defiantly yet calmly sat in their assigned chairs as the general congregation proceeded without interruption. They refused to allow the threats of terrorist attack to turn them from their duties. How the world had changed . . . or had it? Countless centuries of wars, destruction, terror, plague, and obscene slaughter had preceded this moment, much of it directly involving the members of the Body of Christ—either as perpetrators or victims. The wars of the past few years—including ethnic cleansings, genocides, chemical assaults on target populations, widespread terrorist strikes around the world—had brought a new level of fear to people everywhere, Christians, Jews, Muslims, people of other religions or no religious belief. Each new event ratcheted up the fear but was followed by numbness even more than anger. What was to be done? Was there any hope at all that peace might be achieved in this generation of man? As the bishops met in the darkening nave, which even the newest, brightest lights could not illumine without creating ever deeper shadows beyond, they murmured with discontent and even anger at the seemingly impossible task that they now faced. Whence would come the strength and grace to lift them above their own fears and doubts so that they might tend to the real, urgent, and implacable needs of their flocks?

"Brothers in Christ," Archbishop Min began in loud, ringing tones that belied his slight stature and impassive face, "we are called to this session of the holy council to vote on the matters before us—matters of great concern to the people of God in a time of great uncertainty. Like the apostles and the missionaries of old, like so many of the previous generations, we believe that Christ may appear among us at any time—in the next few moments or days, in a year or a century from now. We are not given to know the day and time of His coming, only that He shall come to judge all of us, the living and the dead. We believe that we shall rise from our poor tombs of dust and stand before Him to be held accountable for every thought and action in our little lives, hoping that He may show us mercy and lead us to stand, with Him, before the Father."

Small and unassuming, the Chinese prelate seemed to cast the longest shadow of all as he stood in the intense spotlight before his confreres and the hundreds of guests and observers for this crucial voting process, for which no one except God Himself yet knew the outcome. "Christ Himself told Peter three times, 'Feed my sheep.' How many times must he tell us, the successors of the apostles, to feed His sheep, to attend to their spiritual and temporal needs as His people?" Almost doll-like, Min stood motionless, his small hands raised to shoulder level, palms out in a gesture of openness and supplication. His steel-rimmed glasses reflected pinpoints of light back at the audience.

"Our Holy Father, too, asks us to reflect and to act according to our inspired conscience as the fathers of this holy council. Therefore, we will hear the summary of the declaration on holy orders read by the secretary to the council, and then we shall vote yes or no upon its adoption." He stood to one side, joined his hands as if in prayer, and gave over the chair's microphone to the Italian bishop who served as one of the three cosecretaries of the ecumenical council. Bishop Carmine Rigio of Anagni began to read the Latin summary, which would be followed by even briefer digests in Italian, English, Spanish, and French. As he droned on, a stirring arose among the council fathers at the farthest end of the nave, near the basilica entrance. Some of the bishops rose from their chairs to see the cause of the disturbance.

A tall figure walked slowly along the northern side of the central aisle, moving along the ranks of bishops who reached out to him to touch him, and among the priests and assistants in white albs and black cassocks who were positioned there along the aisle as assistants to the council fathers. As the man in white reached the halfway point of the nave, Bishop Rigio stopped reading. Among the audience of bishops and others rose at first a smattering of applause and a few shouts, which became a louder wave of clapping and stomping that shook the bleacher upon which the council members sat; they rose in a standing ovation that climaxed as the pontiff, Celestine VI, aproached the presidents' table. He turned, faced his fellow prelates, and gave a swift papal blessing, swinging his hands in the familiar sign of the cross, a rueful smile on his pale face.

Min strode quickly over to him, bowed and kissed the Fisherman's Ring on his hand. "What are you doing, Holy Father? Is there something wrong?" His dark eyes searched the papal face.

"No, no, dear Archbishop," Mulrennan said. "Nothing wrong. I was simply prompted to come. By the Spirit, I think," he added.

Within several yards of the pope converged, from every direction, security men. Tyrone stirred from his chair and moved with surprising quickness for an aroused giant to the pope's side, and Biagi came from behind the table where he had been conferring with an aide and greeted his pontiff with a gleaming smile and open arms. Thus surrounded by the three copresidents and ringed by security officers, Timothy Mulrennan turned and waved again to the still-applauding and cheering assembly. Everyone in St. Peter's was stunned by his sudden appearance among them, the first time in many, many centuries, perhaps ever, that a sitting pope had faced a council in this particular way—before a vote on one of the core definitions of doctrine. It was unexpected, too, because they knew that until recently he had been undergoing both chemotherapy and physical therapy in this period of recovery from his cancer. His smile, while a bit tentative, was genuine as he acknowledged the applause and shouts from bishops, cardinals, journalists, interfaith delegates, *periti* (yes, men and women), lay and religious assistants, even the usually immpassive security staff. The Roman Pontiff gestured for quiet, which eventually settled on the chamber.

"Council fathers and friends, brothers and sisters in Christ," the pope said, "I come here this evening with sincere apologies for interrupting this very important vote, which I did not intend to do. I thought you might have already accomplished this and moved onto other business—but I made the mistake, as I have in the past, of assuming that we might one day achieve some level of efficiency in our service to the Lord, that we might do what we say we're going to do in the time we say we're going to do it!"

He spoke these first words in English, and as his comments were simultaneously translated and fed into the episcopal headsets, laughter arose in pockets then caught on throughout the vast chamber. They appreciated his humor, even in this somber, historic moment.

He then spoke in his somewhat halting Italian, which was understandable to more of his listeners without translation: "So, I come here to be among you, as a sign of my solidarity and kinship with you. These are just words, and they have an old, somewhat blemished political meaning—but what I mean is, simply and unambiguously, I am with you. I am no different than you, even though the Petrine ministry sets me apart at times, compels me to wear these special vestments, and gives me a diocese as small and contentious as Old Rome." Again, there arose a smattering of laughter, especially among the Italian and other southern European council fathers. "It reminds me so much of the parish where I first served, in New Jersey. Our people gave the poor pastor a stroke—and in candor I should add that the priests contributed mightily to the man's misfortune." Again, some titters from the audience as his words were translated.

"We are brothers, and I look to you for counsel and for the affirmation of these documents of our council which you have so carefully crafted and debated. What you have done, in a very short time, is to lift up the Church before the world and put her on display so that all can examine her mind, her doctrine, her faith. And any who put her to the test can say that the ancient deposit of faith had not been violated, that it is intact in that beautiful vessel that St. Irenaeus wrote about so long ago. Let us pour it out from that vessel—and empty ourselves as well—for the sake of the whole world.

"I cannot say that this council has been free of conflict and contention—but that is what councils have always been: a time for men of faith and sincere motivation to put forward their views to be tested, challenged by others. This you have done. I agree with many of the conclusions of this council, and I accept all, for it has acted with wisdom and love for the good of all the Church, of all the people of Christ and all people of the world."

As he spoke, he was thinking, Get to the point, Your High Holy Popeship. You got a few laughs, but now you're turning superserious and more than a bit pompous. Be careful. Say what you came to say, then leave as quickly and gracefully as possible. He had learned to check himself in such momentous public occasions, always conscious of the impact a simple word or gesture might have on a listening communicant—or tens of millions of them. . . . He looked toward Cardinal Leandro Biagi, his trusted confidant, and saw the same caution in his Florentine eyes.

From their privileged position among a group of other cardinals, Alfons Stalnaker and Henry Vennholme listened with unconcealed impatience to the pope's unexpected, and to them unwelcome, remarks. They could not help but view him as an interloper, a temporary phenomenon, a passing problem—but a problem nonetheless. So far, everything they had thrown in his path he had somehow sidestepped or hurdled—most importantly, every attempt to thwart this very council. Yet they took solace in his troubled health, the wan look that shadowed his face, presaging death. Yes, death itself would be their ally, sooner or later, and they would be prepared. Vennholme especially meditated on the pontiff's slate-colored pallor, the slight tremor in one hand, noticeable only if one was seeking it. He uttered a silent prayer for forgiveness for his evil thoughts, but could not stop them from crowding into his mind. Indeed, he looked forward to this man's funeral.

As if reading the thoughts of the man who had baldly opposed him at every step of this journey, Mulrennan spoke of tolerance.

"I request of you and demand of myself that when we come out of this difficult day we love each other as we have never loved each other before. In fact, Christ Himself commands us in this. However hurt or offended any one of us may feel, he must put aside his feelings and accept the will of God as expressed in the decisions and declarations of the council. Even the pope must swallow the pill he has prescribed for the Church. If you think he is a poor physician, you should see him as a patient!"

He felt his energy level fall off dramatically and gulped a lung-ful of air—and with it the accumulated atmosphere of popes and pilgrims who had populated this place ever since the martyrdom of Peter and the grandiose tribute of Constantine. He summoned strength from within and went on: "I will break with protocol, as I already have, to urge you to vote in favor of the apostolic constitution before you, on the doctrine of Holy Orders and—for the sake of God and mankind—the institution of a new order, the permanent diaconate for women. I have followed the debates, prayed intently for the wisdom to see the correct path, and I now believe that the document as it has been reviewed and amended—which recognizes the right and responsibility of women as dea-cons of the Church—is correct and necessary.

"I also request that you consider the discipline of priestly cel-ibacy in your further deliberations and include that subject in your redrafted decree for my approval. I shall not instruct you further in this matter, but await your decision and recommendation, with the Holy Spirit in your hearts."

Mulrennan did not address the smallpox reports that had erupted earlier in the evening. But now he was hoping against hope and common sense that these men would be able to give their attention to their duty here without distraction. Would they stay the course in the face of this newest threat?

CHAPTER EIGHTEEN

Rome, April 2, 2004, 5:47 A.M.

On the final morning of the first session of the Third Ecumenical Council of the Vatican, the pope arose and walked with the now-accustomed pain to the southeast-facing window and pushed it open fully to look out upon St. Peter's Square, which rested undisturbed before sunrise like a wide gray stone pool. Beneath that smooth, hard surface lay another city, or cities, that dated back to antiquity and now lay buried under the strata of centuries of life and earth and garbage. Like Roman pontiffs before him, Celestine VI dearly desired to undertake new excavations during his pontificate, but time was the enemy of such ambitions, and other genuine crises and concerns occupied his mind and the resources at his disposal. The ancient sites had been buried and forgotten for millennia now, so they could surely await another day of discovery. The pope breathed in the cold spring air of the Roman morning before it was fouled with automobile exhaust and other human pollutants: Never was it fresher and more invigorating than at a moment like this, and never did he feel more spiritually connected to the apostolic tradition of his 263 predecessors. Would he ever get used to being the Supreme Pastor of the Universal Church? He doubted it; he doubted that he would have enough time. . . . Based on his recent medical history, which had been such a shock to him and to his family and friends, he might have only another year or two to live. A bolt of anger shot through him, and he stood motionless for several seconds, his eyes clenched shut as he looked within himself. Nonetheless, the pontiff allowed the predawn breezes off the Mediterranean to wash over his uplifted face, and he awaited the first yellowish tinge on the horizon that would signal the gift of a new day on God's earth.

This day, just this one day, promised to provide a climax to his still-young pontificate. He again looked down onto the piazza. There a few overfed pigeons swirled in a magic dance around the thrusting obelisk of Caligula upon which an orb and cross had long ago been appended to give a Christian visage to a pagan monument that had stood in Nero's circus on the Vatican plain. Like so much in the long history of the Roman church, outward symbols and practices had been adapted from Greeks, Romans, Asian cultures, making her—the one holy Catholic and apostolic Church—both an anachronism and a powerful contemporary institution. Like the first Christian emperor of Rome, Constantine, who sought to extend and solidify his rule for the ages (and succeeded to a great degree), the Church today looked beyond Rome, to the farthest corners of the earth, for new strength and new ideas that she might embrace, adapt, and make her own.

This is what Timothy Mulrennan, Pope Celestine, saw as he gazed upon the empty expanse of the Piazza di San Pietro. Now, a signal of light, like a silent golden note from an invisible trumpet, drew his eye to the horizon, beyond the splendid dome of the basilica, and even beyond the distant harbor city of Ostia. There: the first finger of the dawning. Above, a shelf of gray and white clouds hung stubbornly in the sky but the tendrils of sunlight reached out to touch their underside and turn them to gold and magenta. The promise of shadow brought new contrasts to the stones and statues in the square, yet to be defined. Mulrennan knew that the spirits of his friends, Philip Calabrese and Jaime De Guzman, walked there in the piazza on this day, perhaps were looking up at him as he stood framed by the apostolic window searching for the light. He remembered his visions of the popes, dream images, during the conclaves of the past year, so long ago. Perhaps they smiled at the anxieties of his mind, for they knew that these earthly cares would pass into dust, even as the stones endured, for that was the way of God whose Name they professed.

And Il Santo Papa, the holiest of men, where was he on this

morning of great moment? Mulrennan felt the stern yet truly loving embrace of the man who had been his friend, his mentor, his
pastor, the one who had placed the pallium upon his shoulders.
He had been gone for more than two years, but his legacy would
remain in and with the Church forever. Like Gregory the Great
and Innocent III and John XXIII, giants of late antiquity, the middle ages, and the twentieth century, he had restored the papacy
to new levels of power and prestige, serving the people of God
with every fiber of his being; he had brought a powerful intellect
and pastoral passion to every single minute of his long pontificate.
What were his followers to do? It was a difficult task, unless one
simply accepted that to serve after him was to walk in the long,
engulfing shadows of greatness.

Each man and woman, Mulrennan believed, held within the
capacity for greatness, for miracles, for salvation in Christ. In his
time as director of a rehabilitation center for troubled clergy, he
had attended many open meetings of A.A. and other twelve-step
programs of recovery, impressed with the simplicity and clarity
of the spiritual message that the people passed on to each other
there, much like the earliest Christians. One of the simple—some
would say simple-minded—affirmations that he had often heard
was: "God doesn't make junk!" This he knew to be true, if more
eloquently stated in Scripture and other spiritual writings. Not
every human being had the capacity for greatness that Karol Wojtyla possessed, nor the occasion to display the fullness of his humanity in such a dramatic way.

If he was not smiling upon the pope and the council at this
moment—as many of his bishops certainly were not—then John
Paul II was praying for them and for the precious and holy institution to which he had devoted his life. He would have made very
different choices and decisions, in a different style and language
than Timothy Mulrennan. No one knew that more than Mulrennan himself. Yet . . . into the hands of the Supreme Pontiff are
placed the keys of the kingdom, in heaven and earth, and he shall
have the power to loose or unloose as he chooses . . . and only
the Father could ultimately judge the rightness of a man's actions
and sins, even a pope's. Celestine said a silent prayer for his great

predecessor, who had been mourned in this same piazza that now, at last, was flushed with the first real light and shadow of the day.

He prayed, too, for the people of China, especially for those Christians for whom the dawn promised only darkness and death. He prayed for the people whose lives were threatened by war and terrorism, around the world and in his own land, that they may always seek justice, not revenge. When the council was finished, he vowed that he would devote even more time and prayer to the dire situation that threatened every person who believed in God and loved God more than life. Cardinal Vennholme's mission had been partially successful but had only begun.

The first sound from the street, a horn blast from a rumbling omnibus, shattered the near-perfect serenity of the moment for the observer. The pope smiled sadly. He clung to the awareness of his temporary isolation from everyone and everything else in the world; this was both the gift and the curse of the papacy— the bubble of security and "privacy" which enveloped him. He loved the promise of quiet and solitude, always had, sometimes thought he should have entered a cloistered order devoted to prayer and contemplation. But he knew, too, that he craved people in his daily life, needed the interaction with them in order to remain sane and feel fully human.

With some reluctance and regret he turned away from the window and the cool spring air. As he did every morning, he set a pot of coffee to brew, then, before his shave and shower, he knelt on the simple prie-dieu at the foot of his bed to pray. Today he prayed the rosary, a simple, formulaic means to focus his mind on Mary and the Holy Trinity, and a way to give himself over to the spiritual cadence and language of prayer. By the time he had finished, the coffee was ready, and he attended to his daily ablutions, during which he also put his thoughts toward the mysteries of God. What, he wondered, had Karl Rahner thought about in the morning as he dressed for the day? The great Jesuit theologian, often criticized for the opacity of his writing and the radical, if not heretical tendencies of his ideas, had no doubt composed densely reasoned Teutonic paragraphs in his bath! Rahner had emerged at Vatican II as one of the leading postmodern thinkers, given the requisite pat on the head when he wasn't being shuffled off to the side and out of the mainstream. His writing, so critical of the "schools"—that is, the neo-Thomistic nonthinking of most of the twentieth century, since Pius X at least—had just avoided censorship by the then-Holy Office and the *odium theologicum* of his brothers. Now, reading Rahner at midnight would put even the most anxious pontiff to sleep! He must try it, he told himself, if his nightly difficulties persisted: a chapter or two from the German's magnum opus, *Foundations of Christian Faith* might be just the ticket for a ten-hour trip to oblivion. . . .

In truth, he respected the men who were able to synthesize and advance the complex streams of Christian thought through the ages. It was a special talent that few were given to possess.

Refreshed and clean, dressed for the morning, having been awake for nearly an hour, the pope felt as prepared as possible for the day of pomp and politics that lay ahead. The past seventy-two hours had been days of decision and action, as the council concluded its business for the first five-week-long session. It had dragged on longer than most had expected—or wanted. But the majority of the bishops had hung in there through the tense and often tedious committee meetings and general assemblies to complete the task their Holy Father had placed before them. An open question, which only the pope himself could answer, was, Will there be a second session of Vatican III, or has enough been accomplished—or had the atmosphere become too poisoned by fear of biological attack, rational or not? That question in itself would engender months of debate, no doubt. Holy Week and Easter lay ahead, and each residential bishop who remained was anxious to return to his diocese to be with his flock during the highest and holiest season of the liturgical year.

The exploding smallpox scare in Rome had been echoed in other parts of the world, including the United States and Israel— but it turned out to be a false alarm. Nevertheless, people everywhere isolated and quarantined themselves. Within the first week of the scare, nearly four hundred bishops had fled to their homelands. Hundreds of others had stayed in their hotel rooms for several days. Barely a quorum was raised for the vote on the proposed change in the discipline of priestly celibacy. It passed by a few votes, and therefore its validity would be challenged. The council tabled a vote on permitting women to be ordained as deacons and took up an inconsequential debate on the creation of a new rank of holy orders that would be open to men and women, married and celibate.

Cardinal Stalnaker had called again for the adjournment of the council. The vote failed, but only by an extremely slender majority. Surprisingly, Tyrone had voted against adjournment. It was clear—to the pope, at least—that the council had unraveled, and he himself had assigned an end date to the session: today.

One of the assistant secretaries, a young French priest named Martin, greeted him, somewhat sheepishly, as Pope Celestine emerged from his bedroom. Father James Wiezevich was not there. He chose not to question the absence, assuming that the American priest had probably been at his cluttered desk since five A.M., finalizing the pope's schedule and poring over his final homily before the council session was officially closed this evening. Before then, there would be a series of private audiences with council fathers from many nations, non-Catholic clergy, a group of *periti* who had worked so hard before and during the council, representatives of various lay organizations and other pilgrims in Rome for the closing ceremonies. But the first audience of the day, immediately after breakfast, was with Jack Rath, to hear his latest report.

When the time came, Rath awaited the pontiff in his study and began, without ceremony: "Your Holiness, so far our investigation has been as thorough as possible in such a short time, and there are still loose ends that we're now attempting to tie up. So this is just a preliminary report, not enough to take into a courtroom. My investigative team is top-notch, extremely reliable, some of them ex-FBI with solid counterterrorist credentials. Anyhow, I assembled a task force of about twelve men from the U.S. and Europe, some of them with Interpol connections, one former Mossad agent. Quite useful. In fact, most of the police and intelligence agencies we contacted were very cooperative, and those that weren't we were able to work around. The Italian national police were good—and I suggest you meet with the top brass at some point to thank them. They will appreciate it."

"I'll do that when the council session is over and these bishops are out of my hair. How much more time do you need?" the pope asked.

"Could be weeks, possibly months, but we have now established a credible list of potential suspects, motives, connections—and a trail of money that flows through the whole scenario, going back to the reporter who was killed near St. Peter's shortly after your election."

"How could he be a target of these people? Everything he printed was against me."

"We think he was paid by the conspirators, then he must have outlived his usefulness. Nothing like a boss who doesn't need your services any more." Rath shifted in the leather chair, an unlabeled manila file folder in his hands. He had the sad, resigned look of a man used to conveying bad news to others, like a physician or a priest. "In any case, we know who killed him." He looked down at his lap. "You may be surprised, Holy Father."

"I hope I am. I'd hate to think I knew, even though I have my own suspicions."

"We are convinced that the American businessman Frank Darragh, an important lay officer of Evangelium Christi, financed most or all of these activities—including the assassination of De Guzman, Pope Innocent, I mean. It will be extremely difficult to prove, maybe impossible, because he had to work through a number of different organizations, use blinds and cutouts to launder the money. Ultimately, his cash paid for the materiel used by the rebel Muslim sect who 'volunteered' to perform the 'execution.' There was only a small cell involved, three or four including the girl who carried the bomb. But we can trace the money back to one presumed Evangelium Christi contact in the suburbs of Manila."

"And that's how you connect Frank Darragh?"

"There is other circumstantial evidence—again, not enough to indict, let alone convict. One of the links is an American priest." The security man consulted a page in his report. "Father

Mark Ciccone, a diocesan priest from Philadelphia."

Pope Celestine felt as if he had been slugged by a heavyweight fighter and could barely breathe. He sat still and silent for a long moment, assessing the implications. "And Phil Calabrese?"

"No evidence of money in that case. But other physical and forensic evidence there and in the Schulhafer-Boehmer murders centers on a single suspect. Oddly, not the same as the reporter."

"Another priest, I assume?" The words were bitterly ironic— and from a former military man.

"No, sir," Rath answered crisply. "We don't have a name yet, but he's sophisticated, possibly American-trained, military background, a professional. Possibly death-squad related, from Central America."

"Is there an Evangelium connection that you can prove to me, if not to a court?"

"We're almost there, but not yet."

"Not good enough."

"I know. Your Holiness, I'm giving you everything we have, hard facts as well as informed speculation. We're closer than anyone has ever been to the truth."

The pontiff, mentally and emotionally straining to absorb everything that was being laid out before him, knitted his brow as if he were suffering from a severe headache. His skin was pale, his palms clammy. The entire world that he had constructed in his mind was crumbling as if it were an empire of dust. What a fool I have been, he accused himself silently. Maybe I haven't wanted to know the truth. It is just too ugly to contemplate, too much like a Borgia scenario to be believed. Why have we not put that evil behind us forever? Why have we not learned to trust and love one another, even when we fundamentally disagree on important matters?

He longed for the innocence that he had briefly experienced and clung to this very morning upon rising from his bed to face the new day. Cleanse and make us whole again, dear Lord, he prayed silently to the Savior of all mankind. Give me the strength and wisdom to act rightly, to prosecute Your will, with utter human ruthlessness if necessary.

"No more reports of smallpox?"

"There have been no confirmed cases anywhere in the world—just rumors. I think it was a coordinated disinformation campaign. And it worked."

"Well," he asked, changing the subject, "what about today's events, the closing ceremony of the first session? All secure?"

"We have taken every measure, as we did with the convocation, and we have tripled the local police presence, the carabinieri, and the Swiss Guard. You don't have to appear in the square—TV works just fine."

"If they want to get to us, they do it," the pope said, fatalistically. "God's will be done."

Rome, April 2, 2004, 7:23 A.M.

"I'm late already. He'll wonder where I am." Jim Wiezevich felt the awful conflict once again, but knew it was for the last time.

"I wonder where you are," Demetra said. "You're not here with me any more."

"You're right, I know. I want to be with you, but I can't. I have to go. Can you understand?"

"No. Not very well. I'm not stupid, Jim, but I feel stupid, and helpless. If we want to make it work, we can—despite everything. I know we can."

First light touched her face, her arms, as she sat unclothed in her favorite kitchen chair. They had never been to his apartment because it was in the Vatican; it was always a risk for him to spend the night at hers because he might be missed. Luckily, he carried his cell phone at all times, for just such emergencies. But he could not live on the edge like this any more; it had to end, for the sake of his own sanity—and his soul. Never had she looked more beautiful as she did in this moment, vulnerable yet unafraid, naked yet innocent as a lamb. She lit a cigarette.

"I love you, Demetra. I have since I saw you the very first time, fourteen years ago. I wish you had married and moved to Los Angeles or someplace."

"A rich Greek dentist in Boca Raton, more likely. But I never met anyone else, in all those years. Fourteen? I refuse to believe it. I always remembered you and hated you for leaving me the first time."

"Today is the final day of the council session."

"You think I don't know that? It was simply the most incredibly stupid idea for your great hero to call a council. He put himself and everyone else at risk."

"That's why he had to do it. Not physical risk, I mean, but to bring the bishops together to talk face-to-face about the important issues."

"And this is not the end of it, believe me, there'll be more."

"You mean another session?"

"How can there not be? This one was so good."

"You're teasing me, now. Insulting me. I understand it, but it still hurts."

"When I was a girl, up until I was eleven or twelve, I believed with my whole heart and soul in Jesus and the Greek Orthodox Church and the Virgin Mary—all of that crap. I really did. I was a perfect kid in school, went to church every chance I got."

"I believe it," Wiezevich said with a stupid, painful smile.

"Anyway, one of the public school girls hated me—why, I never knew, but she would go out of her way to tease me, to beat me up, to humiliate me in front of the other girls. I hated her but I prayed for her. I thought of myself as a martyr for Jesus. You know—ready to endure any kind of pain and suffering for Him." Demetra Matoulis took a long puff on her cigarette. Smoke streamed from her nostrils as she spoke. "One day in front of everyone else she called me a 'holy ass.' Just those words: 'You're a holy ass, Matoulis.' Nothing she ever said or did before or after hurt me as much as that. I don't even remember most of the rest of it—just that dismissive, hurtful name. Never forgot it."

"Is that why you stopped believing?"

"Don't you get it, Father? I never did stop believing, just never let guys like you know how much I believe, how deeply. You know, I could have been a nun for all the whoopee I've made over all these years. I'm closing in on forty, never married, no kids, same job. Why not a veil and a cloister?" She lifted her coffee mug, and Jim saw a tear fall into the black liquid. With her other hand she held the cigarette like a shield or a mask. "Goddamn you."

He had been up for hours, shaved, showered, could have left at six, but he felt as if he had lead shoes on, unable to move from where he stood. He wanted to cry but felt too angry and hurt and confused. She was right—wasn't she?

"I'm a likely candidate," he said. "For hell, that is. But not for lack of trying to claw my way into heaven. Maybe it's just not meant to be. That I can accept. Your disdain I can't accept. I would say I'm sorry—I would say anything—if I thought it would make a difference. But I'm not sorry, Demetra. I am happy we've been together. Even this little slice of time . . . for me it is a whole lifetime."

"I stand by my earlier statement: Goddamn you. You're a good person, Jim. Isn't that awful—an awful thing to say? It's true, though, in your case. Despite yourself."

"Thanks a lot. I guess I'll leave on that note."

He came to her, stood over her as she sat there and smoked and looked at her coffee cup, her bare elbows on the dingy table, the detritus of Roman domestic life—pencils, sugar boxes, telephone directory, spoons—scattered before her. The beautiful brown-gold hair of a goddess spilled forward recklessly over her pinkish, bony shoulders. He wanted to snatch it up and take it with him. Why? To keep in a box and never to look at it—at her—again?

"Good-bye," she said.

He did not touch her. He was afraid he might break her, though he knew better. She was stronger than she looked, stronger than he was, in fact. Her shoulder blades. He contemplated the image for several seconds. They did not move, nor did he. She said something, but he did not catch the words. "What?" he said.

"Good-bye," she said again.

This time he heard her and understood.

Rome, April 2, 2004, 9:02 A.M.

The last day of my life, Arturo Wilderotter thought. It seemed a strange, rasping idea, a loud clashing of metal and morality within his mind. It provided him a sense of peace.

He had written it all out, just like his father had. But it had taken such a short time, a few hours. He had imagined it might take days to record the whole story, but, surprisingly, he captured it all in about thirty scrawled pages. Would anyone be able to read them? He wondered.

For days he had thought of little other than his wife and children. They would be hurt and disappointed, perhaps even appalled, when they received the news. Could not be helped . . . a roll of the dice in the sacred game, and his number had come up on the losing side this time. Or had it? He had done his duty, accomplished much in his lifetime. Few men could say the same. Even the "diary" he would leave behind recorded only one aspect of his life, his secret actions on behalf of the Evangelium Christi cause, not any of the myriad other aspects of his career. There were no names of any other Evangelium members or superiors in those papers, no record in writing or on computer files. Over the past year he had been careful to purge and destroy anything remotely connected to his spiritual work. And it was only within the past seventy-two hours that he had conceived of this idea: leaving a written testament, as his father had.

A beautiful morning. God's breath. The window was wide open, and he could smell Easter in the air, resurrection. He thought of the business deals he had consummated, the women he had slept with, the many cities around the world he had seen. None of those glittering memories gave him a tincture of satisfaction or comfort. The view of the as yet shadowed courtyard of the Hotel Columbus, cool and damp beyond the reach of the morning sun, was enough for him. The Roman morning, God's breath stirring his heart, having run the race and reached the finish point: This momentary awareness was what he had lived his life for, up to this very second.

Salvation comes to the man who seeks it with his whole heart and soul, who acts with knowledge of right, who dares to put his own life on the line to make the world better, safer, more godly for his brother. Salvation comes to him if a man acts for the right, no matter the personal price or the ugly nature of that action; throughout history saints and soldiers have been confronted with this difficult choice. Arturo Wilderotter, though he did not consider himself a saint, certainly considered himself a soldier in the Army of Right, with the archangels standing behind him and urging him to fight on to victory. What more thrilling achievement than to enter the battle and engage the enemy—and to win!

Would his son see the wisdom and rightness of his father's actions? Would his wife and daughter grieve at his passing? Would the world be quickened and enlightened when it learned the truth of who he was? These things he probably would not be given to know, for he would be sheltered in the loving arms of his God, comforted in the tears of the Virgin.

He secured the handwritten manuscript in an envelope, which he addressed to his son, and upon which he affixed Vatican postage in the proper amount. He called for the concierge, to take this and another letter—this to his wife—to the Vatican post office a few blocks away. He realized he had not written to his daughter, but now it was too late. He consulted his wristwatch. The room must be perfect, spartan. He had disposed of all his clothing and miscellaneous possessions over the past few days, giving away some things and money to the poor, throwing others away in the garbage, tossing a few things into the Tiber, including the weapon he had used to kill the American priest, Calabrese. After the concierge had retrieved his final epistles, he sat on a chair by the window and ate a piece of fruit from the bowl there and poured a flute of chilled champagne. He would not get drunk, but he appreciated the buzz that the drink gave him at this hour of the morning. He had never been a hedonist, a sensualist, though he had not been an angel, nor always faithful to his beloved wife. What man was? It had been a long time since he had known a woman other than Elisabeth, at least a year. In this and so many ways, his life had become narrower, more focused, less cluttered with extraneous considerations and activities. The fruit

and champagne tickled his mouth. Oddly, he thought of his childhood, tastes and smells and feelings he had loved: apples, im-
ported Hershey's chocolate, summer-to-autumn, military parades,
mountain snow.

Was it this easy, this sudden? He rose from the hard-backed
chair at about ten o'clock and took one last look around the place
where he had so often stayed over the years. The last day of my
life . . . again the notion played in his mind . . . at least, life as I
know it. But whether he would live or die was up to God, as ever.
Not a choice for him to make. His task was to make himself
available to the Lord. On the last day of his life as he had
known it.

Rome, April 2, 2004, 8:39 P.M.

Leandro Cardinal Biagi, Bernard Cardinal Tyrone, and Father
James Wiezevich accompanied the pontiff to his apartments in the
Apostolic Palace at his invitation. The day was nearly done, the
council ended—for the moment, an open question as to whether
there would be a second session—and these four men, especially
the pope, were exhausted to the point of blindness. Celestine
asked the valet to pour drinks, whatever his guests pleased; he
asked for a short bourbon with just a splash of cold water. His
physicians advised against drinking alcohol, but he needed something just to take the edge off this evening.

With less pomp and ceremony, apart from the pontifical mass
concelebrated with forty bishops from every corner of the globe,
Pope Celestine VI had closed this first session of the Third Vatican
Council and asked the bishops to return to their dioceses in the
peace of Christ, with the knowledge that their mission in Rome
had been accomplished.

Some would criticize—indeed, some in the press and among
the hierarchy already had begun—the pope and his foreshortened
council session in the same spirit that they had from the moment
he had announced it: Now was not the time, less than forty years
after Vatican II. However, their voices were fewer and less shrill.

Even Cardinal Tyrone, who had ably and sternly led the open opposition bishops, now conceded that the debate had been healthy, if inconclusive.

"I learned a few things," the giant said gruffly, folded into a leather papal sofa halfway across the room from Timothy Mulrennan, the sponsor of the council. Tyrone held a whiskey in one hand, an unlit cigar in the other. Out of respect for the Holy Father, he would not light and smoke the odiferous object. "For one thing, I learned that we need better theologically educated bishops," he added, inevitably.

"Bernard, you never give up. I respect that. But please just stuff it for one evening. You might just find yourself appointed to chair a special committee for the education of bishops," the pontiff threatened, with a smile.

Cardinal Biagi laughed. He sipped enthusiastically from a snifter of fine brandy. "Save us, Holiness, from the New Inquisition! Our dear Lord Cardinal Tyrone is itching to take on the job. He won't know what to do with his most formidable talents now that the council is finished."

"Is it?" Tyrone barked, pulling the dry cigar from his mouth, unsmiling. "I know I did not win any points with Your Holiness—nor with the Secretary of State there—but I told you from the beginning where I stood. But something tells me you are not quite done torturing me with your council."

Pope Celestine turned to Father Wiezevich, who stood off to one side nursing a vodka tonic, craving a cigarette for the first time in years. "Jim, would you be willing to serve as the cardinal's secretary on such a committee? I would be willing to make you a monsignor and double your salary. Even that might not be enough to persuade you, I know. I hear that Tyrone is a tyrant, impossible to work for."

"I'll consider it, if you wish, Holy Father," Jim Wiezevich said, not knowing what else to say.

"Don't abuse the young man," Tyrone put in. "I know that you're pulling my leg, as you Americans say. I'll take a vow of silence for a few days, if you'd like."

"A miracle," Mulrennan said. "Cardinal Biagi, note that,

please, for the file—for my cause for sainthood. The first miracle attributed to direct intercession by Celestine VI."

Tomorrow he would begin another round of chemotherapy. He had deferred the latest regime for two weeks, so that he could be fit to attend to the business of the council. Was it over?

In days past, councils had lasted for as little as a few weeks, and as long as decades of intermittent sessions. The model of Vatican II was less what he had expected than Vatican I, which had lasted a month then been truncated by war on its doorstep. Political pressure, even terror, was not unknown in history, from times when emperors and barbarians invaded Italy with impunity. Were times so different now, in the twenty-first century after Christ, another century born in the blood of innocents?

"I worry about my parish, my parishioners," Wiezevich added.

"I know you do, Jim. I still think about Our Lady of Mercies, twenty-five years later . . . can't get the place out of my mind. It is a beautiful, holy place, and the people are as full of faith as ever, new generations, new families as well as the old. It's not quite the same here in Rome."

"Italians have the worst church attendance in the entire Christian world," Biagi said. "But they live and breathe their Church in a way no one else can—here in the apostolic cradle of our faith. Despite the cynicism and secularism of this city, these people would die for their Holy Father, Il Papa. We must never forget that."

"I know, Allo. Believe me, I haven't forgotten. And after all they have been through these past few weeks . . . I am their bishop, first of all." Mulrennan turned to Tyrone. "How am I doing, Bernard, as their bishop?"

"Your Italian still needs work," the cardinal said.

"A burden for me—and for them," the pope admitted.

A Vatican security officer stuck his nose in the study door and signaled to Wiezevich who conferred briefly with him, then announced Jack Rath. The pope rose from his chair, this time with some distinct, shooting pain in his back and legs and a wave of nearly paralyzing fatigue, which he fought.

"Your Holiness." Rath strode into the room and went straight to the pontiff. "I've just spoken to the national police. They have taken a man into custody—he was on his way to attack a journalist, they think. He was armed, and they also think he is somehow tied to the murder of Monsignor Calabrese."

"Just one man?" Mulrennan asked. "Are they sure?"

"The executioner, possibly. We'll know a lot more soon."

"Who was he going after this time?"

"A woman named Demetra Matoulis."

"I know her," the pope said. "Know of her, that is."

Biagi looked at Wiezevich, who stood like a statue, his face drained of color. "Has she been harmed?" the cardinal asked.

"No. It was strange. He went directly into her office, confronted her. But did nothing, was not armed. He thought he was going to be shot by the security men or the police—was prepared to die, apparently. He spoke to her about the girl in Bosnia who has claimed to be visited by the Blessed Virgin. Ms. Matoulis reported on that story, interviewed the girl last year. You know of it, Your Holiness?"

"Yes, I have followed the story." He did not tell Rath or Biagi that he was deeply interested, had read everything he could about the alleged visitations of the Blessed Virgin in the remote mountainous country in the Balkans. Wiezevich knew, had been following the story as closely as the pope himself. The pontiff had held a private audience with the cardinal from Sarajevo, who had been curiously bland and skeptical about the entire thing.

"The man, whose name is Arturo Wilderotter, is an Argentine businessman and diplomat, a member in good standing of the Evangelium Christi society. He is being held by the national police on suspicion of murder; they are questioning him about Monsignor Calabrese's killing—to start with. There may be other matters, Your Holiness. Other murders."

"Pope Innocent? Did this man have anything to do with De Guzman's assassination, Jack?"

"We don't know yet. My guess is no—that was compartmentalized, probably only involved a very few at the highest level within the organization."

"You mean the Evangelium?"

"Yes, Holiness. They had the motive and the means. But it will be damned hard, if not impossible, to prove. I'm just giving you the straight dope on this."

"I understand. I don't like it." Mulrennan pumped his left fist and slammed it on the arm of his chair. "Vennholme? Stalnaker? Any of our Curia friends? Not to be repeated outside this room." He looked directly at Tyrone, who sat in silence, betraying nothing. The pontiff did not even now know where the Irishman stood on Evangelium Christi—for or against, or perhaps neutral, if that was possible in the hothouse world of the Vatican. "We must have proof."

Rath remained for only a few more awkward minutes, then departed with a dark good-bye. In fact, it was later than the pope had realized. He stood and walked again to his favorite south-facing window; he waited to see if he could spy Jack Rath down in the piazza, but there were only shadows, some moving, some still as paint.

Mulrennan heard movement and looked around to see that Cardinal Tyrone was helping himself to another drink. Biagi and Wiezevich spoke privately across the room, in low tones. The Vicar of Christ stood in his own home, the Apostolic Palace, and felt again, as he had since the moment of his election, that unique loneliness that only those few in history had ever known. Yet, he chided himself, he was not alone, need not ever be if he so chose. Biagi had been a good friend and most valued adviser, and Jim Wiezevich reminded him very much of himself, separated from his parish and longing to return to those mundane toils and tribulations. He would allow Father Wiezevich to go back to New Jersey, he decided, something he himself could never do. And Tyrone, the craggy giant—perhaps he had misunderstood or misjudged him; perhaps the Irish cardinal had a lot to teach him, a lot to contribute to his own theological education.

Perhaps . . .

The Vatican, April 7, 2004

He returned to the *scavi* in the afternoon, to the eerie remnants of the second-century netherworld that had been displaced a thousand times over by time and earth. Easter approached. He felt the change within, the stirring anticipation of the holiest season, as well as the settling of spring upon the bustling city. He was dressed in simple priest's clothing, one of his old black cassocks that had miraculously survived the ruthless purge of the valet and other papal staff. He was exhausted from yesterday's round of chemotherapy, felt the ache in every bone and sinew of his body, the nausea that complemented the pains. Prognosis remained lousy, yet at least his mind was clear and focused as rarely happened these days. The weight of the council, all the bishops, had been lifted. Celestine VI was magnetically drawn, as ever, to the remains, if that is what they were, of the greatest apostle. Peter had suffered martyrdom at the hands of the Romans, according to tradition. Mulrennan had not yet been called to bear such a cross.

A small tour was under way, and he hesitated, then walked ahead, leaving his security behind, at the tomb entrance. Who were these people? he wondered. Perhaps a VIP group or wealthy foreigners. Access to the *scavi* was limited, especially in these few years after the terrorist attacks on the U.S. and elsewhere. . . . A young Italian priest guided the tour of three women—one was a teenage girl, the other older and haggard, distracted, and the third an attractive youngish Mediterranean woman.

He approached along the narrow paved pagan street of the dead.

The girl turned, her pale face like the moon, shining in the darkness. "Il Papa," she said, then something else in a language with which he was unfamiliar. She was smiling electrically as she reached out and touched his black sleeve.

The other woman said, "I am Demetra Matoulis, Your Holiness. We have never met face-to-face but we have friends in common."

"Father Wiezevich and Jack Rath?" the pope asked.

"You've got it. Jim arranged the tour of the *scavi* for me." She introduced the girl and her mother. "They came at my invitation. To see the Holy City of Rome."

"Having fun?" he asked.

"Every minute of every day," Matoulis replied.

"Me too," the pontiff quipped. He smiled and appraised the journalist, wanting to ask her a thousand questions.

Demetra seemed to appreciate what the Holy Father was thinking. "I just bet," she said.

The girl, Mirjana, stepped toward Mulrennan again and said something that Demetra translated roughly: "The Blessed Mother is with you. She heals the sick. She has healed you." Mirjana moved between the pope and the masonry wall that had once housed the remains of a wealthy Roman family. She touched his back, where the surgeon had carved away as much as he could of the tumor on his spine.

Timothy Mulrennan felt nothing, everything. He closed his eyes and tried to breathe but experienced that familiar stifling, cottony claustrophobia, the odor of sanctity mixed with the finely ground dust of mortality. He turned and faced the girl; he blessed her, touched her forehead. She smiled and kissed the Fisherman's Ring on his finger. Her mother watched from the shadow of an ancient mausoleum doorway. Mulrennan, Pope Celestine, drew himself erect as the too-familiar, numbing pain escaped from every pore of his body into the close air of the necropolis.

Demetra Matoulis said, "What happened, Your Holiness?"

"God created man in His own image and likeness," Tim Mulrennan said. "Then He sent His only Son among us for the forgiveness of sins. I believe *that* is what happened. I believe it with all my heart. Let's go upstairs for some tea, ladies."

"That would be nice," Demetra replied.

AUTHOR'S NOTE

I have been blessed professionally and spiritually to enjoy the opportunity to continue this journey with Tim Mulrennan into the first years of his pontificate. Like its predecessor, *Conclave*, this novel and the characters who inhabit its pages have in some significant ways changed my life. How? By the simple expedient of necessity: that is, causing me to search ever more deeply into history and theology and, in fact, into myself for perspectives as to what was, what is, and what might be. It has not been a journey I have taken alone. There are a number of friends and associates who have helped me in so many ways to research and complete this book. From early and repeated readings of the manuscript to concrete suggestions and corrections to prayers and words of encouragement over coffee. I should like to thank them here:

Paul Block, Ian Boyd, Ron Chiarello, Gene Conway, Alan Delozier, Kate Dodds, Tom Doherty, John E. Doran, James Duff, Anthony J. Figueiredo, Daniel Gerger, Maryann Hobbie, Christopher Hynes, Stephanie Lane, Eric Major, Jennifer Marcus, Christopher McCabe, John McTague, Patrick O'Connor (most especially), Dermot Quinn, Linda Quinton, Jodi Rosoff, Arnold Ross and the Creative Crew, Francis R. Seymour, Jacques de Spoelberch, Robert Stanton, Paul Stevens, Tony Taschner, Cheryl Thompson, Dianne Traflet, Robert Vaughan, Robert J. Wister; the sales and marketing team of Forge Books; fellow students, faculty, librarians, and administrators of the Immaculate Conception Seminary School of Theology of Seton Hall University; fellow parishioners (especially the faithful men of the Wednesday A.M. prayer breakfast), clergy, and staff of Our Lady of Sorrows Church; my wife, Maureen, and sons, Patrick and Bryan.

Reflections on the History of Ecumenical Councils

The structure and authority of the ecumenical (i.e., universal or general) councils of the Catholic Church were developed over many centuries. Yet, there are enough key similarities between, say, the Council of Nicea in the early fourth century of the Common Era and the Second Vatican Council of 1962–65 to claim direct spiritual and canonical linkage. The fictional council of this novel, then, follows in the well-established tradition of its real-life predecessors, especially Vatican II.

Why is a council convened, and by whom? The first several councils of Christian antiquity were called by the Roman emperors, primarily to enforce unity and orthodoxy on doctrinal issues that roiled the Church and empire of the day. Constantine the Great invited bishops from throughout the empire to a meeting at the imperial summer residence in Nicea, in the province of Bithynia (present-day Turkey). About 220 to 250 bishops attended, at state expense; the bishop of Rome, Sylvester, did not attend but dispatched priest-representatives. (In fact, only a handful of delegates from the western empire attended, typical of the first several councils.) The Council of Nicea met from May 20 to July 25, 325. Its primary purpose was to address the heresy of Arius, which claimed that Jesus was a creature of God and not a person of the Trinity, co-equal with the Father. We have no official *acta* of this, or many other early councils, but a statement of the Christian *credo* (creed) survives, amended and amplified in later councils, as well as some secondary anecdotes and descriptions.

Subsequently, from later antiquity through the high Middle

Ages and into the modern era, councils were convoked by the popes to define doctrine, heal schisms, address the Protestant Reformation, and confront heresies that threatened the orthodoxy and stability of the existing Church. Vatican II was unique in that it was never intended to condemn any person or perceived error. In other words, no anathemas required.

A brief survey of the twenty-one councils that are recognized as general or ecumenical councils by the Church (by the magisterium, historians, and theologians) will reveal that a) some were obviously more important than others (or less important: remember the Photian schism?) and still influence Roman Catholic beliefs and practices, b) some were more truly universal than others (the total number of bishops in attendance is a guide in this regard), and c) some were political and cultural watershed events, in addition to their purely religious significance.

Among a number of excellent books that were published on the eve of the Second Vatican Council (an event which spurred an outpouring of historical and theological writings on the subject) is Hubert Jedin's concise and thorough survey, *Ecumenical Councils of the Catholic Church*, published in English in 1960; the Paulist Press paperback edition is a handy reference for both casual and serious readers. Following Jedin's basic divisions, adding Vatican II, and boiling down the events and personalities across eighteen centuries, here is an overview that informed the speculation about a near-future "Vatican III" in the novel, *Council*.

The first eight councils fall in the five-hundred-year period of late antiquity, from 325 to 900.

Following Nicea, the Church fathers met in Constantinople (381), another convenient spot, to address the doctrine of the Holy Spirit and to amplify the language of the creed to include a more precise description of the belief in the Spirit. At the next meeting, in Ephesus (430), the fathers gave the Virgin Mary a new title, *Theotokos*, or Mother of God. Twenty years later, at Chalcedon (451), where again there were few western bishops, the fathers tackled Monophysitism, the heresy of a single nature of Christ who does not share in the divine nature of the Father.

It seems the emerging doctrine of the Trinity was difficult for some folks to accept.

Arianism, Monophysitism, Nestorianism, and other heresies kept the bishops busy for another half-millennium, three more times at Constantinople and once again at Nicea.

The councils of the Middle Ages are tagged by Jedin as "the papal councils." Typifying and superseding all seven councils in this period (1123–1314) was the Fourth Council of the Lateran (held in the pope's own cathedral church–residence complex) of 1215. It is notable for a number of reasons: It was very brief, it was exceedingly productive, and it capped one of the greatest pontificates in history.

Innocent III had been elected pope in 1198 at the age of thirty-seven; he was a renowned legal scholar and astute political survivor (among the rival noble families of Rome); he had prosecuted the Fourth Crusade in the East and the bloody crusade against the Cathars of southern France; he had brought the kings of England and France, as well as the Holy Roman Emperor, more or less to heel at times during his eighteen-year reign. A complex, holy, brilliant man, he elevated the papacy itself to one of its highest points of secular power in history. Despite huge achievements (and several equally notable, grand-scale failures) subsequent generations have granted him neither "the Great" after his name, nor "Saint" before it.

Among the canons proclaimed by this council are professions of the faith directed against current heresies, the first official use of the term "transubstantiation" to describe the change at consecration of bread and wine into the Lord's body and blood, and rules against clerical incontinence, drunkenness, gambling, hunting, and wearing secular dress. Most importantly, the council passed the legislation that every Catholic of both genders must confess at least once a year to the parish priest and receive Holy Communion. Another canon was passed that requires Jews and Muslims to wear distinctive clothing, as well as against Jewish userers. If the contemporary Church still retains vestiges of medievalism, it is thanks to the Fourth Lateran Council's far-reaching legislation.

The Second Council of Lyons (1274) saw an attempt to rec-
oncile the eastern and western churches, but failed (the great Thomas Aquinas died on his journey to the council), as did a later
council, in Florence (1438).

As the result of the Great Western Schism, which began in
1378, and immediately following the period of papal exile from
Rome to Avignon, the Church by 1414 had three popes simultaneously, each elected by a faction of the Sacred College of
Cardinals. (The third claimant to the Petrine See had actually been
elected at a council in Pisa—which only complicated matters.)
This state of affairs proved embarrassing—to say the least—and
had severely wounded the unity of the *one* true apostolic faith.
How could there be three "Peters" at once? The stirrings of reformation began to be publicly heard and felt, causing alarm
within the Catholic hierarchy.

A historic ecumenical council convened in the windswept
Swiss city of Constance (October 1414) by the emperor Sigis-
mund. It was one of the largest and most colorful—as well as
controversial—gatherings in the history of the councils. More
than 600 cardinals, archbishops, bishops and abbots attended—
some with their own luxurious courts. By October 1417, there
was but one pope, Martin V.

The next three councils each stand alone in time and purpose.
They are Trent, Vatican I, and Vatican II.

Trent was the longest and perhaps one of the most important
councils of all. First convened in December 1545 and met intermittently for eighteen years. Trent gave us purgatory and the first
comprehensive catechism, as well as the authoritative list of accepted Catholic Scriptures, a uniform version of the Latin mass,
and the seminary system for the formation of priests—among
many other liturgical and theological breakthroughs.

Trent was in large measure a response to the Protestant Reformation, which was a stinging critique of scandals and excesses
among the Catholic clergy and hierarchy, as well as a cry for
doctrinal reform. The council fathers, though they dragged out
the sessions of the council perhaps needlessly for nearly two decades (there were some reluctant popes in the mix), succeeded in

protecting and defining the deposit of faith in a comprehensive way as no other council had for four hundred years.

The First Council of the Vatican was one of the shorter but more significant councils (December 8, 1869 to October 28, 1870). Convened by Pope Pius IX, the longest-reigning pontiff in Church history (thirty-two years), it was held during wartime and was suspended but never formally closed. At the same time, the papal states disappeared virtually overnight, eleven hundred years after the original donation of King Pepin! What the Church "gained" was the definition of the infallibility of the Holy Father when he speaks *ex cathedra* on matters of faith and morals. Sound easy? Not really. There was deep division among the church fathers as to whether it was correct, or whether it was time to define something that was generally accepted by Catholics. An American bishop, Edward Fitzgerald of Little Rock, Arkansas, was one of only two who voted against the definition when it was presented (533 in favor).

The impact on the life of the Church of the Second Ecumenical Council of the Vatican cannot be overstated. Forty years later, the effects of the council fathers' decisions still echo loudly throughout the world, and many of the changes wrought in that era are even today being absorbed and assimilated by local churches—or resisted by them.

Vatican II broke new ground, not doctrinally (because councils do not formulate dogma, rather they "define" and perhaps "reclothe" statements of faith for contemporary believers), but in opening hitherto obscure teachings to more common understanding (e.g., liturgies in the local languages). Although Latin remained the official language of the council, a substantial number of the fathers (notably Richard Cardinal Cushing of Boston) were deficient in their understanding and had to rely upon translation and bluff to get through the lengthy debates. Most importantly, Pope John XXIII stated at the opening of the first council session (October 1962) that his intent was not to condemn any person or teaching, rather to present the sacred deposit of faith to the modern world in terms that could be understood and appreciated by all.

Also, Vatican II was the first council to be held in the age of mass communications. Many middle-aged Catholics easily recall images from television, newspapers, and large-circulation glossy magazines (*Life* and *Look*): the thousands of mitered prelates from every continent on earth assembled in the great nave of the Basilica of St. Peter, presided over by the pudgy, wily peasant-pope who wore the vestments of office loosely, according to the Scriptural admonition, almost comically, according to reporters of the day.

The documents of Vatican II make edifying, if sometimes heavy, reading. After three years of preparation and four years of council sessions, the output of the fathers—supported by scholars and theologians called *periti*—resulted in many volumes of letters, debates, apostolic constitutions, and analysis thereof. In addition, countless doctoral theses, journal articles, homilies, and books have been produced in the generation since the council. Further, the pontificates of Paul VI and John Paul II were spent, in effect, responding to the council—at which both were major players (Paul as a leading progressive cardinal, then pope; John Paul as a young bishop from Krakow in Poland). Like so much in Church history, the council and its aftermath seem to unfold in a never-quite-finished pageant of Hegelian thesis, antithesis, synthesis— or action, reaction, adaptation. It is somewhat obvious to state that the full impact of the Second Vatican Council—the net result of all the documents and all the responses—will continue to be felt for at least another century.

Vatican II met in four sessions, closing in December 1965 in the third year of Paul VI's pontificate. Paul, like today's Church, was arguably the product and the victim of John XXIII's revolution.

The one, holy, catholic, and apostolic Church measures time in centuries and millennia . . . rather a unique perspective on history that boggles the contemporary, high-speed, technologically charged minds accustomed to absorbing news and "sound bytes" in twenty-four-hour cycles! The Church absorbs change—if at all—over decades, accretes power subtly, loses power dramatically. It is an open question as to which direction the Bride of Christ is moving in our day.

Suggested further readings

Jedin, Hubert. *Ecumenical Councils of the Catholic Church: An Historical Outline*. New York: Herder and Herder, 1960.

Hughes, Philip. *The Church in Crisis: A History of the General Councils, 325–1870*. New York: Doubleday, 1961.

Rynne, Xavier. *Vatican Council II*. New York: Farrar, Straus & Giroux, 1968. (Revised edition, Orbis Books, 1999.)

Watkin, E. I. *The Church in Council*. New York: Sheed and Ward, 1960.